Ebook ISBN: 978-1-83889-392-7

Kindle ISBN: 978-1-83889-393-4

Audio CD ISBN: 978-1-83889-389-7

MP3 CD ISBN: 978-1-83889-769-7

Digital audio download ISBN: 978-1-83889-390-3

Boldwood Books Ltd
23 Bowerdean Street
London SW6 3TN
www.boldwoodbooks.com

For my late father, Ralph Hutchinson, who encouraged me right from the start. 'You'll get there, just keep trying'. Words to live by.

1

Adam Fitch and Billy Marshall stood waiting at the front of Stafford Gaol as they had done once a month for the last five years.

The door in the huge brick-built gatehouse was firmly locked and was flanked either side by a tall concrete wall.

Adam's eyes glanced over the women leaning against the wall, awaiting a visit to their menfolk inside. Dressed in rags, some had scruffy children clinging to their worn skirts. Others stood alone as if trying to hide from the stigma of being a convict's spouse. No one spoke. They simply waited patiently for the echoing sound of the key grating in the lock which heralded that their visit time was imminent.

Shuffling from foot to foot, Adam was eager for the wrought iron gates to swing open. He shivered. The spring sunshine gave very little warmth, but Adam realised it was anticipation which was making him shake rather than the cool air.

Lifting his flat cap, he pushed his dark hair back before replacing it. He heard a whisper from a small girl hiding behind her mother.

'Is he a peaky blinder?'

'Don't be so daft!' the woman scolded, but she eyed Adam warily nevertheless.

'Won't be long now, lad, and then we'll not be coming again, God willing,' Billy whispered as he laid a hand on the boy's shoulder.

Adam nodded and glanced around again at the small group of people who were also waiting. Young men with their own flat caps pulled low over watchful eyes, everyone keen to see whoever it was they had come to the prison to visit.

As he attempted to quell his excitement, Adam's mind ran swiftly over the last few years of his fifteen-year-old life. His natural father, a pugilist, had been killed in the boxing ring. Adam and his sister were sold to Reed's Orphanage by his stepfather, who died by the hand of his brother James in a freak accident. When Polly was then sold again to a wealthy family, Adam and his friends broke out to rescue her.

Feeling strong fingers squeeze gently at his arm, Adam glanced at the big man at his side. Billy Marshall, champion pugilist, now retired, had taught him how to box and so defend himself if and when the need arose. Billy had married Adam's mum Minnie four years previously, and they had bought a massive property in Major Street, which was now a children's home.

Whilst on the run from Reed's, Adam and his friends had met up with three boys who were living together, thieving and scavenging to survive. Two of them, Echo and Flash, had joined Adam's ever-expanding family; the third had been apprehended by the police, which was the reason for their visit here today. Adam and Billy were awaiting the release of Digit, who had served five years for theft.

So lost in his thoughts was he that Adam had not heard the warder come to unlock the doors. The squeal of hinges drew his attention and he again glanced at Billy.

'They will let Digit out today, won't they?' he asked in barely more than a whisper.

Billy nodded confidently, and the two watched the small group of people shuffle forward into the yard. Then the huge wooden doors began to close and Adam felt his stomach lurch. Where was Digit? Had something happened since they had last seen him? Was he ill – had he died? Adam pushed the thought aside as he stared at the huge wooden doors, willing them to open.

'Bloody hell, Digit – come on!' Adam muttered.

'Patience, lad – all in good time,' Billy said.

Suddenly the door opened, and a young man stepped out into the yard. Toby Hanley, aka Digit, stood for a moment with the sun shining on his thick black hair, which was long and lank and badly in need of a wash. His dark eyes blinked at the bright sunlight, then they searched for the two friends who had promised to be there on his release. His clothes hung on his frame which had once been thickset and muscled but now after five years in gaol, appeared to have lost a little of that mass, although there was still strength beneath the bedraggled appearance.

The warder gave him a shove in the back and Digit lurched forward. Adam's hands clenched into fists at the rough treatment of his friend. When they reached the gate, the warder pushed Digit through it before dragging it closed again and locking it securely.

'Blimey, we thought you were never coming out!' Adam said as he shook hands with the now smiling Digit. The handshake turned into a warm hug. Adam felt his friend's body shaking and knew he was trying to hold onto his emotions.

Feeling his own eyes tearing up, Adam let go of Digit, who then extended a hand to Billy, saying, 'I want to thank you both so much. If it hadn't been for you two, I'd have gone mad in there.'

'Come on, time to go home,' Billy said with a warm smile.

'God, Digit, Echo's driving everyone insane with his constant "when's Digit coming?"' Adam said with a laugh.

'It will be good to see everyone again,' Digit said quietly.

The three sat on the steam train bound for their hometown of Wolverhampton in the heart of the Black Country. The puffs of smoke plumed before drifting across the platform. Ladies in fine dresses took a step back lest their expensive attire be marked. Some held a lace handkerchief to their noses to fend off the smell of the soot laden smoke. Gentlemen in top hats tapped silver-topped canes impatiently as they awaited their train to another destination. Voices were heard as people passed along the corridor seeking what they thought were the best seats. Ironically, all the seats in third-class carriages were the same – hard wooden benches. They chatted, and Adam updated Digit on what their friends were doing now.

Digit had earned his sobriquet because of his light-fingered picking of wealthy pockets. Thick black hair cascaded over dark eyes, which twinkled as he listened. An only child, Digit had taken to thieving after his mother died and his father went to the same prison he had just left. They had never met again as Hanley senior had lost his life in a knife fight shortly after being incarcerated.

Billy smiled as he watched the two boys converse

before turning his gaze out of the window to soak up the countryside. Before he knew it, they were passing rows of identical filthy brick houses. Each was covered in a thick layer of grime from chimneys both industrial and domestic.

Wolverhampton, in the Black Country's centre in the middle of England, was much the same as any other industrial town. Factories and foundries worked day and night, belching out steam and smoke, which lay in a thick pall over the houses. Ragamuffins played on the cobblestone roads as their mothers stood on doorsteps canting the hours away. Huge Shire horses pulled dray carts delivering casks of ale to the numerous public houses. Carters vied for space on the narrow streets as people meandered around them.

Laughter drew Billy's eyes back to the two sat on the wooden bench of the third-class carriage of the train. After a quick mental calculation he realised Digit was now twenty-one years old – he was a young man now. Billy wondered how he would fit in with the others and whether he would ever find work in the poverty-stricken town. Would anyone employ a light-fingered convict? Would Digit revert to his previous trade if no jobs were forthcoming? Had he learned his lesson by being in jail? Billy hoped so, but only time would tell.

The train slowed as it pulled into Monmore Green Station, and they heard the steam as it was released to float past the windows in great clouds. The great iron beast ground to a halt and they got to their feet before jumping down onto a crowded platform. Pushing through the throngs of people, they made their way to the exit, where Billy hailed a cab. Climbing aboard, they were all excited to be undertaking the last leg of their journey.

* * *

Whilst Digit was being greeted and escorted to his new home, Minnie Marshall had been planning a welcome party.

Mabel Elliot, the cook, and Dilys Linton, the maid, had come to them after deserting Reed's Orphanage, as had Ruth Ashby and Celia Brock. Ruth had taken on the duties of accountant and administrator and Celia had brought her teaching skills to the new children's home, and both were more than happy to be away from the spiteful Una Reed.

Mabel's mob cap wobbled atop her grey hair as she bustled around the large kitchen issuing orders to Dilys like a sergeant major.

'Come on, gel, they'll be back any time now!' she urged as she pushed a plate of sausage rolls into the girl's hands.

Dilys rushed to the dining room and placed the plate at one end of a long table, either side of which were wooden benches. Dashing back to the kitchen, Dilys collected plates of fresh bread, cheese, cold meats, pork pies, and two by two they were transferred to the table.

Polly Fitch, Adam's sister, had now arrived to help and a moment later her friend May Johnson joined them, closely followed by Echo.

The two girls had met at Reed's and had become firm friends. May and her brother Arthur had been sold to Reed's for five shillings each, as had Polly and Adam by their stepfather. It was there that they had met Joe Blunt, Matt Roden and Rodney Dukes. By the end of their stay there – when they all escaped – they had become brothers-in-arms. They had helped

Adam find his missing sister and now in turn, Adam's mum was taking care of them all.

'Thank God you're here. Cook's getting on my very last nerve!' Dilys said to Polly, feeling thoroughly exasperated.

'I bloody heard that!' Mabel retorted.

'You was supposed to!' Dilys fired back as she picked up jugs of home-made lemonade.

Polly and May rolled their eyes and Echo mumbled, 'Supposed to.'

Mabel smiled at the slow-witted boy. At seventeen he had the mind of a child but was fiercely loyal to his *ladies* – Polly and May. He had helped to look out for them before the family had come together once more.

'Echo, glasses for the table please,' Mabel instructed. She watched as he carefully picked up a tray laden with tumblers. With his tongue poking between his teeth, he carried it to the dining room.

'All set out,' Echo said as he returned with the empty tray.

'Good lad, I can always rely on you to do a proper job,' Mabel praised him.

'Proper job,' the boy echoed with a beaming

smile.

Polly and May set out knives and forks, plates and spoons for the jelly which would come later. The aroma of roast chicken filled the kitchen and made mouths water, and as Mabel lifted the cooking tins from the range the hot fat hissed. One by one, four cooked birds were placed on huge platters and surrounded by roast potatoes and parsnips. A rich gravy was made atop the hot plate on the range.

'The dining room looks beautiful, everybody, and ooh, my – that smells delicious,' Minnie said as she eyed the chicken. 'They're all in from work now – oh, Rodney's in the bath in the scullery, girls, just so as you know – so we're just waiting now.'

'Waiting now,' Echo repeated as he left to look through the front room window. Polly and May followed to help keep him from getting over-excited.

'Digit's coming soon,' Echo said as his eyes searched the street.

'It's been a long time since we've seen him, hasn't it, Echo?' Polly asked.

'Long time,' Echo nodded, then he let out a screech as a cab stopped outside.

'Go and tell Mum they're here,' Polly said, pushing the boy away from the window.

'Mum, Mum...' Echo's words trailed off as he rushed back to the kitchen.

In a moment Echo had rounded everyone up and had them in the hall – even Rodney, who was still drying his hair with a towel.

The front door opened and Adam walked in followed by Digit and Billy. An awkward silence lasted only seconds before Echo rushed forward and threw his arms around Digit.

'Digit's home!' he called out as he jumped up and down with glee.

It was as Digit smiled and hugged his friend that the tension was broken, and one by one he was greeted by the friends he had not seen for five years.

'This is my mum, Minnie,' Adam said, 'Mum, meet Digit.'

'Hello lad, welcome home,' Minnie said extending her hand.

Digit looked at her hand then back at her eyes where he saw love and forgiveness. Suddenly it was all too much for him and he lowered his head and began to cry.

Everyone looked at each other, not knowing what to do or say, until Minnie stepped forward and wrapped her arms around the young man. She felt him lurch with each sob that racked his body, and she swallowed the lump in her throat as his arms returned the hug. Minnie tilted her head, and everyone disappeared into the dining room, Polly comforting a distressed Echo.

'Digit's crying!' Echo blubbered.

'I know. He's just overcome, Echo. He'll be all right. Mum will see to him,' Polly assured as she led the boy through the doorway.

'That's it, cry it all out lad. You don't need to be carrying all that misery any longer.' Minnie's words were gentle and quiet as she held the young man whose tears had drenched her apron. 'This is your home now with all of us. We've waited these long years for your return and we're really glad to have you.'

After what seemed like an age, Digit let go of Minnie and wiped his nose on a handkerchief she passed to him.

'Thank you, Minnie. It was your man and your boy who have kept me going. If it wasn't for them...'

his words trailed off.

'When we first found Echo and Flash we discovered what had happened to you. Adam and Polly were determined we should do all we could to help. We couldn't get you out of that awful hellhole, but we could make sure you had some clothes and summat decent to eat,' Minnie said.

'Thank you will never be enough,' Digit said with a sniff.

'I don't need no thanks, lad. What I need is for you to be well fed and get used to sleeping soundly.'

'I have nightmares,' Digit confided.

'I'd be surprised if you didn't, but you don't need to worry none, 'cos you ain't the only one.' Minnie brushed his thick dark hair away from his eyes. 'Now, are you ready for some dinner? 'Cos that lot will be clammed to death.' Tilting her head, she indicated the dining room.

Digit nodded then leaned forward and kissed her cheek. It took Minnie by surprise and she smiled as the young man crooked his arm. Sliding hers through his, they strode to where his new family was waiting for them.

2

It was later that evening, when the younger orphans who had been taken in over the years were settled safely in their beds, that everyone sat in the huge living room. A fire crackled merrily in the inglenook fireplace and the gas lamps shed a warm glow over the room.

Mabel and Dilys brought in hot tea and cake before finding seats to join in the conversations taking place.

'Flash helps me here with the little 'uns, as do May and Echo,' Minnie explained.

'I work in the abattoir,' Rodney said, 'so I get cheaper prices for the meat.'

'He don't half stink when he gets home an' all,' May said with a little laugh.

'At least I have a bath!' Rodney feigned upset but seeing May drop her lower lip teasingly, he howled with laughter.

Digit smiled at their antics; the love this family shared was evident. He wondered briefly if he would ever fit into their way of life.

'I work over at Green Lane Cooperage Works,' Matt put in.

'I've got a job at the brick works,' Arthur added.

'As for me, I've got the night off from working the bar at the Forresters' Arms,' Joe said as he stretched out his long legs and flicked his titian hair from his eyes.

'As you know, Peter, James and I work our allotment gardens so there's plenty of fresh fruit and vegetables. In the winter we help out at the wharves to earn a few bob,' Adam said.

'What about you, Polly?' Digit asked quietly.

'I'm training to be a nurse up at the General Hospital,' she answered.

'I know Billy teaches boxing – he and Adam have kept me pretty well informed on their visits.' Digit's eyes fell to his teacup as he spoke, the nightmare of his incarceration still at the forefront of his mind.

'Well, lad, it's a new beginning for you now,' Minnie said.

'I doubt I'll be able to find work, not when people find out where I've been for the last five years,' Digit said sadly.

'Five years,' this came from Echo and he shook his head.

'You don't need to be worrying about that just now. All you have to think about is building up your strength with Mabel's excellent cooking,' Billy said.

Mabel grinned at the compliment and stood to offer Digit more cake.

Accepting politely, he looked around at the faces he had missed so much. It seemed one minute they were all kids chasing around the streets avoiding the coppers, and the next they were all grown up and re-sponsible adults. Only Echo retained a child's mind and would for the rest of his life, and Digit thought he would be a good reminder of days gone by.

The one who had changed the most was Flash. Born Perry Wilton, he had once challenged them to dare to laugh at his name. Nicknamed Flash because he could run like the wind, he had been confident to the point of arrogance. Now he was a shadow of his former self. Billy had explained they had found him alone and starving, waiting for Digit's return from a thieving expedition. He had been unaware his friend had been taken into police custody. Flash, he noted, was never far from Minnie; he seemed constantly afraid of being left alone again.

As the night wore on, Digit slowly began to relax, something he had been unable to do for years. He'd quickly learned that when you were banged up in jail, you kept your wits about you, otherwise terrible things could happen.

'Now don't be worried if you hear crying in the night, it'll be one of the little 'uns still trying to come to terms with being an orphan. It always happens when we get new kiddies in and it teks a while for them to settle. One of us will see to it,' Minnie said.

'I'm used to it, but it was grown men I could hear sobbing,' Digit said quietly. As sad looks were exchanged, he went on, 'Some couldn't take it and hung themselves. It was really bad in there; filthy and damp. Cold like you've never known in the winter and stifling hot in the summer. Rats and cockroaches for bedfellows at times; other blokes trying to steal your food or pick a fight to stave off the boredom. There was stuff which went on an' all which I ain't going into 'cos there's ladies present. I tried to exercise a lot to build up my muscles as best as I could so I could keep myself safe.'

The only sound in the room was the crackling of the fire and the ticking of the tin clock on the mantle shelf. Then Minnie spoke gently, 'I know it will be hard but you have to put all that behind you now. It's time to look forward.'

Digit nodded, then looking at Mabel asked, 'Can I have some more cake please?'

'O' course you can,' the cook said as she cut a huge chunk from a large cake as yet untouched. 'We need to feed you up I'm thinking.'

Digit smiled his thanks and tucked in. He had been hungry for so long he didn't think he would ever feel full again. Little did he know that at that precise moment Mabel had made it her mission in life to sate that hunger.

As everyone drifted off to bed, it was Adam who showed Digit to his room. It was at the front of the house and faced out onto the sprawling heathland.

Polly had suggested it, saying that having been locked up for so long, Digit might like to see the wide open space. It would be good for him to know he could go out and walk there any time he wanted to.

Adam lit the gas lamp and Digit crossed to look out of the window and sighed. Polly's idea appeared to have been the right one.

'Right, we'll see you for breakfast in the morning,' Adam said.

'Adam – thank you!' Digit hugged his friend in the privacy of the room.

'You're welcome, mate,' Adam said as they parted company. 'Sleep well.'

After Adam left, Digit turned off the lamp and returned to the window to stare out at the silvery beams of moonlight casting shadows on the scrubland. He looked up at the great white orb and felt the hot tears sting his eyes. He thanked God for his good fortune at having met such wonderful people. Feeling safe at last, he allowed himself to cry, relief flowing through him at being free once more.

Downstairs, Minnie and Billy sat by the last embers of the dying fire. Everyone else had retired, leaving the couple to enjoy each other's company.

'Are you happy, Minnie?' Billy asked, taking his wife by surprise.

'I am, lovey. The last of the five-shilling children to be brought into the fold,' she answered.

'That's a strange name to give them,' he said.

'I know, but that's how I think of them.'

'Why?' Billy asked.

'Well, Adam and Polly's stepfather sold them to Reed's for five shillings and you know how long it took me to get them back. May and Arthur were sold to Una Reed for five bob as well. Joe is a true orphan on account of his parents dying of pneumonia, and Matt – his dad died and they carted his mother off to the asylum when she went mad with grief. As for Rodney, his mother couldn't cope with his behaviour, but I'd lay a bet she demanded her five shillings before she left him at that orphanage,' Minnie explained. 'Now they're all growing up and making their own way forward. The other three came to us by the grace of God, but I still think of them as part of the group.' She sighed as if she felt her whole life was changing.

'Oh, my sweetheart, they will always need you no matter how old they are,' Billy said with a smile.

'That poor lad has been to hell and back,' she said as she tilted her head towards the ceiling. 'I can't begin to imagine what it was like for him in that jail.' Minnie gave a little shiver and Billy placed an arm around her shoulder, pulling her closer to him on the settee.

'Me neither, but we have to make sure he's safe and comfortable here. I don't see any problems 'cos he's surrounded by his pals.'

'True, but it's been five years, Billy, it's a long time since seeing them last and people change,' Minnie answered. 'I tell you what though, I'm so proud of you and our Adam for going to visit him every month without complaint.'

'He needed to know we were all here waiting for him, and it gave him something to look forward to. The hardest part was explaining to Echo why he couldn't go with us. I don't think his young mind would have coped with it.' Billy shook his head.

'It's just a good job he has no concept of time, ain't it?' Minnie replied.

'Well, we're all here safe and sound so I think we should climb the wooden hills to Bedfordshire,' Billy said with a grin.

'I'll bet every parent has said that to their kids at some time,' Minnie said as she smiled at the old saying and got to her feet. Putting the guard around the fire she left Billy to douse the lamps, then together they held hands as they went to bed.

* * *

The following morning, Minnie greeted a bleary-eyed Digit as he descended the stairs in the same clothes he had worn the day before.

'Ain't you had no sleep?' she asked.

Digit smiled and shook his head. He chose not to mention that he'd passed the night with the window open in order to breathe in the relatively fresh air, and watched the night sky with the dazzling jewelled stars twinkling above him. He kept to himself that he had cried silently for hours at being free at last. He remained silent about praying to the good Lord and promising never to put himself in the position of risking going to jail again.

'I thought not. Right, breakfast then go and change; there's new clothes in the wardrobe and if you like you can take a bath.'

'Thanks, I could do with one,' Digit said as he sniffed beneath an arm.

'Food first, then I'll get Dilys to heat some water for you,' Minnie said shoving him gently towards the dining room.

There was lots of chatter going on when he entered, and the little ones gave him a cursory glance before continuing to eat.

Mabel and Dilys had pans of water heating for Digit's bath whilst everyone ate, and with help from the lads they filled the tin bath in the scullery. Digit had agreed to help Adam and his two brothers Peter and James on the allotment gardens, and so they waited patiently whilst he scrubbed himself clean. Then they helped empty the tub onto the scrubland outside the back door.

The others set off for the daily grind at their respective employment, and Digit and the Fitch brothers strolled to the allotments in the spring sunshine.

'How was your bath?' Peter asked for wont of something to say.

'Bloody marvellous!' Digit replied and ruffled his

still wet hair. 'It's the first time I've been clean for years.'

Sharing a laugh, they walked on to the top of Major Street and turned onto the site where the gardens were marked out into sections. A rickety old shed contained tools for communal use by those working their plots, as well as hessian sacks used for harvesting.

Grabbing one, Adam shoved it into Digit's hands. 'Let's see what's ready for the table.'

As the morning wore on, jackets were shed and sweat ran freely down the faces of the workers. Stopping for a drink of cold water from the standpipe, they turned as they heard a shout.

'Oh blimey, here comes old Reedy's lot,' James muttered.

Adam explained as he saw Digit's puzzled expression. 'The orphanage we all ran away from – remember?'

Digit nodded as he recalled Adam telling him about the daring escape.

'Well they come from there and they're always spoiling for a fight.' Adam quickly explained how he'd overheard Mabel and Dilys discussing what they'd learned in the market about the boys from Reed's causing trouble in the town. They were rude to people, destructive of property and totally dismissive of any consequences that may ensue from their aberrant behaviour.

'What do we 'ave here then? A new worker. You'm a big bugger ain't you?' one of the boys yelled.

'Clear off!' Peter shouted back.

'Or what? What you gonna do if we don't?' Another of the mob decided to join in the melee.

'Don't answer, it only encourages them,' Adam said.

Digit shrugged and bent to the soil once more.

'Oi big 'un, what you puttin' in there?' the leader called out.

'*You!*' Digit growled loud enough to frighten the little group into taking a step back.

The Fitch brothers tittered then resumed their work.

Suddenly Peter yelped as a stone struck his shin.

'You little bleeder!' Digit said between clenched teeth and in an instant he was up and running.

Not expecting such a reaction, it took the boys a

moment to register that one of the enemy was retaliating. Turning to flee, they were not quite quick enough, and Digit grabbed the collar of the apparent leader.

'Gerroff me!' the boy yelled.

Digit shook him hard making his head wobble.

'Stop it! Leave me alone!' the boy continued to shout.

Digit spun him round and pulled the lad close until they were nose to nose. Then with a voice like a rasp on metal said, 'You hurt my friend.'

The boy gulped and fear showed in his eyes. 'I d'aint mean to.'

'Yes you did. You threw that stone hoping to hit one of us,' Digit's voice was gravelly as he held onto the struggling boy.

'I d'aint, honest,' he gabbled.

'Well, the question now is how you pay for what you did.'

'Let me go or I'll tell on you,' the boy was desperately trying to get away.

'How will you speak with no teeth? And who are you going to tell, you little swine? The bobbies? I doubt it, 'cos you see, I have mates in jail...' Seeing the boy's eyes widen, Digit went on, 'Oh yes, I just got out yesterday.'

'Look mister, I'm sorry. I won't do it again.' The colour had drained from the boy's face at the mention of prison.

'Be sure you don't because we know where you live and going back to jail for wringing your neck don't scare me. Now – bugger off!' Digit threw the boy away from him and watched him run for his life to join his friends waiting for him further up the street.

Going back to the others, Digit's grin was broad. 'That scared 'em.'

Adam was checking Peter's shin and a big red mark was beginning to show. Peter gritted his teeth at the stinging before it began to ease off a little.

'Lucky shot,' James said as he leaned over to look at the injury. 'You'll have a cracker of a bruise there though.'

'Our Polly will enjoy tending to that,' Adam said with a grin.

'Oh no,' Peter sighed. He knew once his sister heard of this she would bandage him until he resembled an Egyptian mummy.

Work resumed with no further interruptions from Reed's orphans, and on their return home in the early evening, Adam's words were proved right. Polly was in her element having a real-life ailment to take care of.

3
____

That night, over at Reed House, the three boys who had challenged the Fitch brothers were in the room shared by the two younger ones and were whispering quietly.

'That bloke said he'd been in prison,' Richard Stanton said to his younger brothers.

'Blimey Dickie, it was close though, I was scared when he had hold of you,' fourteen-year-old Christopher, known as Kit, said.

'Nah, he wouldn't have done nuthin',' Dickie responded, full of bravado.

'He scared me,' Philip said.

'No need to be afraid, Pip,' Dickie replied, 'I'll

look after you.'

'I think we should leave them alone in future,' Kit said with a shudder.

'That fella said he'd wring your neck, Dickie,' Pip wailed quietly.

'Shh. He wouldn't do me harm. There's no way he'd risk going back to jail even if he *has* already been there.' Dickie Stanton could not suppress the shiver and he covered it by saying, 'I'm getting cold so I'm going back to bed. You two settle down and I'll see you for breakfast.'

The boys nodded and climbed into their beds. Dickie checked the coast was clear before returning to his room, completely unaware it was the same one Adam and Joe had shared some years ago.

The Stanton boys were like peas in a pod; all sported thick shaggy fair hair and each had eyes the colour of cornflowers. Their teenage faces looked angelic when they smiled, but beneath Dickie's lay a nastiness he sometimes found it difficult to disguise. His brothers naturally deferred to him as leader as, at fifteen, he was the oldest, and he took full advantage of them being so subservient.

Lying in his bed now, Dickie smiled to himself as

he watched the moon cast shadows in his room. Even old Reedy didn't know what the Stantons got up to when they left the orphanage.

The children at Reed's were allowed to come and go now Una left the gates unlocked. It was as she said, where else did they have to go? Because if they went out during the day, they would always return either for lunch or for the evening meal. Neither Una nor the teacher cared whether they attended class or not, so the Stantons chose the latter option.

Dickie thought about the other kids in the orphanage, who were happy to toe the line, but not he and his brothers. His mind then took him to the reason they had come here in the first place.

It was twelve months ago when their father had lashed them together with rope and dragged them along the street like a line of slaves. Their mother had done nothing to help them, she had merely shaken her head in exasperation at their wilful behaviour as she bounced the baby on her knee.

Dickie remembered the looks on the faces of people they passed as Pip cried harder with every step taken. Their father had ignored their pleas and Pip's sobbing as he yanked on the rope that bound them together. It had all begun when the boys were playing at tossing stones into a ring chalked on the cobbles by the privy wall. Dickie's temper had flared when Kit won, his pebble having landed inside the circle. Furious at losing, Dickie had flung his small brick hard and it had bounced off the wall and ricocheted back to hit the neighbour's window. He winced in the darkness as he heard again in his mind the resounding crash as the pane shattered. The boys had taken to their heels as their father shot through the back door to investigate the commotion. The neighbour was yelling that the window had to be replaced and it was down to Stanton senior to foot the bill.

Dickie shivered beneath the covers as he relived the hiding they had received when they'd eventually plucked up the courage to return home. His father had ranted loudly about being out of work; of having three unruly boys and a new baby to feed and now he had to find the money somehow to pay for the broken window. Before sending them to bed he had told them that they would be going to Reed's orphanage if their behaviour did not improve.

As it turned out, they were not given the chance to change their ways, for the following morning they were sold to Una Reed – for five shillings each.

Dickie turned over, the hatred in his heart burning like a fire. Staring up at the moon, he knew all he had in the world worth caring about now was his brothers. He despised his parents for what they'd done to their children, and no matter how long he lived he would never forgive them.

Next year he would be sixteen and then he could leave this wretched place. He would get a job and find somewhere to live with his brothers, and Una Reed and his parents could all go to hell.

The thought cheered him as he watched the clouds scud past the bright moon. Tomorrow was another day closer to being able at last to live life as he chose rather than having it mapped out for him.

Snuggling down beneath the covers, Dickie closed his eyes, intent on dreaming about the day he could walk out of the orphanage gates a free man.

* * *

The following morning, after breakfast, Una watched from her office window the three boys laughing and jostling each other as they passed through the open gate.

She felt an icy chill creep up her spine as she turned away from the window. It was like déjà vu seeing those boys with their heads together, and the images of three other faces came to mind. Adam Fitch, Joseph Blunt and Rodney Dukes.

Sitting at her desk, Una was unable to suppress the shiver that took her. Those boys had driven her near mad. They had picked locks, stolen confidential information from her office and then broken out of the orphanage before encouraging others to do the same. It was for this reason that Una now left the gates open. She knew that any who ventured out would return as soon as they were hungry.

Returning her thoughts to Adam Fitch she scowled. It was common knowledge his mother had married Billy Marshall, the famous pugilist; the man Una had grown up with and had hoped one day to wed herself.

Adam and the escapees had found their way

home to his mother, and they, along with Una's previous staff, were running an orphanage of their own.

With a brief knock the door opened and a pretty young face peeped in. 'May I come in?' the velvety voice asked from between rosebud lips.

Una nodded, taking in at a glance the trim figure of the young woman. Her brown curls matched exactly the colour of her long skirt and a white high-necked blouse completed the look. Her skin was like fine porcelain and her teeth were white and even.

'What is it?' Una asked irritably.

'Miss Reed, I only have four little darlings in my class and...'

Una sighed loudly. 'Diana, what do you want me to do? Should I go out there,' Una pointed to the window, 'and drag more *little darlings* in off the street?'

'No, of course not, but it hardly seems worth me being here,' Diana Wilton returned.

'I see. May I remind you that I have given you employment despite you not being qualified in your chosen profession? I pay you a wage, feed you and provide more than adequate sleeping quarters, do I not?'

Diana nodded sheepishly.

'Good. Now I suggest you return to your class of four and try to make their day as happy as you have made mine miserable!' Una clamped her lips together as she watched the young woman leave the office, suitably cowed.

With another sigh, Una picked up the newspaper. Even though it was now officially spring, there were still reports of the lowest ever temperature recorded in Aberdeen in February. Una glanced at the window and gave a little shiver; it didn't feel much warmer to her.

Returning her eyes to the newsprint she read on. A young woman by the name of Bridget Cleary had been murdered by her husband in County Tipperary, Ireland. He had then burned the body. The man was convicted and sentenced to prison. 'I should think so,' Una muttered. In his defence the man had claimed he had killed a changeling left in his wife's place after she had been abducted by fairies.

'What a load of rot!' Una exclaimed. 'Bloody man should hang!'

Laying down the paper, Una went to feed the fire, which had burned low. Returning to her desk she pondered. Diana Wilton was right, there were too few in her orphanage to warrant badgering the wealthy to stump up more money. The council were worse than useless, saying they were already funding one orphanage in the town and Reed's must look to appropriating coffers of its own.

She had only seven residents at the present time, four of whom were in the classroom, and the Stanton brothers out somewhere doing God only knew what. There was nothing she could do to fill the empty beds except wait for poverty to tighten its stranglehold. Then maybe parents would be forced to sell their children to her; some adults may even die of starvation and the youngsters would come into her care rather than go into the workhouse.

For now all she could do was continue to write begging letters to the wives of rich men. The merchants themselves would discard her correspondence, but their spouses might be touched by the sad plight of these unfortunate orphans.

Taking paper from the drawer and grabbing a pen, Una tipped back the lid of the inkwell. She had to make a start, and there was no time like the present.

* * *

After leaving Reed's, the Stantons wandered down Vicarage Road. Seeing the rag and bone man's horse pulling a cart, Dickie nudged Kit. They heard the bugle blare calling to householders announcing his arrival. The boys imitated the action and giggled. As the cart drew nearer they began to shout. 'Any old rags.' Then they ran across the road in front of the horse. The animal shied and its eyes rolled in fear.

'Bugger off!' the man yelled.

'Bugger off yerself!' Dickie shouted back.

The man flicked the reins and the horse walked on.

Then the boys ran across its path again, waving their arms and shouting.

The horse halted and struggled in its traces trying to escape the strange noise. The man jumped from the driving seat, whip in hand and saw the boys scatter.

'I'll have the bobbies on you!' he growled, waving his bugle in the air.

The boys aped his actions again as they rounded the corner into All Saints Road.

The man stroked the horse's neck to calm it, before climbing onto the cart and continuing on.

'Dickie, you'll get us into trouble,' Pip said as he dragged his boots over the cobbles.

'Aw shut up, you big baby!' his brother returned. 'It was only a bit of fun.'

Pip hung his head as he trailed after his big brother and Kit wrapped an arm around his shoulder.

'It ain't right, Kit,' Pip went on.

Dickie turned on him with, 'You joined in though didn't you, eh?' He poked a finger at the youngest of them. 'Next time you can stay at old Reedy's!'

'I don't want to – not on my own,' Pip wailed.

'Then shut yer yap and do as you're told!' Dickie shouted into the face now covered in tears.

'Leave him alone, Dickie,' Kit said.

'What! You as well? I don't need this from you two, so go back to the orphanage. I don't want you round me with your snivelling and moaning!' With that Dickie took to his heels, leaving his brothers alone in the street.

'What shall we do now?' Pip asked with a sniff.

'Let's go back 'cos I think Dickie's heading for

trouble and I for one don't want to be part of it,' Kit answered.

Pip nodded and drew his jacket sleeve beneath his nose, then they turned around and slowly retraced their steps back to Reed House.

Dickie was furious with his siblings as he marched down Steelhouse Lane. Coming to the allotment gardens, he stopped to look them over. There was only one old man working his plot and Dickie watched, feeling full of mischief. He wondered where the others were – the ones he threw a stone at yesterday. With a shrug he continued to watch the old man raking the soil slowly and carefully.

Stepping onto the gravel path that ran around the perimeter of the plots, Dickie deliberately stomped across the nearest garden.

'Don't walk on there young man, there's plants growing,' the old man called as he spotted Dickie.

Dickie stopped and looked around him then he began to kick at the neat rows of tiny green shoots.

'Oi! You little bleeder!' the old man yelled as he staggered over towards the boy vandalising the garden.

Dickie laughed at the old fellow brandishing a rake before turning and running away. A little further down the street he stopped and looked back. The old codger was looking down at the mess and shaking his head. With another loud laugh, Dickie went in search of somewhere else to cause havoc.

4

Later that day Peter, James and Digit headed for Chillington Wharf in search of cash-in-hand work. There was not enough to do on the allotment, so Adam went alone. He was surprised to see old Mr Jackson on his knees by Adam's plot.

'Hey up, Mr Jackson,' Adam said as he helped the man to his feet.

'Some little sod kicked your rows about, Adam; I was just trying to salvage what I could for you.'

'That's kind of you. I don't suppose you know who did it, do you?' Adam asked, leading the man to an old chair by the shed.

'I do lad, it was the one who chucked that brick at

your brother. I don't know the kid's name, but I think he's from Reed's.'

'Was he on his own or with the other two?' Adam asked as he lit a match for Mr Jackson's cigarette.

'By his self he was. The others, who I think are his brothers, were nowhere to be seen, but that one was in a temper.' Mr Jackson pulled on his cigarette and blew the grey smoke high into the air. 'I chased him off with my rake. You should have seen him go.' The old fellow chuckled and shook his head, his hands resting on his bony knees.

'Good for you but be careful 'cos you never know what they might do,' Adam warned.

'I will. You gonna work on that lot?' Mr Jackson asked nodding to the damaged garden.

'Yes, I'll make a start now before the rain comes,' Adam said, glancing at the overcast sky.

Quietly Adam worked, pushing the soil up around the tender plants to help protect them from any late frosts. He waved to Mr Jackson, who left a short while later, then packed the tools away tidily in the shed.

He felt the first raindrops as he set off for home. Dark clouds rolled across the sky, threatening to shut out the light. Suddenly the rain began to hammer down and Adam broke into a run. By the time he reached the house he was soaked to the skin and shivering with cold. Dashing upstairs to the room he happily shared with Joe, he stripped off his wet clothing, which he then hung up to dry.

As he dressed in warm dry clothes he smiled at Joe's bed. He still made it as smartly as he had when they had slept in the same bedroom at Reed's.

Running down the stairs, Adam went to the kitchen for a hot cup of tea.

'Hopefully we'll have some produce before too long,' Adam said.

'That'll be lovely,' Mabel answered, her blue eyes twinkling at the thought of home-grown vegetables.

'It will be if that kid from Reed's doesn't completely wreck the allotment first,' Adam responded.

'Why, what's happened son?' Minnie asked, concern showing clearly on her face.

Adam explained what he'd found when he had arrived at the allotment. 'There's three of them, but it's the eldest who's causing problems all over the town according to what I'm hearing.'

'Well don't you be getting involved,' Minnie warned.

'I am already, Mum. It was my plot he kicked around. It can't be allowed to go on,' Adam replied.

'I don't want the coppers on my doorstep because you've pasted the kid. You have to remember you've had boxing lessons...' Minnie began.

'I know Mum, and I'll do my best to settle this peacefully should the need arise,' Adam put in quickly.

Minnie nodded.

'I'd punch his lights out anyway,' Dilys mumbled as she returned from the pantry with cake.

'You keep your opinions to yerself!' Mabel snapped, 'and get on with peeling the spuds.'

'I always get the shi... rotten jobs,' Dilys grumbled, 'just once I'd like to have summat nice to do.' Pushing her fair hair back beneath her maid's cap, her face took on a sulky look.

'Dilys, you're the maid – you do maid-type things.' Mabel rolled her eyes and sighed loudly.

'I bloody know that!' Dilys rapped back.

'All right ladies, let's get cracking on tonight's meal. The little 'uns will be starving when they finish in Celia's classroom,' Minnie said in an effort to prevent an all-out kitchen war.

'Well I have nothing to do so I'll peel the potatoes for you Dilys,' Adam said.

'Ooh ta!' the maid said with a grin.

'In that case, Dilys, would you make a few apple pies for pudding?' Mabel asked.

'Yes! A decent job at last,' Dilys said rushing back to the pantry for ingredients.

Adam and Mabel shared a grin before they proceeded with their jobs.

'Polly's coming!' Echo called excitedly as he shot into the kitchen. Then he went to greet her at the front door.

Minnie smiled at how Echo eagerly awaited the return of his *princess* every day. The lad adored her daughter and May too. They had become such firm friends when they all lived together before Billy brought them home. Billy, her husband of the last four years, was so different from her first husband Gerald. Father to Peter and James, Gerald had been a bully, and it was he who had sold Adam and Polly to Reed's for drinking money.

Minnie shivered before trying to shake off the

feeling. Gerald was dead and gone and now she was wed to the nicest man on earth; Minnie felt fortunate indeed.

'Hello, love,' she said as Polly walked into the kitchen, Echo at her heel.

'Phew, what a day,' Polly plonked herself onto a kitchen chair.

'Day,' Echo mumbled as he poured tea and passed the cup to Polly.

'Thanks Echo, you're an angel,' she said with a smile. As she drank, she told them all about her day at the hospital, then listened attentively as Adam explained about the allotment saga.

Minnie left them to it and went to see how May was getting on changing the beds of their charges. As she walked to the hallway Minnie stopped and looked around. They had been so lucky to have found this huge rambling house which was set on the edge of the sprawling heath.

The kitchen and scullery were on the ground floor along with a living room, parlour and what must have once been a music room. There was also a huge dining room. A great sweeping staircase led to sixteen bedrooms, and a set of back stairs reached a further six rooms for servants' use. Mabel, Dilys, Ruth and Celia occupied these happily and had made them cosy and comfortable.

Minnie smiled as she thought how the *kids*, as she referred to them, still chose to share. Adam and Joe; Matt and Arthur; Polly and May; Echo and Flash; Peter and James, and Digit had been pleased to join Rodney. Friendships so strong were very rare, and she knew they would endure until the end.

As she climbed the stairs Minnie thought back to Billy discovering this place, which had lain deserted for many years. Enquiring at the council, their records had shown it to belong to no one that they could discern. Clearly the family had either all died out or had simply upped and gone, leaving the rambling old building to fall into disrepair. The council could not rightly charge a sale price as the dwelling did not belong to them. Because no family could be traced to approach about a sale, the council officer had said Billy and his family could take it on. The proceeds from Minnie's two-up, two-down and Billy's property had helped with renovations to make the place habitable.

Ruth Ashby, once employed by Una Reed and

now working for Minnie, had badgered the local authority into pledging an annual budget to enable Minnie to open an orphanage of her own.

Minnie met May on the landing as the girl was pushing the last of the laundry into a huge wheeled basket.

'That's it Minnie, all the beds changed,' May said wiping her brow.

'Thanks sweet'eart. Leave that there and I'll get some of the lads to carry it down to the scullery. Go and get a cuppa now and have a rest,' Minnie answered.

The two descended the stairs together and Minnie went to the old music room which had been converted into an office. Ruth was going over the accounts when Minnie entered.

'Ruth, if I tell you what I have planned, you can then tell me if we can afford it.'

'You'd best have a seat then,' Ruth replied with a smile, making her bright blue eyes glisten.

5

Whilst Minnie and Ruth were poring over their ledgers, Mr Jackson grabbed his walking cane and ambled slowly over to Reed's orphanage. He wanted a word with the woman in charge about the young man who had vandalised the allotment garden.

Entering the grounds, he walked carefully along the gravel path that wove between the trees. Coming to the building, he mounted the steps and yanked on the bell pull. A moment later the door opened to reveal a pair of questioning eyes.

'I'd like to see the person who runs this place,' Mr Jackson announced.

The door opened wider to allow him to step inside. Closing the door again the woman beckoned him to follow her.

Limping along behind the young woman, Mr Jackson had the distinct impression she was very unhappy. Pointing to a door the woman turned and walked away.

Knocking, Mr Jackson waited.

'Come!' The voice in the room beyond boomed out loudly.

Mr Jackson pushed the door open and shuffled into the office. The officious looking woman who sat behind her desk looked up.

'Yes, what is it?'

'I'd like a word about one of your – residents,' Mr Jackson answered, a little unsure of how to address the children in her care.

'Which one?' Una asked.

'I'm afraid I don't know his name but he's about thirteen or fourteen years old and has a shock of blonde hair,' Mr Jackson said as he leaned on his stick.

'Please take a seat,' Una pointed to a straight-backed chair.

Mr Jackson nodded and sat down, grateful to take the weight off his arthritic leg.

'I think I know which boy you are referring to. What's he done?' Una leaned back in her well-padded chair.

'He kicked the hell out of our allotment garden is what he's done!' Mr Jackson said sternly.

'I take it you witnessed this?' Una asked.

'Yes. I chased him off, but the damage was done and he only laughed.'

'Then I must apologise...' Una began.

'Don't bother with apologies – just deal with it.' Mr Jackson's words cut her off. 'Give the lad a bloody good hiding so he won't do it again.'

'Be assured, I will punish the child responsible,' Una answered, feeling a little annoyed at being told how to deal with her wards.

'Make sure you do because if it happens again I'll have the bobbies down here quicker than you can blink.' With a curt nod, Mr Jackson got to his feet with a groan. 'Good day to you.'

Una watched him leave her office drawing her lips into a thin line.

Dickie Stanton again!

He would be back when it was time to eat and that's when she would tackle him. She realised then that the old man had made no mention of Dickie's brothers, which was curious because they almost always went everywhere together. Clearly something had happened to split them up. She would find out later when they stood in line for supper.

Hearing a commotion, Una left her office and made her way to where all the shouting was taking place, namely the foyer.

'What is going on here?' she yelled as she approached the boys. 'Ah, the Stantons. I might have guessed. Richard, to my office, you others find something to do – quietly.'

Una's side-button boots tapped along the corridor behind Dickie's shuffling ones. The boy stopped directly in front of her office door and Una grabbed his jacket collar and hoisted him back a step. Opening the door, she marched inside and sat at her desk.

Dickie sauntered through, leaving the door open but with a withering look from Una, he turned and closed it. Facing her once more he waited.

The defiant look on his face brought forth in her mind an image of another boy, Rodney Dukes, and Una inwardly raged.

'Would you mind telling me what all that noise was about?' she asked as she shook off the image that seemed to haunt her.

Dickie shrugged his shoulders but said nothing.

'I see. You were yelling at your brothers loud enough to wake the dead, young man, which is wholly inappropriate behaviour.' Una paused as she glared at the boy stood in front of her desk. 'Not only are you causing a commotion here, but I have also received a complaint from one of the townsfolk regarding a misdeed carried out by yourself earlier today.'

Dickie rolled his eyes and shifted his weight to one leg as he shoved his hands in his trouser pockets.

The movement incensed Una and she drew in a breath through flared nostrils. 'Take your hands out of your pockets and stand up straight, boy! I will not put up with slovenliness.'

Dickie was taken by surprise and instantly did as he was ordered.

'Now then, explain to me what you were doing up at the allotment gardens and why you wrecked a plot there.' Una's glare was fierce, and a black anger showed clearly in her brown eyes. Fighting to keep control of her temper, Una patted her dark hair, checking it was still in place. It was her way of showing the boy she was not about to jump up and tear him limb from limb.

'It weren't me,' Dickie answered.

'It wasn't me!' Even as she corrected his grammar she knew she was wasting her time. 'You were seen, Richard!'

Shrugging again, Dickie merely raised his eyebrows.

'Due to your actions, I may be forced to lock the gates, which would be unfair on those who wish to enjoy their little jaunts into town. Those who know how to behave properly, and they would blame you for curtailing their freedom,' Una went on.

'Do what you like, I don't care,' Dickie responded.

'Fair enough. I will inform the other children that because of you their free time will be spent confined to the orphanage's grounds, and it's my guess they will not be happy about it,' Una said.

'Miss Reed, I really don't give a shit!'

Una shot from her chair and delivered a sharp slap to the boy's cheek. 'Watch your mouth Master Stanton, I will not have bad language in my house!'

Dickie clamped his teeth together in an effort to prevent more of the same spewing forth.

Una pushed her face close to his and growled, 'If I receive just one more complaint about you Stanton, be assured I will deal with you most severely.' Poking his shoulder, she continued, 'You will go without supper this evening, but you will sit in the dining hall and watch everyone else enjoy theirs. Anyone who should try to smuggle food to you will be in trouble up to their ears. Do you understand?'

Dickie was shaking with anger as he stared at the woman he hated.

'Do – you – understand?' Una repeated.

Dickie nodded.

'Right. You are dismissed.' Una flicked her fingers and was gratified to see the boy flinch before he turned and left the office.

Una retook her seat and closed her eyes tightly.

For five years she'd had no trouble from the youngsters in her care, not since...

The pictures floating in her mind of the Fitch
children and their entourage made her snap open
her eyes in an effort to dispel them. That little band
had caused her no end of problems; breaking out of
her building, bringing police on her doorstep – the
list went on and on. Now she had the Stanton brothers, but she'd be damned if she would suffer the
same indignations again. The time had come to
stamp out their unruly behaviour, and this evening
they would see the other side of Una Reed.

* * *

Watching the children line up for their meal later,
Una scowled. Holding up the flat of her hand to the
cook as a signal to not yet begin to serve, she spun on
her heel and marched from the dining room. Taking
the stairs two at a time she stomped along the
landing and threw open the door to Richard Stanton's bedroom.

The boy was sitting on his bed and his head

snapped round at the sudden intrusion into his privacy.

Striding to Dickie, she grabbed his ear and yanked him to his feet, then she led him down the stairs and deposited him at the end of the line of waiting children. Nodding to the cook to serve the food, Una watched the faces turn away from her. She followed along as the queue shortened until it was Dickie's turn.

'There will be no supper for this young hooligan,' she said in a voice which carried across the room. 'Go and sit down, Richard.' She gave the boy a shove and when he was seated she went on. 'Master Stanton was seen vandalising one of the allotment gardens today and as a consequence he will forego his meal. Anyone caught passing food to him will be severely punished. Also because of his disgraceful behaviour I am forced to lock the gates. Therefore no one will be allowed out until such time as *Dickie* can be trusted to conduct himself in an appropriate manner.'

There was a chorus of moans from the other children at this news and Una pointed to the boy who was the cause of their dismay.

'You have this young man to thank for calling a halt to your liberty.' She watched as all eyes turned to Dickie and heard the low grumblings of discontent.

Nodding with satisfaction she took her seat at the top table to enjoy her meal, her smouldering eyes firmly glued to Richard Stanton.

6

That same evening, Polly and Adam sat in the living room chatting as was their wont. When they had all moved in, Minnie had dismissed the label of 'orphanage' as she said it only served to remind the children of their unfortunate circumstances. Therefore it was now known as Marshall's Children's Home, and each night since, brother and sister had cemented their tight bond by spending time together – just the two of them.

'Polly, can you remember when we were at old Reedy's...?'

'Oh Ad, don't!' she cut across his words.

'No, just hang on a minute. Think back to when

Rodney came. Do you recall how he and I couldn't get along at first? How he was always in trouble and spent a lot of the time in the *box*?'

Polly shivered at the memory as she nodded.

'Well, I think that lad who wrecked the allotment is the same as Rodney was,' Adam said.

'How do you mean?' Polly asked with a frown.

'I suspect he's top dog there and probably bullies all the others.'

'But why spoil the garden?' Polly asked.

'Maybe he was trying to reinforce his dominance over old Mr Jackson,' Adam reasoned.

'What will happen now? Are you going to tackle him, Ad?'

'Only if he asks for it,' her brother said quietly.

'I recall you saying that about Rodney before you hammered him!' Polly said with a sheepish grin.

'My worry is what he'll do next, though,' Adam said, trying not to frighten his sister.

'In what way?' Despite his efforts Polly felt a frisson of fear shudder through her.

'I don't really know. He could go back and completely ruin all our hard work, or he could threaten Mr Jackson. The old fella would be no match for him, Polly, and I'm concerned he could get hurt.' Adam laid a hand on Polly's arm as he spoke. 'I don't want you to fret about all this, I'm just thinking out loud.'

'Ad, we've always told each other everything so I understand. Is there any way we can protect Mr Jackson?' Polly asked.

'I was wondering the same thing. Maybe if I had a word with Peter and James we could arrange for one of us to be at the allotment all day every day,' Adam confided.

'Is there enough to do to warrant that, though? After all, it's early in the growing season yet.' Polly's mind was ticking over, trying every possible way to help Adam.

'Not really, but we have to do something,' he replied.

'Speak to James and Peter and let me know what you decide. I can help out on my days off from the hospital as well.'

'Good idea, you could bring our lunch,' Adam said with a cheeky flick of his eyebrows.

'Now you're pushing your luck, Adam Fitch!' Polly answered with mock indignation.

With a laugh the two continued to talk until yawns said it was time for bed.

* * *

The following morning Dickie didn't bother trying to pick the gate lock as his predecessors had, he simply climbed up and over, dropping to the ground at the other side. Pleased with his efforts, he strolled along the street in search of mischief.

Scratching his head through his thick mop of hair, Dickie wondered what the day would have in store for him.

The sun was struggling to make an appearance, and the early morning chill had Dickie fasten the only button on his jacket before shoving his hands into his trouser pockets.

Passing the boot and shoe manufactory he breathed in the lovely smell of leather, which was quickly replaced by the tantalising aroma of freshly baked bread. The baker's panniers either side of his horse were stuffed to the brim, but the man kept a wary eye on the boy across the street in fear of being robbed.

Dickie moved on, deciding against attempting to steal from the baker. He pulled his flat cap down over his eyes and returned his hand to his pocket. Kicking a stone, he watched it bounce off the cobbles before coming to rest further down the street. As he walked, he wondered what his brothers were doing. After the incident with the rag and bone man, Dickie had made up his mind they were sissies and he was better off on his own, but he had to admit he was missing their company.

Turning into Cleveland Road, he sauntered past the General Hospital. The huge building was spread over a wide area and although it was a place of healing, people feared the thought of having to go there. They were of the opinion that, once inside, the only way out was in a box. Moving on towards the Union Workhouse, which he had seen countless times, he called the building to mind. The wrought iron gates were always locked and the porter in his little lodge held the key. The structure itself was in a radial shape but all that could be seen from the road was the frontage. The poor people of the town were more afraid of this place than they were of the hospital. Even Dickie knew that accepting the ticket into the workhouse meant you were destitute and had no other choice – unless you wanted to die on the street from starvation. Unable to face that dreadful place, he cut down Jenner Street. Dickie walked past the place which had originally been Reed's orphanage and he curled his lip in derision. He wondered if it still lay empty and was tempted to go and see, but the thought of having to climb the gates deterred him. On he went into Steelhouse Lane until he found himself once more by the allotments. Just as he was about to enter, he was halted by a shout.

'Hey, you here again? I thought I told you to clear off!'

Looking in the direction of the voice, Dickie saw it was the old man who had chased him with a rake.

'So?' he challenged.

'You do any more damage and the bobbies will lock you up,' Mr Jackson yelled.

Dickie walked across to face the man, heedless of crushing the little green plants beneath his boots. 'Was it you who reported me to old Reedy?' Dickie growled.

'What if it was?' Mr Jackson returned.

'I had no supper 'cos of you!'

'You should have thought of that when you smashed up that plot!' Mr Jackson pointed his cane towards Adam's garden.

'Why, you miserable old bugger!' Dickie clenched his fists and stepped forward towards the man now leaning on his stick.

'Morning, Mr Jackson.' The pleasant voice sailed across to the two squaring up to each other. Adam walked swiftly to where they stood. 'Problems?'

'This is the little bugger who spoiled your work,' Mr Jackson responded as he pointed a bony finger in Dickie's direction.

'Is that right?' Adam turned to face the boy accused and said, 'My name is Adam Fitch, who are you?'

'Dickie Stanton, though it ain't any of your business!' came the reply.

'It is when you vandalise my property,' Adam returned calmly.

'I d'aint, that old sod is lying,' Dickie grinned as he tilted his head towards Mr Jackson.

'You calling me a liar? I'll wring your scrawny neck!' Mr Jackson took an unsteady step forward but was held back by Adam.

'It's all right Mr Jackson, I'll deal with this. Now then Dickie, I'll tell you this just once. You stay away from my land and Mr Jackson otherwise you and I will fall out, and you wouldn't want that, believe me.' Adam pursed his lips and raised his eyebrows.

'You don't scare me. I could flatten you easy as anything,' Dickie retorted.

Adam adjusted his stance to one foot in front of the other, his weight balanced solidly on his back foot. Clenching his hands into fists he raised them to his face as Billy had taught him. 'Come on then, if you think you're tough enough, although I warn you I've knocked bigger lads than you out cold,' Adam said with a grin.

Dickie was taken aback. Adam looked to be a boxer and used to sparring if not actually fighting. Suddenly he didn't fancy his chances and felt his bravado begin to crumble.

Turning and walking away, Dickie called over his shoulder, 'I ain't got time today.' Walking swiftly up the street, he considered himself lucky to have avoided getting a bashing. However, as he made his way back to Reed's, he felt anger rise in him. Adam Fitch had made him look a fool and he had heard him and the old man laughing as he had taken his leave of them.

I'll get you for this, Fitch! Somehow, some way I'll make you suffer, so watch your back!

Coming to the gate at the orphanage he saw it was still locked. His fury now at boiling point, he shook them with all his might before kicking out, only to hurt his toe. Hopping around on one foot he felt close to tears. His foot was throbbing, Fitch had humiliated him and now he had to climb the gate and try to land without injuring his toe further.

Dickie Stanton felt the fates had colluded against him and dealt him a bitter blow. Climbing the gate and mumbling under his breath, he steeled himself for the drop. When the landing came, it made him howl with pain before he limped up the gravel path.

From an upstairs window a pair of eyes had watched the whole debacle and Una Reed laughed loudly at the disgruntled boy dragging himself indoors.

* * *

Back at the allotment, Adam and Mr Jackson were discussing Dickie Stanton.

'Don't take him on, Mr Jackson,' Adam said.

'I'm not afraid of him, Adam,' came the reply.

'I know that but I'd still rather you left him to me. James, Peter or I will be here every day to keep a look out,' Adam assured.

'You don't need to babysit me, young man,' Mr Jackson responded.

'We have no intention of doing so, I'm only concerned for Mum's vegetables. If I don't deliver she'll skin my hide.' Adam laughed to help relieve the tension. He had told Mr Jackson a fib and felt badly about that but keeping an eye on the elderly gentleman – as well as the produce – was reason enough for the little white lie.

'I've got some fresh scones with butter and jam if you fancy sharing,' Adam said once they had stopped laughing.

'You bet! I've not had any since my wife passed. Lead the way, Adam my boy!'

Mr Jackson perched on the one chair and Adam sat on the ground. Unwrapping the parcel of baking they shared what Adam had been given by Mabel.

Chatting whilst they ate, Adam learned that Mr Jackson's wife had died around the time he was in Reed's himself. The old gent had managed on his own for five years, but he was frail, and Adam worried for him. There were no children from the marriage and seeing the sad look in the rheumy old eyes, Adam didn't probe as to why. It became clear that Mr Jackson was extremely lonely as they talked and Adam shared stories about his family.

Mr Jackson asked many questions: who lived at the house? How many were there? What jobs did they have? What were their names? Adam answered them all patiently. It was nice that the old man was taking such an interest.

'You're lucky to have so many friends and good parents, Adam, cherish them whilst you can,' Mr Jackson said.

'Oh, I do Mr Jackson.' Adam suddenly found himself relating the story of how he and Polly had become so close.

'Our stepfather sold Polly and me to Reed's for five shillings each.'

'Why just you two?'

'Gerald Fitch was Peter and James's real father,

but Polly and I had a different one,' Adam explained a little sheepishly.

'How do you feel about that?'

'We're all right with it although it came as a shock when we first found out. Anyway, old Reedy sold our Polly to a wealthy family as a companion for their daughter who was nine years old – the same as our Polly.'

'Good Lord!'

'Yes, well, it hit me hard, Mr Jackson, so I decided to run away to find her.'

'How old were you at that time?'

'Ten.'

Mr Jackson blew out his cheeks. 'Quite an undertaking for one so young.'

'I had to find out where Polly had gone so Rodney picked the lock on Miss Reed's office door whilst Joe kept watch. I found the address and then the lads helped me to get out. I went to the address and waited and when Polly came out with a lady and the other child I followed. I sang a little song our mum used to sing and Polly heard it and saw me. Dashing past I shouted "Run!" and then we were long gone. We got the others out of Reed's as well, then we met Flash, Digit and Echo. Eventually I went to Billy who had taught me to box and it turned out he knew my real dad. He found our mum and brought her to see us at his house.'

'It was a miracle that you all came together again at the end,' Mr Jackson said shaking his head in wonder.

'Polly said she'll come here on her day off, you'll like her Mr Jackson, everybody does,' Adam said with a warm smile.

'I'll look forward to her visit.' Mr Jackson raised his eyes to the sky. 'Looks like we're in for more rain so I'd best get off. Thank you for sharing your lunch with me, Adam.'

'You're most welcome Mr Jackson, and hopefully we can chat some more next time.'

Adam watched the old man limp away and hoped he would get home before the downpour, for he had no one to look after him if he caught a chill.

Collecting up the tools, Adam put them away in the shed and took a last look around the plots. Satisfied all was well, he left the gardens and walked away wondering what Mr Jackson did with everything he grew. Surely there was too much for one person to eat, so what happened to the rest?

It suddenly dawned on Adam that today had been the first time he had really talked to Mr Jackson, other than just a polite greeting. He made himself a promise to natter with the old man every day from now on, as well as look out for his welfare.

The sky began to darken and steel grey clouds rolled over the town, blotting out the weak sun. The air chilled and Adam shivered. The first heavy raindrops splatted down, making Adam increase his step. As if to match him, the rain came down faster until it was bouncing off the cobblestones.

Pulling up his jacket collar, Adam broke into a run, desperately trying to outpace the torrent now lashing his body. He breathed a sigh of relief as he shot in through the front door. Shaking himself down he pushed his wet hair out of his eyes and stood a moment to catch his breath. Then he went upstairs to change into dry clothing once more.

* * *

Whilst Adam had been chatting with Mr Jackson,

Minnie had again gone over the figures with Ruth Ashby. They had agreed there was more than enough in the bank to cover the first of Minnie's ideas, which she intended to announce when they all sat down to their evening meal. Marshall's Children's Home was to have electric lights fitted.

Leaving the office, Minnie heard laughter and she smiled. May and Echo were chuckling together over something or other. The sound of boots on the stairs had her turn. 'Oh blimey, looks like you got soaked again,' she said.

'Yes, now I need a hot cuppa,' Adam answered as he wrapped a loving arm around his mum's shoulder.

In the kitchen, Adam related the morning's events with Echo's echoes sounding intermittently.

'Poor old bugger,' Mabel said as she cut bread and cheese as a snack for everyone.

'Isn't there anything we can do to help this Mr Jackson?' May asked.

Echo nodded eagerly as he pushed his chair closer to May's.

'He enjoyed your baking, Mabel, that's for sure,' Adam said with a grin.

'Well maybe I could pack a little picnic for him, what do you say Minnie?' the cook asked.

'It's all right with me, but would Mr Jackson see it as charity?' Minnie answered with her own question.

Mabel nodded, 'He might.'

'Minnie, if I went with Adam after my chores, maybe I could get to know Mr Jackson and in time he might let me befriend him a little, you know – help a bit around his home,' May volunteered.

'And me!' Echo added.

'It's worth a try,' Adam said.

'Right, but you two take umbrellas when you go 'cos our Adam's got soaked twice now,' Minnie said sternly.

'Tomorrow, then, Echo and May will be off to make a new friend. Oh and Adam, invite Mr Jackson to tea on a day of his choosing.' Minnie gave a curt nod, telling everyone she would brook no arguments.

7

Having already eaten that evening, Mabel and Dilys served everyone's meal then stood waiting to hear the big announcement.

'Just to let you all know,' Minnie called out over the clatter and scraping of cutlery on plates, 'next week we are having electric lights installed!'

Spontaneous applause took her by surprise as she sat to enjoy her food. Then a little voice sounded, 'Installed!' Giggles lasted but for only a moment before everyone resumed eating and chatting quietly.

'I'll let Peter and James know what we have planned regarding Mr Jackson, Mum,' Adam said, and Minnie nodded.

Dinners of potatoes, vegetables and faggots in a thick onion gravy were polished off in no time and dirty plates were piled up, the cutlery tossed into a massive enamel bowl filled with water. One by one they queued up for home-made rice pudding and jam.

With a rota drawn up for helping with the dishes, each went to their allotted task without complaint. Later, May read to the little ones before they went to their beds. Echo sat on the floor listening intently.

Adam and Polly went to enjoy their ritual exchange of news and Peter, James, Digit and Flash played cards in the corner of the living room, with Arthur, Matt and Rodney looking on, awaiting their turn.

Minnie and Billy joined the other adults in the kitchen for a cup of tea and a discussion about how much upheaval could be expected the following week.

* * *

Over at Reed's, the evening meal was taking place also.

Una sauntered past the children waiting quietly in line to be served their stew.

'How's the toe, Richard?' she asked loudly.

Dickie's face coloured as eyes turned to look at him. Una laughed and moved on.

So she knew – she must have seen him scale the gate after trying to kick it open in a temper. Was she going to punish him? Apparently not, otherwise she would have done so already.

Truth be told, Dickie didn't much care either way, he was still intent on getting out of the grounds. He had a score to settle with Adam Fitch; the question was how to do it.

Sitting with a bowl of thick glutinous stew he ate automatically, his mind trying to find a way of besting Fitch without actually having to fight. The boy was a boxer, that much was certain, so what could Dickie do to get his own back for being humiliated?

All evening Dickie brooded and shunned his brothers when they tried to coax him into playing games. Eventually Kit and Pip left him to his black mood and went to play dominoes on their own.

Finding no solution, Dickie stomped off to bed, feeling angry and frustrated.

* * *

The following morning the sun shone down full and bright, glinting on the small puddles of rainwater left behind from the deluge the day before.

Mabel had packed two picnic baskets with bottles of home-made lemonade, bread, cheese, chunks of ham carved from the bone, scones and little lemon cakes.

'Blimey, Mabel, there's enough to feed the five thousand there!' Adam said with a grin as he gave the cook a hug. They both turned in surprise as Echo began to count on his fingers, 'One thousand, two thousand...'

'Ready,' Echo muttered, picking up a basket.

'You can always bring back what you don't eat,' Mabel answered, knowing full well everything would be consumed.

Adam grabbed the other hamper and he and Echo went to the hall to wait for May. A moment later she appeared in a pale blue cotton dress reaching to her ankles, a straw boater in her hand.

'Ooh May, lovely,' Echo said timidly.

'Thank you, Echo. Right gents, shall we be off?' she asked with a beaming smile.

'After you, milady,' Adam said as he held open the front door.

'Milady,' Echo laughed.

Chatting and laughing as they went, it was not long before they reached their destination.

Mr Jackson was already on site and waved as he saw them approach. He had been sitting on the old rickety chair watching other gardeners tend their plots laughing and joking as they worked. One man whistled a little tune as he got to his knees to weed his small garden. Although the sections weren't officially marked out with fences, each person was aware of the boundaries, but they weren't averse to helping out another if needed.

'Mr Jackson, meet May Johnson and Echo,' Adam said.

'Echo,' the boy repeated proudly.

'I'm very pleased to meet you both,' the old man said. 'Miss May, won't you take a seat?' Mr Jackson indicated the old rickety chair, which he dusted off with his handkerchief.

'Thank you, kind sir,' May said with a flounce of her skirt.

The boys laid the baskets on the ground beside her and she added, 'We've brought lunch.'

Mr Jackson rubbed his hands together a little clumsily as he was still holding onto his walking stick.

Echo wandered off, carefully stepping between the rows of planted vegetables.

May and Mr Jackson instantly struck up a conversation and Adam began to weed his plot. No one noticed the fair-haired boy casually leaning against the shed on the other side of the gravel path – except Adam.

Dickie Stanton watched and felt a pang of jealousy at how well the little group were getting on. For a moment he wished he was a part of their enjoyment until his eyes landed on Adam. Then the familiar feeling of embarrassed resentment grew in him once again. He shifted his gaze to the other boy as he heard the call.

'Ooh look May – a bumbly!' Echo shouted as he

pointed to a bumble bee buzzing around the greenery.

The boy's an idiot, he ain't right in the head, he thought as he saw Echo on his hands and knees watching the insect with fascination.

May's laughter drew his attention back to her. Beneath her hat, blonde curls bounced as she talked animatedly. Her skin was clear and glowing, and her teeth were white and even; Dickie could just make out she had blue eyes. She was as pretty as a picture and Dickie's eyes lingered dreamily on her. *When I'm old enough I'd like to marry a girl like that*, he found himself thinking. Sitting himself comfortably on the ground, Dickie continued to watch all morning. It was as May began to unpack the food that Dickie realised how hungry he was. The slop old Reedy had the nerve to call porridge was so thin it was barely more than water, and it certainly didn't satisfy an empty belly.

Picking at the grass around him, Dickie began to chew on it, then with a grimace he spat it out again. He had a choice: he could stay here with a rumbling tummy or he could go back to Reed's and see what muck was being served for lunch. His stomach won out and Dickie got to his feet and ambled away.

Adam watched him go from the corner of his eye. Under other circumstances he would have been happy to share his meal, but he felt sure Dickie Stanton would have seen it as charity and not have wanted to accept. Instead of improving the situation between them it would most probably have damaged it further. Adam felt sorry for the boy having to live at Reed's, for he and Polly – and their friends – had been in that same situation years ago.

Mr Jackson caught Adam's eye and flicked up his eyebrows as his eyes slid to the direction Dickie had taken. So Mr Jackson had spotted the boy too. Adam winked in response to the unspoken message, and man and boy shared a knowing smile.

Making his way up Steelhouse Lane, Dickie suddenly felt loneliness wrap itself around him. Yes, he was top dog in the orphanage, but out here on the streets he was completely alone. He dragged his feet as he shuffled along like an old man, his chin on his chest and flat cap perched precariously on his thick hair.

He had so wanted, if only for a moment, to be a

part of that little gathering; to laugh and have no worries. He wanted to eat decent food for a change but most of all he needed to feel wanted.

Ambling along, Dickie felt the hot sting of tears and swallowed them back. He would not weep, he was almost a man now and Black Country men didn't cry. But he couldn't fight the fear which enveloped him. What would become of him? How would he cope on his own when old Reedy threw him out when he turned sixteen? Where would he live? And then there was the prospect of trying to find work. It would be nigh on impossible having had virtually no schooling. He could write his name so he didn't have to make his mark and he could add up simple numbers, but that didn't bode well with so many applying for so few jobs.

Arriving at Reed's he scaled the gate, feeling the saddest he'd ever been in his life. Hearing the hand bell ring calling everyone to the dining room, Dickie sprinted up the driveway. Whatever was for lunch, it would be better than nothing.

8

At the end of the week, Polly Fitch arrived home in floods of tears. Echo paced the kitchen wringing his hands as he listened to his *lady* cry. Her nursing training had finished and she had been dismissed from the hospital along with the other trainees. Cutbacks in funding was the reason given, and only the most senior and experienced nurses were to be kept on. Years of hard work and devotion to duty were gone in the blink of an eye. The hospital was very sorry – but there it was.

It was Adam that Polly turned to for comfort, and Minnie looked on as brother held sister whilst she wept. It should have been her that Polly turned to in her hour of need, but Minnie knew the bond the siblings shared was far stronger. It made her sad that this was the case, but she knew the reasons. Adam was the one who had rescued Polly when Una Reed sold her to a wealthy family. Adam had taken care of her during the time they lived on the streets, and Minnie knew in her heart that the love her children shared was deep and unbreakable.

Adam led Polly to the living room where she could be consoled a little more privately; everyone else remained in the kitchen, feeling wretched for the girl.

Echo began to wail as Polly left the room and Minnie caught the boy in her arms and talked to him quietly. 'Don't take on so, lad, Adam will make our Polly feel better. She'll be right as rain soon you'll see.'

'Polly... crying...' Echo said through his own tears.

'Echo, we have to be strong for Polly now and show our support. She needs to know we all love her,' May said.

Echo nodded and Minnie released him.

'I'll tell you what, let's go and find some wild

flowers and you can give them to Polly later.' May held out a hand and Echo grasped it eagerly.

'Later.'

The two slipped quietly out of the back door in search of a posy for Polly. Minnie smiled at the gesture as everyone resumed their business silently.

In the living room, Polly's tears had subsided as the shock began to wear off.

'What shall I do now?' she asked.

'You'll just have to nurse us lot,' Adam answered with a tiny smile.

'Ad, I need to be earning and I can't do that here.' Polly shook her head and sniffed.

'Polly, you can't move away if that's what you're thinking. I couldn't bear it and it would break Mum's heart. Besides, there's no saying you'd be taken on anywhere else. Wolverhampton is a big town and if they are cutting back...' Adam paused allowing his words to sink in.

'I know you're right but – oh Ad, I feel so helpless!'

'It's not your fault, Polly, and the sooner you realise that the quicker you can get over it. Look, I'm not trying to be dismissive 'cos I know how much it means to you, but we have to look forward now.' Adam squeezed Polly's hand in a supportive manner.

'All right, Ad,' Polly said, and he was transported back to when they were small, coaxing her into doing something for the best outcome despite her reluctance.

'You know you scared the life out of Echo, the poor fella was beside himself with worry,' Adam added.

'He's such a sweetheart,' Polly acknowledged.

'You ready to face the music?' Adam asked.

Polly nodded and got to her feet. Throwing her arms around him she whispered, 'I love you, Ad.'

'I love you too, Pol,' he answered and just about managed to swallow the lump in his throat.

Back in the kitchen over tea, Polly explained again the events of the day. Slowly the others joined them as their workday ended.

'Makes you want to take up alcohol again,' Ruth said as she eyed Celia, her one-time drinking friend.

'Not in this house,' Minnie answered warningly.

The two women had taken to the bottle whilst in Una Reed's employ but had quit when they joined Minnie's family.

'Set up on your own,' Digit said – still a man of few words.

'It wouldn't be possible, Digit,' Polly responded.

'Why not?' Flash asked.

'Well – erm,' Polly searched for an answer.

'You could, you're clever enough,' Rodney put in.

'He's right,' Matt concurred, pushing his dark hair out of his eyes.

'Maybe May could be your assistant,' Arthur volunteered.

'Go on, Polly, give it a go. Nothing ventured and all that,' Joe encouraged, his ginger eyebrows bouncing as if on springs.

Polly smiled at the faces surrounding her and was about to speak when Echo burst in through the door. 'Polly – flowers!' he said on a breath. May followed indoors and watched as Echo presented his other *lady* with the posy.

'Oh, Echo, how beautiful!' Polly said as she took the ragged bunch of weeds and held them to her nose. 'Thank you, now I feel so much better.' Polly kissed Echo's cheek and the boy flushed with pride.

'No more crying?' he asked.

'No, I won't cry again,' Polly assured him.

'Right, I have an idea,' Adam said, 'but it will need Mum and Billy's approval so maybe when the little 'uns are in bed we could have a meeting in the living room.'

With all in agreement, Polly and Echo went in search of a vase for her flowers.

After their meal of meat and potato pie with fresh vegetables followed by fruit, Minnie and May settled the younger members into their beds before retiring to the living room.

Once everyone was in attendance and comfortable, Adam began. 'I've had an idea and wanted an opinion from you all. We all know Polly's training has finished up at the hospital so here's what I suggest. Mum and Billy, it will depend on what you think as well as our Polly. One of the empty rooms upstairs could be turned into a sick room for want of a better description. Polly could be in charge and sort out medicines and bandages and such like, and if anyone is poorly she can look after them in there. We could put a couple of beds in and some cupboards and things to help out. The thing is, Polly will need to be paid 'cos she'd be an on-site nurse.' Adam looked around at the faces watching him before he went on. 'I don't know about the finances of this place so, Mum, you and Ruth would have to work that out. That's my idea – what do you think?'

Everyone began speaking at once and Adam called for order. 'One at a time please.'

'That will take up a room, so what happens if we have more kiddies come in?' Mabel asked.

'We'll manage, it's not as though we're short of space at the moment. Besides, when anyone gets ill, it's Mum who is run ragged taking care of them. This way Polly can help relieve that burden,' Adam answered.

'It makes sense, Mum,' Polly concurred.

Discussions went on long into the evening around putting Polly's training to good use and how to set up the room utilising the space to the best advantage. The subject of having electricity installed was also talked about at great length, along with the upheaval it would cause, to say nothing of the mess to be cleaned up. Then at last it was decided to give it a go, and excited chatter ensued around planning.

'Monday morning the electric company are coming to make a start so I suggest Polly's ward should be first,' Minnie said.

'Thanks, Mum,' Polly beamed with delight.

'You lads will have to transfer the beds from the other spare rooms and just hope we don't have any more kiddies come in just yet,' Minnie added.

The excitement in the room was palpable as suggestions were made and ideas exchanged, until at last yawns said it was time for bed.

Polly and Minnie were soon the only two left in the living room and before she left, Polly threw her arms around her mother. 'Thank you, Mum, I love you so much.'

Minnie's eyes misted over as she held her daughter tightly. 'I'm so proud of you sweetheart. My love for you and Adam has never wavered, not even when... we were apart.'

'This is a big undertaking for me especially as I'm still not qualified,' Polly said as they left the room arm in arm.

'Yes, but you can see to colds and cuts and bruises. For anything major you can call the doctor in if you don't feel confident enough to tackle it. Anyway, you know more about medical stuff than all of us put together,' Minnie said with a grin.

'It's all so exciting!' Polly said on a breath.

'Ar, well, you'd best get some sleep then 'cos we've a busy time ahead of us.'

Parting company with a kiss, Minnie watched her girl skip along the landing. She felt so very lucky her family was reunited and prayed they would never be parted again.

* * *

Every day throughout the week Dickie Stanton had visited the allotments alone. Kit and Pip, he learned, had joined Miss Wilton's class with the four young pupils. He had been furious with them for deserting him, although strictly speaking it was he who had shunned them.

Now he wandered the streets on his own and he found making mischief was not nearly so much fun by himself. As each day passed his mood blackened; frustration and depression weighing heavily on him. He was missing his brothers and the fun they had together.

Every day he had watched Adam Fitch and his little entourage come and go from the gardens, but of the one who had been in prison there had been no sign. He wondered where the big fella was, but he had no way of knowing Digit was working at Chillington Wharf.

On Saturday morning, Dickie arrived to watch the work at the allotment but was surprised to see no one there. Even the old man had not put in an appearance and he couldn't work out what had happened. Mr Jackson was there every day, no matter the weather, but not today. Had he died in the night? Why were the others not there either?

In his now customary place by the shed, Dickie waited. Squinting in the bright sunlight he pulled his cap down to shield his eyes. Sitting down he leaned his back against the old wooden structure, and as the minutes ticked away he felt more and more forlorn.

Then suddenly the clip-clip of a horse's hooves drew his attention to the cobbled street. He watched as the cab came to a halt in front of a house across from where he sat. He was surprised to see Adam Fitch jump out and enter the house. A moment later he emerged with Mr Jackson on his arm. They climbed into the carriage, which the driver turned around before it rolled away, leaving Dickie to wonder where they were off to.

Deciding to find out, Dickie ran along behind the cab, ignoring the disgruntled grumbles of people he passed. Eventually he saw the carriage stop outside a massive building at the end of Major Street.

So that's where they live, he thought as he watched them alight. He knew of the place even though he could not read its sign.

Leaning against a brick wall a little way off, Dickie wondered if residing there would be any better than Reed's; something told him it would be, and he wished with all his heart he could be inside with everyone else.

9

As the cab halted outside Marshall's Children's Home and Adam helped Mr Jackson to alight, Minnie and Billy were waiting in the hall to greet them. Adam introduced them, and Mr Jackson grasped Billy's hand in a firm shake.

'Billy Marshall! I've watched you box many times,' Mr Jackson said with a smile.

The two men chatted happily as Minnie led them to the living room for tea and cake, where more introductions took place.

The morning wore on and eventually the conversation came round to Dickie Stanton.

'The boy's a menace!' Mr Jackson said.

'I suspect he's unhappy, Mr Jackson, and that's why he causes trouble,' Adam replied.

'There's a lot of folk who are not happy, Adam, but they don't go wrecking other people's property,' Mr Jackson answered irritably.

'We were all as miserable as sin when we lived at Reed's until Adam helped us to break out,' Joe said with a grin. His pale face held blue eyes which twinkled mischievously as he recounted the tale for Mr Jackson's benefit. He explained how Rodney had picked the gate lock to enable them to escape, before joining Adam who had left previously in search of his missing sister Polly.

Echo's repetition of words dotted the conversation then Adam told of meeting Digit, Flash and Echo and how they had come to live together for a while.

'Good Lord! I had no idea you'd been through so much in your young lives,' Mr Jackson said.

Minnie had sat and listened, and although the boys had made it all sound like a grand adventure, she knew what her children had gone through. She had suffered the same agonies of being separated from them and being unable to do anything about it. Watching the little ones playing on the floor with building blocks, Minnie thought of the last child born to her. Taken by a fever, John had been less than a year old and Minnie still had no idea where her deceased first husband had buried the child. The pain of the loss stung again and never seemed to lessen. It wasn't, or shouldn't be, the natural order of nature for children to die before their parents. Minnie's eyes moved to her other children and she gave a silent prayer that they were fit and well. She watched as Polly got down on the floor to settle an argument as to whether it should be a castle or a fort that was being built with the wooden blocks, and her pride threatened to overwhelm her.

As her eye scanned the coterie gathered in the living room, they came at last to Billy. Minnie smiled as he winked at her and she felt the love surge through her. Her attention was drawn away from her adoring husband as the door opened and Dilys announced lunch was ready. An extra place had been set for Mr Jackson next to Billy, and throughout the meal the two men talked boxing.

Tea washed down a delicious lunch of potatoes,

fresh vegetables, steak and kidney pie and thick onion gravy, then Mr Jackson stood to take his leave.

The cabbie had been paid handsomely to wait and he had dozed contentedly in the warm sunshine.

Giving his thanks for being so well fed and welcomed so warmly, Mr Jackson walked unsteadily outside. Everyone piled out to see him off.

Adam helped the old man into the carriage then climbed in beside him. Only Adam saw the boy leaning against the wall of an old dilapidated building a little way off. Dickie, however, was not watching Adam – he had eyes only for the dark-haired beauty who was Polly Fitch.

Dickie stared at the girl whose features were so like Adam's; they were unmistakably siblings. He had admired May with her blonde curls, but this girl had taken his breath away. He felt his pulse quicken as he watched her laughing and waving at the departing cab. He had a longing in his heart to come to know her and knew he had to find a way to do just that.

When she went back indoors, Dickie felt a sudden sadness stab him which was almost like a bereavement. His eyes searched the windows in the hope of one last look at the beautiful girl, but alas it was not meant to be. She had disappeared from his sight and Dickie felt the loss keenly. With a heavy heart he wandered off, and all the way home he saw only the image imprinted on his mind. Somehow he had to meet the girl who had stolen his heart in an instant, the one who didn't even know he existed.

Climbing over the gate at Reed's, Dickie was oblivious to the eyes watching him from an upstairs window. Una had considered taking the boy to task about his absconding every day, but in all honesty she didn't relish the consequences which would undoubtedly follow. It wouldn't stop him and he would most likely cause more problems in the town with his temper. For now she would bide her time and keep a close eye on the boy. Una frowned at Dickie, who was dragging himself up the drive looking forlorn and lost in his own thoughts. She wondered where he'd been this time. Just then the dinner bell sounded, and patting her hair into place, Una swung away from the window. Her dark skirt swished around her legs as she crossed the room. Locking the office door behind her she swept down the staircase and entered the dining room.

'Glad to see you have graced us with your

presence, Master Stanton,' she said as she marched past Dickie, who now stood in line for his meal.

The boy scowled and Una smiled. Wherever he had been, he had returned in a foul mood.

Sitting at the table with his bowl of broth he swirled the few floating vegetables with his spoon.

'Where have you been?' Kit asked in a whisper.

Dickie glanced at his younger brother. 'None of your business!' he snapped back.

'I was only asking,' Kit said with a hurt look.

'Well, don't!' Dickie's reply was sharp.

Kit and Pip exchanged a glance and Pip's shoulders shrugged as he slurped his soup.

'Dickie, you'll get in awful trouble with old Reedy if you're not careful,' Kit persisted.

'Kit, I don't care!' Dickie said in an explosive whisper.

'You should 'cos she'll lock you in the box,' Pip added with a shiver.

Dickie closed his eyes tight for a second and let out a sigh as he brought his temper under control. It was not fair to take his misery out on his brothers. It wasn't their fault they were in this place, or that he was feeling so desperate to meet the girl of his dreams.

'I went to Marshall's,' he whispered conspiratorially.

'What for?' Pip asked as he bit into a hard chunk of bread.

Dickie hastily explained as his brothers listened intently.

'Blimey, our Dickie's in love,' Pip said with a grin.

Shoving his spoon in his brother's face Dickie growled, 'Do *not* push this, Pip, I'm warning you!'

'All right Dickie, he meant no harm,' Kit said as he shoved one brother's hand away from the other.

'You gonna marry her then?' Pip could not help himself.

Dickie saw the question was asked in innocence and said thoughtfully, 'I wish.'

'What's her name?' asked Kit.

'I don't know as yet but I intend to find out,' Dickie answered.

'How?' Pip enquired.

'I ain't got a clue,' Dickie said with a faraway look.

Una's banging of her spoon on the table for silence brought the boys' attention back to their meal.

After lunch the boys went out into the garden in the sunshine. Saturday meant no lessons, so they were free to enjoy their leisure time. The Stantons talked for a long while about how Dickie could meet the girl he'd fallen for and he revelled at once more being friendly with his brothers.

'However you manage it you'll have to be better behaved,' Kit ventured.

Dickie nodded.

'And tidy yourself up,' Pip added as he looked at Dickie's scuffed boots.

Dickie felt deflated as he too glanced at his worn-out footwear, then his old jacket and trousers. Having no money, he could not replace the ragged clothes Una doled out, and his spirits dropped.

'You could always pinch some stuff from the market,' Pip suggested without thinking it through to the possible consequences of being caught.

'That's not a bad idea!' Dickie said his mood lifting again.

'Pip! Don't encourage him into thieving. You really should engage your brain before you speak,' Kit reprimanded.

'No, he's got a point. It's the only way I could get

some decent togs,' Dickie said excitedly as he mentally arranged a visit to the market.

'Dickie, if you get caught you'll go to Stafford Gaol!' Kit said with exasperation.

'I'd best not get caught, then,' Dickie answered with a grin.

'Get me a new cap when you go,' Pip said, and the three burst out laughing.

A couple of days later Dickie was up bright and early. He set off for the market feeling excited but fearful. He was determined to try to steal some clothes, but he was afraid of being nabbed by the bobbies and sent to jail.

Sweat formed on his brow as he entered the market and he ran a finger around his shirt collar. His eyes darted this way and that on the lookout for any signs of the police and he began to think that maybe this was not such a good idea after all.

The noise was deafening, with vendors calling out prices and handcarts being dragged around. As he walked, he smelled exotic spices imported from faraway countries. Further along the delicate bouquet from cut flowers standing in buckets of water reached him, which soon changed to the sickly sweetness of a confectionary stall. Dickie looked longingly at the trays of pretty coloured sweets and his mouth watered. A fishmonger attracted his attention as he yelled what he had on offer and Dickie grimaced as he saw the dead fish lying on trays waiting to be sold. Chickens and rabbits hung from hooks on a meat stall and suddenly the odour of death threatened to choke him. He rushed to the other side of the market to get away from the cloying odours.

Meandering between the stalls, he searched each one for any clothing in better condition than what he was wearing.

Stopping at a stall, Dickie cast his eyes over a pile of red apples and he swallowed the saliva filling his mouth. In another box were green ones and yet another held pears. Moving on he found a woman selling boots which were tied together in pairs by their laces. Further along he came to a man banging a tin pot with a wooden spoon to draw custom to his array of kitchen utensils. Amid the din Dickie heard a shout.

'Gerrout the way, lad!' a man called as he pushed a handcart piled high with small crates of vegetables.

Dickie stepped aside, allowing the man to pass

by before resuming his search. Seeing a stall laden with flat caps, he glanced around furtively. In one swift movement he walked past, snatching a cap and moving on. Folding the hat, he shoved it into his pocket as sweat ran down his face. Stealing a jacket or trousers was not going to be nearly as easy he thought to himself. At least Pip would be pleased to have a new cap; Dickie smiled inwardly.

With no opportunities presenting themselves to acquire new clothing, he left the market feeling thoroughly miserable. How would he catch the eye of that girl now? She wouldn't spare him a passing glance dressed as he was. Dickie picked his way back to Reed's with a heavy heart. He would have to find another way to get to know the dark-haired beauty from the Children's Home.

Monday morning arrived and with it came workers from the Electric Light Company. James, Peter and Digit set off for the wharf to find work for the day. Polly, May, Echo and Celia Brock took the youngsters for a picnic in East Park and with everyone else at their respective jobs, Minnie sat in the kitchen with Mabel, Dilys and Ruth.

'Best keep out of the way whilst the work is going on,' she said.

'I 'ope they don't leave too much mess behind,' Dilys answered.

'It will be wonderful to have light at the flick of a switch!' Ruth added with an excited air.

'I bet old Reedy ain't got the 'lectrics yet,' Dilys put in.

'I suspect not,' Ruth concurred. 'That woman is far too fond of money to part with any of it for the benefit of those in her care.'

The others nodded in agreement then winced as the hammering began.

'We'll all 'ave a yedache by the finish of this lot,' Dilys said as she covered her ears with her hands.

'Why don't you and Mabel get off to the market and get the shopping in?' Minnie suggested.

'Bloody good idea!' Mabel said as she grabbed her shawl.

'Take your time, them blokes could be here a while,' Minnie added.

Ruth poured more tea and nodded a farewell to the cook and maid as they left via the back door.

Whistling and shouting could be heard as the men brought cables and wiring through to each room.

'At least there are plenty of workers,' Ruth commented.

'Ar, I told 'em I wanted it all done as soon as,' Minnie replied. 'They said as it would be about a fortnight which was when I told 'em to stick it up their arses. I said as I'd go to Birmingham and get them to come and do the job.'

'What did they say to that?' Ruth asked.

'We'll mek sure it's finished by the end of the week, madam,' Minnie mimicked.

'That will take some doing,' Ruth said as she glanced out of the window.

'We'll see. I'll be glad when they stop all that banging though and no mistake!'

Ruth nodded and they set about making preparations for an evening meal of sorts. It would be cold portions today – salad, cheese and meats which could be covered away from the dust.

Outside and a little way off stood Dickie Stanton, watching the comings and goings of the workmen. He was hoping to spot the dark-haired girl again but she was nowhere to be seen. Had she gone out and he'd missed her? He cursed himself for being later than usual because old Reedy had lectured them at breakfast about good behaviour.

Muttering under his breath, Dickie wandered away. Passing the Borough Hospital he wrinkled his nose. People with infectious diseases went in there and were damned lucky if they came out again. At the top of Pond Lane he crossed a patch of scrubland towards All Saints Road.

'You should be in school!' a woman said sharply as they passed each other.

'I've left and I'm looking for work!' Dickie snapped back.

'Oh,' the woman responded as she faced him.

'Ar, so next time don't be so quick to judge!' Dickie sniffed and turned away.

'Sorry, lad.'

'S'all right, you d'aint know,' Dickie said sullenly.

'Good luck finding a job, son, for I fear there ain't much to be had.'

'Ta, missus.' Dickie strode away, feeling a little better for having stood his ground despite the lie he'd told the woman.

As he walked on he wondered if finding work was what he should be doing, but he knew the woman was right – it would be difficult, if not nigh on impossible. The questions and answers whispered in his mind; why work – he didn't need to. He was fed at Reed's, albeit poorly. Jobs paid money and although it would be nice to have cash in his pocket, he managed without. He wouldn't be able to roam about free to cause trouble if he was stuck in a foundry or the like.

Climbing the gate, Dickie then sauntered into the orphanage. It was quiet indoors with the others still in the classroom. With a sigh, he ran up the stairs to his room. Lying on his bed he smiled as his mind conjured an image of the girl he could not forget.

The clanging of the dinner bell woke him, and Dickie leapt to his feet. Running downstairs, he joined the line in the dining room where he heard the question from Pip.

'Where you been?'

'Marshall's,' he said quietly.

'What for?' asked Kit.

'It ain't none of your business.' Dickie grinned and Kit nodded.

'Did you see her? That girl you like.'

'Kit, keep yer nose out,' Dickie responded gently not wishing to cause a ruckus. 'The kids' home is havin' 'lectrics put in.'

'Electricity, Master Stanton,' Una Reed corrected with a slap to his head as she swept past, her skirts rustling as she went.

Dickie started; he'd not known she was behind him.

Collecting his two boiled potatoes, one faggot and a chunk of hard bread he took a seat with his brothers. Looking at the food he shook his head. It was no fit meal for a growing boy. His eyes moved to Una, who was rubbing her hands together. When he saw her meal he sighed. No wonder she was happy. If he had pork and crackling, potatoes, vegetables and gravy he would be happy too.

'It's better than nowt,' Kit said as he dug Dickie in the ribs and pointed his fork at the plate in front of him.

'It's a bloody disgrace is what it is!' Dickie rasped through clenched teeth. His rumbling stomach told him to get on and eat it regardless of how unappetising it appeared.

After lunch, when the others filed back into the classroom, Dickie went roaming once more.

Una Reed watched from her office window as the boy scaled the gate effortlessly. So the Marshalls were having electricity installed, were they? Moving to her desk she drew out her ledger and scanned the figures. Not nearly enough in her coffers, she would have to stay with gas lamps for a while yet. Slamming the heavy book back into the drawer she scowled. Then a thought struck – maybe she could use the need for electricity in her begging letters. She could point out how fortunate the wealthy were to already have it in their homes when these poor orphans were forced to use candles to save on the gas bill.

Whilst Una composed a suitably worded letter, Dickie meandered his way back to Major Street to watch the men at work. It was mid-afternoon when he was rewarded with a sight for sore eyes. The dark-haired girl, her blonde friend, a woman and some youngsters were walking towards where he was standing. Dickie felt a flutter in his stomach as they drew near and heard a little one call out a name.

'Are we nearly there yet, Polly?'

'Yes, sweetheart, almost.'

So her name was Polly! Dickie's eyes followed her, and he blushed to the roots of his shock of hair when she gave him a dazzling smile.

'Hello,' she said.

'Erm... hello,' Dickie mumbled, wondering why his tongue felt like it was twice its normal size.

The little group continued on their way and Dickie watched until they disappeared into the massive building. Turning away he thought he had died and gone to heaven, so light was his step. His grin stretched from ear to ear and was set to remain that way for the rest of the day at least.

Nodding a greeting to those he passed on his way home, Dickie had a warm feeling at the nods and smiles sent his way. This was much better than being yelled at or scorned and he liked it. Maybe being nice to people was the way to go in the future; perhaps he could be happy like this all the time.

Whistling as he walked, Dickie arrived back at Reed House. Climbing the gate he looked at the building. Not as nice as that other place but it was home – for now anyway.

* * *

Indoors, Minnie hugged the little ones and said they could play outside on the heath behind the house provided they didn't stray.

'Echo, would you be in charge and keep an eye on them for me?'

'Yes, Mum,' came the excited answer.

Minnie smiled at the way Echo had taken to calling her 'Mum'. She knew he was imitating Polly, but she welcomed it nevertheless.

Celia Brock was in the kitchen now having a much needed cup of tea and listening to the complaints about all the noise when Minnie joined them.

'What have you got there? Minnie asked, seeing the paper in Celia's hand.

'Echo's work. You know how he sometimes comes into class to join in? Well, the other day he joined us and produced this.'

Minnie took a look at the paper and her mouth dropped open.

Celia nodded as Mabel glanced over Minnie's shoulder.

'It can't be – can it?' Mabel asked.

'It is, I assure you,' Celia confirmed.

'Polly, have a squint at this,' Minnie said.

'Blimey! I knew he loved his numbers, but I didn't know his mathematics were this good. I've watched him lots of times playing number games with the little ones outside using stones.'

Polly passed the paper back to Celia who said,

'I'd like to try something.' Walking to the back door she yelled for Echo, who was in the middle of a crowd of yelling children.

Rushing indoors, Echo asked, 'Yes?'

'I've just been showing everyone your good work and Polly tells me you love number games.'

'Yes,' he nodded.

'Will you play one with me now?' Celia asked.

Again the boy nodded and sat at the table.

'Right, if I gave the butcher two pounds and it came to one pound ten shillings...'

'Ten shillings change,' Echo put in quickly.

Mabel and Minnie stared in disbelief at how rapidly the lad had reckoned it up in his head.

'Crikey, Echo, you worked that out fast,' Minnie said.

Echo nodded and watched as Celia decided to give him a little challenge. She asked him to add and subtract figures she gave him, and everyone was astonished that he came back with the answers almost immediately. Whoever had said this boy was dim-witted had been mistaken in their assumption.

Echo was enjoying what he saw as the numbers game and encouraged Celia to give him more sums to work out. For half an hour they played the *game* and each time, Echo gave the correct answers, the questions becoming harder the longer they went on. Hundreds, tens and units appeared to give him no problems and Celia praised him often.

Mabel sat with an open mouth as she listened to the questions and answers, hardly believing her ears. Dilys applauded Echo's efforts and he revelled in the attention he was given.

'I think that's enough for now. Well done!' Celia said.

Echo beamed and dashed back to his playmates outside.

Others drifted in as time passed and listened quietly as Echo proved time and again he was a brilliant mathematician. Eventually Ruth joined them and marvelled at the lad as she poured herself some tea.

Having exhausted the topic of Echo's amazing calculations, the subject turned to the outing.

'Who was that lad you spoke to when we came home Polly?' May asked.

'I'm not sure but I wonder if he's from Reed's,' Polly answered.

'Big chap with blonde hair?' Dilys asked, having recently arrived back from the market with Mabel.

Polly nodded.

'Ar, I've seen him afore. He stands there a lot just watching.'

'I wonder why,' Polly said as she poured herself a cup of tea.

'No idea, you could ask Adam when he gets in, maybe he'll know,' Minnie answered.

It was gone six o'clock when Adam arrived home, weary from working the allotment. The workmen had long since gone to their homes with the promise of an early start the following day.

In the dining room, low chatter accompanied the food as everyone enjoyed discussing their day.

Polly and Adam sat together later in the sitting room and it was then that Polly raised the subject of the boy watching the house.

'It sounds like Dickie Stanton,' Adam said.

'I wonder why he stands there,' Polly mused.

Adam shook his head. 'I think he's lonely.'

'That's a shame. Does he not have any friends?' Polly asked.

'Unlikely, Polly, he's a bit cocksure. Although he's

got a couple of brothers, I think. Why?'

'I was just wondering. Maybe we should try and make friends with them,' Polly suggested.

'We could do that, but be careful Polly, he has a temper on him,' Adam warned.

'I will. I'll take Echo with me next time I see him.'

Adam nodded. Surely even Dickie Stanton wouldn't pick on a girl or someone like Echo? 'Any trouble and you let me know straight away, agreed?'

'Agreed.' Polly grinned at her brother, the person she loved most in the world.

Polly went to the kitchen in search of her mother to relay her discussion with Adam.

'You just watch what you're doing with that one, our Polly,' Minnie said.

'I will, Mum.'

'Mum...' Echo said, having followed in Polly's wake.

'You'll be with me, won't you Echo?' Polly asked.

'Yes! I'll look after my lady,' the boy said feeling full of self-importance.

'Fair enough,' Minnie conceded.

Polly led Echo away to discuss a strategy of how they could make friends with Dickie Stanton.

11

'It won't be long before you have some new potatoes for your mum's table,' Mr Jackson said from his chair on the allotment.

'You'll come and share with us, won't you?' Adam asked.

'Ar lad, it would be a pleasure.'

'Mr Jackson, what do you do with everything you grow?' Adam asked.

The old man smiled. 'There's a carter comes by once a week and I swap my goods for his. My lettuces for some tea; tomatoes for sugar and so on.'

Adam grinned. 'Clever idea, but what about when you've nothing to swap?'

'I've plenty in my larder to see me through the slow times such as now. You know, lad, you should get a stall on the market when you have stuff to sell. That way you'll have coppers for seeds for the next season.'

'That's good thinking, I wonder if Polly and May might be interested,' Adam reasoned.

'You can but ask. I see that lad from Reed's don't come by any more.'

'He's taken to standing by our place, Mr Jackson. I think he's taken a fancy to May.' Adam gave a little laugh.

'Let's hope not, eh? You can do without the likes of him hanging around, the young hooligan.' Mr Jackson drew on his cigarette and shook his head.

'He's not so bad, he just needs friends, someone to show him life is better without violence and destruction,' Adam said gently.

'You've a big heart, Adam Fitch, you mind that bugger don't break it.'

'How do you mean?'

Mr Jackson shook his head. 'Never mind. Tell me what you know of that boy and his brothers and how they might be living at the orphanage.'

Adam said he didn't know too much about the Stantons, but he knew plenty about Reed's. He told the old man about the poor food served, probably because Una wouldn't spend the money. He related about being punished, 'Rodney's the one to ask about that,' he said. 'He was afraid and unhappy, as were we all, but Rodney was the one who got put in the *box*.' He explained with a shiver how Una would lock children inside a cold dark cupboard if they misbehaved. 'I wouldn't be at all surprised to find out Dickie has been in there more than once.'

'I wonder if I've misjudged that young man after what you've told me,' Mr Jackson muttered quietly.

The old man got wearily to his feet. 'I thank you for sharing your lunch with me again, but now I think it's time I went home for a nap. I'll see you tomorrow, Adam.'

'Turrah, Mr Jackson, mind how you go.' Adam watched as the sweet old gent hobbled away leaning heavily on his cane. *I wonder what he meant about Dickie Stanton breaking my heart.* He couldn't fathom what the reasoning was for the statement, and with a shrug he began to clear away the tools.

That evening Adam told everyone about Mr Jackson's idea of procuring a market stall and to his delight Polly and May couldn't wait to get started. So, it was decided that when there was enough produce they would approach the market inspector for a pitch. In the meantime, they would continue to help Minnie out running the children's home.

'We could knock together a couple of barrows for you,' Joe said.

'I'll see what pallets are laying around at work,' Rodney added. Seeing Polly wrinkle her nose he added, 'We can wash 'em down first.'

'Pallets from the abattoir – they'll stink to high heaven!' May said with a grimace.

'Not if we paint them for you,' Matt put in.

'Ooh, in rainbow colours,' May said dreamily.

'With whatever we can get for free,' Arthur countered.

The evening wore on with everyone making excited plans. The wait for things to grow would seem interminable but at least the barrows could be made in the meantime.

The next day, Adam was surprised that Mr Jackson was not in his usual place in the garden. *Maybe he's slept in*, Adam thought as he began weeding and hoeing. However, by lunchtime Adam was getting worried. He decided to pay a visit to Mr Jackson's house to check on the old man.

Adam banged on the front door and waited. He knew it would take a while for Mr Jackson to shuffle along to answer. After a moment Adam peeped into the window. It was dark inside and he couldn't see much so he trotted around to the back. Knocking on the back door he waited again. Maybe Mr Jackson had gone out for the day, but Adam thought it unlikely. Seeing no signs of movement through the kitchen window, Adam felt his nerves twang. Something was wrong. Trying the door handle he found it locked. Now he was really worried. What if Mr Jackson had fallen and couldn't get up? The doors were secured, as were the windows, a quick check revealed. He had to get inside somehow. *Think!* he told himself.

Looking around the yard there was nothing that could help; no ladder, no brick to smash a window. Adam felt the panic begin to rise in him. Mr Jackson could be hurt and Adam couldn't get to him! Standing for a moment, Adam took stock. Mr Jackson could have gone to the market – but then he never went anywhere but the allotment. Adam could break in – but it would cost his mum the price of a window – and he would be in trouble if Mr Jackson was just resting today.

'Christ!' he muttered now unable to decide what to do. 'Oh, bugger it!'

Taking off his jacket, he wound it around his arm and facing away he hammered his elbow against the kitchen pane. With a crash like thunder the glass gave way and shattered into hundreds of tiny pieces. Pushing out the loose shards with his bound arm, Adam then climbed inside. Shaking out his jacket he donned it once more as he stepped through the dark house.

'Mr Jackson,' he called. No answer.

Again, 'Mr Jackson!' Nothing. Checking the living room and finding no one there, Adam began ascending the stairs calling out at intervals.

Opening a bedroom door, he was surprised that it was completely empty, devoid of furniture. Going to the next room, Adam turned the knob, a feeling of dread coursing through him.

He saw the hump in the bed and as he stepped nearer he realised there was no sound of breathing.

'Mr Jackson?' Adam stood by the bed and looked down on the old man whose skin was a waxy grey. 'Oh Mr Jackson!' Adam felt for a pulse and pulled back sharply from the cold body. 'Rest in peace.'

Going back downstairs, Adam unlocked the front door. Closing it behind him he ran hell for leather for home. His mum would know what to do.

'Hey up, lad, what's amiss?' Minnie asked as Adam rushed in through the front door.

'Mum, you have to come!' Adam panted.

'Whoa, catch your breath lad,' Minnie said.

'Mum, it's Mr Jackson – I think he's dead!' Adam managed between gasps.

'Oh blimey,' Minnie said sadly. 'Right, you show me the way and I'll get Mabel to come with me.' Minnie grabbed a shawl and yelled for the cook. 'Mabel, get yer coat – we might have a laying out to do.'

Rushing into the hall Mabel asked, 'Who?'

'Old Mr Jackson. Our Adam just found him. Right lad – lead the way.'

Adam explained about the window and how he had found his aged friend still in bed.

'Don't fret about the winder, son, I'll get one of

the lads to board it up later,' Minnie assured him. 'Has he got any family? I can't remember.'

'No Mum, he was all alone.' Adam's answer was full of sadness and he felt tears prick his eyes. 'I should have...'

'Let's have none of that!' Minnie said sharply, then seeing her boy crumple she went on a little gentler. 'You did as much as you could, we all did. Just be thankful he slipped away in his sleep. He wouldn't have known anything about it.'

Adam nodded as he led them in through the front door he'd left on the sneck.

'Adam, have a look around for a will or a savings book,' Minnie said quietly.

'Mum!' Adam was shocked to think his mum could be so mercenary.

'We need to know if he had a savings plan with the funeral parlour, sweetheart, and a will for a solicitor,' Minnie explained carefully.

'Oh, right. Sorry, Mum I thought...' Adam apologised.

'I know you did. No harm done so go on – look around whilst we make sure Mr Jackson...'

Adam nodded and went into the living room. He

felt badly about having to snoop through Mr Jackson's things but knew it had to be done.

Pulling open a drawer he mumbled, 'Sorry, Mr Jackson, but I'm sure you'd understand.' He found a little book and peeped inside. He breathed a sigh of relief – Mr Jackson's funeral was all paid for, they just had to contact the undertaker. He drew out a large envelope which was sealed and addressed to a solicitor. The will, Adam surmised. Taking both upstairs he showed them to Minnie.

'Right, you drop the book into the undertaker. Then deliver the letter to the solicitor. When that's done fetch a hammer and nails and one of the others to help board the winder up.' Minnie was taking everything in her stride as she usually did, and Adam was glad to leave it all in her capable hands.

Just as Adam turned, she called out, 'Oh and Adam, fetch the doctor first.'

'It's a bit late for that, Mum.'

'For the death certificate, lad.'

'Oh yes, of course.' Adam's mind was in turmoil and he couldn't think straight. Giving himself a mental shake he set off on his errands.

'Poor old devil,' Minnie said as she rifled through

the wardrobe to find some clothes to lay the old man out in. She found a black suit and laid it across a chair in readiness.

'Better than bein' run over by a hoss and cart!' Mabel said as she found a pair of black dress shoes.

'Mabel Elliot!' Minnie snapped.

'What? It's right ain't it?'

Minnie sighed and nodded.

'Fancy a cup of tea whilst we wait?' Mabel asked and seeing Minnie's surprised look she added, 'Mr Jackson wouldn't mind, 'sides he won't be needin' it now, will he?'

'True. I don't suppose it would hurt,' Minnie said.

Half an hour later, Digit and Adam arrived to board up the window and a few minutes after them came the doctor. Minnie paid for the death certificate from the purse always kept in her apron pocket. With the kitchen secure once more, Adam and Digit left for home and Minnie and Mabel washed and dressed Mr Jackson ready for the undertaker.

That evening the mood was subdued around the dining table with everyone lost in their own private thoughts. Not only were they dwelling on Mr Jackson's passing, but also on their own mortality and that of their friends and family.

Later in the sitting room they talked in hushed tones about Mr Jackson and what a good old boy he had been.

Adam listened quietly, trying to stifle the emotions he felt were suffocating him. Excusing himself, he went to his bed early, where he could give free rein to the tears which were choking him.

12

Over the next couple of days, Polly did her best to cheer Adam up, knowing he was feeling Mr Jackson's loss keenly. They talked together for hours after everyone else had gone to bed and Polly realised only time would ease Adam's suffering.

Minnie had been informed that the funeral would take place the following Friday, by which time the installation of the electricity would be complete.

Adam continued to visit the allotment, but it wasn't the same without Mr Jackson. All the enjoyment had gone. Nevertheless, Adam found solace in tending the old man's plot as well as his own.

Word had spread of the death when neighbours

had watched the undertaker come and go through dirty curtains. Adam also kept an eye on the house to ensure it was not broken into and robbed of its meagre contents.

Adam nodded a greeting to Dickie Stanton as he passed him each morning but could not find it in himself to strike up a conversation. Then one morning Adam was taken by surprise. As he walked up Major Street, Dickie stepped forward. 'Hey, mate, I was sorry to hear about the old man.'

Adam stopped and gave his thanks. The two stood awkwardly, neither knowing what to say next.

'I'd best be off,' Adam said eventually.

Dickie nodded and looked down at his scuffed boots.

After a few steps Adam turned back and called, 'Fancy helping me in the garden?'

'Yeah, all right.' Dickie beamed his delight at being asked.

The boys walked in silence until they reached the allotment and Dickie stopped. 'I... erm... I'm sorry about wrecking yer garden... you know... before.'

'Forget it, it's in the past,' Adam said. 'Come on, I'll show you what needs doing.'

All morning the boys worked together tilling and watering, and at lunchtime Adam shared his food as they sat in the weak sunshine.

Suddenly Dickie asked, 'Who's Polly?'

'She's my sister, Polly Fitch.'

'You look alike,' Dickie went on.

Adam explained that James and Peter were his brothers and the others were close friends.

'I got two brothers an' all. Kit and Pip; they're in class at old Reedy's,' Dickie explained.

'That's what we called her when we were there,' Adam confided.

'You – at Reed's?' Dickie could not hide his surprise.

Adam nodded, and as they relaxed after lunch he told Dickie his tale.

'Blimey! I thought we was hard done by!' Dickie said when Adam had finished speaking. 'I hate it there, Adam. I wish I could get me brothers out and we could live somewhere together.'

'You would need to work and earn money to feed yourselves; pay rent, gas or candles – it's expensive. At least at Reed's you are fed and have a bed,' Adam said.

'Old Reedy has it in for me all the time,' Dickie moaned.

'She was like that with Rodney too until he out-witted her.' Adam went on to explain about Rodney picking the lock of her office door so Adam could find the address Polly had been sold on to.

'Crikey! I'll bet she was mad about that,' Dickie said, in awe of their antics.

'She wasn't best pleased,' Adam said and they both burst out laughing.

'She used to put Rodney in the box and he'd kick and yell all night long,' Adam said as his mind took him back five years. He saw Dickie shiver at the thought and added, 'It did no good so he gave up in the end.'

'So how did you get out?' Dickie asked.

'Through a hole in the hedge, but the others went through the gate after Rodney worked his magic on the lock.' Adam wiggled his fingers and they laughed again.

'I just climb over it, but Pip and Kit would never manage,' Dickie said sadly.

'Getting your brothers out would be the easy bit.

The difficult part would be where you all go once you're free.'

'Anywhere is better than there!' Dickie said vehemently.

'I know how you feel, believe me, but think about how you'd feed your brothers. How would they feel about not having a warm bed to sleep in every night?' Adam could see where the conversation was heading and was trying to encourage the boy to think clearly.

Dickie dragged his hands down his face and sighed loudly. 'You're right, they'd be miserable.'

'How come you're in there, anyway?' Adam asked.

Dickie told him about being dragged through the streets with a rope around their necks.

Adam nodded, recalling Gerald Fitch pulling Polly and himself along those same streets.

Before they had realised it, the sun had begun to dip towards the horizon and the air held a slight chill.

'Time for tea, or whatever slop old Reedy is serving tonight,' Dickie said with a sneer.

'You coming again tomorrow?' Adam asked.

'Be all right, would it?'

'Yes, I enjoyed our chat.'

'Me an' all. See yer tomorrer Adam.'

'I'll bring some lunch for both of us,' Adam yelled as they parted company.

* * *

'Well, I never!' Minnie said when Adam told them all about his day spent with Dickie Stanton.

'He was very interested in our Polly,' Adam said with a grin.

'Me?' she asked.

'Yes, you. I think that's why he's been hanging around, so he could see you.'

Polly blushed.

Echo scowled and moved closer to Polly in a protective gesture.

'Anyway, he's coming to help again tomorrow. Maybe you could bring us some lunch, Polly, and you can get to meet him,' Adam teased.

'Take your own lunch!' she snapped.

'Lunch!' Echo repeated with a firm nod of his head in emphasis.

'All right, you two, give over,' Minnie said. 'Sounds like the lad is badly in need of some friends.'

'He's desperate to get out of Reed's and take his brothers with him,' Adam replied.

'Well, we have room but if he's sweet on our Polly I'm not sure it would be a good idea.' Minnie was thinking aloud rather than speaking to anyone in particular.

'I agree, Mum,' Polly put in.

'Tell you what, bring him back here for his dinner about one o'clock and we'll see what's what.'

'What!' Echo echoed.

'All those *whats* – bloody hell, I'm confused!' Dilys said, causing laughter to fill the room.

'I think I might be out somewhere doing something,' Polly mumbled.

'You'll be here as always, my girl,' Minnie said, and Polly knew better than to argue.

The following morning Celia and May took the little ones onto the heath for a nature ramble, and to be out of the way of the workmen. Polly and Echo took a basket and set off to collect herbs, the others having left earlier for their respective employment.

Flash continued to follow Minnie like a shadow and said very little.

When Adam arrived at the allotment Dickie was waiting for him, having set out the tools in a neat row.

After a greeting Adam said, 'Mum says you are to come home with me for lunch.'

'Honest?' Dickie asked incredulously.

Adam nodded.

'Bostin'!' Dickie's face sported a grin that split his face. 'Right, where do we start?'

'Over there,' Adam said pointing to Mr Jackson's plot.

As they toiled, Adam explained there would be no work the next day as it was the day of Mr Jackson's funeral.

'Can I come?' Dickie asked.

'Anyone can. It's at St George's at eleven o'clock.'

Dickie nodded.

'Time to knock off and get some dinner, I'm famished. Mum likes us to eat at one o'clock, it's a consistent routine and helps the little ones who can't tell the time yet.' Adam packed the tools away and the boys set off for Marshall's.

'You all right?' Adam asked as they walked.

'Yes, why?' Dickie answered with a question of his own.

'You're quiet, that's all. You nervous?'

'A bit. I won't know anyone,' Dickie said before swallowing loudly.

'It'll be fine. You'll be made welcome,' Adam assured him.

Reaching home, they entered by the front door.

'Blimey!' Dickie gasped as he looked around the huge foyer.

'That you, our Adam?' Minnie's voice floated to them from the kitchen.

'Yes, Mum – and Dickie.'

Minnie came bustling through. 'Hello lad, I hope you're hungry.'

Dickie nodded, suddenly feeling even more shy.

'Good. Now both of you – to the kitchen and get washed, and then we can eat.'

In the next few minutes there was a flurry of activity as youngsters ran into the dining room, followed by the adults. Dickie was introduced and stood in line for lunch.

'It's the same as at Reed's, grab some food and find a seat,' Adam advised.

The aroma of chicken made his mouth water, and taking a plate and cutlery from a table at the beginning of the line, Dickie moved forward slowly. There was a lot of chatter – something Una Reed would never allow.

Dickie held out his plate and Mabel piled it high with chicken, vegetables and potatoes, then Dilys poured a ladle of rich brown gravy on the top. Finding a seat, Dickie settled himself and waited.

'Eat up before it gets cold.'

Looking up, he blushed at the girl who spoke to him.

Polly smiled. She had determined she would make him feel welcome despite the teasing she'd get later from the others.

Dickie ploughed his way through the massive dinner and sighed with pleasure as he laid down his knife and fork.

Polly refilled his tumbler with water and he smiled his thanks. The room was filled with laughter and the scraping of cutlery on crockery.

'I know what you're thinking,' Polly said.

'What?'

'You are wishing it was like this at Reed's.'

'Yeah, but that's like wishing for the moon,' Dickie said sadly.

'I remember. We hated it there too.'

'Adam told me. I think you were all very brave.'

'Not really. We all stuck together – we became a family and looked out for each other. We still do.' Polly looked around at Digit, James, Peter and Adam.

'Still do...' Echo had pushed in beside Polly where he could protect her if needed.

Dickie was tempted to ask if the boy was simple-minded but refrained for fear of upsetting anyone.

'Come on, let's get some afters,' Polly urged.

Stacking their plates on another table, their cutlery dropped into a huge enamel bowl filled with soapy water, they each took a dish and spoon.

Steaming rice pudding was ladled into his dish and Dickie's eyes grew wide.

'Jam or treacle over there, lad,' Mabel said tilting her head. 'Help yourself.'

'Thanks,' Dickie said but retook his seat instead. It had been an age since he'd had rice pudding and he wanted to enjoy it without enhancements.

Once finished, he disposed of his bowl and spoon. He caught Mabel watching him and he wandered over to her.

'You want some more, lovey?'

Dickie shook his head and blew out his cheeks, his hands stretching over his full belly. 'Thank you,' he whispered.

'You're more than welcome. It's worth cooking when it's eaten and enjoyed.'

Dickie smiled and turned, finding himself face to face with Polly. 'Come into the living room and let your dinner go down before our Adam drags you back to the allotment,' she said.

Dickie followed Polly and Echo into the huge room where the others had congregated. He was on cloud nine to be so close to the girl he had dreamed about every night since he'd first seen her. His pulse raced as he caught a whiff of soap from her hair, which shone in the light from the window.

Here again voices sounded and the little ones rushed outside to play before afternoon lessons.

Dickie joined in conversations and realised how much he was enjoying being here with these lovely people.

Before long it was time to return to work, and giving his thanks, Dickie, along with Adam, left and sauntered up Major Street.

'I am stuffed,' Dickie said rubbing his belly. 'I should have saved some for my brothers.' He sighed guiltily. Goodness knows what they'd had to eat but one thing was for sure: their stomachs would not be full.

'It's a shame they couldn't have come with you,' Adam said.

'I feel badly about eating so much and they're going hungry,' Dickie responded.

'Bring them with you next time,' Adam suggested.

'Next time?'

It was Adam's turn to nod.

'I know they'd love it, but I can't get them out. Old Reedy locks the bloody gate!' Dickie's frustration bubbled over.

'That's not a problem...' Adam grinned as he wriggled his fingers as he had previously, denoting Rodney's expertise with picking locks.

They fell about laughing and on reaching the garden they sat in the dirt to make plans.

Minnie wouldn't be happy about it, but Adam could stand by no longer knowing the Stanton brothers were suffering at Reed's. He had to gather their little coterie together once more to plan, and it had to be executed early tomorrow morning when everyone had time off from work to attend the funeral. There would never be a better time for Adam and his friends to aid the unfortunate Stanton brothers.

13

The two boys parted company, each with firm instructions. Dickie was to get his brothers out quietly and wait at the gate at five in the morning.

As Adam trudged home he debated whether to tell his mother what they were planning beforehand, or would it be better afterwards? Maybe he should ask the others their opinion first.

Reaching home, he immediately went in search of Polly.

'You can't be serious? Ad, Mum will play hell!' Polly said with quiet urgency.

'It's a risk we have to take. Polly, I can't leave those kids at Una Reed's any longer – they'll starve to death!' Adam was determined to do all he could to help. 'Have you forgotten how she sold you without so much as a by-your-leave?'

'No, but...'

'What about that slop she fed us on? Can you re-member going to bed hungry?'

'Yes, but...'

'Well then. She was – is – cruel, Polly. She still puts kids in the box and it was only by the grace of God you and I weren't shoved in there. Ask Rodney what it was like for him.'

'All right, all right! After tea we'll speak to the others – quietly. Just don't let Mum know yet 'til we hear what they have to say.' Polly relented as her mind took her back to that sorrowful time.

Adam gave her a hug, saying, 'Thanks Pol, I knew you'd help.'

Polly shook her head but her smile told him she could refuse him nothing.

'I'll tell May and Arthur to meet us outside after we've eaten. You speak to Joe, Matt and Rodney – and for goodness' sake keep it quiet!' Polly said as she went to the dining room.

Adam moved along the line and whispered a message. 'Meeting outside after.'

Three nods confirmed the boys would be there, despite their questioning frowns. Arthur and May also inclined their heads as Adam caught their eye.

An hour later the group was all there and Adam said, 'There's to be another break-out!'

The friends turned to each other and surprised looks changed to grins.

In the meantime, Dickie had returned to Reed's and sought out his brothers. Dragging them into the garden, he told them of his day at Marshall's. Their tummies rumbled as he described his lunch and their eyes widened when he said talking was allowed in the dining room. He explained there was no box there and the children were not punished.

'Can we go there, Dickie?' Pip asked innocently.

'It sounds too good to be true,' Kit added sceptically.

'It is true Kit, believe me. And you know what? We can get out of here if you two can get up really early tomorrow morning. We have to be as silent as the grave though, we *cannot* let old Reedy hear us,' Dickie said excitedly.

'The gate will be locked, soft lad!' Kit muttered.

'Don't worry about that – Adam has a plan.'

'Who's Adam?' Pip asked.

'That lad from the allotment. He's going to help us 'cos it's his mum who runs the children's home,' Dickie explained patiently.

'We'll miss breakfast,' Pip complained.

'No, we won't. I think Mrs Marshall will make sure we're fed, she won't see us go without.'

'Then what?' Kit asked as he shoved his hands in his trouser pockets. 'Where do we go once we're out of this place?'

'Adam said his mum would most likely take us in,' Dickie answered.

'Most likely? And what if she won't?' Kit rounded on his big brother. 'Bloody hell Dickie! You ain't thought this through properly, have you?'

Dickie blew through his teeth then said, 'We have! You have to trust me! Mind you, you can always stay here and me and Pip will go.'

'You *have* to come as well, Kit!' Pip was becoming distressed.

'What time do we get up then?' Kit asked, not wanting his little brother to get upset.

'We have to be at the gate at five o'clock before anyone else gets up,' Dickie said.

'All right, but if I have to go without brekky I'll bash you!' Kit said indignantly.

Dickie sighed with relief. 'Just remember, don't say anything about this again in case old Reedy hears.'

As they walked back into the house, none of them noticed Una watching them from her office window.

With a shiver, she moved to the fire and held out her hands to the dancing flames. The image that haunted her was that of another bunch who used to get their heads together plotting mischief. The Fitches and their little entourage. Were the Stanton boys doing the same thing?

Una dismissed the idea with a shake of her head. Dickie was a thug; he didn't have the brains to plan anything. He was an opportunist when it came to causing trouble. As for Kit and Pip – they simply tagged along behind, doing as they were told.

The little meeting she had just witnessed was surely no more than Dickie telling his brothers where he'd been all day. Satisfied with the explanation, Una retired to the kitchen for a cup of hot coffee.

* * *

Having related his proposal to the others, Adam waited for their response.

It was May who spoke first. 'I think we should let your mum know.'

'Yes, I agree. She was good enough to take us all in and this seems a bit – disloyal,' Matt added.

'I won't have any trouble picking the gate lock,' Rodney said with a grin, 'but I have to say I think Matt is right.'

'What if your mum won't take the Stantons in?' Arthur asked.

'It's my contention she wouldn't turn them away, but consider her feelings for a minute,' Joe put in.

'What do you mean?' Adam asked.

'She might consider we don't trust her enough to include her,' Joe answered.

Adam dragged a hand through his thick dark hair in exasperation. He'd made the arrangements with Dickie on an impulse. At five o'clock in the morning the lad and his kin would be waiting for them. Adam felt he couldn't let them down now.

'Ad, let's take this to Mum,' Polly said quietly.

'Mum...' came the echo and all turned to see Echo peeping around the corner of the building.

'That's done it,' Joe whispered.

'Looks like we'll have to speak to Mum – and Billy – after all,' Adam said resignedly.

The little ones were tucked up in their beds and everyone else was sitting in the living room when Adam broached the subject of breaking the Stantons out of Reed's.

Echo sat between Polly and May on the long sofa, and Digit lounged in an armchair with Flash on the floor by his feet. The others settled on a variety of seats as they listened to what Adam had to say.

Eventually Minnie spoke up. 'Why break them out? Why not just pay Una Reed for their release?'

'No way!' Adam exploded. 'Mum, it wasn't that long ago that she sold your daughter to a wealthy family!'

'Calm down, lad,' Billy intervened gently.

'Sorry. Mum, please – we can't leave those kids in

there, we have to do something to help,' Adam pleaded.

'What if Una goes to the bobbies and says we've stolen 'em away?' Minnie asked.

'The boys would argue that's not the case; they would tell it like it is.' Adam was clearly fretting that the whole thing was falling apart.

'I can see you ain't gonna let this go, are you?' Minnie asked.

Adam shook his head. 'I promised, Mum, and you brought us up to never break a promise made.'

Minnie's eyes moved to her husband. Billy raised his eyebrows, a tiny smile forming on his lips. Looking back to her son, Minnie nodded.

The whole room erupted in cheers and applause and even Minnie couldn't resist a grin. When the noise subsided Minnie held up her hands for attention. 'I don't want the coppers on my doorstep, so don't you lot bloody well get caught!'

'We won't,' Adam assured her.

'We didn't last time,' Rodney added. He ducked as Minnie threw a cushion at him and laughter filled the room.

'We'll need that big bedroom sorted out so the

three can share,' Minnie said as she eyed her family, which was soon to grow yet again. 'You lads shift the beds from the storeroom. Polly and May, there's bed linen in the ottoman on the landing, Echo you can help with that. Matt, Flash and Digit we'll need another table and chairs for the dining room, they'll be in the same room as the beds. Joe, Arthur and Rodney grab a chest of drawers and a tallboy, then you can all sort out any clothes you can spare 'cos them boys will only have what they stand up in.'

Adam threw his arms around his mother. 'Thanks Mum!'

Minnie hugged him back then said, 'Go on and help the others.' Then she called out, 'Quietly! I don't want the little 'uns woken.'

When they filed out whispering excitedly, Billy spoke. 'You're a soft touch, Minnie Marshall.'

'Don't I bloody know it!' she said with a laugh.

'Looks as though you might have some more students joining your class, Celia,' Billy added.

'The more the merrier,' Miss Brock said.

'Three more places to set for breakfast then, Dilys,' Mabel said.

'I know, I ain't daft!' the maid retorted.

'I have to say I ain't happy about this, but what could I do? They would have gone ahead with it anyway,' Minnie said with a frown.

'At least they'll be looked after better here,' Ruth countered.

'And fed well an' all,' Mabel said with a perfunctory nod.

'I can't help thinking this will lead to trouble with Una Reed,' Minnie mumbled.

'One step at a time, my love,' Billy said. 'Let's get them here safe and sound first.'

Minnie nodded but she couldn't shake the feeling of foreboding that settled heavily on her shoulders.

14

Early the following morning Adam, Rodney, Joe and Arthur stole quietly from the house so as not to wake the other residents. There was a chill in the air and a light mist hung sullenly in the streets. The town was still sleeping so as yet there was no cart traffic, and the silence was eerie. The boys walked down the road, the only sound being their boots tapping on the cobblestones.

'I feel like I'm up to no good,' Adam whispered.

'Well you are – in a way,' Arthur replied in the same hushed tones.

They shared a little laugh, more to cover their uneasiness than anything else.

It was not long after that they arrived at Reed House gates.

'Oh no!' Adam said in a loud whisper.

'What?' asked Joe.

'The door will be locked, they won't be able to get out of the house!'

'Bugger!' Arthur's exclamation was quiet but forceful.

'Never fear Musketeers, d'Artagnan to the rescue!' With a flourish, Rodney pulled out a small leather pouch, which showed an array of metal hooks nestled inside.

Adam patted his back. 'Hurry up.'

Rodney slid one of the hooks into the lock on the gate and fiddled it around until it sprang open whilst the others kept their eyes on the windows. With a sigh of relief they slowly pushed the gate open, holding their breath again in case it squeaked. One at a time they filed through before the last one pushed it to behind them. After a quick glance around to ensure it was safe, Adam tapped his friends on the shoulder and they ran quietly across the lawns to the door where Rodney repeated his magic with the door lock. All four winced as they heard the click and they waited a few seconds as they listened for any hint of being discovered. With a nod, Adam opened the door carefully and was gratified to see the Stantons standing silently in the hall. Adam quickly lifted a finger to his lips then hooked it for them to come.

'Shh,' he said in the barest of whispers, then led them outside. Closing the door as quietly as he could, he motioned for them to follow. Dashing across the grass, they then stepped as quietly as possible onto the gravel path.

Once through the gate they closed it and then they ran hell for leather down Vicarage Road. Reaching All Saints Road, they slowed to a walk, all panting from their efforts.

'Quite like old times,' Joe said, a grin splitting his face.

'You never did learn how to re-lock doors then, Rodney?' Adam asked, his grin as wide as Joe's.

'Nope.'

'Thanks fellas,' Dickie said. 'This is Kit and Pip.'

'Are we really coming to your house?' Pip asked.

Adam nodded.

'So we won't have to go back to old Reedy?' Kit prayed he was right.

'Never,' Adam answered.

The sky lightened as they walked and chatted, and the sun dragged its head wearily above the horizon.

The aroma of bacon hit them as they entered the house and bellies rumbled loudly. Pip wiped the drool from his chin on his sleeve, a sheepish look on his face.

Adam led them into the kitchen where he introduced them to Mabel and Dilys.

'Sit at that table, boys, and get yourselves a cup of tea,' Mabel instructed.

The huge kitchen table was suddenly surrounded by famished boys chatting excitedly.

'It went all right, then?' All eyes turned to Minnie as she entered the room.

'Sweet as a nut – eventually,' Adam responded before launching into an explanation about the locked door.

Kit and Pip stared at the woman who they were told was Adam's mum.

'Mrs Marshall...' Dickie began.

'Yes, lovey?'

'I just want to say – thank you,' he went on feeling a little embarrassed.

Minnie nodded her acknowledgement. 'I'd be much obliged if you behaved yourselves whilst you're living here with us. If you've got a problem you can bring it to any one of us. We'll help sort it out.'

Pip began to dribble, his eyes never leaving the massive frying pan Mabel was tending.

'I think you'd best feed this 'un first, Mabel, afore we all drown in spit!' Minnie gave the hungry boy a smile but he merely glanced at her before returning his eyes to the cook.

Plates of bacon, eggs, mushrooms and tomatoes were placed in front of the boys with chunks of fresh bread smothered in butter.

'Slowly, else yer'll mek yerself bad,' Mabel said to Pip as he shovelled food into his mouth. The boy nodded but took no heed, he wanted this breakfast gone as fast as possible.

Over more tea, the boys relived their adventure once more. Pip began to wriggle in his seat.

'Privy is out the back sweet'eart, just through that door. When you come back you can have some toast and jam,' Minnie said. She smiled as the boy shot through the door and in a matter of moments he was back.

'Young man, swill your hands in the sink first,' Mabel instructed.

Pip obeyed, dried them on a towel passed by Dilys then retook his seat.

'This one's gonna take some filling, Minnie,' Mabel said with a grin.

'Ta,' Pip said as he tucked in.

Smiles passed from one face to another as they watched the young boy happily consume his food.

After breakfast, Celia began her lessons in the schoolroom, joined by Kit and Pip. Everyone else prepared themselves for Mr Jackson's funeral at St George's Church. Dressed in their best bib and tucker, the group trudged along the street.

'I wonder what Una will do when the boys don't appear today,' Minnie said quietly to Billy.

'I've no idea, but there's not much she *can* do really,' he answered.

'It's my guess she'll be knocking on our door if she's that worried,' Minnie returned.

'I doubt she'll even miss them. Anyway, they're

safe at home, and just now we have other things to think about. We have a final goodbye to say to Mr Jackson.'

With a nod, Minnie focused on putting one foot in front of the other. This was going to be hardest on Adam so she would have to put his needs first.

'You all right, son?' Minnie asked as they passed through the lychgate.

Adam nodded. 'It's sad, though. I miss him, Mum.'

'I know lad, at least the Lord took him whilst he was sleeping. We should all be that lucky.'

Billy wrapped an arm around Adam's shoulder in a supportive gesture.

With a sigh, Adam stepped into the church.

* * *

Whilst Minnie's family settled themselves on the church pews, Una Reed was questioning her cook.

'You are sure?'

'I said so, d'aint I?' Mrs Gibbs replied indignantly. 'Four kiddies for breakfast only. Them Stanton sods were nowhere to be seen!'

Una scowled and turned away. Where were they? What were they up to now? Was this what their little meeting in the garden had been about? Marching to her office, she dragged a chair to the fireside. Sitting before the crackling logs she wondered where they could be. The front door was locked... wasn't it? Jumping to her feet, she rushed headlong down the stairs, holding up her skirts to prevent a tumble. Trying the handle, she gasped when the door swung open. Stepping outside she hurried towards the gate and in but a moment she realised that too was unlocked.

There was no point in re-locking it now, so she returned to her chair by the fire.

Dickie couldn't have opened the door and gate, otherwise he would have done it before rather than climb over. Kit and Pip were content to be in Diana's classroom so it was unlikely to have been them. So, who had picked the locks? Sudden realisation hit her like a sledge hammer. Rodney Dukes! He was the only person she knew who could pick locks. But she knew he was employed at the abattoir so surely he would have been at work early in the morning?

Una puzzled over the debacle for a long time before finally settling to the notion the boys would be back for lunch. Then she would discover exactly how they'd got out and where they had been all morning. Once those questions were answered she would ensure the Stanton boys were punished accordingly.

It would be the *box* for them with no food or water for a day.

Let's see how you like that, Dickie Stanton!

15

Adam eyed the only other mourner at the graveside as Mr Jackson's coffin was lowered into the ground. Who was he? Was he a relative? A friend, maybe?

It was then that Adam realised the vicar had stopped speaking. Slowly they drifted away as the grave digger began to shovel earth onto the fancy wooden casket.

'Excuse me,' Adam heard the call as they reached the lychgate. Turning, he saw it was the man from the graveside. 'May I enquire... would you know of Adam Fitch?'

'That's me.' He was taken by surprise being asked for by name.

'Ah, forgive me, my name is Francis Germaine.'

'The solicitor?' Adam asked, remembering the name neatly printed on the envelope he delivered to an office in the town.

'Indeed.' Lifting his bowler hat, he inclined his head in greeting as the rest of the family gathered around. 'Such a shame about Mr Jackson,' he went on, waving his hat in the direction of the cemetery before replacing it on his head.

'Indeed,' Adam responded, and Germaine grinned.

'Mr Jackson told me you had your head screwed on the right way. Mr Fitch, I wonder if you would do me the honour of accompanying me to my office.'

Adam was taken aback at being addressed so formally.

'May I ask what for?' he asked after a moment.

'There is something you need to know, and it will take a little time,' Germaine said with a smile which didn't reach his eyes.

'I ain't so sure about that,' Minnie intervened, 'after all, we don't know you from Adam – if you'll pardon the pun.'

Francis, to their surprise, burst out laughing. In

his mid-fifties, the shade of his hair matched his brown eyes exactly. Taking out a handkerchief he mopped away tears of mirth.

'It weren't that funny,' Minnie mumbled as she watched the spotlessly clean handkerchief be returned to a trouser pocket.

'Mrs Marshall, I presume?'

'Yes, and how come you seem to know us?' She spread her arm towards her son.

'If you would all join me in my office too I will explain everything fully.'

'Right then, let's get to it, we'll all come,' Minnie said.

Half an hour later, Minnie and Billy were sat before Germaine's desk whilst everyone else stood around.

'I'm sorry there's not much room or enough chairs but I usually have clients singly or in pairs.' Francis drew out an envelope from a drawer and dropped it onto the desktop.

'First of all, thank you Mr Fitch for bringing this here.' He tapped the envelope with a beautifully manicured hand.

'Adam, please call me Adam,' the boy responded.

'As you wish. Now I'm sure you've guessed, that this is Mr Jackson's last will and testament.' Francis looked at the sea of faces before him. 'Yes, well, it concerns yourself, Mr... Adam.'

'Me?' Adam asked, but his eyes went first to Polly, then to his mum.

Francis nodded. 'I don't know if you are aware, but Mr Jackson was a very wealthy man.'

'You'm joking, ain't yer?' Minnie asked incredulously.

'No, Mrs Marshall, I most certainly am not. Having been Mr Jackson's solicitor for many years, I am conversant with his estate, which is quite considerable.'

'I thought... he lived in that little house and...' Adam's words trailed off.

'All the buildings on that expanse of land abutting the allotment gardens belonged to Mr Jackson. The tenants in the houses paid him a nominal amount in rent. He insisted on that, as they are in an impecunious state.' Francis paused as mutters sounded.

'But he swapped his produce for other things so we thought he was living hand to mouth,' Adam said.

'The old fellow enjoyed the exchange system and it was company for him once a week,' Francis explained. 'It was as he told me often – he didn't need much to live on.'

'He never said a word!' Adam gasped.

'He wouldn't, he was a very private man.'

'Why did Mrs Jackson put up with it? I mean, I would have thought she would have wanted to have a bigger house with nice things in it,' Minnie said quietly.

'Mrs Jackson was an invalid, Mrs Marshall. She had some sort of ailment which took the strength from her muscles. It grew steadily worse over the years until her death five years ago.'

'How dreadful.' It was Polly who spoke in a whisper.

'I'm afraid Mr Jackson retreated into himself after her passing, that is until he met you, Adam.'

All eyes turned to the boy in question then back to the solicitor as he took the papers from the envelope and began to read aloud.

* * *

Having left the solicitor's office in a daze, the family walked home in silence. It was later in the living room that they finally discussed what they'd been told by Mr Germaine.

It transpired that the house they now sat in had once belonged to Mr Jackson. Having had no children and with his wife so poorly he had moved them into the small house to better take care of her. Francis had explained that Mr Jackson was fully aware of Billy's investigations into ownership of the huge building.

'Fancy him never saying anything about owning this place,' Billy said.

'Mr Germaine said it was because he knew it was to be a children's home,' Adam added.

'I can't get over him having all those houses an' all,' Minnie put in.

'Old money, passed down from father to son,' Polly mused.

'Poor old Mr Jackson didn't have a son – not by blood, anyway,' May said.

Everyone glanced at Adam and he blushed.

'What was the wording again?' Joe asked. '*To Adam, the son I never had…*'

'Give over, Joe,' Adam said flushing a deeper shade of scarlet.

'Mrs Marshall, Mr Jackson left us each fifty pounds – how many is that?' Kit asked timidly looking at his fingers.

'Celia, that would be your area of expertise, you'll have to find a way to explain.' Then to Kit she said, 'You and your brothers are quite rich young men now.'

'I don't understand,' Dickie put in, 'I was horrible to him and yet he still left us some money – why?'

'Because he knew there was good inside you and one day it would win through,' Polly answered, making Dickie turn beetroot red.

'Win through,' Echo's words sounded half a beat later but he scowled at Dickie. He felt the new boy was getting a little too familiar with Polly and he didn't like it.

'Everyone is rich now,' Billy said. 'You kids need to be careful with the money left to you – make it last.' He looked at each face in turn – James, Peter, Polly, Flash, Digit, May, Arthur, Matt, Rodney, Joe and Echo – and wondered if they had inkling of just how much fifty pounds actually was. The rest, numbering in the thousands, was left to Adam.

'It was so nice of him to include us as well,' Celia said daintily.

'I'm gonna buy me a good winter coat with my money,' Dilys said.

'With the amount you've got now you could buy the shop!' Mabel said with a grin. They too had received fifty pounds each.

'Might I suggest, it would be a good idea to open a bank account each so Mr Germaine can deposit your money for safe keeping until you want to use it,' Billy said.

'Monday morning first thing – everybody to the bank,' Minnie stated, in a way that would brook no arguments. 'Right, let's eat, then we'll get you Stanton boys settled in properly.'

16

Lunchtime came and went with no sign of the
Stanton boys and Una began to wonder if they had
got themselves into trouble. Could it be they'd been
carted off by the police? Sitting by the fire in her office, she pulled up her long brown skirt to warm her
knees. Dragging her woollen shawl tighter around
her shoulders, she sighed. Springtime proper
couldn't come soon enough for her; each year that
passed she felt the cold a little more.

Her thoughts returned to the Stantons and where
they could be. They had missed two meals now and
would be famished. It was as she had an image of

them standing in line that she recalled something Dickie had said.

The kids' home is havin' 'lectrics put in.

Now how would that young rogue know that? Unless he'd been there. Why would he go down to Marshall's? What was so fascinating to draw him there? Maybe he was roaming the town and ended up there. That old man who complained about Dickie kicking up the allotment came to mind and Una knew the gardens were at the top of Major Street. Perhaps he'd been there vandalising again and had wandered further down the street. That must be it because he would have no other reason to visit that particular area.

Re-covering her now warm knees, Una just hoped the old fellow wouldn't be banging on her door again with more complaints. There was still time for the boys to return for their evening meal, but if they didn't? Una pondered the dilemma before her. Should she inform the police if the brothers were still missing by morning? Or should she just count her losses and concentrate on filling their places at Reed House?

Suddenly another thought struck – would

Minnie Marshall have taken them in? Would she have been aware the boys resided here? Then again, she may think they lived on the streets. If that woman had brought them into her fold, was it worth the bother of trying to get them back? Shaking her head, Una thought not. She could do without the constant battle of wits and it was three mouths less to feed.

A knock on the door broke her concentration.

'Come!'

'I'm sorry to bother you,' Diana Wilton said as she stepped into the room, 'but I thought you should know – the children are unwell.'

Una sighed audibly. 'What's wrong with them?'

'Not being a medical professional I really couldn't say. They have a fever and a dry hacking cough. They're sweating but shivering too, and their breathing is erratic. Maybe a doctor should be called in.'

Raising an eyebrow at the young woman daring to challenge her authority, Una shook her head. 'I'm sure there's no need for that. Instruct cook to give them some medicine and put them to bed.'

'I must protest...' Diana began.

'Must you? Forgive me, but I was under the impression I was in charge here!' Una snapped. 'Now carry out my orders. I will visit the children tomorrow to determine whether a doctor's visit is worth the extortionate fee he charges.'

'As you wish.' Diana left the office unhappily, leaving Una to ponder this latest crisis.

With the Stanton brothers still missing the following morning, Una had no time to dwell on their fate. She had far more pressing matters to deal with. The four children left in her orphanage were very poorly and Una despatched the cook to fetch a doctor.

* * *

Going from room to room, the doctor examined the children. Each one coughed and gasped as the sweat ran down their little bodies. Then they shivered uncontrollably, as if they were freezing to death.

Una followed along behind, a handkerchief pressed tightly against her mouth and nose.

'Why was I not called before this?' the doctor demanded to know.

'The children have only just shown signs of being ill!' Una retorted before replacing her face cover.

'These kiddies have pneumonia and have been unwell for a while, Miss Reed, so how come no one noticed?'

Una shook her head, wishing he would hurry up so she could escape to the safety of her office.

'They need to be fed fruit and vegetables – if they will take it. Plenty to drink and they must be kept warm, so bank up the fire and put them all in one room. Open the window for fresh air. I will leave you some medicine for them but I tell you now – it's touch and go as to whether they will live through the night!'

Shaking his head, the doctor placed a large glass bottle with a cork stopper onto the table. 'One teaspoon three times a day. If you need me again, just call.' Then he made his way downstairs, where Una paid his fee and saw him out.

By mid-morning Una chose to quarantine herself until the disease had run its course – just in case.

Returning to her office, she paced the floor and thought through the consequences. Not only having had to pay the doctor, she now was faced with the prospect of paying for four burials. Then her orphanage would be empty for the first time in twenty years. No children meant no more money from patronages. How could it be that there would be no more to fill the empty beds? Poverty in the town had not improved over the last decade, so what had changed? Why were folk no longer selling their kids to her? Was it down to Marshall's opening up?

Una knew that families were still struggling to survive due to the high level of unemployment. She was also aware that it didn't stop women producing children one after another until their childbearing days were over. This then begged the question – how could they afford to feed them all?

Una sighed heavily. If her charges were to die then she would have to close the orphanage. Teacher and cook would have to go and she would be left alone in this great rambling building. She would have no income and her savings would not last forever. How would she survive? Running this place was all she knew how to do.

The night passed slowly for Una, who fretted through the long hours about whether she would be closing her doors for good very soon. However, by the morning she was informed the children were past the worst, their fevers having broken. Now they were feeling a little better. Exhaling with relief, she ate breakfast wondering how she could get more heads in beds.

* * *

Once the fast was broken in the Marshall household, Minnie and Billy were discussing getting everyone along to the bank when Adam joined them.

'What's up, bab?' Minnie asked seeing the perplexed look on her son's face.

'I still can't believe it, Mum. Mr Jackson leaving us all his money, I mean.'

'I know, what a lovely old fella he was,' Minnie said with a smile.

'Now I know what all the questions were about,' Adam said.

'What questions?' Billy asked with a frown.

'When we worked up at the allotments, Mr Jackson was always quizzing me about my family. How many brothers and sisters I had, who else lived here and what jobs they did. He must have been taking it all in so he could alter his will.' Adam shook his head in wonderment.

'What will you do about the houses and tenants you've inherited, son?' Billy asked.

Adam felt his heart lurch at the endearment and saw his mum smile broadly.

'I'm not sure, what's your advice – Dad?' Adam felt a little awkward using the term in case Billy would be embarrassed.

Instead Billy grinned. 'I love the sound of that, Adam, thank you.'

Adam nodded, 'So do I.'

'Well, it's up to you of course, but if it were me I would go and introduce myself to the folks who will be paying you rent,' Billy went on.

'Good idea. I can let them know that nothing will change regarding their payments.'

'You won't increase the rent, then?' Minnie asked.

'No, Mum. From what Mr Germaine said, those people have little enough as it is so I would want them to be assured all will stay the same,' Adam answered.

'I'm proud of you, lad,' Minnie said as her eyes misted over.

Turning to Billy, he asked, 'Would you come with me?'

'Yes, son, I'd be happy to.'

An hour later, Minnie and Billy led the younger ones to the bank to open accounts; the older ones could sort themselves out during their lunch breaks from work. Once that was completed, they filed home clutching tightly to their little bank books.

Dressing in their Sunday best, Adam and Billy set out to get to know the people living in Adam's houses.

17

Deciding to start with the house next door to where Mr Jackson had lived, Adam knocked loudly. A thin woman answered, 'What do you want?'

'My name is Adam Fitch and this is Billy Marshall.'

'You the new landlord then?' the woman asked pointedly and when Adam nodded she went on, 'You'm a bit young, ain't yer?'

Adam and Billy exchanged a glance.

'You'd best come in, we don't want to discuss yer business on the doorstep.' The woman moved aside to allow them entry. 'Go on through to the kitchen, the kettle's on.'

The tiny two-up, two-down, Adam noted, was immaculately clean and smelled of beeswax.

'Sit and have a sup,' the woman instructed.

The pen and notebook Adam had brought with him was laid on the table and the woman eyed them suspiciously.

She filled her two best cups with tea and sat down with her own tin mug. 'I s'pose you've come to tell me you're putting the rent up?'

'How did you know who I was?' Adam asked.

'That solicitor bloke came and told us all you was taking over.' The woman watched as Adam nodded. 'So how much more are we gonna 'ave to pay?'

'Nothing,' Adam replied. 'The rent is to remain the same.'

'Oh!' The woman's eyebrows shot up in surprise. 'So why am you 'ere?'

'I've come to introduce myself and get acquainted with everyone, as well as assure you that there will be no increase in the rent being paid,' Adam answered.

'Well that's bloody nice of yer, young man.'

'May I ask your name?' Adam asked.

'Doris Jones, and I live 'ere with my 'usband Alf.'

Adam made a note in his book.

'We pay one and sixpence a week – 'ave done for many a year,' she added.

Again Adam made a note.

'Does Mr Jones work?'

Doris nodded. 'Ar, he's a smithy over at the back of the 'ospital. What you writing all this down for?'

'It's to help me remember who is who, and if you need any help I can check which number you live at until I know everyone,' Adam said as he closed the book.

'Oh right,' Doris said with a satisfied nod.

'Is there anything I can help you with today?'

'No cocka, we'm doing all right, 'specially as we ain't got to pay you more each week,' Doris said with a smile which softened her features.

'Then we'll take up no more of your time, Mrs Jones. Just to let you know we live at Marshall's Children's Home if you need to contact me for any reason.' Adam and Billy stood to leave and the woman nodded.

'Thank you for the tea. Give our regards to your husband.'

'I will an' all,' Doris said as she saw them out.

Walking to the next house, Billy said, 'Nicely done, lad, I'm proud of you.'

Adam smiled. 'I hope they're all as nice as Mrs Jones.'

The whole of the day was taken up with visiting the houses, numbering twenty-two in all including Mr Jackson's empty one. With a cup of tea in each and the odd visit to the privy, Adam and Billy finally started to make their way home.

'You'll need to get Mr Jackson's house let too, you know,' Billy said gently as they strolled along.

'I'm not sure how to go about that,' Adam responded.

'You'll likely find the neighbours will put the word out, and now they know where you can be found someone will come knocking before long is my guess.'

'So we just wait and see then. Tomorrow I'll open my own bank account and tell Mr Germaine so he knows where to put the rent.' Adam's mind was working overtime with all that being a property owner entailed.

The spring sunshine was warm and Adam removed his jacket and carried it over his shoulder.

Billy did the same and they whistled a little ditty as they sauntered on. Stopping at the allotments, they were surprised to see Dickie on his hands and knees pulling weeds.

'Kit and Pip are in school so I thought I'd help out here, I hope that's all right.'

'It certainly is,' Adam said. 'We'll see you later.'

The two walked on, discussing the change in Dickie Stanton since he'd come to live at Marshall's.

Arriving home, both were hot and tired and grateful that they could now relax.

'So how did it go?' Polly asked eagerly as they entered the kitchen.

'Extremely well,' Billy put in quickly. 'Everyone took to Adam straight away.'

Refusing tea offered by Mabel, they went to change out of their best togs.

Later, in the sitting room, Adam and Polly had their usual evening chat. Adam told her about his meetings and Polly praised him for being so kind.

'How was your day?' he asked eventually.

'Oh Ad, I'm fed up with nothing to do except lend a hand here. I need to feel useful and I don't at the moment,' Polly wailed.

'I take it there's no one in your sick room at the moment?'

Polly shook her head. 'Don't get me wrong, I'm glad everyone is well but I'm at a loose end all the time.'

'What about chasing up the idea of a market stall? I know you and May were quite excited about it when it was mentioned previously.'

'I know but I want to do something that fulfils me and a market stall won't do that.'

'Well, now you have some money why don't you set up a little business?' Adam suggested.

'Doing what?'

'Anything you want to. I know you've trained as a nurse which will always come in handy, but why not try something different? Anyway, have a think on it – ask the others, they may have some ideas.' Adam felt sorry for his sister, who thought she was wasting her life away in the children's home.

Before long the room began to fill as the workers returned and the younger children were set free from the school room. When Polly mentioned her discussion with Adam, ideas did indeed pour forth.

'You could train as a teacher as I did,' Celia said.

'Or a cook like me,' Mabel offered.

When Rodney suggested a lock-pick everyone groaned and threw cushions at him.

Polly had a lot of notions to consider by the time she went to bed, and Adam said she could help at the allotment whilst she made up her mind.

The following morning, the dawn chorus was a cacophony of bird calls, and the sun rose promising a warm day.

It was as Adam was readying himself for a few hours tending his plot that a woman called to see him. She was stick thin and wearing a patched dress. Her hair was mousy brown and caught at the back with a clip. Eyes dark and serious appeared too large for her face and her hands were calloused.

'I've come to ask about the 'ouse you 'ave to rent,' she said quietly.

'What's your name?' Adam asked.

'Jillian Ferguson. But please call me Jill.'

'Right, Jill, let's chat in the kitchen over a cup of tea,' Adam said.

Following along, Jill was given a seat at the table where Mabel poured tea and presented a large slice of cake.

'Thank you kindly,' the woman said with a gaunt smile, giving her face a macabre expression.

'How did you know I had a house to rent?' Adam asked.

'I went to the market to scav... get some food and the stall holders were talking about it. They said you were the new landlord for the houses along Derry Street and old Mr Jackson's place was empty now he'd passed,' Jill answered.

Between bites, Jill explained that she had four children. She was a widow, her husband having died of miner's lung – a euphemism for tuberculosis. Now she went to people's houses to do their washing in exchange for a few pennies.

'The rent paid by everyone else is one and six-pence a week,' Adam said, knowing what the woman's answer would be.

Getting to her feet, Jill thanked them and turned to leave. 'I'm sorry I wasted yer time, Mr Fitch, but I can't afford that.'

'Jill, please stay a minute. Tell me, where are you living now?' Adam probed.

'On the heath at the back of the railway line,' she answered meekly.

'I didn't know there were any houses out that way,' Minnie put in.

'There ain't,' Jill whispered lowering her head.

'Jill, are you living outdoors with four kiddies?' Adam asked.

A nod her answer, Jill tried to stifle the sob in her throat.

'Mabel – a hamper if you'd be so kind,' Minnie said and watched the cook shoot off to the pantry to carry out the request.

'Jill, move your family in today,' said Adam.

'But I can't pay…'

'Never mind that. Get those children some shelter from the cold nights. I'll be along later to see if there's anything you need.'

'Oh, Mr Fitch, God bless you. You'm an angel. All of yer – angels!' Jill sobbed.

Seeing the size of the baskets packed with food, Adam said, 'On second thoughts, I'll come now and carry these for you.'

'Take Echo with you, he can help,' Minnie said.

'I can't thank you enough,' Jill said as she wiped away her tears on the sleeve of her tattered dress.

Minnie shouted for Echo, who came hurtling

through the door. 'Good lad. You give Adam a hand with the lady's baskets please.'

'...baskets please,' Echo repeated.

Jill smiled indulgently, realising immediately that the boy was dim-witted.

Minnie shook her head as she watched them leaving hearing Adam say, 'We'll take this to the house and you fetch your children.'

'Christ, Mabel, I thought the wench might die of starvation right here in the kitchen!' Minnie said after they had left.

'Me an' all. By but she was skinny. Your lad though – he's a bloody diamond,' Mabel answered.

Minnie puffed up her chest in pride at the compliment. After all that boy had been through and he still thought of others before himself.

An hour later, the boys were back and calling for Polly.

'I've a favour to ask,' Adam said.

Echo was bouncing from foot to foot with excitement. '...ask.'

'Could you order four beds to be delivered today for Mr Jackson's house; they can send me the bill. Jill said she'd be more than happy to sleep in his bed so we'll need five new sets of bed linen too. Then can you and May take some money and fill the larder, oh and get some clothes for the family living there now.' Adam gave her a scrap of paper with sizes he'd had to guess on seeing the youngsters. 'Echo's going to the coal yard to get an order sent so they'll have a fire tonight.'

Echo beamed at being given such an important task. 'Now, you remember the message Echo?' Adam asked.

Nodding frantically, the boy collected his thoughts. 'Coal shed filled at number twenty-seven Derry Street. Invoice Adam Fitch at Marshall's Children's Home.'

'Well done! Right, off you go.' Adam's praise gave the boy a grin that split his face before he scampered away.

'I'll get going too,' Polly said as she accepted the money Adam had drawn from the bank on his way home.

'God bless you, son,' Minnie muttered.

'Oh Mum, you should see those kids! Filthy dirty and thin as laths. It's a wonder they're still alive. Jill said her next step was going to be to take them to the workhouse when she left here. I couldn't let that happen, Mum – I just couldn't!' Adam was distraught at the thought. 'Anyway, I said we'd come to an arrangement about the rent at a later date, but I can't see it happening. I don't care about that as long as that family are safe and warm.'

'Seems to me like Mr Jackson was very clever leaving you all that money and property. He knew you'd be wise in the spending of it,' Minnie said.

'I hope you're right, Mum.'

Just then a knock sounded on the front door and Dilys was sent to answer it. A moment later she was back, followed by a policeman.

18

'Mrs Marshall?' the constable asked, looking down his nose at Minnie, who nodded.

'In my station I have one Christopher Stanton, aka *Kit*,' he spat the word with emphasis on the last letter.

Minnie sighed heavily. The boy was supposed to be in class with his brother Pip. Clearly he'd sneaked out whilst no one was looking.

'What's he done?' Minnie asked.

'He's assaulted a woman is what he's done!'

'Assaulted? He's a fourteen-year-old kid, constable,' Minnie replied.

'At this moment I have two women waging war

and a boy who's screaming blue bloody murder!' The constable glared at Minnie who took a deep breath and glared back.

'Right, let's go and see what all this is about,' she said.

'I'll come with you, Mum,' Adam volunteered.

Minnie nodded, and mother and son followed the policeman out of the house.

A while later Polly arrived back from her errand pleased with her accomplishment, and was hearing the tale of Kit when Echo rushed in.

'Coal delivered!' he said with a pant.

'Well done, Echo,' Polly praised.

'I took the coalman there,' Echo added.

'Why?' Polly asked.

'So he d'aint get lost!' came the reply. 'This is for Adam.' Echo held out a piece of paper to Polly.

'Thank you, you're very considerate.' Polly took the invoice and added it to her own.

'Where's Adam?' Echo asked.

'He's gone to the police station with Mum,' Polly replied.

Echo immediately threw his hands to his ears

and began to wail loudly. He banged his head and shuffled from foot to foot.

'Echo, it's all right, he's not in any trouble!' Polly said as she put her arms around the boy to calm him.

Slowly Echo settled as Polly explained fully the reason. She mentally berated herself for not having done this in the first place, knowing Echo had to be told everything as though he were a five-year-old.

'Kit naughty,' the boy said on a sob.

'We're not sure what happened yet,' Polly said gently, 'but Adam will tell us when he gets home.'

'...home,' Echo repeated with a nod.

'Now tell me all about your visit to the coal yard,' Polly encouraged.

* * *

Minnie couldn't believe the noise as they entered the police station. Shouting and yelling, loud enough to wake the dead, assaulted her ears.

The sergeant sat behind a huge desk as he watched the two women trade insults, and Kit Stanton stood with his hands in his pockets, a sullen look on his face. There was a row of kitchen chairs opposite the desk beneath a window, and to the side of the room were two doors.

The women continued to argue with the occasional interruption from Kit pleading his case.

'Quiet!' the sergeant yelled and instantly all fell silent. 'You,' he glared at a large woman, 'in there with the constable.' He then pointed to one of the doors. 'You, sit down and keep yer mouth shut, and you, young man, give over before I clap you in irons and send you to the cells!' He indicated the other door with a jerk of his thumb.

Minnie's eyes rested on the woman told to sit; it was none other than Una Reed. Adam went over to Kit to console him.

'This lad says he's in your care, Mrs Marshall,' the sergeant began.

Una opened her mouth to speak but closed it again as the sergeant raised a finger in warning.

'He is, now what's going on?' Minnie answered.

'It appears the boy went looking for his brother Dickie when Miss Reed caught him by the arm and attempted to drag him away.'

'That is not what happened!' Una snapped.

The sergeant sighed and said, 'I told you to be

quiet, you'll get your turn to speak so for now – button your lip!' Turning back to Minnie he went on, 'That is what Kit told us and it was borne out by the lady in there.' He tilted his head to the other room. 'However, Miss Reed denies this, saying she merely wanted to speak to the boy.'

'So, where does the assault come into all this?' Minnie asked.

'Kit kicked Miss Reed to force her to release him so he could go home to you.'

Minnie turned to the boy in question, and asked, 'Is that correct?'

'Yes! She tried to drag me back to Reed's and I wouldn't go!' Kit answered angrily.

'I believe you, lad, so calm down,' Minnie said, then, turning back to the sergeant asked, 'So what's to be done now?'

'Just get the boy home and keep a better eye on him in the future.'

'He should be locked up!' Una spat.

'I'll lock you up if you don't behave!' Clearly at the end of his tether, the sergeant went on, 'Kit and that woman both say you accosted the boy before he assaulted you. Now I'm inclined to believe that is what occurred, so I suggest you get off home and think yourself lucky I don't bang you in jail for the night!'

Una jumped to her feet and marched away indignantly.

The sergeant blew his cheeks out then called to the constable. Speaking to the large woman he said, 'Thank you for your help, madam, it was most fortunate you were on the scene.'

The woman gave a curt nod and smiled at Kit as she went on her way to relay the gossip to anyone who would listen.

'Right, young man, I don't want to see you in my station again – understand?'

'Yes, thank you, sir,' Kit replied.

Thanking the sergeant, Minnie led Kit and Adam out of the building, listening to Kit explaining the incident again.

Once in the kitchen, Minnie related the tale yet again, then asked Kit, 'Why were you not in class?'

'I went to find our Dickie, I told you!'

'Kit, be respectful!' Dickie remonstrated. 'You promised you'd stay in school.'

Kit looked suitably chastised.

'Well I think you did the right thing kicking Una Reed,' Mabel said.

'I'm not so sure, you should never do that,' Dickie replied.

'She *was* trying to abdicate him!' Dilys put in.

'Abduct Dilys. If you ain't sure of the word then don't use it,' Mabel corrected.

'I was sure of it. I just d'aint know it was the wrong one!' Dilys said with a pout.

'Let's get back to the matter in hand, shall we?' Minnie interjected. 'Kit, you can go out any time you want, just let someone know so we don't worry.'

'Thanks, I'm sorry I caused a problem but I ain't sorry I kicked old Reedy.' Kit folded his arms and clamped his lips together.

'What did Una say when she grabbed you?' Minnie asked.

'She said I should be at her place and not yours,' Kit answered. 'I told her to... bugger off.'

Minnie stifled the grin about to erupt and nodded. 'Time I had a word with that woman, I think.'

'Mum, it's all over and done now, maybe we should let sleeping dogs lie,' Adam said.

Seeing the look that crossed her son's face, Minnie nodded. 'Fair enough.'

'Kit, it's important for you to get an education. Suddenly I've found myself to be a businessman and I'm glad I learned to read and write as well as do my numbers,' Adam said quietly. Turning to Dickie, he added, 'Kit was out looking for you, not realising you were at the allotment garden I would guess, so how would you fancy taking over the allotment for me? Then Kit and Pip could help at weekends if they want.'

'What about Peter and James; how would they feel about that?' Dickie asked.

'I think it will be all right with them as they spend most of their time working the wharves now anyway.'

'Go on, Dickie, then we can help,' Kit urged.

'Righto. Thanks Adam.'

'Mum, May's coming with me to the market, is there anything you need?' Polly asked.

'No thanks, gel, but you two watch what you're doing,' Minnie warned.

'...doing,' came the echo.

Adam turned to the boy, saying, 'How did you get

on with the coalman, Echo?' He knew Polly and May wanted to visit the market by themselves without having Echo tag along, so it was his way of distracting the boy.

Echo excitedly related his tale yet again and beamed when Adam praised his efforts.

'Right, no kids washed, no pigeons 'ome,' Minnie said as she got to her feet, meaning that sitting around was getting no work done.

Polly and May donned straw boaters and set off, chatting quietly about the debacle between Kit and Una Reed.

As they walked up Steelhouse Lane they heard the flutter of wings as a group of pigeons took to the air. The girls watched the passerine of birds soar and dip in a graceful dance of the sky. All along the street, pigeon flyers opened their loft doors to free their birds, and suddenly the clouds were blotted out by the little grey bodies. Tiny feathers fluttered down to land gently on the cobbles.

After enjoying the moment, Polly and May moved on, leaving behind the sound of bird seed rattling in tin cans calling the birds home, and the grating noise of lofts being scraped clean.

A little dog yapped and ran to the gate of a house where Polly stopped to stroke its nose through the laths.

Further along, May wrinkled her nose at a carter's horse which had stopped to deposit a steaming pile of manure into the sack tied beneath its rear end. They hurried on to escape the foul odour.

Coming to the Union Workhouse, Polly stopped dead in her tracks. 'May, look at that.'

19

Standing at the wrought iron gates of the workhouse was a man with two small children. Dressed in rags, the two little girls were sobbing and the man was doing his best to console them.

'We have to do something!' Polly said.

'Like what?' May asked.

'May, that man is about to put those children into the workhouse!'

'I can see that, but I ask again, what can *we* do about it?'

Polly's eyes flitted left and right as she forced her brain to find a solution. Settling once more on the man now down on one knee, an arm around each of his daughters, Polly's heart went out to them.

'We can take them home with us,' she said in a sudden flash of inspiration.

'Polly, you don't know that man! He could be a murderer!' May was aghast at her friend's suggestion.

'For God's sake, May! Look at him – does he look like a murderer?'

'No, but he could be a drunk or violent – Polly, be sensible, please!' May begged.

'Any minute now those girls will be forced through the gates and will probably never see their father again. Could you live with that on your conscience? They will have a life of hell in that bloody awful place!'

May sighed heavily. 'Please God, don't let us regret this,' she muttered as she followed Polly, who strode purposefully forward.

'Excuse me,' she said and the man turned to look at her. 'Please don't put your children in there.'

'I ain't got no choice, lass,' the man said woefully.

'You have. My mum runs a children's home, you could bring them there,' Polly urged.

Just then the porter arrived to open the gates. 'You comin' in or what?'

The man glanced at the porter then his eyes returned to Polly. 'I can't pay...'

'You don't need to. Come with us and you'll see. I promise you won't regret it.' Polly was adamant those girls would not be subjected to a life in the workhouse.

'Mek yer mind up!' the porter snapped.

The man shook his head and the porter harrumphed and walked away back to his cosy lodge.

Polly sighed with relief, then bending down she spoke to the girls. 'Here, take these.' Pulling two chocolate bars from her bag, Polly offered them to the children.

'Where did you get those?' May asked incredulously.

'From the pantry, I thought we might get hungry but their need is greater than ours.'

Tears subsided as the girls looked to their father for permission to take the confectionary. With a nod the man gave his daughters leave to accept.

'Thank you,' he muttered, as tears filled his eyes at the kindness shown to his family by strangers.

'My name is Polly and this is May. Come on and we'll show you the way. You can meet my mum, Minnie, and make your decision then about what you want to do.' Polly then smiled down at the girls who were listening intently as they munched on their treat. To them she said, 'We have a school room and a lovely teacher, and your dad can visit any time he wants.'

Polly and May led the way, chatting as they went, but Polly had seen the look of fear cross the children's faces at the thought of living in a strange place without their father. She shuddered as she recalled that same feeling when she was sold to Reed's. At least the girls had each other, as Polly had had Adam, which might give some small comfort.

May's banter was lost to her as Polly realised what she'd done. What if Minnie refused to take the girls for some reason? No, her mum would never do such a thing. How would Minnie react to her daughter bringing home a strange family? Would it be the same as May when Polly suggested the rescue in the first place? In all reality Polly should have asked her mother before making the offer but the situation was dire. The man, who said his name was

Ted, was on the cusp of making the worst decision of his life – through sheer desperation. Polly felt this justified her impulsive action, which she would defend with vigour if the need arose.

Looking again at the bedraggled family, Polly knew her decision to bring this family home with her had been the right one.

On their arrival, Polly took them straight to the kitchen. 'Mum, I found these people at the workhouse gates and...'

'You did the right thing,' Minnie said straight away on seeing the state of the wretchedly poor family. Then to the man with a child clinging to each trouser leg she added, 'Come in and have a cup of tea.'

The man nodded and Minnie saw the look in his eyes. Relief, gratitude and fierce pride shone forth as he did as he was bid.

'Mabel, is that broth ready yet, 'cos we have some hungry bellies to fill,' Minnie said as she poured the tea.

'Thank you. I'm Ted Freeman and this is Dora and Gertie,' the man said indicating his girls in turn.

'Hello, girls, you ready for some dinner?'

Blue eyes twinkled at Minnie as they nodded, each with their fingers in their mouths.

Lamb stew with chunks of fresh bread was laid before the family and Minnie was surprised when the girls clasped their hands in prayer.

'May the Lord make us truly thankful,' Ted said before they tucked in with gusto.

'So Ted, our Polly says you were at the work-house gates. Was it your intention to...' Minnie nodded towards the girls, whose attention was firmly on their food.

'Yes, Mrs Marshall,' he replied with eyes full of regret.

'That bloody awful place should be shut down!' Mabel intervened as she cut more bread which she handed to the girls and their father.

'If it was closed there would be many more folk out on the streets left to die of starvation,' Ted countered, with a nod of thanks for the bread.

'I suppose so,' Mabel relented.

'When did you last have summat to eat?' Dilys asked innocently.

'My girls had a little bit the day before yesterday.'

'What about you?' Minnie asked.

Ted shook his head, evidently unable to remember.

Minnie's heart ached for the man, who had been forced into a terrible situation which was clearly not of his own making.

Whilst the family ate, Dilys was instructed to fill the two tin baths with warm water out in the scullery. May went to the cupboard where spare clothes were kept to find something for the girls to wear.

Mabel made a fresh brew and Echo watched eagerly, hoping he had two more friends to play with.

Fresh fruit followed, then Minnie said, 'You two little 'uns go with Polly and get washed and changed whilst I chat to your dad.'

The Freeman girls hesitated and looked to their father. 'Go on, do as Mrs Marshall says. I'll be here when you're done.'

Given permission, they went happily with Polly and May.

Just then Billy walked in, his boxing lessons having finished for the day. He was introduced to the man at the table with a brief explanation of how he came to be there.

'Now then, Ted, what's occurring?' Minnie asked.

The man with chocolate brown eyes drew in a breath and began. 'I work at the coal yard and last year my wife died giving birth. The babby was lost an' all.'

'I'm sorry to hear that,' Minnie said quietly.

Ted nodded his thanks and went on. 'I've been working but I 'ave to leave my little wenches at home on their own, I can't afford to send 'em to school you see. Anyway, my wages are just enough to pay rent and buy a bit of food now and then.'

Minnie saw the tears forming in his eyes as he spoke.

'My girls were starving to death, Mrs Marshall, and I couldn't stand to watch it any more! One is my breath and the other my body and I couldn't let them die 'cos I can't feed them!' Suddenly Ted's shoulders heaved and months of sadness burst forth as he cried like a baby.

Billy closed his eyes tightly for a moment as he watched this grown man sobbing. How could life be so cruel?

It was Echo who wrapped an arm around the man's shoulder as he sobbed. 'Be better now,' Echo soothed.

Eventually Ted brought his emotions under control and he turned to Echo. 'Thanks, lad.'

'Ted, you can leave Dora and Gertie here with us so you can still work. Now before you say anything, you don't have to pay 'cos we have council funding. They'll be safe here with us; well fed and schooled and you can come and visit any time you like. You can take 'em out for walks and things and bring them back in time for food and bed. How does that sound?'

'Mrs Marshall, I'll never be able to thank you enough,' Ted said and smiled as he heard, '...enough.'

'Can I ask – why didn't you go to Reed's?' Minnie asked.

'From what I hear, it's not much better than the workhouse,' Ted responded.

'Didn't you know about us?' Billy asked.

'Yes sir, I did, but I thought I would have to pay and I just couldn't find the money. I will say though that Marshall's has a good reputation around the town. People sing your praises.'

'Well, that's nice to know,' Minnie said.

Given another cup of tea, Ted nodded his thanks

as Minnie spoke again. 'It's clear to everyone how much you love those girls and how well behaved they are. You've brought them up well and should be proud.'

'Oh, I am!' Ted smiled.

'Like I said, Dora and Gertie can stay here with us if you trust us to look after them in your stead.' Minnie looked to Billy for approval and when he nodded she went on. 'I know we're strangers as yet but I'm sure we'll get to know each other in time. However, the decision must be yours to make and if you agree you know you can come back for them once you're on your feet again. No one from here gets sold on or thrown out – be assured.'

'Thank you both very much,' then turning his eyes to Billy, Ted asked. 'Pardon me for asking, but are you the boxer?'

'I am.'

'Well I'll go to the foot of our stairs! I've watched you win many a fight. You're a fine bloke.'

'He is that,' Minnie said with a grin.

She was telling Ted about who lived at Marshall's when the girls came rushing back into the kitchen all clean and tidy.

'Well now look at you two. Pretty as pictures,' Ted beamed his pride as he hugged his daughters. 'Mrs Marshall has very kindly said you can stay here whilst I'm at work, would you like that?'

The girls nodded, and laughed when Echo clapped his hands.

'I'll come and see you every Sunday,' Ted added.

'In that case we'll set an extra place at the dinner table,' Minnie said with a grin.

'Thank you – everyone.' Ted's eyes misted over again as he stood to take his leave.

'I'm going now because I have to get back to work,' he said, with a catch in his throat.

Instantly the girls rushed to him and flung their arms around his legs holding on for dear life, tears streaming down their faces.

'Daddy!' Dora sobbed.

'Please don't go!' Gertie pleaded.

Ted retook his seat and lifted a daughter onto each knee. 'I want you to listen to me. I know it will be hard but you are big girls now. You're six years old, Dora, and you are five, Gertie.' As he spoke he tenderly stroked their dark hair. The girls' brown eyes looked up adoringly into the eyes of their father, the colour matching exactly. 'I know you'd rather be at home with me, and that's what I'd love as well, but it's not possible at the moment. So, we all have to be brave and soldier on until Sundays come round and I can visit and take you for outings. Can you do that for me?'

The children nodded.

'Good girls. If Mrs Marshall agrees you can come and wave me off.' Lifting his daughters from his knees he set them onto their feet.

'By all means,' Minnie said. 'Echo, will you be in charge please?'

The boy nodded eagerly and held out his hands, which the girls grasped.

Ted smiled at Minnie, shook hands with Billy and turned to leave, unable to trust himself to say anything more without breaking down again. He walked away with tears pouring from his eyes and didn't turn to wave until he was certain the girls could not see them.

Echo, Dora and Gertie stood by the front door and waved until Ted was out of sight then went back inside. The girls were shown the bedroom they would share as Dilys made up the beds, then Echo took them outside to play 'tag' for a while.

'How many rooms do we have spare now?' Minnie asked as Ruth Ashby joined them in the kitchen.

'Three now,' Polly replied.

'Ruth, you and I need a meeting, I think,' Minnie said.

'Uh-oh, why do I get the feeling spending money will come into this?' Ruth said with a chuckle.

'If our Polly rescues any more kiddies we are gonna need more bedrooms.' Minnie grinned as her daughter walked in after she and May had emptied the tin baths onto the wasteland out the back. 'Don't worry, Pol, I can see how you had to bring that family back. The girls are playing lovely outside with Echo so I think they'll settle in well.'

Adam had been sitting quietly thinking, and when Ruth and his mum went to the office to discuss finances, he asked if he could join them.

20

Whilst the Freeman family were being fed at Marshall's, Una Reed was in her office quietly fuming. Her shin bone was sore where Kit Stanton had kicked her, and the police had been of no use whatsoever.

She had seen the boy in the street and had indeed grabbed his arm in order to converse with him. That had been a mistake on her part, she should have merely called out to him. On reflection she should be more honest with herself. She had fully intended to drag the boy back to the orphanage and give him a hiding. Then when his brothers came looking for him she would paste them too. Following that, they would have a night each in the *box*. However, what's done is done, and now at least she knew where the Stanton brothers were – Marshall's Children's Home.

Rubbing her aching leg, Una winced. *Little swine*, she thought. Knowing she should look to filling her own orphanage, her mind kept returning to seeing Minnie at the police station. That woman had set up business right under Una's nose and with council funding, which she'd discovered on applying for the same herself and being refused, and it looked as if she was doing very nicely. Not only that but she had married Billy Marshall, the man Una had grown up with and who had been the love of her life.

Gazing out of the window, Una saw nothing of the sunshine lighting up the lawns or the trees which had long since woken from their winter slumber. The squirrels chased up and down the trunks to hide in the canopy of leaves, and birds chattered loudly regarding the best nesting sites. All of this slipped past Una as she stared, seeing only Minnie's face. Although she hated the woman with a vengeance, she had to concentrate on her own future, for the moment at least.

Things were not looking too rosy with only four children in the home. If no more came in, and once her current charges were gone, Una would find herself out of business. She *had* to do something, and soon.

* * *

That evening James Fitch came home with a face longer than a wet weekend. He spoke to no one and pushed his food around on the plate with a distasteful look.

'Summat on yer mind, son?' Minnie asked.

'No, I'm just tired,' James replied sullenly. 'I think I'll just head off to bed.' Leaving the table, James climbed the stairs wearily.

Adam watched him go then glanced at Minnie who nodded. Following his brother, Adam knocked on the bedroom door.

'What?' James shouted.

'It's Adam, can I come in?'

'I s'pose.'

Entering the room, Adam closed the door quietly behind him and went to sit on the chair near the bed.

'So, what's happened?' Adam asked gently.

James was sitting on the side of his bed and he dragged his hands down his face.

'Come on, brother, it can't be as bad as all that,' Adam prompted.

'It's worse Adam. If I tell you, please keep it to yourself.' James eyed the boy sitting opposite him and saw Adam nod.

'I've been walking out with this girl and – she's pregnant!' It came out in a rush before James released a heavy sigh.

Adam sucked in a surprised breath. 'You're a dark horse; no one knew you even had a sweetheart,' he said at last.

'She wanted to keep it quiet,' James said in response.

'Well, the question now is what will you do about it?'

'I want to marry her, Adam, but her parents are

well-to-do and there ain't no way they'll allow it!' James rubbed a hand across his mouth as if trying to erase the words spoken.

'Hence keeping the relationship quiet,' Adam said almost to himself. 'Do her parents know?'

James shook his head. 'Not yet. Fliss – Felicity – is going to tell them tonight and I'm worried sick. What if they throw her out? What if they make her try to get rid of it? Christ, what a mess!'

'Don't meet trouble around the corner James. It might be they'll understand that you want to wed each other.' Adam looked hard at his brother. 'You do, don't you?'

'Yes! We're in love but I'm a penny-a-day man – I work at the wharf! They will want her to marry a doctor or lawyer. Adam, I don't know what to do!' James's eyes filled with tears and Adam went to sit next to him. Wrapping his arms around his big brother, he held him whilst he wept. Adam wondered why James had not mentioned his inheritance but now was not the time to ask. He felt his brother would tell him in his own good time, for now James had more than enough to cope with.

'The first thing is to tell Mum. If anyone can sort this out it's her, and don't worry, I'm sure she'll be all right about it in the end.' Adam spoke in soothing tones and eventually he released James as the weeping ceased. 'Come on, there's no time like the present.'

The two boys trundled downstairs and into the living room where all but the youngest were gathered.

'Mum, I need to talk to you,' James said following a reassuring nod from Adam. Silence, save the odd mimic from Echo, ensued whilst James spoke. 'In private.'

Minnie glanced at Billy who nodded. 'Let's go into the office then.'

Mother and son sat in the room dedicated to paperwork and accounts and Minnie eyed her boy. Whatever he needed to tell her must be important and by the looks of the misery on his face it would be hard in the telling.

'Mum...' James began, but then words failed him. How could he explain so she would understand and not be disappointed in him?

'I can see that something is eating at you lad, but if I don't know what it is, I can't help.' Minnie said gently.

James stared at his shoes, unable to meet his mother's eye. Taking a deep breath, he plunged in. 'I have a sweetheart; her name is Felicity.' He risked a quick glance at his mum to gauge her reaction so far.

Minnie kept her counsel and waited for what she had now guessed would come.

'I love her, Mum, and I want to marry her,' James went on.

Still Minnie waited.

'The thing is...'

Here it comes! Minnie thought.

'She's pregnant.' James's head remained low and only his eyes looked up.

Minnie sighed loudly; her surmise was correct. 'Oh, lad! I thought you knew better.'

'I do and I'm sorry. I just – got carried away.' James's sorrowful eyes gazed at his mum as he waited for the outburst he felt would surely come.

Minnie's emotions flowed and ebbed as she looked at her first-born. She was angry he'd put himself in that situation but sad that he was upset. She was glad he had found the courage to talk to her about it but sorry that he was in the position he needed to. She was cross that this Felicity had allowed it to happen but disappointed that James could not control himself.

'Mum, please say something – anything!'

'I'm thinking.' Minnie muttered as her thoughts turned to Adam and Polly, the two children she'd had by another man whilst being unhappily married to James's father. Could she condemn her son for his actions whilst hers had been no better? No, she felt she couldn't.

James's face spoke volumes. Clearly he was haunted by having let his mother down, and Minnie could bear it no longer.

With a deep breath she said, 'There's to be a wedding, then, and I don't give a bugger what folks say! First thing, you fetch her here to meet us and we can thrash out a plan. Don't be fretting now, son, if you love her then so will we.'

'Thanks, Mum,' James said giving her a huge hug. Then he told her all about Felicity Hargreaves.

When they returned to the living room, James's

eyes moved to Adam's and the brotherly love they shared shone out as bright as day.

Once they had retaken their seats Minnie nodded to James and she saw him shake his head. He couldn't bear having to tell it all again to everyone so it would be up to her.

'Our James is to be married,' Minnie announced, 'to a young lady called Felicity Hargreaves – who is carrying his child.'

Gasps sounded as shocked faces looked at James then back to Minnie. James hung his head in guilty shame, and seeing the distress weigh heavy on him again she went on. 'I've told you all bluntly because let's face it, there's no other way to say it. He's not the first to have to face this and God knows he won't be the last, but he needs our support. Felicity comes from a wealthy family and her folks will be all fired up when they hear the news. It's my guess they'll come gunning for James and although it takes two, the blame will be put squarely on his shoulders. However, we'll deal with that as and when. So having said that, I suggest we look on this as a happy event – a new addition to our family. Mabel, let's crack open a bottle of something I know you keep in the pantry and toast James and Felicity.'

The grateful smile she received from James as he shared a hug with Adam melted Minnie's heart.

Congratulations were given and Mabel and Dilys ran to the kitchen to prepare drinks for everyone – alcohol for the adults and lemonade for the younger ones.

'Mum wasn't overjoyed when I told her,' James admitted.

'What did you expect? But I did say she'd be all right with it once she thought about it, didn't I?'

'Thanks, Adam. I'm proud you are my brother.'

'Half-brother,' Adam reminded him and the significance of their mother's indiscretion finally dawned on James. With a chuckle they clinked glasses.

* * *

Minnie called for attention and when silence fell she said, 'To change the subject for a minute, there's summat else needs discussing,' Minnie went on. 'I think this place needs extending to accommodate any more little waifs our Pol might pick up. Our Adam is in agreement and has offered to use some of the money left to him by Mr Jackson to see it done.'

Suddenly everyone began to speak at once and Minnie called for order. 'One at a time! You'll all get your chance to speak, so let's go round, starting with Billy.'

After a couple of hours of intense talk it was agreed to find an architect and a builder to get things underway.

Drifting away to their respective beds, there was only Adam and Polly left in the sitting room.

'I wondered why you went to the office with Mum and Ruth,' she said.

'All that will be the easy part, but this upset with James I fear will cause trouble,' Adam responded.

'I agree. We have to reassure him he has his family at his back whatever happens,' Polly concurred.

'It never rains but it pours in this house,' Adam said with a little laugh.

'Ain't that the truth!' Polly grinned as Adam got to his feet.

Kissing his sister's cheek, he bid her goodnight and left her to her thoughts.

Early the next morning, James duly arrived with his very nervous intended. A petite girl with skin like porcelain, Felicity Hargreaves had thick fair hair and eyes of sparkling blue. She gave the impression of being subservient, but this actually belied her true nature.

Minnie was in the kitchen with Mabel and Dilys when they arrived, with all the others already out at work or in the schoolroom. Adam and Polly joined them shortly afterwards and were introduced.

Sitting around the table, Fliss was given tea before the discussions began.

'Now then, Fliss, James has told us what's happened but I'd like to hear what you have to say,' Minnie said.

'James and I... we're in love and want to marry,' Fliss said, full of confidence. 'We're expecting a baby in the autumn and wish to wed as soon as possible so our child won't be born out of wedlock.' Fliss held her head high, a sign of good bearing, and had no hesitation in speaking her mind.

'Sensible, providing you both feel the same,' Minnie said with a nod.

'I'm glad you feel that way, Mrs Marshall, for my parents most certainly do not,' Fliss replied.

'You told them then?' James asked with a gulp.

One curt nod answered his question. 'They are at this precise moment discussing sending me to my aunt in Essex to have the baby. Once born they are insisting I give it up for adoption before returning home.'

Adam and Polly exchanged a glance but neither spoke.

'How do you feel about that?' asked Minnie.

'I won't go! There is no way on this earth I will give up our child!'

Our child. Minnie picked up that the girl had not said *her* child. That one word told her all she needed to know.

'So what's to be done about your folks?' Minnie pursued.

'Nothing. It is my intention to remove my belongings from their home as soon as I can find accommodation elsewhere.' Fliss looked to James for support and he provided it. Coming to stand behind her chair, he laid his hands on her shoulders.

'I'm going to see the vicar today to see when we can get married. It will have to be a quiet affair as I only have enough saved to pay what's needed.'

Fliss laid a hand on one of his and smiled up at him.

Minnie saw the love emanate from Fliss's brilliant blue eyes, which was returned by James. It was then that Minnie wondered why James had not mentioned his inheritance money. Had he not told his betrothed of it? If not, why not?

Minnie felt sure everyone was thinking the same thing, but no one spoke of it. Should she say something? No, if James wanted Fliss to know he would tell her; it was not Minnie's, or anyone else's place to do so. What she did do, however, was set herself a mental reminder to ask James about it in private when the opportunity presented itself.

'Supposing you were lucky enough to find somewhere to live, what will you live on? Our James don't make much working the wharf, which I'm sure you know,' Minnie said.

'I do indeed, and although I have no training as

such, I'm prepared to find work until my birthing time.' Fliss didn't miss a beat; clearly she and James had discussed this down to the last detail.

'She could have had Mr Jackson's house, Mum, but I've just let it,' Adam added.

'You two may be in love but you can't eat that, and you have my grandchild there to think about.' Minnie's words suddenly registered with everyone and all eyes went to her.

'So, this is what I propose.'

21

Una Reed listened intently to the gossip being re-layed by her cook, Mrs Gibbs. Where the woman got her information from was beyond Una, but nine times out of ten she was right.

'Ever'body up at Marshall's got a bit of summat, but young Adam Fitch was the best off. He got most of the money and all them houses along of Derry Street,' the cook said.

So, the old man who had complained about Dickie Stanton's behaviour had passed away and left his fortune and property to the Fitch family. How lucky could a boy get? Here was Una desperately trying to keep her orphanage open and the Fitches were handed money on a silver platter.

'They've already had the 'lectrics put in and there's talk of them having water piped in and even indoor lavvies!' Mrs Gibbs droned on and Una snapped her attention back.

'Surely there would not be enough room even in that monstrosity of a building for that,' Una said with a scowl.

'Not at the moment there ain't, but I heard tell they'm building on to it,' the cook responded.

'A new wing,' Una muttered.

'Ar, well they can afford it now, can't they?'

'How did the old man come to leave all that money to the Fitches in the first place?' Una asked.

'Mr Jackson and Adam was great friends. They worked the allotments together,' Cook answered.

Had Adam inveigled his way into the old fellow's affections in order to inherit his money? Or had Adam not known Mr Jackson was wealthy and it had come as a surprise? Either way, that family must now be amongst the richest in the town.

The thought was like a barb to Una's heart, and she stamped from the kitchen in a huff.

'Oh dear, summat else to make her ladyship even more moody,' Cook muttered as she propped her feet on a three-legged stool.

Una donned her coat, grabbed her bag and marched from Reed House. She needed some fresh air and peace and quiet to consider what she should do next.

* * *

As Una strode to East Park to take a stroll around the boating lake, back at Marshall's the discussions were becoming heated.

'I will tell you now – they won't come!' Fliss insisted.

Minnie's suggestion had been to invite Mr and Mrs Hargreaves to supper, whereupon she would endeavour to encourage them to allow their daughter to marry her son.

'We can only try,' Minnie said.

'What then, Mum – if they refuse?' James asked feeling full of woe.

'If they do, they do,' Minnie said simply.

'James, this is the first step. Let's await the outcome before deciding what to do next.' It was Adam who spoke placatingly.

'I suppose I should be getting home. Thank you all for your kindness and understanding,' Fliss said as she stood to leave.

'James, see the girl home safely then come back here,' Minnie said.

James nodded and the couple left.

'What do you make of that, Mum?' Polly asked.

'I think that wench is right, her folks won't visit us here.' After a moment's thought she added, 'Then again, they just might, if only to see what we have and how we live. If that should prove the case – won't they be in for a surprise? They could change their tune when they know about the inheritances.'

'Do you think James has told Fliss that he has fifty pounds behind him now?'

'I was wondering the same thing. It's my guess he hasn't, otherwise he would have mentioned it earlier,' Minnie answered.

'I wonder why not?' Polly asked.

'I'm guessing he wants to be certain she wants to marry him for himself and not what he's worth,' Minnie answered.

'A shrewd move,' Polly added.

'I also think those kids will wed no matter what her parents say or do.' Minnie screwed up her mouth as another thought struck – one she kept to herself. Would they be forced to run away to marry because of her family's attitude?

A short while later James returned wearing a glum expression.

'All right, bab?' Minnie asked.

James shrugged his shoulders. 'I didn't want to leave her to face the music on her own, Mum, but she insisted.'

'I know, lad, and I'm proud of you. Now don't you get worrying 'cos if her folks won't meet with us, then it may be that she'll have to come here to us.' Minnie laced an arm around her son's shoulder, acutely aware he was taller than her. How had that happened? With all that life had thrown at them she'd not noticed her children growing up into fine young men and women.

Minnie looked at James, now sitting at the table, with new eyes. Cornflower eyes beneath an unruly shock of blonde hair, broad back and bulging arm muscles; legs like tree trunks. Her first-born was a man now. Before long he would be a father himself and Minnie's eyes misted over as past memories crowded her mind.

She recalled how James had stepped in and saved her from a beating from his father. The knife Minnie had been holding for protection somehow finding its way into James's hand before ending up in his father's body. A terrible accident which she, James and Peter covered up before burying the man out on the heath.

Giving herself a mental shake Minnie said, 'Right, no kids washed, no pigeons 'ome.'

'I'll get off to the wharf and find our Peter, it will take my mind off things,' James said. Wrapping his arms around his mother he whispered, 'I love you, Mum.'

Minnie's tears formed again as she replied, 'I love you an' all, son.'

Then in a trice, James was out of the door and on his way to discover where his brother might be.

* * *

Una had walked around the boating pool twice before she began to feel decidedly unwell. Thinking the stress of filling the orphanage was getting to her, she made up her mind to return home and rest.

Una trudged through the streets feeling more and more breathless. In her mind she cursed middle age, as perspiration pricked her forehead. A slight tingling in her left arm caused her to give it a rub in the hope of dispelling it. Walking slowly down Sutherland Avenue lined both sides by trees, Una was glad of the shade. Crossing the bridge over the railway line, she paused to take a rest. Feeling slightly better, she moved on to skirt the Monmore Green schools in order to cross the tramway.

Taking the tunnel beneath the Stour Valley train line, Una felt a slight compression in her chest. She needed to get home but shortness of breath would not allow her to increase her pace.

Eventually reaching Steelhouse Lane, she was relieved to know she was almost there. Navigating a couple more streets would see her at Reed House. Without realising, Una began to drag her feet and her posture became a stoop. She felt the pain in her chest increase and a fear gripped her.

It didn't register with her that her left arm was

numb as it hung limply by her side: all she could think about was resting on her bed.

Coming to the house, she was panting hard but glad to be home. Loping up the driveway she leaned against the door. A flight of stairs was the only obstacle in her way now. Opening the door, she stepped inside, and closing it behind her she winced at the fire in her chest.

Slowly and carefully she mounted the stairs and threw open her bedroom door. Hobbling to her bed, Una lay down, grateful to be able to rest at last.

Suddenly pain exploded in her chest and her eyes rolled back. In the next moment Una Reed was unconscious.

Downstairs in the kitchen Mrs Gibbs was complaining about Una's punctuality.

'She's not normally late for a meal,' Diana Wilton said.

'Well, she is today! You'd best go and see what she's doing. I know she's here 'cos I heard her come in.'

With a sigh, Diana did as she was bid.

Mrs Gibbs almost jumped out of her skin when she heard the scream.

22

Mrs Gibbs leapt the stairs two at a time, her bulky skirts held high to prevent a trip or fall. Dashing into Una's room, she took in the situation at a glance. Diana Wilton was standing by the window sobbing and Una lay on the bed looking deathly white.

'She's dead!' Diana wailed.

Mrs Gibbs moved to the prostrate woman and leaned her head close to Una's, listening for the sound of breathing.

'She ain't dead, but she will be if we don't get the doctor straight away.'

Turning to Diana, who hadn't moved a muscle, she yelled, 'Now, Diana! Fetch the doctor!'

Diana fled the room like the devil himself was hot on her heels.

Folding the side of the eiderdown over Una, Mrs Gibbs muttered, 'I knew this would happen one day, Una Reed, and now it has. It's your own bloody fault for being such an evil bugger over the years. I'll tell you summat else an' all, you won't be running this place again that's for sure. Who's gonna take care of them kiddies now, eh? Me and Diana, that's who, as well as looking after you!'

Sitting on the chair by the bed, Mrs Gibbs shook her head and sat silently, waiting for the doctor to arrive.

Two hours later Una was taken to the hospital to recover from what the doctor was sure was a heart attack.

Diana and Mrs Gibbs sat in the kitchen that evening when their charges were safely tucked up in bed.

'You'll have to see to the money part of this,' Mrs Gibbs said, ''cos I'll be busy with seeing to feeding us all.'

Diana nodded, although the thought of sorting through Una's papers filled her with dread. Una kept her office locked and no one was allowed in there unless on her say-so. Goodness knows what Una would say when she discovered Diana had been meddling in her desk.

'I'll do it tomorrow,' the teacher replied.

'You think she'll ever come out of the 'ospital?' the cook asked.

'I don't know, Mrs Gibbs, but if she does it will be down to us to care for her as well as the children.'

The women sighed in unison then fell silent as they considered the implications of Una's convalescence. Bad-tempered at the best of times, they knew Una would be a nightmare having to leave everything to her *minions*. How would they cope if they were having to be at her beck and call? This was presupposing Una returned – but what if she didn't? Who would run the place if Una remained in hospital? What would happen if she died? Had she left a will? Diana knew she would have to find out – just in case.

Mrs Gibbs had been having much the same thoughts, and with another collective sigh they shook their heads in doubt.

* * *

Early the following morning, Minnie rushed into the hallway when she heard crying and angry voices.

Fliss had arrived with a small bag of clothes, sobbing that her parents had thrown her out after she had told them she *would* marry James, no matter what they said.

James was pacing angrily, threatening to go and sort out his future father-in-law with a punch to the nose.

'You two – kitchen, now!' Minnie yelled over the noise. Following along behind, she waited until James and Fliss were seated before asking, 'What's going on?'

James began. 'Fliss's parents have chucked her out, Mum!'

Turning her eyes to the girl Minnie asked, 'Is this the way of it?'

Fliss nodded as she mopped her tears with a lace handkerchief.

'Right, then. As I see it there's only one course of action open to us. You'll have to move in here with us.' Minnie saw the relief on the girl's face as she spoke. 'However, you'll have a room of yer own until such time as you're wed.'

'Mum, it's a bit late for that,' James said sheepishly.

'Maybe, but I'll have no hanky-panky under my roof, so the offer is there – take it or leave it.'

'Thank you, Mrs Marshall. I was so worried,' Fliss gushed.

Minnie nodded. 'I'll ask May to make a bed up for you but I warn you, you'll muck in and help where you can. Everybody does, no one gets a free ride here.'

'Of course, I'll be glad to,' Fliss answered sweetly.

'First, you write a letter telling your folks where you are. Ask them to send your things if you don't want to go back to collect them. Now, as I see it, there seems no point in waiting too long for you to be wed, so James you get off and see the vicar. The quicker you are married, the sooner you can be together.'

With a grin from ear to ear, James shot out of the back door, eager to track down the vicar and arrange his wedding.

'Pop into the schoolroom, Fliss, and get some paper and pen and ink and get that letter written,' Minnie said. She watched as Fliss rose from her seat and was certain she caught a wry grin grace the girl's lips. A strange feeling crept over her, but Minnie couldn't account for it. All she knew was that something suddenly didn't feel quite right about all this. Quickly dismissing it, she went about her work helping in the kitchen.

During the morning, Polly and May made up the bed in a spare room ready for Fliss.

'What do you make of this?' May asked.

'I don't know, May, but it's all rather sudden, don't you think?' Polly answered.

May nodded and the two girls returned to the kitchen just as James bustled in.

'The vicar says three weeks' time!' he panted. Clearly he had run all the way back with his exciting news.

Fliss rushed into his arms and kissed him.

'Do you mind – this is my kitchen!' Mabel said sternly.

'Sorry,' James said quietly.

Minnie noted Fliss did not apologise but she let it go – for now. She had every intention of keeping a close eye on this young woman, for they had only just met and now she was to live in this house.

With a beaming smile, Fliss settled herself once more on a kitchen chair, looking for all the world like a queen.

'Don't get too comfortable, miss, there's work to be done,' Minnie said.

'Mum, she's pregnant!' James cried.

'Yes she is, but that doesn't mean she can't help out. So you get off and find some work and I'll look after her.' Minnie raised her eyebrows, telling her son to do as he was bid.

'See you later, then,' James said, giving his intended a wide grin.

'Right, madam, you can help Mabel prepare tea,' Minnie said.

'Tea? Don't you mean supper?' Fliss asked.

'In this house we have breakfast, dinner, tea and if anyone wants to eat before bed – supper. So, you'd best get used to the idea.' Minnie rose from her seat and marched from the kitchen, Flash close on her heels.

'Take my advice, gel, don't cross Minnie Marshall, not if you know what's good for you,' Mabel whispered as she pushed a knife into Fliss's hand and nodded to the carrots.

23

Una Reed lay in the hospital bed feeling wretched.

'Is there anything I can get you?' a nurse asked.

'Yes, you can get me out of this place!' It was barely more than a whisper, but it left the nurse in no doubt she had been snapped at.

'Miss Reed, you have had a heart attack and it will be a while before you can go home,' the nurse said as she fiddled with the bedclothes. 'Now you must rest. I'll be back later to check on you.' With that the nurse walked away, the sound of her boots tapping on the stone floor receding with every step.

Una raised her head and glanced around. She was in a large ward, and a couple of beds down from her lay a woman on her back looking for all the world as though she was already dead. On the other side, another woman was yelling for the nurse, complaining she needed to use the privy. Next to her was yet another who was coughing her life up into a handkerchief. Laying her head back on the pillow, Una prayed for the Lord to either make her well quickly so she could go home, or take her to Him now.

She had no idea how long she would be kept in this awful place and the thought made her more miserable than she had ever been. Hearing the tapping of the nurse's boots once more, she again raised her head to see what was happening. She watched as the woman on her back was tipped over onto her side, a bolster propped behind her to prevent her rolling backwards out of bed. Then the nurse went back to her station at the other end of the ward.

Lying there, Una felt lost and alone. How had she come to this? What had caused her to have a heart attack? She'd had no trouble with her heart before as far as she was aware, and hadn't felt unwell until she had strolled around the park. Surely that would not have been enough to see her collapse and be carted off to the General Hospital – would it?

Suddenly her thoughts turned to her orphanage. Who would run it whilst she was stuck in here? Diana Wilton would probably take over that task until Una's health improved sufficiently for her to resume her duties. The cook could manage to feed the four children in care for now at least. Certainly there was nothing she could do from her hospital bed other than to accept the fact that she was very ill, and fretting about things would do no good.

Listening to the woman still calling for the nurse, Una closed her eyes tight and prayed yet again. *Please God, shut that woman up!*

The day dragged by for Una, but despite the goings on in the ward she managed to get some sleep. However, her mood blackened each time she was woken to be given some foul-tasting medicine or have her temperature taken by the nurse.

Why could they not leave her in peace? The doctor made his visit, telling her she had to take things easy if she wanted to get well. Wasn't she doing just that by being confined to this bed?

As the day moved into evening, Una felt herself

becoming more and more depressed. She wanted to cry as frustration built inside her. She couldn't remember a time when she had been ill and now she was all but incapacitated. If she felt like this on the first day, how would she be feeling after a few weeks?

She *had* to find a way out of this place – and soon.

* * *

Over at Reed House, Diana let herself into Una's office, having found the keys on the bedside cabinet. She shivered as she glanced around; it felt wrong to be in here alone. She felt guilty, although she knew she had to rummage in the desk to find papers pertaining to the business and possibly Una's will.

'God, I hate this place,' Diana muttered to herself. 'This office, the house and you too Una Reed, and I've made my mind up – when you get back, I'm leaving!'

Moving to the desk she opened a drawer and pulled out a huge ledger. Glancing through it she noted the figures in neat columns. All was as it should be with enough in the bank to pay for what was needed. But with a frown she realised she could not access these funds without Una's written permission. How would they buy food or pay bills with no money to hand? Replacing the ledger, Diana tried another drawer. Inside was a large envelope, which on opening revealed enough money to tide them over. She released a pent-up breath in relief.

Searching the office thoroughly, Diana found no evidence of a will. Taking the money envelope she returned to the kitchen to explain her findings to Mrs Gibbs.

'That's all well and good, but what about our wages?' the cook asked.

'I don't know, but we have to keep this money for food, at least then we won't starve,' Diana answered.

'This is a right bloody mess and no mistake!' Mrs Gibbs boomed.

'There was no will either that I could see,' Diana added.

'Oh, it just gets better and better don't it?' Mrs Gibbs said with a shake of her head.

'Look, all we can do is go on as we are until we know what's happening with Una.'

'And how will we know that?'

'One of us will have to visit her in the hospital,' Diana said with a grimace.

* * *

That evening, Adam was surprised to see Polly and Dickie deep in conversation and he wondered if his sister would join him later for their usual discussions. He was glad Polly and Dickie were getting on well together but he had also noticed the scowl on Echo's face as he pushed his way closer to Polly. He made a mental note to mention to Polly to be aware that Echo was becoming very jealous of her being so friendly with Dickie, and if they weren't careful there could be ructions there.

James and Fliss were ensconced on a settee in the corner of the room with their heads together and he smiled. They were probably making wedding plans. Adam was pleased his brother was so happy and inwardly he wished them well.

Sitting in an armchair Adam glanced around the room. His mum and Billy were laughing at something or other; some were playing cards or dominoes, and the little ones were playing happily on the carpet. May was trying her best to conquer the art of knitting with help from Dilys. The whole family scene brought joy to his heart and he silently thanked the Lord for His mercy in bringing them all together once more, including Digit, who had settled in remarkably well after his ordeal in gaol.

Adam was reading the newspaper when Polly came to join him.

'Anything interesting in there?' she asked as she tilted her head to the paper Adam was now folding up.

'I was reading an article about Oscar Wilde being arrested in London after losing the criminal libel case against the Marquess of Queensbury.' Seeing her disinterest, he asked, 'What's on your mind?'

'May and I agree there's something amiss with Fliss,' Polly said in a whisper.

'You're a poet – did you know it?' Adam joked.

'I'm serious, Ad. May thinks she's false and I think she's lying about being thrown out.'

'Why?'

'I don't know! I just have this feeling!' Polly said with an urgency that made Adam sit up and take notice.

'Calm down, Pol, and tell me,' Adam said.

'I have no idea why I feel this way about her Adam, it's something in her manner. She gives me the impression she thinks she's better than us,' Polly went on.

'She comes from money, Polly, and people like that always tend to look down on others.'

'I understand that. She always has to be told what to do, it's as though she can't think for herself.'

'She's quite bright, Pol, I'm sure it's because she's never had to do jobs around the house before.'

'Maybe,' Polly relented.

'Why do you think she's lying about her parents throwing her out?'

Polly shook her head and sighed. 'All that crying and wailing – they were false tears if ever I saw them!'

'That seems a bit harsh, Polly, and not like you at all,' Adam said gently so as not to enrage his sister any more than she was already.

'Why are you taking her side?' Polly asked irately.

'I'm not, I'm just playing devil's advocate. All right look at it this way – if you're right, what can we do about it?'

'Nothing as yet, but if I *am* right then it will come out sooner or later.'

'Then we just watch the situation carefully and see what happens.'

The two chatted quietly for a time before Polly went to bed. Adam lingered a while, thinking on what his sister had said. If Polly was right and Fliss was playing them false, how long would it take for her true colours to show through?

Adam didn't have long to find out, for the following morning he witnessed a scene in the kitchen between Fliss and his mother.

'I'm not doing that, it will make me sick, which will not be good for the baby!' Fliss said vehemently as she covered her stomach with her hands.

'So you're happy to piddle in the guzunders but not empty them – is that right?' Minnie asked.

'Fliss, we all have to help out at times,' James said as he laid a hand on her arm.

Shaking his hand free she snapped, 'Maybe, but that's one job I simply won't do! Besides, I have to – go – in the night now because of...'

Minnie cut her off with, 'I know, the baby.'

'Precisely!' Fliss said, her eyes imploring James to support her.

'Let me tell you, milady, I've had five kids and I had to empty the piddle-pots despite being pregnant, and it didn't hurt me or them.' She thrust out a hand towards her children.

'Five?' Fliss questioned, clearly of a mind to distract Minnie.

'Yes, our John died of fever when he was a babby, which had nothing to do with emptying chamber pots!' Minnie said sternly.

Adam hid the grin he felt forming on his lips. Fliss had challenged the wrong one and now she would see a side of his mother she probably wouldn't like.

'Well, I'm sorry but I won't do it. That's a job for a maid,' Fliss said, casting a glance at Dilys.

'Fliss, for goodness' sake!' James jumped in.

'Who do you think you are, you cheeky bugger!' Dilys was fuming and took a step forward in confrontation.

'Calm down, lass,' Mabel said as she grabbed the maid's arm and held her back.

'I won't! Lady muck over there casting aspirations...'

Fliss laughed loudly. 'The word is aspersions, Dilys.'

'I don't care what it is, you ain't no better than me!'

'My dear girl, I am infinitely better than you – for I have money!' Fliss retaliated.

'Not no more you don't! You got chucked out, remember? And if my guess is right you'll be disinherited!' Dilys silently congratulated herself for using the correct word at last.

Fliss visibly paled as the words sank in.

'Fliss, I will not have you speaking to the people of this family in that manner!' James yelled.

'Enough!' Minnie shouted. 'I told you when you came you would have to muck in and help. Now, if you're not prepared to do that – you don't eat. No work, no food, 'cos this ain't a charity!'

At that Fliss burst into tears and fled the kitchen, with an irate James right behind her.

'Mum, can I have a word in private please?' Adam asked.

Minnie nodded, trying to calm her temper.

Mother and son retired to the office, where Adam explained Polly and May's concerns regarding Fliss.

'I'm of the same opinion, lad,' Minnie said when he had finished speaking. 'I thought she was sweet at first and it seemed evident they were in love; now I'm not so sure. I tell you this, though – she'll have to change her attitude if she's going to marry into this family.'

'Let's see how things go over the next week. Maybe that little contretemps in the kitchen will have done the trick,' said Adam.

'All right but I warn you, I won't put up with her playing the Lady Bountiful,' Minnie said huffily.

As they emerged from their little meeting, Minnie was gratified to see Fliss carrying the waste bucket downstairs to be emptied into the privy. She smiled at the grimace clearly showing on the girl's face.

Obviously James had warned his betrothed not to mess with his mother.

24

The next morning Mabel was counting up her money after a visit to the market when Ruth joined her in the kitchen.

'You all right?' Mabel asked.

'I have another headache,' Ruth said rubbing her temples. 'Poring over the books makes my eyes hurt and every single time my head bangs for hours afterwards.'

'Sounds like you might need spectacles,' Dilys said.

'Probably.' Ruth sat with her elbow on the table and her forehead resting in her hand. She closed her eyes and sighed with relief as the pain began to subside just a little.

'You should talk to Polly, maybe she knows a way you can get rid of it,' Minnie said.

'I will, but first I'd like to ask you something.'

'Go on, then,' Minnie encouraged.

'Minnie,' she said at last, 'do you remember a while ago when we watched Echo doing his mathematics with Celia?'

Minnie nodded. 'I do indeed, he's a bloody marvel!'

'It is patently obvious that Echo is clever enough to take over the books, you know, at least judging by what I saw. That way I'll be able to give a hand with this place and I won't suffer with these blasted headaches!'

'Would you feel comfortable about it, Ruth?'

'Yes. In fact, I'd rather like not having to pore over the figures so much. I think he'd do a grand job if you were of a mind to let him.'

Minnie was relieved that it was Ruth who had come to the same conclusion as she had herself not long after the boy had shown his expertise.

Minnie yelled for Echo and he came rushing in straight away.

'We've just been talking about how good you are at the number game, and Ruth thinks you would do an excellent job with our accounts books. What do you think, Echo? Would you like to be my book-keeper?' Minnie asked.

'Ooh, yes please!' came the reply.

Everyone applauded and Echo beamed his pleasure.

'Who taught you to do this with numbers, Echo?' Polly asked.

'Nobody. I just can,' the boy replied simply.

'Well, come with me and I'll show you the books and then you can tell me if you want to do it,' Minnie said.

An hour later they reappeared when Echo, in his innocence, called out, 'I found mistake!'

Ruth looked up from the job of peeling potatoes she had volunteered for and the boy's face fell.

'Sorry,' he mumbled.

'No, Echo, that's good.' Ruth smiled at the lad's stricken face. 'Did you put it right?' He nodded. 'Good. See I told you, I knew you'd be better at it than me,' Ruth said. 'Was it a big mistake?'

'No, just a tanner,' Echo grinned.

'Sixpence, goodness I must have had a real bad headache that day. Thank you for sorting it out.'

'Welcome,' he mumbled before ambling away to wait for the youngsters to finish class so they could all play outside.

* * *

For once the children at Reed's Orphanage had been given a good breakfast of creamy porridge followed by toast and jam and a cup of tea before being allowed out in the gardens to play.

Mrs Gibbs pulled a penny from her apron pocket, tossed it into the air and slapped it down on the back of her other hand.

'Heads or tails?' she asked.

'What?' Diana questioned.

'Choose.'

'Why?' Diana asked.

'Just bloody choose!' the cook snapped.

'Oh all right, heads.'

Removing the hand covering the coin Mrs Gibbs showed it to the teacher. 'Tails, you lose.'

'Mrs Gibbs, what is all this about?'

'You lose, so you have to go and visit Una in hospital,' the other woman said with a grin.

'Oh, no!'

'Oh, yes!' the cook said emphatically. 'Look, we need to know if Una is going to live or turn up her toes.'

'But...' Diana began, but seeing the look on Mrs Gibbs' face she relented. 'Oh, all right then.'

Grabbing her best coat and hat, Diana left the orphanage and trudged wearily to the General Hospital. She wasn't looking forward to it; she didn't know what she'd find when she got there. Una could be dead already for all she knew.

It wasn't far and as Diana walked up Vicarage Road, she heard the birds twittering. The sun's rays were already warm and it promised to be a beautiful day.

Too nice to be visiting the sick, she thought, then berated herself for being so uncharitable. Una Reed had no family that Diana was aware of; she only had her employees.

Turning the corner into Cleveland Road, she glanced across at the tramway depot as she strolled along. Arriving at the hospital entrance, she stopped and stared up at the imposing building.

Striding through the double doors she came to a lady sitting at a desk. She requested to see Una Reed, explaining she was from the orphanage and Una was her employer and had no family of her own. She was directed to a ward via the stairs at the end of a long corridor.

Entering the ward, she spoke with the nurse who pointed her in the direction of Una's bed.

'Hello, Una,' she said quietly as she approached.

'Well! I never expected to see you,' Una returned.

'How are you feeling?' Diana asked, her own feeling being decidedly uncomfortable.

'How do you think? I had a heart attack and now I'm stuck in here with this lot!' Una cast her eyes around indicating the others in the ward.

'It must be dreadful for you. Are you recovering well enough, do the doctors know?'

'Apparently if I take it easy I will be fine soon enough. In the meantime, I have to stay here unless... Diana, you have to get me out of this place!' Una was practically begging for help.

'I don't think that is such a good idea, Una, if the doctors...' Diana began.

'The doctors don't know everything! I'm going mad in here with that one dying under my nose, and that one constantly screeching for the nurse! Please, Diana, tell them I'm well enough to go home. Tell them you will look after me... anything, just take me home!'

'I'll have a word with the nurse, then,' Diana said and turned to walk back to the nursing station.

'Thank you,' Una mumbled.

A moment later she was back. 'The nurse can't give permission for you to leave, it has to be the doctor and he's not due on his rounds for a few hours yet.'

'Oh, God, I'll be insane by that time.'

'Is it so bad here, Una? I mean to say, they're looking after you very well from what I can see. You're being fed and medicated and bed rest is surely the best thing for you now,' Diana said as she sat in the chair next to the bed.

'The food is atrocious, Diana, it's like pigswill. God only knows what the medicine is but it tastes like horse piddle! There's comings and goings at all hours which makes it impossible to sleep, and when I can manage a few hours they wake me up again. I can't rest for thinking about Reed House, so I would get well quicker if I were back there.' Una became fractious.

'I understand that, but you needn't worry, Mrs Gibbs and I have things under control until you come back.'

They both winced as the screeching patient yet again let out a wail loud enough that even the deaf could hear.

'Listen Diana, in the drawer of my desk there's an envelope with some money inside. Use it for household expenses. I'm telling you in case the doctor won't let me out.' Una said quietly.

'All right, I'll see to it.' Diana couldn't find it within herself to say she had already found the envelope. She didn't want Una to think she'd been snooping in the office. 'I have to say I'm surprised you are looking so well. I mean, we thought...'

'You thought I was dead; you can say it, Diana.'

'Well, yes, at first I did. I expected to see you unconscious still maybe. It is nice to see you – well, better.' Diana was finding it hard to say exactly what she thought, which was that Una looked like death warmed up.

'I just feel tired, not ill,' Una responded.

'The rest in here will do you good, and then when you come home you can take over Reed House again just like always.'

Una nodded.

'I can see you are weary now, so I'll go and leave you in peace.' Diana stood and smiled down at the woman she really didn't like very much.

'You don't need to leave yet, you've only just got here,' Una said with a gasp.

'I must, I'm afraid, there's the children to see to after all,' Diana replied, desperately wanting to be away.

'Mrs Gibbs can...'

'Mrs Gibbs will be at her wits' end is my guess,' Diana said, 'so I'd best get going...'

'All right, thank you for coming, it means a lot to me,' Una said.

'I'll come again if... Goodbye for now.' With that, Diana turned and walked swiftly away, breathing a sigh of relief that the visit was over. She couldn't get out of the place quick enough.

Walking briskly back to the orphanage, Diana breathed in the warm air. By the time she arrived, she was feeling calm again.

'Well, how did it go?' Mrs Gibbs asked as Diana walked into the kitchen.

'It was awful! She looks dreadful, pale and tired. She's desperate to come back here so we can take care of her. She told me about the envelope with the money in and to use it for expenses,' Diana said, taking off her hat and coat.

'Blimey! She must be poorly!' Mrs Gibbs gushed as she poured tea for her friend.

'She begged me to get her out of the hospital, Mrs Gibbs, and I asked the nurse but it's the doctor who must discharge her. I know it's a wretched thing to say, but this place is far nicer without her, it's more relaxed.' Diana hung her head in shame for saying what she'd been thinking.

'I agree. The longer she's in there the better off we'll be is my thinking.'

'You know, when she does come back I'm giving in my notice. I can't work here any more, Mrs Gibbs. That woman is cruel and spiteful and doesn't deserve to be in charge of orphans!' Diana was giving vent to her pent-up feelings which she'd harboured almost from the time of starting work at Reed's.

'What will you do?'

'I don't know, but anything is better than this.'

'I'm inclined to agree with you. In fact, I might well do the same,' Mrs Gibbs said with a shrug of her shoulders.

'I wonder how she would cope being left alone with four children,' Diana mused.

'Christ knows, but it won't be our problem will it?' Mrs Gibbs asked.

'No, but it's the children I worry for. Anyway, I'll have to go back tomorrow and see what the doctor has said about releasing her,' Diana said with a grimace.

'Good luck with that!' Mrs Gibbs replied glibly.

'Of course, you could go instead,' Diana said hopefully.

'I could but I don't intend to. Now fetch those kiddies indoors and do your job – teach them something useful.'

'What, like how to share responsibility?' Diana muttered sarcastically under her breath as she went out into the garden.

25

Throughout the day, Minnie watched Fliss closely, then in the mid-afternoon she and Echo went to the office to work on the accounts.

Mabel took this time to visit the market, and everyone else was busy with various household chores.

Dilys was washing the dishes when Fliss sidled in. 'When you've finished there you can pop upstairs and make my bed.'

Turning to face the speaker, Dilys' face held a look of incredulity. 'I don't think so, I ain't your hand-maid you know.'

'You would do well to remember your place,' Felicity said as she picked up a knife and began to turn it in her fingers.

Dilys watched the movement and her stomach clenched.

'Sharp these, aren't they?' Fliss asked as she brought the blade close to the maid's face.

Dilys recoiled from the knife and swallowed the lump in her throat. Was this a threat? Did Fliss intend to harm her if she didn't agree to pander to the girl's wishes?

Fliss gave a sickly smile, saying, 'This could cause a lot of damage if one is not careful.' Twisting the knife again it glinted in the light from the window. 'So I take it you will be kind enough to see to my bed – as a favour, of course?'

Dilys found herself nodding, quite sure now that this was a veiled threat.

'Good.' Fliss threw the knife into the soapy water in the sink and marched from the kitchen.

Flopping onto a chair, Dilys could hardly believe what had just happened. Her hand moved to her face where the knife had almost touched her skin. Her mind slowly began to formulate its thoughts; should she do as she was told to keep herself safe?

After all, if she didn't comply she would be looking over her shoulder constantly. This episode had taken her completely by surprise for she would never have thought it of the girl. They had already crossed swords – but this?

Dilys then considered the ramifications of her other option. She could tell Minnie what had occurred. Would Minnie believe her? If she wasn't believed it could be construed as spite. Would that lead on to a reprimand or even dismissal? Then again, if Minnie believed what she was told, there would be a confrontation. This in turn would cause upset between Minnie and James for he would invariably take Fliss's side. If Minnie asked Fliss to leave then almost certainly James would go too, causing a family rift.

A shiver overtook her as she sat pondering the best course of action. *Damned if you do, damned if you don't.*

Dilys felt sick to her stomach. She had no idea how long she sat there feeling wretched and afraid, but the back door slamming shut snapped her attention back.

'Having a little rest, were we?' Mabel asked sarcastically as she placed the shopping bags on the table.

'I...' Dilys muttered.

Looking at the girl, Mabel was instantly concerned. 'Are you all right, wench? You look as white as a sheet.'

Shaking her head, the maid burst into tears.

'Whatever is the matter?' Mabel asked as she laid an arm on the maid's shoulder.

Dilys shook her head, wiping her nose on her sleeve.

'You'd best get yourself back to bed. I'll bring you a cuppa then you can sleep it off,' Mabel said as she helped Dilys to stand. She watched the girl leave the kitchen, dragging her feet as she went. Setting the kettle to boil, Mabel wondered what was ailing her young friend. Whatever it was it had come on very suddenly because she had been fine earlier that morning. Making tea, she set a tray and took it upstairs to Dilys' room. Knocking gently, she entered and laid the tray on the dressing table.

'Right, get that down you then get into bed. You stay there 'til you feel better. I'll explain to Minnie you're feeling poorly.'

Leaving quietly, Mabel was puzzled by the rapid onset of the illness. She knew it wasn't pregnancy, for Dilys didn't have a beau and hardly ever went out alone. What could it be? Maybe a head cold setting in. Satisfied with that explanation, Mabel returned to the kitchen to unpack the shopping.

A little while later Minnie emerged from the office, happy that Echo was doing a grand job with the books. Going to the kitchen, she was informed that Dilys was sick.

'We'll see how she goes and if she's no better tomorrow she can move to Polly's ward, then if needs be we'll call the doctor out,' Minnie said. Then she asked, 'Have you seen Fliss?'

Mabel shook her head. 'No, not seen her at all today. Maybe she's having a lie-in.' The cook grinned as Minnie scowled.

'We'll see about that!' Turning on her heel, Minnie marched from the kitchen. Going to the room allocated to Fliss she knocked on the door before opening it.

Fliss was lying on the bed she had made herself reading the newspaper. She looked up as Minnie entered.

'Why are you lying there when there's work to be done?' Minnie snapped.

'I didn't know what needed doing and you were nowhere to be found to ask,' Fliss said, as she unconcernedly folded the paper and laid it on the bed.

'You don't need me to tell you what to do! You go round and ask if anyone needs help with their allotted task!' Minnie was furious at the girl's blatant laziness. 'Get up off your arse and come with me,' she added sternly.

Fliss sighed loudly and followed along behind Minnie.

Going outside at the back of the house, Minnie grabbed a pail and scrubbing brush and thrust them at Fliss. 'Privy needs cleaning.'

'I refuse to do it!' Fliss said with horror.

'You use it, don't you?' Minnie asked.

'Yes.'

'Then you take a turn at cleaning it, same as everybody else.' With that Minnie stomped back into the kitchen.

'Trouble?' Mabel asked.

'She was only lying down reading the bloody paper! I tell you, Mabel, there's going to be a falling out with that one if she doesn't buck her ideas up!'

Mabel blew out her cheeks and continued to peel the mountain of potatoes sat in front of her.

That evening, Minnie peeped in on Dilys. Seeing that she was sleeping peacefully she retreated quietly. Finding Polly, she explained that her nursing skills might be needed if the maid was no better by morning.

Sitting with her knitting in the living room, Minnie kept a surreptitious eye on Fliss, who was smiling sweetly at James.

May's right, you are a false bugger, she thought. The sweethearts said they were going for a stroll before darkness set in, and James laughed as catcalls and whistles sounded.

'You're quiet tonight, my love, is everything all right?' Billy asked.

'I'll tell you later – when we go to bed,' Minnie whispered.

Billy frowned with curiosity but nodded his acceptance that whatever it was it could wait a while.

Before they retired for the night Minnie assured

herself Dilys was no worse. Then once in bed she related the tale of Fliss's laziness to her husband.

* * *

Early the next morning Diana Wilton set out once more to visit Una. Again, it was a lovely warm day and she would rather have been having a stroll around East Park.

She was surprised to see Una sitting in a chair when she arrived.

'Hello. My goodness, you're looking a lot better,' she said airily.

'I'm feeling better,' Una responded. She watched Diana drag another chair close and sit down.

'What happened to the lady from that bed?' she asked.

'No idea, she was gone when I woke up.'

'Oh dear, I hope she didn't...' Changing tack she went on, 'At least the noisy one is quiet today.'

Una nodded. 'They insisted I have a walk about, so I went over there and told her if she didn't shut up I would drown her in her own chamber pot!'

Diana giggled but with a glance at the woman in

question and registering the scowl, she turned away quickly. 'What did the doctors tell you?'

'Provided I have someone to take care of me and if I promise to do only gentle exercise I can go home tomorrow. Apparently they need the beds.' Una was clearly relieved, for a tiny smile played at the corners of her mouth.

'So, you will need me to collect you?' Diana asked.

Una gave a curt nod.

'Very well. I'll get back now and help Mrs Gibbs. I'll see you in the morning.' Diana put the chair back in its rightful place and gave Una a smile.

'Thank you, Diana,' Una said, but Diana knew it was said grudgingly.

Returning to Reed House, she knew she and Mrs Gibbs would have their work cut out for them. No matter what they did, Una would find fault with it. Whatever she thought of Una, Diana could not abandon the children. She had been adamant about leaving when discussing the matter with Mrs Gibbs previously, and she hadn't changed her mind since, but the thought of those kiddies remaining in Una's sole care with her being so poorly sent a shiver down her spine. There was no telling what might happen, and if any harm befell those children Diana would forever hold herself responsible.

In retrospect she also knew it would be quite a while before either of them could put in their notice, certainly until something could be sorted out regarding their charges. Una would be convalescing for God knew how long so she would need the help of both.

Diana heaved a heavy sigh as she entered the orphanage. She was trapped and would be for the conceivable future.

Now she had to inform Mrs Gibbs that Lady Muck would be home the following day.

26

Meanwhile at the children's home Dilys had risen, dressed and gone to the kitchen to begin work.

'You feeling better today?' Mabel asked.

Dilys merely nodded. She couldn't trust herself to speak lest yesterday's encounter with Fliss should slip out or she would burst into tears again. Going about her business, Dilys dreaded seeing Fliss, for part of her was afraid, and part of her was angry and wanted to challenge the girl. The love for the Marshall family and what it could do to them was what kept her quiet.

With breakfast over and everyone at their tasks, Dilys wondered how she could slip away in order to

make Fliss's bed and tidy her room. Normally assigned to kitchen duties, it would be difficult to find
an excuse to leave for any length of time. As the
morning wore on, she became more and more agitated. Unable to concentrate she began to make silly
mistakes until at last Mabel yelled at her.

'I don't know what's going on in that head of
yours, gel, but you need to sort yourself out.'

Dilys nodded, her eyes brimming with tears.

'Take yourself out in the garden for a little while;
let the fresh air blow the cobwebs away,' Mabel said.

Dilys almost ran from the kitchen. This was the
chance she'd been waiting for. Rushing up the stairs,
she shot into Fliss's room and closed the door behind
her. Looking around, she gasped. Where had all
these clothes come from? Strewn on the bed and
floor were dresses and skirts, underwear and boots.

In a mad flurry of activity, she began to shove
things in drawers and the wardrobe. Pulling the bedclothes straight, she nodded and ran back to the
kitchen. That would have to do. At least she'd made
the effort, but it still worried her as to where all that
stuff had come from.

Settling into her familiar routine now, Dilys

chatted quietly with Mabel as the chores were completed.

It was around mid-morning when Fliss strolled into the kitchen. 'I'm ready for a cup of tea,' she announced.

'Kettle is over there, you can make one for us whilst you're at it,' Mabel retorted.

Dilys glanced at the girl, who set the kettle to boil and received a nod in return. The maid let out a breath, and Fliss appeared satisfied with her efforts. Then Dilys began to fret about how she could manage to complete the extra task given her every day without being discovered.

'If you're making tea, I'll have one an' all,' Minnie said as she bustled in and sat at the table.

Fliss nodded and turned away with a scowl.

'Oh there you are, Mum, have you seen my red cardigan? Is it in for wash can you remember?' Polly asked as she joined them.

'No, love, it's just bedding to be washed today as far as I know,' Minnie answered.

Dilys shot a look at Fliss who gave her a warning glance. That red cardigan was one of the items the maid had shoved in a drawer in Fliss's room. *So that's her game!* Now Dilys had two secrets to keep – how many more would come to light?

The more she thought on it, the more puzzled she became. Surely Fliss wouldn't be able to wear the clothes she had taken from Polly and probably May too, so what would she do with them? Was it her plan to sell them and keep the money? Second-hand clothes would not fetch more than a few pennies so Fliss wouldn't amass a fortune. Why then was she stealing from the family who had so kindly taken her in? How could Dilys find out?

After tea and cake provided by Mabel, Minnie asked Fliss to help Polly strip the beds, saying there was clean linen in the ottoman on the landing. A sulky look and an audible sigh was the reply. However, Fliss followed Polly to get started.

Minnie chatted with Dilys and asked after her health and the maid kept her answers short – almost clipped.

Flash and Echo went to collect and bring down the sheets ready for washing, and Minnie asked, 'What's on your mind, Dilys?'

The maid was taken aback at the direct question and mumbled, 'Nothing.'

Minnie gave a curt nod and let the matter rest – for now. Whatever was ailing the girl, there was only one person who could find out. Minnie determined she would approach her son when he returned home later. Adam, she felt, was the one who could sort this out, for Minnie was sure that there was something terribly wrong.

Flash and Echo dragged the mangle outside from the scullery, and Minnie and Dilys began to fill the tub with hot water from pans bubbling on the range. With soap added, Polly pushed in a couple of sheets and began pounding them with the dolly, which looked like an upturned three-legged stool attached to a sturdy broom stale. After a good wash she drew out each with large strong wooden tongs. Allowing the sheet to drip a little, she then passed it to the boys who threaded it through the mangle then dropped it into another tub filled with clean cold water. Swishing it around to remove the soap, they then 'mangled' it again before pegging it on the clothesline to dry. With so much bed linen, washday occurred twice a week with a prayer the weather would stay fine and bright.

Adam arrived home just before lunch and imme-diately Minnie ushered him into the office.

'I don't want any business discussed in front of Fliss, lad, we don't know her well enough as yet to trust her,' Minnie explained.

Adam nodded his agreement. 'Mr Germaine was very helpful, Mum, he gave me the name and ad-dress of a reliable builders, so I went round to see them. They live at the bottom of Pond Lane,' Adam volunteered.

'Oh, just across the way, that's handy,' Minnie said.

'Yes, and they deal with the local brickworks so building materials will only have to be brought over that patch of scrubland at the back of us.'

'Who are these builders, are we sure they're trustworthy?'

'Rewcastles, they're from the north – Geordies. They moved down here looking for work. There's the father, Ray, and five big strap-ping sons. They were eager for the work of ex-tending this place and Ray said he knew an architect who he would ask to come and see us as soon as he can. Then we can draw up some plans and hopefully get going,' Adam said with a smile.

'Good. Now – I have a favour to ask.'

* * *

Diana arrived at the General Hospital at the duly appointed time and entered the ward to collect her employer. Una was dressed and sat in the chair eagerly awaiting the doctor who would give her leave to go home. It was an hour later when Una finally walked from the building and breathed a sigh of relief. 'If and when I die, it will not be in a place such as that!'

'Una, they most likely saved your life,' Diana said as they walked slowly home.

'Yes, and I'm grateful, but there are people more in need of that bed than I,' Una responded.

'Well when we get back to Reed House you are under strict orders to rest, otherwise you might well find yourself back in that bed.' Diana had determined that she would take no nonsense from Una regarding the instructions given by the doctor. Plenty of rest with a little gentle exercise every day, good nourishing food, and masses of fresh air.

Hearing Una harrumph she went on, 'Una, you had a heart attack – you could have died!'

'Well, I didn't!'

'No, but you still could if you don't abide by the rules,' Diana pushed.

Una relented with a nod. Already she was feeling short of breath and they were only halfway home.

'How are things?' she asked between pants.

'Fine. You've only been gone a couple of days, what could change in that time?'

'It only takes a minute for your whole world to turn upside down – look at me for instance,' Una managed. 'I need to stop for a moment.'

Diana saw Una's complexion had turned grey and she worried the woman might collapse right here in the street. She chided herself for not hailing a cab, but then Una would have baulked at the cost. Had she thought more she would have realised Una would struggle even with this short distance. 'Lean on me. Take your time, we have all day and it's not too far now.'

Una's look spoke volumes as she took Diana's arm. She knew precisely how far they had left to go for she'd lived in the area all her life. Catching her breath, she nodded and they moved on arm in arm.

Approaching the gate Una actually smiled. She was home and all would be well now. Slowly walking up the drive they reached the steps, and Una leaned against the wall whilst Diana threw open the door.

Hearing children laughing and playing Una scowled.

'What did you expect? I couldn't bring them with me, and Mrs Gibbs is busy in the kitchen,' Diana said.

'I know,' was all Una managed as she allowed herself to be led inside and taken to the kitchen.

'Well now, here you are. Cup of tea?' Mrs Gibbs asked.

With a nod, Una noted the cook had not said *welcome home*.

Sitting at the table, her breath still coming in gasps, Una realised just how weak she was. Would she ever be well enough to run the orphanage again? Or would she have to take a step back and leave it to the cook and teacher? Nodding her thanks for the tea passed to her, Una knew she had a lot of thinking to do.

27

'Why me?' Adam asked.

"Cos you have a way with people,' Minnie answered. 'There's summat not right with Dilys and I want to know what it is.'

Sighing heavily, Adam thought about the favour his mother had asked – find out what was ailing their maid.

'If she needed help, surely she would ask for it,' Adam said at last.

'Would she, though?'

Seeing his mum's worried look he relented. 'All right, I'll have a word.'

'Good lad. Do it quietly out of the way of that Fliss,' Minnie said.

'You don't like her much, do you?'

'No, son, I don't. I think she's idle and has a bob on herself.'

Adam smiled at the term but had to agree – Fliss did consider herself above everyone else. 'Our James thinks the world of her.'

'Does he? Or does he feel responsible for her predicament? It takes two to tango, Adam, and she's as much to blame,' Minnie countered.

'You think he's just *doing the right thing* by her in getting married?'

Minnie nodded.

Adam considered this as he blew out his cheeks.

'Will you have a word with Dilys now, then?' Minnie asked.

'It's as good a time as any.'

'I'll go and send her through to you in here.' With that Minnie left the office quickly in case her son changed his mind.

A few moments later Dilys knocked the door and walked in. Taking the seat Adam indicated she waited.

She was shaking, Adam noted, and her face was still pale. 'Dilys, we're all worried about you. Clearly something has upset you and if you don't share it, we can't help to put it right.'

Tears formed in her eyes as she shook her head.

'Oh, Dilys! Whatever it is, it has you in a mess. Look at the state of you,' Adam said as he leaned forward and took her hand.

'I can't...' she murmured.

'Why not?' Adam probed gently. Seeing her head shake again he went on in barely more than a whisper. 'Are you in trouble of some sort?'

'No.'

'Have you done something wrong?'

'No.'

'Dilys, I want to help, but if you won't talk to me – how can I?'

A sob escaped the girl's throat, then the flood gates opened and she cried her heart out.

Adam waited patiently, after passing her his clean handkerchief, until her tears began to subside.

'Has someone threatened you, Dilys?'

Terrified eyes flicked up, and in that moment he knew he'd hit the nail squarely on the head.

'I see. I think you had better tell me everything and then we can see where we go from there.' Seeing her nod, he added, 'Let's start at the beginning.'

Listening intently, Adam was shocked at what he was hearing. Dilys related being threatened with a knife by Fliss and revealed the girl was stealing clothes from Polly certainly and possibly May too. When she had finished speaking, she looked up at Adam.

'Can I ask, why didn't you tell anyone?'

"Cos it would cause ructions! Fliss would say I was lying and James would take her side. If Minnie threw her out James would go too and there would be a rift between mother and son. I couldn't risk that happening!' Dily was becoming agitated and Adam realised he needed to calm the situation.

'I can understand your thinking and it was very brave of you to take that stance. However, Fliss cannot be allowed to get away with this. We can't have you in fear for your life every minute of every day. Therefore, this is what I propose.'

Speaking in whispers again, Adam laid out his plan and by the end Dilys was looking much happier.

'Right, you go back to the kitchen and don't say a word to anyone – and no more worrying.'

'Thanks, Adam, I'm sorry if I caused you grief.'

'You haven't, I'm just glad we've got to the bottom of all this. Now off you go and I'll be along in a minute.' Adam watched the maid leave the office, closing the door with a quiet click behind her, before he released a huge sigh.

'Where have you been?' Mabel asked sharply as Dilys walked into the kitchen.

'It ain't none of your business!' the maid snapped, feeling quite like her old self again.

Minnie shot Mabel a warning glance, shifting her eyes to Fliss who was sitting at the table taking an interest in the conversation.

Mabel's eyebrows flicked up in acknowledgement. 'Well, now you're back, there's spuds to be peeled.'

'Fliss can do them for you, Mabel,' Minnie said.

The girl made to object, but seeing the look on Minnie's face thought better of it.

'Any chance of a cuppa?' Adam's jovial voice came as he walked in.

'In the pot,' Minnie said as she looked into his

eyes. Seeing his eyebrows dancing she knew he had got to the bottom of the problem and she smiled.

'Mum, when you have a minute, I'd like to go over the figures for the extension again, just to be sure we've allowed enough money to see it completed,' Adam said.

'Get your tea first then,' Minnie replied.

Fliss had not moved but was clearly listening intently.

'You, madam, get off your backside and get those potatoes peeled,' Minnie said as she got to her feet. 'I'll see you in the office when you're ready, Adam.'

A little while later Adam joined his mother in the office and began to explain.

'You what!' Minnie exclaimed as Adam explained what he'd learned from Dilys. 'Bloody hell! I knew there was something wrong – but this?'

'I know. Dilys was afraid for her life, Mum, and didn't want to cause trouble between you and James,' Adam added.

'The question is: what are we going to do about all this?' Minnie asked.

'I've told Dilys she's not to clean Fliss's room or make her bed. I said someone will be with her every minute, and when she retires for the night she must lock the door and not open it for anyone. I'll have a quiet word with the others although those at work can only help safeguard her when they have time off. Polly and May will stay close, I'm sure.'

'Why don't we call in the police?'

'It's one word against another, Mum. Besides, Dilys wasn't hurt, and it's up to us to ensure that doesn't happen.'

'I think we should confront that little madam!' Minnie said exasperatedly.

'Let's go with this plan for now and see how it pans out. My worry is that in a couple of weeks James will be marrying her.'

'Christ, I almost forgot about that!' Minnie's face drained of colour.

'Don't worry, we'll sort something out before then. In the meantime, I'll call a clandestine meeting and see what we can come up with.'

Minnie nodded as Adam added, 'For now, let's make sure everything stays as normal as possible.'

Throughout the day and on into the early evening Adam gathered his forces around him, surreptitiously informing them a meeting was needed.

'What about Echo?' Polly asked as she was approached in the hall.

'Yes, Echo too, he's part of the family and I'm certain he can be relied upon,' Adam assured her.

That night, Minnie and Billy retired once Mabel and Dilys had gone up. Fliss was not far behind and James went to say goodnight to his sweetheart, adding that he was also ready for his bed.

Everyone else listened in shocked silence at what Adam had to say.

Polly broke the spell when she said, 'At least I know where my red cardigan went.'

'We have to watch Fliss carefully but not let her know we're aware of all this. Echo, this is a secret so – not a word.'

'Secret, Adam,' the boy answered, clearly happy to be part of the gathering.

'We have to catch Fliss out before the wedding takes place otherwise our brother will...' Adam began.

'Be in shit up to his eyeballs!' Rodney finished.

Despite the gravity of the situation, a few titters sounded.

'So how do we get Fliss to drop herself in that sh...?' Matt asked.

'Shit,' Echo supplied.

Ideas went back and forth and the hour grew late. In the end, they decided with luck an opportunity would present itself.

Going to their beds quietly, each was lost in thought about what they'd learned about Felicity Hargreaves.

28

Dilys slept fitfully, despite having locked her door, and by the morning she was tired and tense. Up and dressed, she ran down the back stairs and stepped out onto the landing to see Polly waiting for her.

'We had a meeting,' Polly whispered.

A tiny smile appeared on Dilys' lips. 'Thank you,' she mouthed before they walked to the kitchen together.

Mabel nodded and tipped them a wink, letting them know she was in on the secret too.

Dilys visibly relaxed and set to helping to prepare breakfast.

Minnie kept a close eye on Fliss as everyone sat

down to eat. She was shocked when she saw the girl catch Dilys' eye and raise her knife. *So Dilys was telling the truth!* Her eyes went to the maid and saw her shake her head. Shooting her look back to Fliss, she saw anger crossing her face.

Minnie smiled inwardly. Dilys was goading the high and mighty Fliss. Would this make her drop her guard and do something silly? Time would tell.

'I had a word with Mabel,' Minnie whispered to Adam and he nodded. 'Did you see that a moment ago?'

'I did, Mum. We need to watch her very carefully, I'm thinking.'

'Me an' all, lad.'

* * *

Across at Reed House, Una had woken in her own bed and was thankful. Rising, it took her a long time to dress, having to rest frequently to catch her breath. Slowly and carefully she made her way to the kitchen and by the time she got there she felt exhausted.

'You should have stayed in bed,' Mrs Gibbs announced.

'Good morning to you, too. I'm all right,' Una replied but in her mind she agreed with the cook's statement. Accepting the hot tea offered, she wondered how quickly she could regain good health. The thought of being an invalid for the rest of her days gave her great cause for concern.

Mrs Gibbs shrugged and continued with making breakfast.

A moment later Diana joined them and was surprised to see Una sitting at the table. 'How are you today?'

'Better – thank you,' Una said quietly, the lie having slipped easily from her lips.

Cook and teacher exchanged a brief glance in amazement. Perhaps the stay in hospital had helped improve Una's manners. Both wondered how long this change for the better would last before their employer reverted to her old and spiteful ways.

'After breakfast, I'll get the children back into the classroom,' Diana said.

'I will have lunches to prepare,' Mrs Gibbs put in,

unwilling to put herself in the position of babysitting Una.

'I may take the day to rest in my room, I have a lot to think about.'

Once they had eaten, Una dragged herself to her feet and slowly padded from the kitchen.

'Phew! I thought for a minute there I'd be stuck with her all day!' Mrs Gibbs confided. 'I wonder what she will be pondering.'

'Probably how she will run this place in her weakened state,' Diana replied.

'Do you think she'll close up?'

'It's a possibility. Let's face it, she's in no fit condition to take any more children, so what options are left open to her?'

'So, it's possible we'll be sacked, then.' It was a statement rather than a question. 'I don't know about you but I've nowhere to go and no money to go with,' Mrs Gibbs said, a worried look crossing her face.

Her mind took her back to the conversation they'd had when they had agreed to up and leave. The bravado she'd felt then began to crumble a little at thought of living on the streets, especially during the wintertime. On the other hand she had said she would join Diana and they would go together, but was giving her word enough to see herself homeless? She didn't want to stay, in truth, but she was afraid of the consequences if she went.

'I'm in the same boat as yourself, Mrs Gibbs. There are four youngsters here to consider also.'

'What would happen to them? Surely even Una wouldn't throw them out onto the streets?'

'She may do, but it's my contention she would send them to Marshall's, telling them to beg to be taken in.'

'Do you think they'd have room for you and me as well?' Mrs Gibbs asked hopefully.

'It's unlikely, it is a children's home after all, and I suspect they already have a cook and teacher in their employ.'

'Oh bugger!'

'Precisely.'

Standing silently in the hall, Una had heard every word. With quiet steps she climbed the stairs one at a time, stopping frequently to catch her breath. She ambled to her bedroom, panting heavily, before collapsing on her bed, now feeling terribly ill again. Her staff had discussed exactly what she had

been thinking over the previous days. Now it was up
to her to decide not only their futures but also
her own.

Lying on her bed, Una stared at the ceiling. What
to do? The council had refused her funding when
she had applied previously and there was precious
little coming in from the wealthy. So how could she
afford to continue to pay the staff? True, she could
pack the children off to Marshall's but that would be
admitting defeat. The thought stuck in her craw as
she imagined Minnie gloating over the closure of
Reed House. No matter how she looked at this
predicament, she could see no other way out.
Closing her eyes, Una decided that for the moment
she would rest and recuperate.

* * *

With breakfast finished, the morning routine at Marshall's began. The ones with work to go to grabbed
their snap tins for lunchtime and set off. Dilys
washed the dishes, Polly dried and May put them
away. Mabel began to prepare the ingredients for
bread making and Adam said he would use the day

to call in on his tenants. Minnie asked for any clothes to be washed to be put in the large basket on the landing.

It was later, when sorting this washing, that Minnie pulled out Polly's red cardigan. Had Fliss put it in there in fear of being caught? In a way it was a shame, for if she had been accused of stealing, there was now no evidence to prove it.

Minnie had two weeks left before the wedding to catch the girl out, but how she would do this she had no idea.

Over afternoon tea, Minnie told Polly she'd found the elusive cardigan. She noted Fliss's eyes flick up at hearing this.

'Where was it?' Polly asked.

'In the washing basket. I swear our Pol, you're as blind as a bat at times.' Minnie and Polly shared a knowing look, and Polly addressed Fliss.

'Speaking of clothes, have your parents sent yours on yet, Fliss?'

'No. I only have what I brought with me.'

'That's strange. I would have thought they would have realised you would need them and so forwarded them straight away,' Polly pursued.

Fliss shrugged.

Minnie watched the exchange with interest. Polly was trying her best to stimulate the girl into action but Fliss was not biting.

'You did write to them, didn't you?' Polly went on.

'Yes!'

'No need to snap, I only asked.' Polly feigned hurt as she spoke.

'I don't see what business it is of yours,' Fliss countered.

'It will be if you start to smell!' Polly snapped.

'I do not smell! I may not have much in the way of attire, but what I do have is clean!'

'Not yet you don't, but give it a few more days...' Polly left her words hanging.

Dilys sniggered and the look Fliss shot in her direction was hot enough to burn her to a crisp.

'Polly's right, Fliss, maybe we could find you something to tide you over,' Minnie added.

'No, I'll manage, and I'll thank you all to keep your noses out of my affairs!' With that she jumped to her feet and ran from the kitchen.

'Stuck up little madam,' Mabel said, and everyone grinned.

It was an hour or so later when Fliss returned to help prepare the evening meal.

'I've just got to pop to the lav,' Dilys said, wiping her hands on her apron before walking through the open back door.

Minnie was chopping cabbage at the table and from the corner of her eye saw Fliss slip outside too.

Mabel turned to Minnie with a look of concern.

Minnie nodded and held up a finger for them to wait and listen. Sure enough they heard a croak, and Minnie was on her feet in an instant. Rushing through the door she stepped smartly to the privy and pushed her way inside.

'You all right, Dilys?' she asked and was relieved to see the maid nod. 'What are you doing in here? There's another lav next door you can use,' Minnie's words directed at Fliss were sharp.

'I thought it was engaged,' Fliss answered feebly.

'Well, it ain't!' Minnie grabbed the girl by the shoulders, twisted her around and pushed her out through the door.

Dilys was rubbing her forearm and when Minnie examined it she could see red finger-marks on the pale skin.

'You're all right. Do what you have to, and I'll stand guard,' Minnie said.

'Thanks,' Dilys whispered.

When they returned to the kitchen, Fliss was already there sitting with a bad-tempered expression on her face.

A moment later they heard laughter coming from the hallway. Minnie trundled through to see Polly and Dickie chatting animatedly.

'Hello, lad, tea's mashing if you fancy a cup,' Minnie said.

'Thanks, I'm parched,' Dickie replied.

Minnie caught the look the youngsters shared, thinking they were being discreet. *Even a blind man could have seen that!* It looked like young Stanton and her daughter could be walking out together before too long. Quite what Adam would have to say about that was anyone's guess, but the person Minnie was most worried about was Echo.

Right from the start the boy had considered Polly and May to be *his* ladies and he treated them like queens. Minnie knew how close to Polly he stayed when Dickie was around. *God only knows how he will react when he knows they are sweethearts*, Minnie thought.

Plodding along behind them, Minnie had more pressing matters on her mind right now, namely keeping Dilys safe from Fliss's spite – and stopping the upcoming marriage.

29

'I'm sorry, ladies, but I simply have no other choice,'
Una said. She had just finished telling her cook and
teacher that she was considering closing the orphanage.

'And what about us? Where will we go? How will
we live?' Mrs Gibbs asked, full of woe.

'What else can I do?' Una placed a hand on her
chest when her heart felt like it was missing a beat.

'How are you going to look after yourself?'

Questions came one after another, but no answers were forthcoming.

'Look, before you decide anything for definite,
why don't we discuss this calmly over a cup of tea

and a slice of Mrs Gibbs' excellent cake.' Diana tried her best to subdue the argument she could see brewing.

Una nodded and the cook brought out a sponge cake. Diana poured tea and each ate and drank in silence.

Then Diana spoke again. 'Una, you will need Mrs Gibbs to cook for you. You will need me to take care of you. You will need us both to do the washing and cleaning. As I see it, the only ones you can do without are – and it pains me to say it – the children.'

'True, but if there is no money coming in then how do I pay you?'

'Bed and board. I'd be happy with that for now, how about you, Mrs Gibbs?' Diana asked.

The cook nodded eagerly. At least they would have somewhere to sleep and a full belly until they were in a better position to leave.

'Then what happens when the money and food run out?' Una asked scathingly.

'We cross that bridge when we come to it. For now, we have to decide what is to be done with the children,' Diana answered.

'We can't turn them out onto the street!' Mrs Gibbs blustered.

'Agreed,' Diana replied, 'so – Una?'

'They'll have to go to Marshall's if that woman will have them.'

'The next question is – who will take them there?' Diana asked feeling dread crawl up her spine.

'Well, I certainly can't! I can barely walk two steps before I have to rest.' Again, her hand went to her chest and Una felt the discomfort there.

'Then you must write to Mrs Marshall and explain,' Diana said sternly.

'Why can't you do it? You're the teacher!' Una boomed.

'Because it is *your* orphanage and the children are *your* wards!' Diana blasted back.

Una harrumphed then nodded. She was beginning to feel completely exhausted and just wanted to get back to bed.

'All you have to do is say due to extreme ill health you find you can no longer take care of those four children. Explain you will not be admitting any more and *request* that she takes them under her wing,' Diana said more quietly.

'All right!' Una barked. Knowing Diana was right, it still riled her to have to go cap in hand to Minnie Marshall.

'Might I suggest that now would be a good time? The sooner the children are settled in their new home the better,' Diana pushed.

With a curt nod, Una got to her feet unsteadily before slowly shuffling away to the office.

Cook and teacher exchanged a glance and Diana went to the door to check Una had gone. Satisfied they were alone, she returned to the table.

'I am determined to leave this place but in my heart I cannot justify doing so until these children are in safe hands,' Diana whispered.

'I wondered why you suddenly suggested to stay on with bed and board and I was going to ask but thought better of it,' Mrs Gibbs answered.

'We will have shelter in the interim,' Diana said her eyes constantly darting to the door in case Una should return.

'When the kiddies have gone, what then?'

'We do the same,' Diana said simply.

As she sat at her desk Una realised that she suddenly felt superfluous. Mrs Gibbs and Diana Wilton appeared to have thought all this through very carefully and had reached a conclusion that suited them both. Una's destiny had been taken out of her own hands. She was being treated as a means to an end in that whilst she was ill, the others had food and housing. There was no other recourse open to her; Una had to accept it. That didn't mean she had to like it though.

Flipping open the lid of the inkwell, she took up her pen. Diana was right – the sooner this was done, the better it would be for all.

* * *

Polly had requested a meeting with Adam and now they sat in the office.

'Ad, we have to do something – we can't let James marry Fliss!'

'I'm not sure there's anything we *can* do,' came his reply. He had returned from visiting his tenants and was happy all was well with them.

'If our James marries that harridan he will regret it for the rest of his life!' Polly said disconsolately.

'Pol, I'm in agreement with you on this but – he loves her.'

Polly's hand moved to her brow and she sighed loudly. 'We all know she's not right for him. She's a thief and a liar. I'm of the opinion she never wrote to her parents at all. In fact, I'll bet they didn't throw her out and could be worried stiff not knowing where she is.'

'What do you want me to do, Polly?' Adam asked sharply.

'I don't know! Can't you talk to James?'

'And say what? *You're making a mistake because Fliss has threatened Dilys with a knife? Because she stole Polly's cardigan?*'

'Well, she did! It sounds ridiculous when said out loud but it's true. We cannot ignore the fact that Dilys has to be chaperoned every minute of the day. That won't stop when they do get wed because they will still be living here until they find a place of their own.' Polly was becoming exasperated as she tried her best to make Adam understand her fears.

'She's taken up a room which should rightfully be for children in need,' Polly went on.

'I can't argue with that, although we do have two

empty rooms which are full of spare furniture at the moment,' Adam concurred.

'Exactly! What happens if more kiddies turn up here? How can we take them in?'

'There are another two spare rooms in the servants' quarters...' Adam began.

'What – so we put Fliss up there where she can readily get to Dilys? I don't think so!'

'Look, Polly, I'll have a word with Mum and see what she says.' It was the best he could come up with at that moment and it seemed to mollify Polly.

Late that afternoon a knock came to the front door and as Minnie was passing through the hall, she answered it.

'Mrs Marshall?' the well-dressed man asked.

'Yes.'

'I am Josiah Holbrook. Ray Rewcastle asked that I call on you regarding drawing up plans for an extension to your building.'

'Oh yes, please come in, Mr Holbrook.'

'Josiah,' the man beamed.

'Fancy a cuppa, Josiah?'

'I do indeed, Mrs Marshall.'

'Minnie.'

'Then lead the way, Minnie,' he said, his grin lighting up his whole face.

Introduced to those in the kitchen at that time and given hot tea and a wedge of cake large enough to feed the five thousand, Josiah joined in the chit-chat around the table.

'I'd like Adam to join us in the office if that's all right with you, Josiah,' Minnie said.

'Most certainly.'

The three left the kitchen and Minnie noted the sullen face of Fliss. Clearly the girl was disgruntled at not being privy to the discussions about to take place.

After two hours, they emerged from the office and took a stroll around outside. Josiah made more jottings in the small notebook he had brought with him.

Coming to the back of the building Josiah said, 'I see you have a standpipe for water.' Seeing Minnie's curious look he went on, 'It would be an easy thing to pipe water to the house and then – money permitting of course – you could do away with that privy block and have an indoor bathroom or even two given the number of residents.'

'Oh, now that *would* be nice, don't you think, Adam?' Minnie cooed.

'It sounds like an excellent idea to me, Mum. More hygienic too.'

'Would it be an imposition to take a peek into the bedrooms so we can decide the best location for said bathrooms?' Josiah asked.

'Follow me!' Minnie said, like a general leading troops into battle.

It was gone eight o'clock when Josiah left Marshall's, saying he would draw up the plans as soon as possible for them to consider.

Minnie and Adam ate their meal, which had been saved by Mabel, in the kitchen and despite the questions thrown at them, they remained tight-lipped. They were not about to discuss any details of their meeting whilst Fliss was around to overhear, although they had agreed Minnie would explain it all to Billy in the quiet of their bedroom later that night.

30

Time was marching on and the weather improved immensely. The sun's rays beamed down and insects buzzed lazily around the wild flowers growing on the scrubland at the back of the house. It promised to be a hot day with only a whisper of a breeze to cool everyone as they went about their daily chores. Mabel was delighted with the fresh vegetables Dickie brought home from the allotments every day. Celia, May, Echo and amazingly Flash, took the children out on the heath for nature rambles in the sunshine, and Minnie threw open all the doors and windows for a breath of clean air. Washing fluttered gently on the lines and Polly boiled eggs to go with the salad for lunch. The postman arrived and with him came a letter addressed to Minnie.

'Well, I never!' she said as she finished reading.

'What?' Mabel asked.

Minnie passed the letter over for Mabel to read, her eyes sliding to Fliss who was watching them avidly. The girl had relented finally and accepted some clothes given to her by Polly and May so her own could be washed.

'What do you make of that?' Mabel asked as she passed the paper back to Minnie.

'Anything I can help with?' Fliss asked.

'No, it's private business,' Minnie replied pointedly.

'Suit yourself. I was thinking I'd take a walk as it's such a lovely day.'

'Were you? Well, before you do there's the hall floor to mop, windows to clean, rugs to beat and food to help prepare,' Minnie replied.

Dilys sniggered quietly.

'Do you think that's funny?' Fliss rounded on the girl.

'It was a bit,' the maid answered, the smile still gracing her face.

Minnie watched with interest, wondering where this would lead.

'Why do you all hate me so much? Is it because I'm pregnant and will be taking your precious son away from you?' Fliss's words were directed at Minnie as she clearly realised she'd get no further with the maid.

'Fliss, James didn't do it on his own – you were involved as well, so don't be laying all the blame on him,' Minnie answered.

'We're in love and that love got away from us one time!'

'That's all it can take – one time.'

'What would you know about love – you're old!' Fliss snapped. Suddenly realising her mistake, Fliss immediately apologised. 'I'm sorry, I shouldn't have said that.' She needed to keep Minnie onside as before long they would be related.

Minnie bristled as Mabel and Dilys drew in sharp breaths at the insult. 'Older than you, I admit, but as I see it that also makes me wiser. Now, I will warn you once – do not attempt to cross swords with me, miss, for you will not win. I've battled worse than you in my time and I haven't lost yet!' An image of

Una Reed rushed into her mind as she spoke and she wondered if the woman's fighting days were truly over now.

Minnie's words caused Fliss's temper to rise and she could no longer hold back, spurred on by memories of talking over her problems with James.

She had discussed the situation with James but he had dismissed it, saying with so many women in the house there were bound to be disagreements. He had suggested she tried harder in her dealings with his family.

'You make me sick – all of you! You whisper behind my back; you shut me out of discussions...' Fliss began.

'That's because it's none of your business!' Minnie yelled.

'I thought I was to be part of this family, especially as I'm providing you with a grandchild!'

'*Do not* use that child as a tool to bargain with!' Minnie was on her feet and Mabel and Dilys exchanged a worried glance.

'Mum, calm down,' Polly said, trying to assuage the animus radiating from both women.

'No, Polly, that was a step too far!' Turning back

to Fliss she went on, 'You are a nasty piece of work, madam, and I for one will not put up with it. Either you change your attitude and quick – or you leave my house!' Minnie's finger had jabbed in the girl's direction as she spoke. Watching tears form in Fliss's eyes she continued. 'Crying won't do you any good; it won't wash with me. So, whilst you mop the hall you think about what I've said. Now get to it!'

Fliss fled the kitchen and Minnie dropped onto her chair. With closed eyes, she sighed long and hard.

Mabel nodded to the kettle and Dilys duly complied. The perfect panacea for a time like this was always a cup of tea.

Polly joined her mum at the table and Minnie pushed the letter across its surface for her to read. Still angry, she didn't trust herself to speak for fear of snapping at her daughter.

Returning the letter to its envelope, Polly asked quietly, 'Would you like me to come with you?'

'No, child, I don't want you anywhere near Una Reed ever again.'

'Please take someone with you,' Polly urged.

'I agree with Polly,' Mabel put in, 'the mood you're in you're liable to do old Reedy in!'

Minnie couldn't help but laugh at the comment and everyone breathed a sigh of relief. The dark moment had passed.

'Echo would be the best person, Mum. If those kiddies are coming here then he can comfort them and they won't be so afraid.'

'Good idea, gel. I'll wait until they get back and then we'll go and visit Una and see what's what.'

Dilys passed over a cup of tea, saying, 'Thanks, Minnie. I'm grateful that you're all looking out for me.'

'That's what families do for each other and you're part of this ever-growing one.' The two shared a warm smile as Minnie settled down to await Echo's return.

It wasn't long before Fliss's voice rose to a crescendo as she berated the returning children for stepping on the clean hall floor.

Minnie got to her feet. 'Here we go again.' She stifled a smirk whilst watching the excited kiddies milling around the foyer. They were bursting to tell anyone who would listen about their outing, and their voices grew louder as they tried to be heard over the adults shouting at each other. Celia was trying to apologise and Fliss was yelling her disgust.

Clapping her hands twice, Minnie saw all movement stop instantly. 'Celia, take this lot into the schoolroom please. Echo, I have a job for you, and Fliss – stop shouting.'

The teacher nodded and ushered her charges away. Echo and May retreated into the kitchen and Minnie glared at Fliss. Holding up a finger in warning she growled, 'One more time – just give me the excuse, lady!'

Turning her back, she made her way back to the kitchen to enlist Echo's help. Explaining quietly what she needed, Minnie was pleased when Echo nodded eagerly.

'Good lad. I tell you what, we'll come back by cab,' she said.

'...by cab.' The familiar repetition made everyone smile.

Shoving the letter into her bag, Minnie beckoned to Echo and winked. 'We'll go through the front. That will upset her ladyship!' she whispered.

Striding out and crossing the hall, Minnie

nodded to the girl standing watching them. Throwing down the mop, Fliss crossed her arms and scowled.

Minnie and Echo howled with laughter as they left via the front door.

Minnie reiterated what she'd told Echo previously as they walked up past the allotment gardens. Seeing Dickie on his hands and knees, Minnie returned his wave. Traversing All Saints Road they then turned into Vicarage Road. As they entered the grounds of Reed House, Minnie suppressed a shiver. Her mind had instantly returned to the time she came here once before looking for her children, only to be told Polly had been sold on, and Adam had run away in an effort to locate and rescue his sister.

The hairs on the back of her neck stood up as she rapped the knocker. Momentarily the door was opened by a pretty young woman.

'I'm Minnie Marshall.'

'Ah, yes, please do come in.' Diana closed the door after Minnie and Echo had stepped inside. 'Una is in the kitchen; the stairs are proving somewhat of a problem for her at the present time. I am Diana Wilton, the teacher.'

Minnie nodded, and along with Echo followed Diana to where Una was resting.

'Una, Mrs Marshall is here with...?' Diana began.

'Echo.'

Diana's eyebrows rose in surprise as she looked at the boy.

'You hurt my Polly!' Echo snapped.

Minnie laid a hand on his arm saying, 'Now is not the time, lad; the lady is very poorly.'

Fuming inwardly, Echo sealed his lips.

'I was sorry to hear you are ill, Una. I've received your letter.' Minnie said as she stared at the woman, who appeared to be a shadow of her former self. Grey and haggard, Una had lost weight and her cheeks were sunken. The fire had disappeared from her eyes and she looked at least ten years older than her age.

'We have four children – two girls and two boys. As you can see for yourself, I am in no fit state to continue to care for them. The question is, can you take them in?'

'What can you tell me about them?' Minnie asked pointedly.

Una sighed. Was it too much to ask for the woman to just take the children and go?

'All one family,' Una snapped.

'Michael is eight years old, David is seven, June is six and Bella is five. Their surname is Watkins,' Diana explained helpfully.

'How is it they came to you?' Minnie asked Una.

'Their father was a sailor who went to sea from Liverpool docks and never returned. The mother couldn't cope; she had no work and was unable to feed them, so she brought them here.'

'And went away twenty shillings better off, I'll be bound.' Minnie couldn't help making the snide remark.

Una bristled but didn't take the bait. She needed Minnie's help and causing an argument wouldn't aid her task of rehoming the little family.

'Are you willing to have them?'

Turning to Diana, Minnie went on. 'Get them ready and I'll take them with me now.'

Diana nodded.

'Would you care for tea?' Mrs Gibbs offered.

'No, thanks. I'll be on my way as soon as the kiddies are here. Has anyone told them they are moving?'

Mrs Gibbs and Una shook their heads in unison.

'I guessed as much, that's why I brought my right-hand man with me,' she said gesturing to Echo who beamed at the compliment, 'He'll settle them if they get upset.'

Una was clearly feeling guilty, her eyes darting to the door constantly.

'Here we are,' Diana said as she ushered the children into the kitchen.

Bending down to their level, Minnie said, 'My name is Minnie Marshall and because Miss Reed is sick you'll be coming to live at my children's home. This is Echo and he'll tell you all about it as we go and – guess what? We're going in a cab!' Looking at the faces watching her, Minnie smiled.

The four blonde children stood in a huddle, their blue eyes watching Minnie fearfully. They were rail thin and the old clothes they had been given were all but worn through. The boys' long trousers ended halfway down their shins and on closer inspection they wore no socks inside their battered boots. The shirts had ragged collars and cuffs and were far too small. The girls fared no better, with cotton dresses, which should have been knee length, coming down to their equally tattered boots.

Bella gripped Michael's hand tightly as she glanced from face to face, and June's eyes filled with tears. Hearing her give a little sob, David put his arm around her shoulder and drew her to him. It was clear to all that these siblings were very close and would look out for each other no matter what.

They were afraid, and no wonder, having been sold to Reeds, and now they were on the move again. They were five-shilling children just like Polly and Adam and so many more who had suffered the same fate over the years.

'Echo, you're in charge,' Minnie said eventually. 'Here, take these and share them out if you would.' She handed the boy a bag of boiled sweets she had pulled from the pantry before leaving home, thinking they would be useful to ease the children's transition.

Echo took the sweets and herded his new charges towards the front door.

'Find a cab please, Echo,' Minnie called after him. Then to Una, 'I'll be off then.'

A nod being the only reply given, Minnie shook her head in disgust and walked out of Reed House for the very last time. Never again would she grace this place with her presence if she could help it and what went on there in the future would be none of her concern.

The cab was waiting on the road and Echo and the children were already inside. She could hear the laughter as she approached. Polly's idea to bring the lad with her had been a good one.

31

'You are one miserable mare, Una Reed!' Mrs Gibbs said once Minnie and the children had departed. 'You never even thanked that woman and those kiddies left with nowt but the clothes they stood up in!'

'That's how they came to me, Mrs Gibbs!' Una retaliated.

'I don't give a bugger. You are spiteful and vindictive and it's time someone told you so.'

Diana kept quiet as the argument raged on.

'How dare you speak to me in that manner?'

'I dare because you are relying on us now.'

Una drew in a sharp breath, knowing the cook

was correct; she was totally reliant upon the two women staring at her.

'Things have changed now, Una, and you'd best get used to the idea. Diana and I are here under duress; you threatened to throw us out with no money and nowhere to go. So don't come with those high and mighty ways with me any more. We'll never be friends, but at least we can be civil to each other whilst we are in this situation.'

'As you wish,' Una said, feeling thoroughly beaten. What had she expected on her release from hospital – that she would be able to continue to work straight away? This whole matter had been taken out of her hands and the loss of control had her head spinning. She now had to treat these women as equals and it galled her. With a heavy sigh she knew she had no other choice.

* * *

Climbing out of the cab at Marshall's, the four children stood in a line and looked up at their new home. Minnie paid the cabbie and watched with interest, allowing Echo to take the lead.

'It's nice,' Echo said gently. He could see they were afraid, and he wanted to make them feel comfortable about coming here. They had relaxed a little on the carriage ride and he had made them laugh, but he knew this move was daunting for them.

'Michael, David, June, Bella,' he counted their names on his fingers as the Watkins children watched him. 'I remembered.'

The fear was still evident in the eyes that stared at him and Echo wondered how to get them indoors. Thinking back, he recalled Adam once saying he and Polly were always hungry when they were at Reed's, and the memory sparked an idea.

'Dinner time! Come on.' Holding out his hands to June and Bella, he smiled as they grasped tightly. Then he had another thought. Standing them in line one behind the other, with Michael bringing up the rear, he took his place at the front.

'Quick march!' he called out and stepped smartly forward.

Minnie shook her head with a grin as she watched Echo lead his line of soldiers into the house.

She followed them into the kitchen, where Mabel and Dilys were already preparing food.

'It's all hands to the pumps, now,' Minnie said, 'we have to shift the spare furniture out of those two remaining rooms for these kiddies.'

Echo and Flash, Polly and May, Fliss and Ruth as well as Minnie and Adam trundled up the stairs to begin work.

'Leave two beds in each room, a wardrobe and chest of drawers. Everything else will have to come out,' Minnie called out.

'Where shall we put the extra stuff, Mum?' Polly asked.

'We'll have to stack it outside next to the privy and hope it doesn't rain.'

Peter, James and Digit arrived back from the wharf early and immediately set themselves to helping.

With Dickie in next, the work was completed in record time. The girls made up the beds and sorted out some spare clothes for the drawers.

Then Echo took the new arrivals up to see their rooms.

Minnie collapsed onto a kitchen chair and checked the teapot.

'I'll do it,' Dilys said preparing a cup for Minnie.

'Ta, gel, I'm exhausted. That's all of our rooms full now save the two up by you,' Minnie said as she glanced at the cook and maid.

'How long will it take to build the extension?' Mabel asked.

'How long is a piece of string?' Minnie answered.

'If any more kids come in, I don't mind sharing,' Dilys offered.

'That's good of you, pet; let's just hope we don't have any more in yet for a while,' Minnie said with a smile. She was gratified that Echo had taken the new children under his wing, showing them around and explaining how the place was run. After her tea, she sought Polly out.

In the living room, she asked, 'Are you and Dickie walking out together?'

Polly blushed beetroot red and nodded. 'Do you mind about it, Mum?'

'No, sweetheart, but I'll have to try and explain it to Echo. You know how protective he is with you and May.'

'Thanks, Mum,' Polly said as she hugged her mother.

Minnie watched as her daughter left the room.

Polly was a young woman now and Minnie felt a pang of regret. Her children were all grown up and she realised before too long they would be going their individual ways. They would find partners and have homes of their own. There would still be children at Marshall's, of course, but they wouldn't be hers.

Her thoughts shifted to the child Fliss carried – it would be her first grandchild. Would she be able to love it, knowing who and what its mother was? She felt sure she could if she thought of it as James's child.

The next person she had to seek out was Echo. Finding him still in the kitchen, she asked if he would spare her a moment in the office.

'Echo, you know Polly is a grown-up lady now, don't you?' The boy nodded. 'Well, I know how much you care for her but there comes a time when...'

'Dickie,' Echo put in.

'Yes, lovey.'

'Hate Dickie!' he growled.

'Why?' Minnie asked. 'Is it because he's Polly's sweetheart?'

Echo shook his head violently.

'Then why?' Minnie probed.

'Trust,' Echo answered simply.

'You don't trust him?'

'No.'

'I understand but we have to let them get on with it. Maybe it won't last and in time Polly might find a new partner.'

'Hope so,' Echo said sadly.

'Now, to the children from Reed's. Thank you for today, you were a tremendous help,' Minnie praised.

'Problem?'

'I'm worried they might not settle well,' Minnie fibbed.

'Echo see to it,' the boy said, jerking his thumb towards his chest.

'Oh, thank you!' Minnie said on a breath for effect.

'Go now?' Echo asked.

'Yes, and thanks again.' Minnie smiled as Echo shot out to take care of his new companions.

Again, Minnie sat for a moment in the quiet of the office and allowed her thoughts to roam.

Echo, everyone seemed to think, was a dimwit, but he was far from it. He was wise beyond his years at times. He was observant, for hadn't he seen the relationship growing between Polly and Dickie? He was bright enough to know he couldn't change it and wise enough to accept it. Minnie suspected he would continue to watch over Polly – but from a distance.

Satisfied their little meeting had gone better than she could have hoped for, Minnie turned her mind to her eldest son. James was besotted with the girl he was betrothed to, and only his discovering what she truly was would upset that.

Time was passing and the wedding was drawing nearer. If something didn't happen soon, it would be too late for James to realise his mistake.

Minnie had considered talking to James about marrying Fliss but had refrained from doing so for fear of alienating him. One wrong word and she could lose him forever, and she couldn't risk that. She wondered if her other children were harbouring the same fear, for none had confronted James regarding pointing out the folly of his decision.

With a sigh, she closed her eyes.

Please God watch over my boy, help him to come to his senses sooner rather than later.

Minnie left the office, the prayer still lingering in her mind.

That evening, when everyone was in the living room, Polly brought up the subject of clothes once more.

'Fliss, what are you going to do about a wedding gown?'

Minnie's ears pricked up.

Taken by surprise, Fliss glared. 'I have no idea, besides, surely that's my business and not yours.'

James's eyes shot to his mother's and Minnie gave an imperceptible shake of her head. *Don't you dare offer to buy one for her!* The warning was clear.

'I'm buying a new hat for the wedding,' Dilys said in innocent excitement at the prospect of the occasion.

'And just how can you afford a new hat?' Fliss asked nastily.

'I...' Dilys began but stopped as Minnie's eyes flashed in her direction. 'Surely that's my business and not yours!' *Touché!* Dilys silently congratulated herself for standing up to the girl.

'Well, I wouldn't bother because you are not invited!' Fliss snapped back with a self-satisfied smile.

'Fliss!' James growled.

Fliss's head snapped round to look at her betrothed.

'We will invite everyone, including Dilys,' James said sternly.

'James, this will be *my* day and I will invite who I want!' Fliss retorted.

Minnie saw the angry look on his face. Was he beginning to see through the sweetness Fliss so often portrayed?

'This is supposed to be *our* day, Fliss, it's not just about you!' James replied hotly.

Fliss scowled but kept her counsel.

Disappointed beyond belief, Dilys was resolute when she said, 'It don't matter; I'll spend my money on something else then. Would you come to the bank with me, Minnie, to draw out some funds?'

Minnie nodded as she stifled a grin.

Fliss was agog that the maid had a bank account, let alone money in it.

Polly and May exchanged a look which said they were both disgusted at Fliss's spite.

'Nasty!' Echo put in.

'You shut your mouth, you idiot!' Fliss yelled.

Echo hung his head but Polly was on her feet in an instant. The sharp slap she delivered to Fliss's cheek resounded in the now quiet room. 'Don't you *ever* call Echo an idiot again or I will not be responsible for my actions!'

There was a collective intake of breath and everyone waited as Polly stood over Fliss, a look of thunder on her countenance.

Polly's blood was up now. 'You are a spiteful person, Felicity Hargreaves! I'll tell you something else as well – I know about the cardigan!'

'James...' Fliss began with a sob.

'Polly! Calm down! How could you do such a thing?' James yelled.

'Oh, God! I'm sorry,' Polly said as she saw the girl's stricken face.

Turning to Fliss, James went on, 'What Polly did was very wrong and I cannot condone anyone striking a woman, especially one who is pregnant. However, had you not provoked her it would never have happened. You simply cannot continue to behave in such a manner, Fliss, I will not stand for it.'

The colour drained from Fliss's face at that and she jumped to her feet and ran from the room.

Well done, son! Minnie thought as she watched James calmly retake his seat.

32

'I don't have time for all this running around after
her ladyship!' Mrs Gibbs said in exasperation.

'Nor do I,' Diana replied.

Una had fallen into a depressed slump and had
taken to staying in her room. She had brought the
dinner bell with her and rang it loudly when she
wanted something.

'I thought the doctor said she had to have gentle
exercise,' Mrs Gibbs huffed.

'He did, but she won't even go for a walk. I've
tried to coax her, but she just bites my head off!'
Diana explained. 'I don't see what else I can do.'

'Well this ain't fair on either of us. We're cooking,

cleaning and washing and what do we get in return? A bed and meals! She's running us ragged, Diana, and it can't go on!'

'I'm at a loss as to how to change things, Mrs Gibbs, believe me.'

Just then the bell rang again and both women sighed loudly.

'What does she want this time, I wonder?' Mrs Gibbs asked.

'I'll go and see.' Diana got to her feet wearily and went to Una's room.

'Ah, there you are. I'm ready for a cup of tea and can you see if Mrs Gibbs has a scone and butter?' Una said from where she lay on her bed, an open book on her lap. 'I'd like the newspaper as well.'

'You could come down for tea, Una. It would save me having to run up and down stairs every five minutes,' Diana responded.

'I'm not nearly well enough for that yet!' came the sharp answer.

'What about what the hospital doctor said about exercise?' Diana asked tentatively.

'All in good time. For now the rest is helping. Now what about that scone and tea?'

Diana nodded and plodded back to the kitchen.

As she prepared a tray Mrs Gibbs muttered, 'We could always just up and leave her to it.' She cast a glance at the teacher and the look she received in return said Diana was seriously thinking about the idea.

'We could, but where would we go?'

'That's the problem isn't it? There's nowhere.'

Wolverhampton had a prolific bicycle trade which had begun in 1868 and was still going strong but as fast as jobs became available they were refilled. The town was also famous for its woollen trade but again, openings for work were scarce. The lock-making factories were fully staffed too, as the men standing in the *bread line* could attest to.

Finding a house to share would be impossible; the women knew the best they could hope for would be a room in a boarding house which would still require payment.

'Let's face it, Mrs Gibbs, we're trapped.' Diana's sadness was evident as she placed the folded newspaper on the tray next to the plate holding two scones.

As she put the small teapot on the tray, Mrs

Gibbs went on, 'Right, take that up to her and tell her if she wants anything else she'll have to get it herself.'

'But we're supposed to be looking after her!'

'That doesn't mean we have to pander to her every whim! No, go on and be firm with her,' Mrs Gibbs said sharply.

Lifting the tray Diana nodded.

'Tea, scones and newspaper as requested,' Diana said as she entered Una's room.

'Just put it there,' Una said indicating the bedside cabinet.

'Mrs Gibbs says that as we're both very busy cooking and cleaning, if you need anything more to please get it yourself.' Diana's shoulders rose as she waited for the barrage to come.

'Did she, indeed? Well, you tell Mrs Gibbs from me that she is living here under my say-so. She should be grateful to have a roof over her head and food in her belly. Now go away and leave me in peace!'

Diana all but ran from the room, glad to be out of the firing line.

Mrs Gibbs stormed around the kitchen in a fit of temper when Diana repeated Una's words. 'That's it!

I'm doing no more for that ungrateful witch! She ain't been home but five minutes and I'm sick to the back teeth of her already!'

'Calm down, Mrs Gibbs, or you will be the next one to have a heart attack,' Diana said in earnest.

'I've had it with her, Diana,' the other woman said as she dropped onto a chair. 'After we've had our meal, I'm packing my bags. In the morning I'm off!'

'Where to?'

'I'm going to try my luck at Minnie Marshall's place.'

'What if she can't help?'

'Then I'll sleep in the bloody park!'

Diana's mouth formed an 'O' as she drew in a breath. Then on impulse she said, 'I'm coming with you!'

Mrs Gibbs cooked a hearty meal that evening. Potatoes, fresh vegetables and a leg of lamb covered in rich gravy. Diana took Una hers on a tray, saying she would bring her a hot drink before bedtime.

As the cook and teacher ate they made whispered plans about leaving the following day.

'I don't have much to pack,' Mrs Gibbs said.

'Neither do I,' Diana answered with a grim smile.

Each knew the other had no family that they could approach for help and had gathered few possessions over the years. Therefore it was likely everything they owned could be pushed into one large bag or suitcase.

'Good – less to carry.'

'Aren't you concerned about Mrs Marshall turning us away?'

'Yes, but like I said I ain't staying here any longer than is absolutely necessary.' Mrs Gibbs said then she nodded at the meat on her plate. 'That's a nice bit of lamb, tender and cuts lovely.'

'Yes indeed,' Diana agreed.

'Tomorrow we'll have us a real good breakfast because it might have to last us all day.'

Diana munched on her food as she considered the implications of being homeless, and the huge gamble they were taking by just walking out. She prayed Minnie would find them a room and a job. She didn't think it was likely to happen but she hoped nevertheless.

Later, after taking Una a bedtime drink, Diana said goodnight. Then she and Mrs Gibbs slunk away to do their packing – quietly.

In the morning the woman prepared bacon, eggs, tomatoes and mushrooms, followed by toast and jam. Then Diana took Una's upstairs.

'We thought a hearty breakfast would do you good,' she said warily.

'As long as it's not every day, I'm not made of money, you know,' Una said curtly.

'Will you be coming downstairs today, do you think?'

'No. I'll take a few more days of rest and see how I feel then.'

Diana breathed a sigh of relief as she left the room. Running downstairs, skirts held high, she rushed into the kitchen. 'Una is staying put for another few days.'

'Good. Now get that down you, then we'll be off,' Mrs Gibbs said pushing the plate of food towards her friend. Seeing Diana's hesitation, she added, 'Eat up. It might be the last you have for a while.'

Diana nodded and tucked in. Once finished she made to begin washing the dishes.

'Leave them. We need to be away as soon as possible in case Una changes her mind and comes down.'

On tiptoes they went to their rooms, grabbed their bags and descended the stairs like thieves in the night. Quietly closing the front door behind them they hurried down the drive and away from Reed House.

* * *

The dining room at Marshall's was quiet at breakfast time after the fracas of the previous evening.

Shortly after Fliss had sped from the room, James had followed, leaving the others to discuss the debacle.

The couple had not come down to break their fast and everyone wondered if James had managed to talk some sense into his fiancée.

It was as work began in the kitchen washing, drying and putting away crockery and cutlery that a knock sounded at the front door.

'I'll go,' Dilys said as she dried her hands on her apron. A moment later she returned. 'Minnie, there's two ladies to see you. They're in the hall – with their bags.'

Minnie frowned. Who would be calling at this

early hour? Going through, her question was answered in an instant; it was the staff members from Reed House.

'Come through to the living room. You can leave your baggage there, it will be safe enough.'

The two women followed Minnie and took the seats offered.

'I have a feeling I know what's coming but I'll ask regardless. What can I do for you?'

Looking at each other, it was Mrs Gibbs who spoke first.

'We've left Reed's. Una has us run ragged and now she can't pay us.'

'I did wonder about that when I came for the kiddies,' Minnie confessed.

'We had bed and board but only until the money runs out,' Mrs Gibbs added.

'So, is Una on her own then?'

'Mrs Marshall, please don't judge us until you hear what we have to say,' Diana put in carefully.

'I wasn't judging you, I was merely asking,' Minnie responded.

The two women explained between them how demanding and spiteful Una had been during their time at Reed House, and that it was Diana's idea to approach Minnie to request the four orphans be transferred. They told about Una's use of the *box* and the children's fear of her.

'So, you are the teacher as I recall?' Minnie asked.

Diana nodded. 'I have to confess I am, as yet, un-qualified, as seeking work took precedence over my studies.'

'And you are?'

'Josie Gibbs – the cook.'

Diana shot a quick look at her friend.

'Problem?' Minnie asked as she caught the movement.

'My apologies. It's just in the five years we have been at Reed's I didn't know Mrs Gibbs' first name. We always knew her as – well, Mrs Gibbs,' Diana answered.

'So ladies, I'm not surprised in the least that you've walked out. May I ask what Una's reaction was?'

The women's eyes lowered to their hands in their laps.

'I see. You didn't tell her.'

Heads shook in unison.

'I have to admit I feel very guilty about just leaving without a word, but I could not face yet another barrage of abuse,' Diana said.

'So you've come to me in the hope of...?' Minnie questioned.

'Work,' Mrs Gibbs said simply.

'We understand you must already employ a cook and teacher and that your funding will only stretch so far, but...' Diana was saying.

'And we'll understand if you ain't in a position to give us a job. We wouldn't ask, only we're desperate. We've had no wages and now we don't have a home either,' Josie put in quickly.

Standing up, Minnie beckoned to the women to follow her. Taking them to the kitchen, she requested they be given tea. She introduced them and asked Adam and Polly to give her a minute of their time.

Back in the living room once more, she explained the plight of the women and asked her children's advice.

'Well, there are two rooms still empty in the servants' quarters, Mum,' Polly reminded her.

'Is there enough money to pay them?' Adam asked.

'Yes. My concern is how they will fit in with Celia and Mabel,' Minnie confided.

'The new teacher is not qualified, you say?' Adam asked.

'So she tells me.'

'Then she would have to be an assistant to Celia. As for Mrs Gibbs, she would have to do the same where Mabel is concerned,' Adam said wisely.

'Two cooks in the same kitchen smacks of disaster, if you ask me,' Minnie responded.

'The rules would have to be laid out and adhered to,' Polly said. 'What do you reckon, Mum, are you going to add them to our ever-increasing family?'

33

Una rang the large hand bell for the third time, all the while becoming more and more annoyed. She wondered if Diana was deliberately ignoring her call.

In the end, and feeling thoroughly disgruntled, Una made her way downstairs slowly and carefully.

In the kitchen she caught her breath. Dirty plates and cups were still on the table, the frying pan handle was sticking out from a sink of soapy water. The smell of bacon pervaded the air and most noticeable was the sound of silence.

Una shivered at the eerie feeling that crept over her. Never in the years she had been here had the house been so quiet.

Sitting on the nearest chair, she knew instinctively what had happened. She had been deserted. The two people she relied upon had upped and left without as much as a þy-your-leave. She had no friends or family, no staff or orphans; she was totally alone.

She made herself a cup of tea and sat listening to the odd creaks of the house which she'd not heard before. It was unnerving, and she mentally berated herself for allowing the strange sounds to unsettle her.

It's an old house, it's bound to creak and groan, she told herself.

'They couldn't even clean up after themselves,' she muttered as she stared at the dirty crocks. 'Well, at least I only have myself to consider now.'

As she cleared the table and washed the dishes her mind dwelt on the two women who had so cruelly forsaken her. Where had they gone? Had they planned this together? Why had they said nothing to her about leaving? How would they live with no money or a roof over their heads? Would they return when life became too difficult to bear? Or would they end up in the workhouse? Moreover, would *she* find herself in that dreadful place?

Fear at that last thought crawled up Una's spine. She had to ensure that didn't happen to her.

Lingering over more tea, she wondered if her staff had defected to Marshall's. Thought of Minnie filled her with hate; that woman had taken everything from her. Minnie had stolen Billy Marshall – the man Una had thought to marry one day. She had not only her own children back but their friends too. She had taken in Mabel and Dilys who had once worked for Una and now probably Mrs Gibbs and Diana.

Slamming her cup on the table, she took no heed of the cold tea slopping onto its surface. Minnie Marshall was the bane of her life. But she was in no fit state to fight the woman any longer. All that was left to her was to live out her days in this big rambling house alone.

* * *

Whilst Minnie had been meeting with Polly and

Adam, Josie Gibbs had been comparing notes with Mabel regarding Una Reed.

'She's not changed much, then, by the sounds of things,' Mabel said.

'It would seem not,' Josie concurred.

'We walked out for all the same reasons and were fortunate to have met Minnie.'

'I feel bad about sneaking away without a word,' Diana muttered.

'Not nearly bad enough to go back though, eh?' Josie asked.

'No. I'm afraid you are right there, Mrs Gibbs.'

'Things are different here though, aren't they, Mabel?' Dilys put in.

'Yes, we're like a big family. They don't treat us like staff; they include us in everything. The kiddies are well looked after and as happy as they can be having lost their own parents one way or another.'

'It sounds idyllic,' Diana mused.

'Oh, we have our upsets at times, ain't that right, Dilys?'

The girl nodded, her mind immediately turning to Fliss. It had not gone unnoticed that the young woman hadn't yet put in an appearance. Evidently she was too ashamed to show her face at breakfast and was, as far as anyone knew, still in her room sulking.

'Mrs Marshall is taking a long time, it doesn't bode well for us, I'm thinking, Mrs Gibbs,' Diana said with a worried look.

Unbeknown to them, Minnie had gone into the schoolroom to have a word with Celia. Polly and Adam waited for her return and chatted in hushed tones.

In a moment Minnie was back. 'Celia says she could do with the help. Now you two can go about your business, but Pol, can you ask Mabel to come through first?'

'You wanted to see me?' Mabel asked as she trundled in.

'I want your opinion about taking Josie Gibbs and Diana Wilton in. Celia needs help in her class so she's agreed. What I want to know is – how would you feel having another cook in your kitchen?'

'Like in any family there would have to be rules. The pecking order needs to be clear so there's no falling out,' Mabel answered.

'Fair enough. What about Fliss? Do we tell them about her?' Minnie asked.

'I think we would have to 'cos that girl picks a fight at every given opportunity. It might look bad if there's constant bickering and they don't know why.'

'Right then. I think they'll have to share a room up by you, which will leave one spare for emergencies. Agreed?'

Mabel nodded.

'Let's go and welcome them into the fold then,' Minnie said. 'I swear we'll need a massive extension at this rate.'

Returning to the kitchen, Minnie sat down and began to speak. 'You can move in here with us, although I'll have to discuss it with Billy, my husband. I can't see him raising any objections but you need to know regardless. You will have to share a room until the extension is completed so we can keep a room in readiness in case of an emergency intake. Diana, Celia is happy to have you in her classroom as an assistant. Do you agree to that?'

'Yes indeed! Thank you, Mrs Marshall.'

'Minnie. All first names here.' Turning to Josie she continued. 'Mabel is head chef here but will gladly share her kitchen providing you understand she's the boss. Do you accept?'

'Yes, and I thank you, too – Minnie,' Josie answered before giving a deferential nod to Mabel.

'Good. I'll get Polly to show you to your room and you can get settled in. You'll get to know the others as and when they get in from work.' Calling for her daughter, Minnie then added, 'We'll speak about wages later in private, as there's something else you'll need to know about.'

Diana and Josie exchanged a puzzled look before following Polly up the back stairs.

Polly left them with a 'Welcome to Marshall's' and the two began to unpack their belongings.

'I wonder what all that was about,' Diana said.

'We'll find out soon enough. For now, I'm just bloody glad we've landed on our feet. I'll be forever grateful to Minnie Marshall for this,' Josie said as her eyes swept the room.

A knock came on the door and Josie opened it.

'Hello, I'm May. I've brought you some clean bed linen and towels.'

'Thanks, I'm Josie and this is Diana.'

'Welcome. When you're ready there's always hot

tea in the kitchen. See you later.' Then she was gone.

They found pillows and eiderdowns in the wardrobe and began to make up their beds.

'You know what, Diana? I'm thinking we'll be very happy here,' Josie said.

'I concur,' came the reply.

* * *

After yet more tea, Minnie invited her two new employees to join her in the office. Giving each a slip of paper which informed them about their wages she was glad to see their surprise. Clearly more than they had been earning. Then she gave them a potted history of the Fliss affair.

'So, no business is discussed in front of her, and everyone watches over Dilys,' Minnie finished.

'What will you do about the wedding, then?' Josie asked.

Minnie shook her head. 'I don't know. It's only a few days away and I'm no further forward. I think maybe the time has come to speak to our James and let him know the truth of it all.'

'If we can help in any way...' Diana began.

'Ta, lass. I'll let you know.' With that, the three returned to the kitchen where the preparation of lunch was well under way.

'Anyone seen Fliss this morning?' Minnie called out.

Shaking heads gave the answer.

Minnie growled and stamped away. Going to the room Fliss occupied, she knocked once and walked in.

Fliss was up and dressed, and stood staring out of the window.

'There's work to be done and two new members of staff to meet, so get a shimmy on,' Minnie said gruffly. Without waiting for a reply, she walked out, leaving the door open behind her.

Downstairs once more, Minnie asked Echo to add Josie and Diana's name on the books, which he duly did.

Fliss joined them meekly and was introduced before Minnie asked her to set two more places in the dining room. The girl did as she was bid without a word but with a sullen look on her face. When she returned, joviality filled the kitchen and yet again she felt like an outsider.

34

Lunch consisted of lettuce, tomatoes, pickled beet-root, home-made pork pies, ham off the bone, cheese, boiled eggs, apple slices, chutney and bread and butter. For afters there was fresh fruit and honey cakes. Josie nodded approvingly as she tucked in.

In the afternoon, Diana joined Celia in the classroom and everyone else set to washing dishes and re-setting the tables in readiness for the evening meal.

It was around four o'clock when Peter, Digit and James sauntered in. Minnie immediately asked James to join her in the office where they wouldn't be disturbed.

Coming in from the privy, Fliss asked, 'Was that James's voice I heard?'

'It was,' Mabel answered.

'Oh good, I need to speak with him. Where is he?'

'He's in the office with his mum.' Again it was Mabel who answered.

'I'll go and find him then.'

'I wouldn't bother. They're in a *private* meeting,' Polly emphasised.

'Well, he'll see me,' Fliss pushed arrogantly.

'Fliss, do you understand the meaning of *private*?' Polly asked pointedly.

'Of course I do!'

'Then you'll have to wait until they're finished!' Polly snapped.

Fliss huffed and walked out.

Polly and Mabel exchanged a look and Mabel nodded towards the door. Polly stood and wandered from the kitchen.

'You won't hear anything,' she said as she spied Fliss with her ear pinned to the office door.

The girl almost jumped out of her skin. 'I was just wondering if they'd finished.' She said by way of explanation.

'Clearly they haven't, so it would help if you would chop the vegetables,' Polly said, pointing back to the kitchen.

With a last look at the office door, Fliss nodded and retreated.

Polly followed, thinking it was ridiculous that they had to keep an eye on Fliss at all times. She hated the friction the girl was causing in the household, and really didn't know how much longer it could go on before there was a big falling out. She guessed Minnie was tackling James about it at that very moment and wondered how her brother would react when confronted with the truth about his intended.

Peter and Digit were telling the others about their day at the wharf.

'There's not much work there at the moment, though,' Digit said.

'We might have to try another if things don't pick up,' Peter added.

'Well there's plenty of wharves and canal basins to choose from,' Mabel said as she passed over a thick slice of cheese and a hunk of fresh bread to keep the boys going until their next meal.

'Thanks, Mabel,' Digit said his eyes lighting up.

'I swear I don't know where you put it all, lad.'

'After five years of being constantly hungry, I'm not sure I'll ever feel full again,' the young man responded.

'We'll see. You leave that up to me,' Mabel answered with a grin.

In the office, Minnie began. 'I need to talk to you son, and I want you to listen without flying off the handle. Everything I'm about to tell you is true – as God is my witness.'

Minnie laid it all out for James to hear. The incident with the knife; the stealing of Polly's cardigan and other clothes; the trapping of Dilys in the privy. She told him of the arguments and Fliss's attitude and laziness. When she had finished, she looked at her boy. He had listened without interruption and Minnie was surprised he didn't instantly jump to Fliss's defence, wanting to shout her innocence from the roof tops.

'I swear it's all true, son, and I'm desperately worried that if you wed her next week you'll be making the biggest mistake of your life.'

'Mum, I promised to marry her, she's carrying my child after all,' he replied quietly.

'Is she? Is it yours? Can you be certain?'

'No, I can't but...'

'Well, then. The other thing is – why haven't her parents sent her stuff over – her clothes and things?'

'She wrote and asked them to, didn't she?' James asked.

'Yes, but did she post the letter?'

'Oh, Mum, this is all such a mess!'

'James, I'm going to ask this once and I want an honest answer. Do you love her?'

'I thought I did.'

'Now you're not so sure?'

James shook his head. 'I've been having second thoughts for a while, Mum, but I didn't know what to do about it.'

'In that case I would recommend you call off the wedding. This needs sorting out and quickly because that girl is causing untold grief in this house.'

'How do I do that? She'll have nowhere to go!'

'She can go home to her folks.'

'What about the baby?'

'James, I don't think we should make any decisions about that until it's born and that's a while away yet. Let's deal with one problem at a time.'

'She'll never forgive me!'

'That might be the best thing all round.'

'I know you're right, Mum, but I'm dreading it,' James said miserably.

'Come on, let's get it over with and remember – you have your family at your back.'

'There you are, sweetheart!' Fliss said on a breath as James walked into the room.

'I need to talk to you, Fliss. Shall we go into the living room?' James said awkwardly.

'There's no need, my love, I'm not one for keeping secrets,' Fliss answered as her gaze swept the room.

Dilys snorted and Mabel shot her a warning glance to keep quiet.

'Fliss I... I can't marry you,' James hung his head and waited.

'What? James, whatever do you mean?' Fliss's face turned a pale shade of grey.

'I know everything, Fliss. Mum's explained it all.'

The silence in the kitchen was palpable as all eyes and ears were riveted on the couple.

'Maybe we should discuss this in private, after all,' Fliss said as she took a step forward.

James held up a hand. 'It's too late, Fliss! Everyone has known for a while – everyone except me, I was the last to find out!'

'Find out about what?' Fliss asked.

'Everything! Your attitude, the stealing, the knife at Dilys' throat – everything!' James said angrily.

Minnie could see the fury building in her son and she laid a hand on his arm both to calm him and reassure him he had his family's support.

'You don't understand...' Fliss began.

James cut her off with, 'I have one question for you, Fliss. Are you even pregnant?'

The hiss of mouths drawing in breath was loud as Fliss looked around her. 'How could you ask me that?' she yelled.

'Are you?'

'I... James, I love you!'

'So, do I take it that the answer is no?' James asked.

Shocked looks passed from one face to another at the revelation.

'Why? Why would you lie about something like

that? What did you hope to gain?' James asked, disgust showing clearly on his face.

'I want to marry you and I thought you'd never ask!'

James shuddered at the venom in her voice. 'I wish I hadn't, now,' he replied in no more than a whisper.

'James, we can sort this out if only you will give me a chance!'

'No, Fliss, you had the opportunity to come clean but you kept up this charade. I'm disappointed, I had thought better of you.'

Fliss began to cry and beg for forgiveness but James shouted her down. 'Just get your things, I'm taking you home to your folks!'

'You can't just throw me away like a dirty rag!' Fliss bawled.

'Don't make this any worse than it already is,' James said, suddenly feeling very tired. 'Get your things.'

'Don't bother, I can take myself!' Fliss boomed. 'As for you, Minnie Marshall – you're a very spiteful woman! It's all your fault this has happened!'

'You brought it on yourself, Fliss, I just pointed it

out to James. Now I'd be pleased if you would leave my house.'

Fliss glanced around at the faces watching her before she ran from the kitchen. A moment later the front door shut with a bang.

35

Josie Gibbs wondered what she'd let herself in for as she watched the confrontation take place, but as everyone settled she felt the tension disappear with the girl who had caused it.

James sat with his head in his hands. The discomfort for the lad eventually drove everyone back to their work and it was Polly who then led her brother to the quiet of the living room.

'I'm sorry, James,' she whispered.

'It's all right, I just wish I'd known earlier.'

'We didn't know how to tell you. Dilys was afraid it would mean trouble between you and Mum so she kept her mouth shut.'

James nodded. 'I hate to say this, Polly, but I'm relieved.'

'There's plenty of time to find someone new and have a family in the proper order,' she said with a sheepish grin.

A knock sounded and Adam walked in, closing the door after him. 'Are you all right, James?'

'Yes. Adam, I want to say thanks – for everything. I might never have known if not for you.'

'I'm just sorry it all turned out like this,' Adam replied.

'It's for the best and I'm better off out of it,' James said resignedly.

'Will you do me a favour? Don't go courting for a while yet, eh?' Adam asked.

Despite the gravity of the situation James could not help but laugh. 'I'm done with women,' he said.

As they all stood to leave, James laced his arms around his brother and sister in a hug which they returned with fervour.

In the meantime, Minnie and May went to clean out Fliss's room. Minnie found the letter Fliss had supposedly sent to her parents. Opening the envelope addressed only to Mr and Mrs Hargreaves she snorted – inside was a blank sheet of paper.

'This is mine!' May gasped holding up a white blouse. 'And this and…' One after another she pulled out garments that belonged to her but had not been seen in a while.

'Look at this,' Minnie said nodding to the drawer in the bedside cabinet. Lip creams, jewellery and money lay inside.

'Where did all that come from?' May asked in astonishment.

'We'll find out when we take it all downstairs,' Minnie answered.

Clearly Felicity Hargreaves had been rifling through other people's rooms and helping herself to anything that took her fancy.

Shoving the sheets into the large basket on the landing, they then took Fliss's *stash* to the kitchen to try and match the items with their owners.

It was later when Adam said to Polly, 'James took the whole thing quite well, don't you think?'

'No Ad, I don't. Or rather I think he took it *too* well. I can't help thinking he either knew beforehand, which I doubt, or we'll see the extent of his un-happiness in the next few days.'

'He seemed relieved that he wasn't going to be a father after all,' Adam said.

'Tinged with disappointment, maybe?'

'Possibly, but now he's free to find a nice girl to settle down with. I wonder if we'll see any more of Fliss?'

'I hope not, because we've enough to be dealing with at the moment without more upset and argu-ments,' Polly said with a shudder.

'I was surprised when Josie and Diana came knocking though. Now old Reedy is on her own.'

'Ad, you're not feeling sorry for her, are you?'

'In a way I am. No one deserves to be alone, Pol, even though she brought it on herself.'

'She'll get no sympathy from me after what she put this family through. I sometimes still hear Rod-ney's screams when he first arrived and she locked him in the *box*!' Polly said, unable to suppress the shiver that overtook her. 'What about when she sold me to the Bellamy family?'

Adam's mind took him back to that fateful day

when he watched from a window his little sister being led into a carriage. He saw in his mind's eye the cab roll away down the drive, and he felt again the pain that cracked his heart. In his memory he heard the howl of agony that sounded like a badly wounded animal before he realised it had come from his own mouth.

'I see you remember it well,' Polly added.

'I'll never forget it, Polly. I thought I was going to die; unable to bear the pain of the loss,' he replied in a whisper.

'Well then, don't feel sorry for Una Reed. Now I'm going to bed, I'm worn out.' she said as she kissed him lightly on the cheek.

'Me too,' he said, 'tomorrow is another day.'

* * *

The woman the siblings had been discussing sat in her kitchen, which seemed massive with only her in it. Una looked around and felt the sting of loneliness.

She knew she would have to pull herself together and stop moping about. Everyone was gone and she had to get used to the idea.

Coming at it from the opposite angle she

thought, *I only have myself to think about now.* She had savings in the bank and at least Diana had left the money in the envelope on the table. They may have left but they hadn't robbed her into the bargain. She had just herself to feed so that would cut down on expenses. The summer was coming so she would save on coal and could get out for walks and fresh air once she felt better, rather than be cooped up in the house. But what about winter? She'd be holed up for months. With every positive thought a negative one countered it and she sighed loudly into the quiet of the room.

Would it have been better if she had died from that heart attack? She chided herself for the maudlin thought. No, she simply had to make the best of what she had.

Starting tomorrow she would begin a new life, she would be a lady of leisure. Feeling a little cheerier, she made her way back to rest in bed.

* * *

Bright and early the next morning, James rose and dressed quietly.

'You're off quick, aren't you?' Peter said through the fug of sleep.

'I have something to do before work,' James replied.

Shrugging, Peter closed his eyes and snuggled deeper beneath the bedclothes.

James let himself out of the house as silently as possible and breathed in the cool spring air. As he walked up Major Street he heard the birds twittering their little hearts out. His boots tapped out a steady rhythm and all around him was still. On into the town he went, past the Union Workhouse and towards the Smithy.

Slowly, noise from cartwheels on the cobbles began to break his peaceful reverie. The town was coming to life. Turning left into Cleveland Road he heard hammering coming from the carriage manufactory, the clang of metal on metal loud in his ears. Cutting down Hospital Street he emerged onto Bilston Street. The smell from the abattoir hit him like a punch in the face and he heard the bellow of cows in the cattle market.

Doubling back onto Walsall Street, James breathed fresher air once more. He was almost there.

He was heading for a house on one corner of St James' Square. Fliss's parents' house.

When he arrived he stood looking at the building. His mind was swamped with questions. Was Fliss in there? How had her parents reacted to her return? Why had she lied to him about carrying his child? Had she told her folks that same untruth? What made her want to marry him in the first place? And finally – should he knock and endeavour to find answers?

36

Over at Reed House, Una was also up early. Knowing she had insufficient strength to carry her to her destination, she hailed a cab. Giving the address to the cabbie, she settled herself for a bumpy ride.

As the carriage rolled to a halt, Una alighted and called out, 'Wait here.'

Going into the Servants' Registry building she walked to the woman sitting behind a huge desk.

'I'm in need of a maid, someone who can cook and clean to a high standard.'

'Live in?' the woman asked.

'Yes.'

'Where?'

'Reed House.' Una watched the woman's head snap up from looking at a large ledger.

'Miss Reed, I take it.'

'Correct.'

'Hmm,' the woman consulted her book again.

'As soon as possible, if you don't mind,' Una snapped.

'I'll have someone round to you this afternoon.'

Una gave a curt nod and with a straight back she marched out. On her ride home she smiled to herself. It would cost her to have a maid again but at least she wouldn't be alone.

Back at Reed House she paid the cabbie and watched him drive away. By later in the day she would have someone to talk to. Going indoors she was glad she had requested a maid. To have a cook would have cost a good deal more in wages and often they would not undertake any other duties. A maid would be happy to do almost anything for a paltry amount. Of course, it would eat into her savings but if she continued to write begging letters to the wealthy perhaps they would respond with donations. She didn't have to mention that there were no longer any children staying here, and if and when they found out it would be too late. Then again, she could always dismiss the maid when her money ran too low.

Making tea, Una took it to the living room to await her new employee's arrival.

* * *

'James took off early, Mum, he told me he had something to do before work,' Peter said.

'Oh, I wonder what that could be,' Minnie replied as they all trooped into the dining room for breakfast.

Peter shook his head, and grabbing a plate, he joined the queue to collect his food at the hatch between the dining room and kitchen.

Sitting next to Adam, Minnie asked, 'Do you know where Fliss lived before she came here?'

'No, Mum, why?'

'I think our James has gone looking for her,' Minnie answered. At Adam's puzzled look she explained what Peter had told her.

'Oh, Lord!' Adam exclaimed.

'...Lord,' Echo mimicked from a couple of seats away.

'Exactly. I have a feeling we may not have seen the last of that girl,' Minnie said quietly.

'I hope that's not the case, Mum. James needs time to come to terms with what's happened. It came as a blow to him, I'm afraid.'

'It did, lad, but given time he'll get over it,' Minnie said. Who was she trying to convince here?

Around mid-morning, Polly, May, Echo and the two teachers took the children out for a picnic packed for them by Mabel and Josie.

Diana and Josie had slipped into the Marshall way of life as if they had always been there and Minnie was pleased it had all worked out well.

Taking her tea to the office where she could think in peace, Minnie had a lot to mull over.

James, she was sure, had gone looking for Fliss, or more likely he was searching for answers. What that would result in she had no idea but her heart said it wouldn't be anything good.

The children's home was almost full and they were awaiting the plans for the extension from Josiah Holbrook, the architect. Then they could agree a price with the Rewcastle family of builders. The extension would need electricity put in and also water would need to be piped to new bathrooms and the kitchen. It was a big undertaking and Minnie prayed it would all go smoothly as well as quickly.

The older boys all appeared happy in their jobs and the two younger Stantons had settled nicely into school.

Echo had taken to doing the books like a duck to water, and still loved to play out with the little ones.

Adam had come into his own, finding himself a landlord and a very wealthy young man.

Her staff were happy in their roles within the household, and her husband Billy was content giving boxing lessons in a room lent by the chapel.

May had taken over the duties of housekeeping, which left Polly and Dickie. Their relationship was growing stronger by the day and Minnie's feeling was there could be a wedding announcement before too long. Polly was young yet to be thinking of marriage, she had only just turned fifteen, after all. However, that was a bridge to be crossed when reached.

Overall, Minnie considered herself fortunate, although worry for James was still uppermost in her mind. Unable to do anything about that now, she just had to wait for his return. Then they could discuss things more fully.

Minnie returned her empty cup to the kitchen and listened to the light-hearted banter taking place between the cooks.

* * *

Across town, James was still staring at the Hargreaves' residence. He knew the only way to get answers to his questions was to knock and ask them. Then again, did he really want to know? Could he face more arguments and tears? Would he feel so sorry for Fliss that he would take her back? If he did, it would most certainly upset his family and he couldn't risk that.

Turning, he ambled away, resigned to the fact that his questions would remain unanswered and now he had to get on with his life.

'You missed breakfast,' Minnie said as he walked into the kitchen.

James explained where he'd been and the reasons behind his early morning outing as Mabel prepared a plate of eggs and bacon for him.

'I guessed as much and that you'd come home rather than go to work,' Minnie said. 'James, lad, she ain't worth the worry.'

'I know, Mum, it's just that I don't understand what she hoped to gain.'

'Did you tell her about your inheritance?' Minnie asked, suddenly remembering she had planned to ask but had forgotten until now.

'No, why?'

'I wondered if that was what she was after, is all,' Minnie responded.

"Scuse me for interrupting, but it was all over the town about that money coming to your family,' Josie put in.

'So she could have known about it all along,' Minnie said.

Thanking Mabel for his food, James nodded. 'I suppose it's to be expected, nothing remains a secret for long.'

Minnie saw the look her son gave her and realised instantly he was recalling burying his father out on the heath even though, as it turned out, the man wasn't actually dead. He had been frozen stiff whilst lying in a drunken stupor out in the snow and James, Peter and Minnie had dug a hole and dropped him in it. They had fled the scene, terrified, when Gerald Fitch had moaned from the resting place intended for him. The point of it was that the neighbours discovered the truth somehow but had thankfully kept their counsel.

Minnie patted her son's shoulder, saying, 'The best thing is not to dwell on it. Clearly you two being together was not meant to be.' *Although I had once thought it to be the case.* Minnie kept the thought to herself.

'I'd best get off to the wharf and find Digit and our Peter,' James said.

Minnie nodded and watched her boy leave, a sadness settling on her heart. He'd had more than most to deal with in his young life, and Minnie prayed he would have some good luck now.

'I'm going to see the folks in Derry Street, Mum, I'll see you later,' Adam called out.

Minnie nodded. She smiled at his humility; Adam was still unable to call them his tenants, always referring to them as *folks* almost as though they were his friends.

As he strolled along in the sunshine, Adam's thoughts turned to Jill Ferguson, the woman who had lived out in the open with her four children. He had learned on his last visit that she had acquired a job in a small lock-making factory and was now paying rent along with all the others. A neighbour was looking after her offspring for a few pennies a week so she could go out to work. Adam had originally offered her a lifeline and she had grabbed it with both hands, hauling herself out of the murky depths of poverty. He was happy for her, and quietly proud of himself for that one good deed.

As he passed the allotment gardens he silently thanked the man who had made it possible. *I hope you are once again with your wife and you are both happy, Mr Jackson.*

37

The spring had slipped easily into summer and the unrelenting sun baked the earth solid. Birds sang endlessly and squirrels scampered up and down trees as though they were playing tag. Red kites flew high in the blue sky in a beautiful balletic dance, soaring and plummeting on the thermals.

Doors and windows were wedged open to allow a welcome flow of air through dark houses, and washing lines held an array of colours dazzling to the eye.

Children too young or poor to attend school screamed and laughed as they played in the streets whilst their mothers chatted over fences and at their gates. Windows were washed and brickwork cleaned as women fought their ongoing battle against the smoke-blackened grime from fires and furnaces.

The sun had brought with it a little joy; respite from the worry of poverty, empty bellies and the biting cold of winter.

Dickie Stanton sat back on his haunches to admire his handiwork on Mr Jackson's plot, for that was still how he thought of it. Green beans climbed wigwams of canes; rows of lettuce, cabbages, carrots, onions, potatoes, beetroot and shallots were helping feed the family who had been so kind to him. He smiled – they were his family now. They had welcomed him into the fold along with his brothers, his past sins forgiven and forgotten. For the first time in his life Dickie felt happy. He had some money in the bank and the most beautiful girl in the world as his sweetheart, the added bonus being her folks approved of the relationship. He had exchanged a few words with Adam as he had passed by and Dickie felt all was well with the world.

He listened a while to the noise emanating from the construction site further down in Steelhouse Lane. A new church was being built, not that Dickie could envisage himself visiting it unless it was to be wed. His smile returned at the thought and way off in the distance he could just make out the chime of St James' church bell calling the hour.

It was midday and Dickie opened his lunch kindly packed for him by Mabel. Leaning his back against the old rickety shed he determined he would build a new one and dedicate it to old Mr Jackson. After lunch he began work on Adam's plot and was happy to do so.

Meanwhile, at Reed House, a young woman sat in Una's kitchen. She had been sent by the Servants' Registry to apply for the post of maid.

Beneath shining black hair, steel grey eyes stared at the woman asking her questions.

'So how did you come by the name of Cherry?' Una asked.

'My mum liked cherries, it was all she wanted when she was pregnant with me,' the girl answered simply.

'It's a good job her craving wasn't for gooseberries,' Una quipped.

No smile graced the girl's lips at Una's attempt at comedy; her name was nothing to laugh at.

'The post is for a maid which includes cooking, cleaning and washing,' Una went on hurriedly. 'The salary is ten pounds per year plus bed and board.'

'It ain't much, is it?' Cherry Banks asked.

'It's what is on offer, take it or leave it.'

The girl nodded.

'Where have you been living?' Una probed.

'I used to rent a room at the back of the railway but I've been chucked out.'

'Why?'

'Because I had no job so I couldn't pay the rent,' Cherry answered honestly.

Una cast a glance at the battered old cardboard suitcase on the floor. 'That, I take it, contains all your worldly goods?'

One curt nod came in answer.

'I shall expect hard work and the utmost respect. I am the lady of the house, after all,' Una said with a glare which could sour milk.

'Fair enough,' Cherry responded.

'I am in recovery from a heart attack so I need to rest frequently, therefore you should be able to work under your own initiative.' Una gave a tired sigh in emphasis.

'I can do that.'

'Good. Then follow me and I will show you to your room.' Una pushed herself to her feet with the aid of an old walking cane she had found in the hall cupboard. She didn't need it, of course, but it all added to her persona of being an invalid. Showing her new maid to the room once used by Mrs Gibbs, she left Cherry to settle in.

'On this one occasion I will make tea, so be quick,' Una called over her shoulder as she went.

It took Cherry two minutes to toss her few clothes into the chest of drawers and stow her case on top of the wardrobe. Then she descended the stairs, having a good look around at the same time.

'There's tea in the pot before you start work,' Una said.

Cherry sat and poured herself a cup. 'I thought this was an orphanage,' she said conversationally.

'It was. Unfortunately, I had to close it due to my ill health.'

'Shame.' Cherry slurped the hot tea and Una grimaced. 'I'll get me a squint around so I know where everything is, then I'll start on tea. What do you fancy?'

'Something cold will do for this evening as the weather is so fine,' Una answered.

'Righto.' With that, Cherry jumped to her feet and began to look into cupboards and drawers, familiarising herself with the layout of the kitchen.

Una winced with each door that was banged shut.

'Quietly!' she boomed.

'What? Oh yes, all right,' the maid said with a little giggle.

'I will be in the office,' Una said already beginning to wonder if she had made a mistake in hiring the girl. She then hobbled away in search of peace, although in truth she felt better at having someone else in the house.

* * *

It was late afternoon when Adam passed by the allotments again, his jacket slung over his shoulder and his shirt sleeves rolled up.

'I wouldn't stay too long, Dickie. It looks like we might have a drop of rain,' he called, pointing to black clouds gathering overhead.

'I won't,' Dickie yelled back and smiled as he watched Adam move on towards home. 'Just another half an hour,' he mumbled to himself.

The sun disappeared behind the clouds rolling his way, and in the distance he heard a faint clap of thunder. The sky turned grey and an eerie darkness covered the land.

'Time to go,' Dickie muttered as he gathered the tools and shoved them into the shed. He closed the door firmly and as he turned to leave he saw a man cutting a cabbage free with a wicked looking knife.

38

'I wonder where Dickie is, it's not like him to be late back,' Polly said, clearly worried.

'I told him to get a move on when I saw the weather beginning to turn,' Adam said, but he could see his words held no comfort for his sister. 'Give him another half an hour and if he's not home I'll go and fetch him.'

'I'll come with you,' Peter said as he returned from the wharf.

'Me an' all,' Digit put in.

'All right, thanks,' Polly said but her eyes remained on the window looking out for her love. She could not know that Dickie was at that moment confronting the man stealing from the allotment.

'What do you think you're doing?' Dickie said angrily.

The man stood, the knife in his hand hanging by his side. 'I thought there was nobody here,' he said.

'Well, there is, and that's stealing!' Dickie yelled.

'Look, mate...' the man began.

'I'm not your mate, and there's no excuse for taking other people's belongings!' Dickie said venomously as he took a step forward.

Instantly the man raised the knife and Dickie stopped. 'It's only a cabbage; I don't want any trouble.'

'Then get off my land and don't come back!'

'I only wanted this to feed my family,' the man went on.

'If you had asked, I would have given it and more, besides...' his words trailed off as the man launched himself at Dickie, his fists raised. Dickie's eyes widened in disbelief as he felt a piercing pain in his stomach. He glared into the man's frightened eyes before looking down at the knife protruding from his belly. The confrontation was over in only a minute.

The man stepped back, and looking at his hands, he whimpered. 'Oh God! What have I done?'

Dickie's legs gave way and he fell to his knees as his hands moved to the source of his pain. 'For a cabbage...' he gasped.

The man, who was shaking uncontrollably, looked around him, not knowing what to do. Then he watched in horror as Dickie fell face first into the dirt. Forgetting the vegetable now, the man took to his heels.

Dickie lay on the ground in agony and felt the first raindrops cool his face. 'Polly...' he whispered. Unable to stand up again, Dickie felt his life blood draining away to be washed into the soil by the rain now coming down hard. 'Polly – I... love... you...' he whispered again before his eyes closed and his last breath left his body.

Wrapped against the weather, Adam, Peter and Digit ran up Major Street in search of Dickie. They were all worried now as it was so late.

It was Adam who saw the boy first.

'Dickie!' he yelled as he shot towards the prone figure.

'Oh Christ!' Peter said, panting hard. 'Is he...?'

Digit moved to where Adam knelt in the dirt, and together they gently turned the boy over.

'He's gone,' Digit confirmed as three pairs of eyes saw the knife simultaneously.

'Whatever could have happened?' Adam asked in disbelief.

'God knows, but we should get him home,' Peter answered.

'Look at this,' Digit said as he kicked the cabbage, 'it's been cut and left.'

'Do you think someone was stealing food?' Adam asked.

'That would be my guess, and I suspect Dickie challenged that person before...' Digit left the words unsaid.

Wiping the lashing rain from his face, Adam nodded. 'Come on, give me a hand.'

'Out of the way,' Digit said as he bent down and lifted the boy like he weighed nothing. Peter picked up the cabbage and stared at it. He shook his head in wonder at the terrible loss of life for a mere vegetable. He followed on in a daze as the others walked away sombrely.

Staring through the living room window, Polly

saw them coming and as she rushed into the hall she screeched at the top of her voice. 'Mum!' Then she dashed through the front door and out into the rain.

Minnie heard the urgent yell and she and the others ran into the hall to see what had happened. She heard her daughter scream, and saw her collapse into Adam's arms. Her eyes registered Digit carrying Dickie and stood back to allow him to come in.

Everyone gasped as they watched Digit carry the boy upstairs.

'Put him in Fliss's room,' Minnie said as she spotted the knife still sticking out of the boy's body. Then her attention went to Polly. Adam was half carrying his sister indoors, her wails loud in the silence of the hall.

'Dilys, fetch the police and the doctor,' she ordered, and the maid scampered away to get her shawl.

Adam took Polly to the living room, where he held her tightly as she sobbed. He understood exactly how she was feeling as he recalled how he felt that day he thought he had lost her forever.

'Ad,' Polly gasped.

'I know, love, I know,' was all he could manage.

His heart was breaking as he watched his sister's cries come from her soul. Was this what Mr Jackson had meant when he said Dickie would break Adam's heart? He had been right after all.

Digit left Dickie in Minnie's care and went to stand outside, allowing the rain to wash away the boy's blood.

Peter stood in the hall holding the cabbage, looking lost and confused.

The others returned to the kitchen, muttering to each other in shock.

It was not long before a constable arrived, and Peter showed him to the room where Minnie sat in silent vigil. He explained haltingly what they suspected might have happened as he thrust the vegetable forward.

The policeman made notes before saying, 'I'm sorry for your loss. We'll make some enquiries but it's unlikely anyone will have seen anything. They seldom do if it means having us on their doorstep, I'm afraid. We'll ask at the houses by the allotments though just in case.' Closing his little notebook, he cast a last glance at Dickie and shook his head. Then he left quietly.

He passed the doctor and Dilys in the hallway and pointed up the stairs. The doctor nodded, and Dilys took herself back to the kitchen.

Pronouncing Dickie dead from the stab wound, the doctor then said, 'The coroner will need to deal with him I'm afraid. I'll inform them and they'll come to collect him straight away.' With a shake of his head he added, 'Such a waste of a young life. Rest in peace, lad.'

Minnie saw the doctor out. 'I'll forward my bill,' he said as he donned his hat.

'Thank you,' Minnie replied, still in a state of shock.

Hearing Polly's cries, Diana had slipped from the classroom to see what the commotion was about. Told what had occurred, she returned to whisper to Celia, whose eyes immediately looked to Kit and Pip. Someone had to tell them their big brother was dead.

Adam stayed with Polly whilst the coroner's wagon came and went. His arms remained around her as she cried endless tears and his own fell at his sister's heartbreak. He knew it would take a very long time for her to get over this – if she ever could.

In the background, he heard Echo's wails also. The lad would be beside himself at Polly's distress, but someone else would have to comfort him, for Adam was not about to leave Polly.

Minnie entered quietly, bearing a tray. Placing it on a nearby table she looked at her sobbing children.

'Can I do anything?' Minnie asked, feeling wretched that she couldn't make everything right for her children.

Adam shook his head and gave her a grim little smile.

Minnie nodded, and she left as silently as she had entered.

In the kitchen, Echo was pacing and banging his head with his hands. He was wailing loudly, and Minnie rushed to wrap him in her arms.

'Echo, listen to me!' she said sharply.

The boy stilled and instantly stopped his noise.

Looking him in the eye, she tried to explain. 'Dickie has been stabbed and he's dead. Polly is crying and will do for quite a while, so we need to be supportive. She's very upset so she will need us close. Do you understand?'

Echo nodded.

'Good lad. Now let's have a nice cup of tea. Adam is looking after Polly.' Seeing May dissolve into tears she added, 'May needs you right now.'

Echo's eyes followed her finger, and he immediately went to the girl who was mopping her eyes.

'Don't cry, Echo's here,' he muttered as he led her to a chair and held her hand.

'You'll have to explain to Kit and Pip,' Mabel said.

'I'll do it now,' Minnie answered with a huge sigh.

'Boys, I have some bad news I'm afraid. Dickie was in a fight with someone at the allotment, we think and – he was stabbed. Adam, Digit and Peter found him and brought him home,' Minnie said as she crouched in front of Pip and Kit.

'Is he all right?' Kit asked in a panic.

'I'm sorry, lad, but he died.'

Kit lowered his head as tears rolled down his face, his young body lurching with each silent sob.

Pip's eyes went to his big brother and then he burst into tears himself, his little body heaving as he caught his breath. It was then that Kit let go and the boys howled out their pain like wounded animals.

Minnie wrapped them both in her arms and held them tight whilst they wept, her heart breaking at the utter distress they were suffering. They had no parents that she was aware of and now they had lost their big brother; Minnie's heart went out to them.

The Stanton brothers had begun to mourn the loss of their brother.

The others returned from work one by one and were told of the incident. Very few had an appetite that evening and all drifted away for an early night – all, that is, except Adam and Polly.

39

News of the murder travelled like wildfire. The police interviewed everyone who lived in Derry Street but to no avail. As they suspected, no one had seen a thing. Rather than have a bobby in the house, folk remained tight-lipped about anything that went on in their area. As a general rule it was fathers and husbands who dealt with any small problems, but murder was another thing entirely and no one wanted to become involved in any way. With no clues to follow, they were forced to close the case, and the coroner released the body for burial.

It transpired that Dickie had made a short will which he had left at the bank for safe keeping. He had left his inheritance to Polly. This discovery had been made by Minnie and Billy who had visited the bank to inform them of Dickie's unfortunate demise.

Polly lapsed into a strange stupor, wandering around the house like a lost soul. She ate sparingly and wasn't sleeping well. Adam was dreadfully worried for her, but he knew only time would help heal her wounds.

Minnie arranged and paid for the funeral which was to take place two days hence. She wanted it over and done with as quickly as possible so her daughter might begin to recover.

The mood was sombre at Marshall's, with everyone being careful about what they said for fear of upsetting Polly, Kit and Pip further.

As they sat as usual in the living room after everyone had retired for the night, Polly said to her brother, 'I still can't understand, Adam.'

'It doesn't make sense to us, Polly, because we're well fed. If whoever did it was starving then it's easier to see why they were stealing.'

'But why kill him?'

'I suspect, and it's only a guess, mind, that Dickie challenged the person. They may have got into a fracas and then – it would have been an unfortunate accident,' Adam said.

'It doesn't make it any easier to bear though,' Polly said through her tears.

'I can only imagine what you're going through, sis, but would Dickie want you to grieve for the rest of your life?'

'No, I don't suppose he would,' she muttered.

'Once he's laid to rest maybe you can begin to re-member the good times you had together,' Adam said wisely.

'I hope so.' Polly gave her brother a hug and went to her bed.

Adam lingered a while, his thoughts centred on the boy he had come to like. Dickie had turned his life around for it only to be snatched away in a tragic accident. The fates could be very cruel at times.

* * *

Although he was sad about Dickie's death and worried for Polly, James was still troubled by Fliss's behaviour. The whole debacle wouldn't let him rest, so the following morning he pulled Adam aside after breakfast.

'Will you come with me to Fliss's parents' house, Adam? I have to know what's going on and why she lied to me. It's eating away at me.'

'I don't think it's such a good idea, but if you have to do this then you shouldn't do it alone.'

'Should we tell Mum where we're going?' James asked.

'I think so, yes. Come on, let's go now.'

Minnie was not happy when her sons explained where they were off to. 'You should just let sleeping dogs lie,' she said.

'Minnie, I know you're worried,' Billy said 'but James is determined, so...'

At her nod he added, 'Just be careful.'

The two young men stopped at the allotment to say a quiet prayer for the departed soul of Dickie Stanton before moving on in earnest.

Eventually arriving at their destination, Adam asked, 'Are you sure you want to do this?'

'Yes, I *have* to get some answers, Adam, then I can let go.'

Rapping the knocker, they waited. A moment later the door was opened by a pretty young maid.

'We've come to see Felicity Hargreaves,' Adam said when he noted his brother's tongue was tied.

'Come in, please,' the maid said. 'If you will wait here I will see if she's available.'

Looking around them, they marvelled at the splendour of the hallway. Paintings adorned the walls and thick curtains hung at the windows.

'May I help you, gentlemen?' A tall man with greying hair and a thick moustache stood before them.

'We're here to see Fliss,' James croaked.

'I am Felicity's father, Norvin Hargreaves. May I ask what you want with my daughter?' Mr Hargreaves asked as his eyes took in James's work clothes.

'Mr Hargreaves, this is James and I am Adam Fitch. Please be assured we are not here to cause trouble, but we would like to ask Felicity some questions.'

'Relating to what exactly?'

'Well, sir – this could take some time,' Adam replied.

'Follow me,' Mr Hargreaves said, leading them

into a comfortable sitting room. 'Sit and explain yourselves.'

Adam took a deep breath and began to relate the reason for their visit.

'I sincerely doubt what you are saying is true, young man. Felicity has been away visiting friends down south and has only recently returned.'

'I'm sorry to tell you, sir, that she has lied to you. She has been living at Marshall's the whole time,' Adam said respectfully.

'I can't believe what you have told me! My daughter would not lie to me, nor would she threaten a maid with a knife. As for stealing clothes – she has more in her wardrobe than there is in a London store!'

'She said she was pregnant and I was the father, then when confronted she owned up that it was yet another lie!' James burst out.

'Dear God, this just gets worse!' Norvin bellowed. 'I'm not sure what you young men hope to gain from this but if it's money...'

'Mr Hargreaves, we are not after financial remuneration – we have money and property of our own,' Adam assured the irate man. 'We only wish to have answers to James's questions. Once we have those, we will leave you in peace and you will never see us again.'

Norvin's eyes bored into the Fitch brothers then he stood and yanked on the bell pull at the side of the fireplace.

A moment later the pretty maid entered and bent her knee.

'Fetch my daughter please,' Norvin said. With another bob the maid left.

'We shall see who is lying when Felicity joins us,' he added.

'She will deny it all, sir,' Adam said confidently. 'May I ask that you watch her reactions when she sees us here and if and when she gives answers to any questions put to her?'

Mr Hargreaves nodded curtly.

The door opened again and in swept Felicity. She stopped dead in her tracks and visibly paled when she spotted the visitors.

Adam glanced at her father, who nodded. Mr Hargreaves had indeed noted her surprise.

'Felicity, take a seat, there are questions to answer and I want the truth from you, my girl!'

Felicity dropped onto an overstuffed armchair, a sullen look on her countenance.

For an hour she denied all the accusations levelled at her as was expected. Then Adam asked Mr Hargreaves, 'Was your daughter wearing a white blouse and a brown skirt the day she returned?'

'Yes, she was, in point of fact. I have to say, I thought it unusual not to see her in one of her fine dresses, but how did you know that?'

'Because those clothes were lent to her by our sister, sir, her own one dress being in the wash,' Adam said.

Father and daughter stared at each other and Felicity burst into tears. It was then he knew she was guilty of everything.

'Why?' Norvin asked. 'You lied to everyone, why would you do these things you have been accused of?'

'Daddy...' Felicity began.

Adam and James shared a knowing look. Felicity Hargreaves was a spoiled brat, clearly used to having all her own way.

'Why, Felicity?' her father demanded.

'I want to be mistress of my own house!' Turning

to James she went on, 'You inherited a fortune, I heard tell. We could have been married and bought a big house where I could have had maids, a cook and a butler!'

'Oh, Fliss, you are so wrong,' James said, 'I inherited, yes, but it was not a fortune. That was Adam. You targeted the wrong brother.'

'What! But I was told...'

'You were lied to and now you know how that feels.' Adam felt no sympathy for the girl as he spoke.

Felicity stared from one face to another in disbelief.

'Are you satisfied, James, that you have your answers?' Adam asked.

James nodded.

'Mr Hargreaves, I am sorry that we brought this upset to your door, but you can see now why we had to,' Adam said.

Norvin nodded. 'Be assured, gentlemen, that I will deal with my daughter appropriately. I extend my thanks for drawing my attention to this and my sorrow at the hurt and upset Felicity caused within your household.'

The brothers stood and quietly left the house. They heard Felicity's cries and her father's shouts as they walked away.

'Feel better now, brother?' Adam asked.

'Yes. Thank you, Adam, I could never have managed that as well as you did.'

'Mum is going to want to know every detail, you know,' Adam said with a grin.

'What's her saying again? *The ins and outs of Meg's arse!*' James said.

The boys burst out laughing as they walked home in the sunshine.

40

It was the morning of Dickie's funeral and Celia and Diana elected to stay home with the children. Pip and Kit were given leave to attend. Mabel, Dilys and Josie also remained behind to prepare lunch.

Everyone gathered in the hall dressed in black or dark clothing following the lead of Queen Victoria who had adopted the tradition, and Polly went to Adam. He nodded and she linked her arm through his. Then Minnie led the procession forward. They walked in silence until they reached the church. Skirting the building itself they made their way to the cemetery where Dickie's coffin sat on a bier at the side of the grave plot.

Crowding around, they listened to the vicar's solemn voice and Minnie kept an eye on Polly, who was leaning against Adam for support.

As the coffin was lifted by its straps and lowered into the ground, Kit and Pip sobbed quietly as they watched their brother's box disappear.

Polly's unearthly wail echoed across the grave-yard and Adam caught her as her knees gave way.

Digit was there in a second and he scooped her up into his strong arms. Catching Minnie's eye, he tilted his head and she nodded. To Adam, he said, 'Come on.'

Walking away in sad silence, the two took a distraught Polly home. Digit carried her every step of the way, his face grim as Polly sobbed onto his chest.

Depositing her in a chair in the living room at last, Digit said, 'Tea.'

Adam smiled briefly – Digit remained a man of few words.

It was Dilys who delivered the tray before silently ducking out of the room.

'You were very brave today,' Adam said as he poured the tea.

Polly dried her eyes and accepted the cup. 'He's gone, Ad – forever,' she whispered.

'I know, but now it's time to heal. It won't happen overnight, we all know that, but gradually you will remember him with fondness as your life takes shape again.'

'Dickie mentioned marriage before...' Polly began.

'I guessed, and we would all have been pleased for you, Pol,' Adam assured her.

She gave him a little smile and he went on, 'Let's celebrate his life rather than the loss. We can keep his memory alive by talking about him. No one should be afraid to speak his name in front of you for fear of upsetting you. Don't you agree?'

Polly nodded and dabbed her eyes once more.

'Good. Drink your tea and tell me more about Dickie and the good times you had together.'

* * *

Over in St James' Square the following day, the arguments were still raging. Felicity's mother had taken to her bed in utter disgust at her daughter's behaviour, leaving her husband to deal with the girl.

'I still cannot believe you stooped so low!' Norvin Hargreaves growled.

'Daddy, I've explained why I wanted to marry James!' Felicity snapped.

'Yes, but to go about it in that manner! You lied to us, Felicity – your own parents!'

'I know, but I have apologised so there's no point in saying it again,' she said with a bored expression.

'I can see that we should have been stricter with you during your formative years,' Norvin said, completely ignoring her statement.

'Well, it's too late now,' Felicity said offhandedly.

'Felicity!' Norvin barked.

'Look, Daddy, it's all over and done with so can't we just forget it?' she asked, totally unconcerned that her father was still furious with her.

'We most certainly cannot! You appear to be oblivious to the mayhem you have caused that family.' Norvin was pacing the sitting room, doing his best to control his temper.

'They'll get over it,' Felicity commented.

'If this becomes common gossip it will besmirch

our good name, Felicity! Once that happens you will have no chance of finding a decent husband.'

'I don't care,' she replied sulkily.

'You will when people will have nothing to do with you! Besides which, it will reflect very badly on your mother and me.'

Felicity blew out her cheeks in a long drawn out sigh. It was looking increasingly likely that she was stuck here for the duration whilst her father ranted on. Staring out of the window, she shut out Norvin's voice and allowed her thoughts to roam.

This was all the fault of that damned maid! If she had kept her mouth shut then none of this would have happened, and she would still be on course to marry James Fitch.

James had said he had money but not the fortune she had expected. She wondered just how much he *did* have. Then she turned her mind back to Dilys. That girl was going to pay one way or another.

Snapping her attention back, she heard her father say, 'Therefore, your mother and I have agreed – we are sending you to a convent.'

'What?' Felicity couldn't believe what she was

hearing. 'A convent! Daddy, you're not being serious surely?'

'I am indeed, Felicity – deadly serious. Get used to the idea, because you are going to be taken into the penitentiary of the Sisters of Mercy Convent where you will be taught how to become a penitent and see the error of your ways.'

* * *

Whilst Dickie Stanton's funeral had been taking place, Cherry had been visiting the market.

Now, the morning after, she was relating to her employer what she'd seen.

Una Reed was listening to her new maid prattling on.

'Another one gone in the ground,' she said. 'I passed the funeral on my way back from the market yesterday morning.'

Una didn't really care two hoots who had shuffled off their mortal coil.

'It was a white coffin,' Cherry went on, 'but it was a big one.'

An older child then. *Ah well, one less mouth to feed,*

Una thought. Then she had a sudden notion – was it someone from Marshall's? She shook the idea away – it could have been anyone, after all, this was a large town. Poverty had taken many to their graves and it would take a great many more.

'It's a shame,' Cherry continued, 'you know, that some people have to die so young, I mean.'

'Are you always so talkative?' Una asked sharply.

'Oh, yes. My mum, God rest her soul, used to say I could talk the hind leg off a donkey. It's a strange expression that is, isn't it?'

Una sighed. She could always get rid of the girl if the chatter became too much, but then she'd find herself alone again. Cherry might be noisy but at least she was company.

'I'll see if I can find out who it was,' the maid said, bringing Una's attention back to her once more.

'Who what was?' Una asked her head beginning to spin in confusion.

'The burial – somebody will know.'

'Oh, yes.'

'There you go – breakfast,' Cherry said with a beaming smile.

Una was surprised when she saw it actually

looked appetising. Two poached eggs, toast and marmalade.

'When you've had that, you and I are going out for a stroll.'

'I'm not sure...' Una began.

'Pfft! You need exercise. We don't want you getting fat and lazy.'

Una bristled, but then decided the girl was probably right. Besides, they needn't go far and when she was tired they could return either on foot or by cab.

'We'll enjoy the sunshine, then I'll do the dishes when we get back whilst you have a rest.'

Una nodded and continued to eat. Initially the thought of going for a walk had unnerved her; what if her heart gave out completely? Brushing the thought aside, she knew the best way to regain her health would be good food and exercise as the doctor had ordered. Besides, she had Cherry to lean on now and there was always the possibility of picking up snippets of gossip as they went. If you wanted to know anything in this town then tittle-tattle was the way to find out. Maybe a jaunt out would be just the thing after all.

41

Over in St James' Square, Felicity had spent the night plotting and planning, and up in her room she decided she would have to run away, now it was clear her father was persisting with his ridiculous idea. First, however, she had to make Dilys pay for bringing her to this. Packing a bag with essentials, she settled down to wait. What she had in mind would have to be carried out tonight under the cover of darkness.

There was no telling when Norvin would send her away, so she couldn't afford to wait to exact her revenge. She planned to steal away when it was dark enough, taking her bag with her. Once she had dealt with that stupid maid, she would flee the town. There were many other places she could live where her father wouldn't be able to find her. However, she would need money, and at the moment she had none, but Norvin had plenty.

Thinking through her plan logically she knew she would have to search her father's office in order to pilfer enough funds to enable her to live comfortably in whichever town she ended up in. She felt sure he would keep some cash in there for the household expenses; certainly enough for her to get away free and clear.

Happy in the knowledge that by tomorrow she would be away from this house and her parents, and having avenged herself, Felicity lay on her bed with an evil smile on her face. All she had to do now was to find the money and then stay out of sight until nightfall.

* * *

Around mid-morning, Josiah Holbrook arrived at Marshall's with scrolls of paper tucked under his arm. He was ushered into the office by Minnie and

Adam, who were excited to see the plans for the extension. Billy had joined them at Minnie's request, and having no students for his boxing class until later in the day he was happy to do so. Dilys followed with a tray of tea before disappearing back to her work.

'Firstly, please accept my condolences on your loss. As you may already know, the news is all around the town. It's a sorry business.'

Minnie nodded her thanks as Adam voiced his.

'It's always sad when a member of your family passes away, but under circumstances such as those... Dickie may be gone but he will not be forgotten, and he would want us to move on with our lives, I'm sure,' Billy said as he pointed to the scrolls.

Unrolling the papers, he laid them out on the desk.

'You were quick doing all this,' Minnie said as she scanned the drawings, but in truth she couldn't make head nor tail of them.

'I was aware of the urgency of the project, Minnie, that the extension be completed as soon as possible,' Josiah said with a smile. 'As you will see, I have made two copies, one for yourselves and one for your builders. I would be most happy to oversee the construction if you so wish.'

'I think that would be for the best, Mum, don't you, just to make sure all goes to plan,' Adam said.

'I agree,' Minnie said nodding her head.

'Then let me walk you through these drawings and we can make any adjustments as we go,' Josiah said.

As it turned out, Minnie and Adam were delighted with the drawings as they were, and hardly any amendments were needed.

'I have taken the liberty of asking Ray Rewcastle to join us at midday, Minnie, I do hope you don't mind.'

'Not at all, it makes sense to thrash it out all in one go,' she replied.

'He can then take a look at these,' Josiah tapped a finger on the plans, 'and give you a price. Having an estimate in mind, I can tell you whether his offer is fair for the work undertaken.'

'Marvellous!' Adam said enthusiastically.

'If you decide to employ the Rewcastles, Ray will then give you a date for starting.'

'The sooner the better,' Minnie mumbled.

The three chatted on about the new extension and Josiah explained his thoughts on the best way to go about it which would cause the least amount of disruption.

At twelve on the dot, Ray Rewcastle was shown into the office. After exchanging greetings, he studied the plans carefully.

'Aye, we could do this nae bother,' he said, his Geordie accent coming through. 'Ah think if the main extension is built first like, then the residents in the room allocated for that bathroom can move over.' He tapped lightly to indicate the room he spoke of – the one Adam shared with Joe Blunt. 'It'll be easy then to turn that room into a second bathroom.'

'That was precisely our thinking,' Josiah agreed.

Taking out a notebook and retrieving the pencil stored behind his ear, Ray scratched out some calculations as the others looked on. The Geordie muttered under his breath as he took into consideration the number of rooms, their sizes, roughly how many bricks and roof tiles would be needed, bathroom fittings and fixtures, piping, plaster – the list went on and on.

Eventually his pencil came to a halt. 'Ah think

that's everything. I've included our charges so there's only one bill to pay, all right hinney?' he said to Minnie as he passed over his notebook.

Minnie gasped at the amount and Adam and Billy took a look before Josiah did the same.

'Bloody hell, it's a lot, ain't it?' Minnie gasped.

'It's a lot of work, but it's a very fair price, Minnie,' Josiah assured her.

'Adam, it's up to you, lad, it is your money after all. What do you think, Billy?' Minnie asked, with a silent prayer her son would agree.

Billy nodded his agreement.

'I only have one question,' Adam said and as all eyes turned to him he went on, 'When can you start?'

Minnie breathed a sigh of relief and everyone shook hands to seal the deal.

'Ah'll get my lads over tomorrow to make a start on the footings,' Ray said. 'Ah'll go across to the brick works and put in my order, then it will be all systems go.' His notebook in his pocket, pencil in place behind his ear once more and his copy of the plan under his arm, Ray said, 'Thanks very much to ya all, it's come at just the right time for my family.'

'For us too, Ray,' Adam said with a warm smile.

'We've had no work on for a couple of weeks now; people canna afford it. I was beginning to worry for my bairns but this job will see us through. Ah'm very grateful.'

Ray took his leave, as did Josiah, saying he would be back bright and early the following morning.

Minnie and Adam returned to the kitchen to inform the others that work would start the next day. They knew there would be little disruption to the household for the time being, as all the work would be going on outside. The land had to be cleared and the foundations dug out so there would be no inconvenience to the everyday life of those indoors. All were excited at the prospect – all, that is, except Polly, who sat staring into space. Adam worried for her, but he could do nothing to ease her pain at losing Dickie.

Peter had informed them he had decided to take over the allotments again before they were overrun by weeds, but James and Digit said it was not safe for him to be alone there. So it was agreed they would join him to keep both Peter and their produce safe from thieves. They didn't think for a minute that

Dickie's murderer would be back, but they wanted to be safe not sorry.

Echo stayed close to Polly and tried not to fret about her distress. All he knew was his *lady* was hurting and he couldn't make it better.

With the others in work and the little ones in class, Echo maintained his silent vigil at Polly's side. Then he had a thought and, grabbing a basket, he dashed out of the back door. He was gone a while, and when he returned the basket was full of willow twigs and flowers. Sitting on the floor in the corner so as not to be in the way, he began to intertwine the things he had collected.

Minnie watched him from the corner of her eye, wondering what the lad was up to now. She didn't have to wait too long to find out.

Echo had produced a rough but pretty wreath which he presented to Polly. 'Later?'

Polly's eyes misted over at the gift. 'Thank you, Echo, will you come with me?'

Echo nodded eagerly. He would accompany Polly to lay the little wreath on Dickie's grave.

Mabel stifled back a tear and Minnie sniffed. What a lovely thing to do for her grieving daughter.

Yet again her mind insisted this boy was no dimwit. His body held a heart of gold and his brain worked perfectly well when given the opportunity.

Polly hung the wreath on a nail hammered into the back door and her hand brushed gently over the wildflowers. Then she gave Echo a hug in thanks for his thoughtfulness. His face beamed in pleasure and a moment later he was sweeping up the mess he'd left in the corner.

42

It was after midnight and all was dark and silent in the Hargreaves house. Felicity slipped from her room with her bag and locked the door behind her, dropping the key into her coat pocket. That way everyone would think she was still sulking and leave her alone.

Tiptoeing to the study, she put down her bag whilst she rifled through the desk drawers as quietly as possible in search of money. She was thankful there was a moon which cast enough silvery beams for her to see what she was doing.

Having stayed in her room and out of her father's way for fear of further arguments, Felicity had had to trust to luck that there would be some funds kept here. It stood to reason Norvin would ensure household expenses were to hand. If not, her plans would be scuppered and she would have to think on her feet.

She smiled when she found what she was looking for, and pushed the pound notes into her pocket alongside the key. Grabbing her bag, she checked she had left everything as it was. Satisfied, she left the room, closing the door with a click. It seemed to echo loudly and Felicity winced.

Going to the kitchen, she grabbed a large knife still lying on its chopping board. Shoving it into her bag, she returned to the hall, casting her eyes around to ensure she was still alone. Without further ado, she crept across to the front door, unlocking it carefully before stepping out into the chill of the night. Closing the door behind her, she jumped from the step onto the soft lawns. With the grass muffling her tread she made her escape.

The streets were lit only by occasional pools of light from the gas lamps. Fliss kept to the shadows as she walked quickly. She wanted to be in position before dawn.

As she went, her eyes darted about, keeping watch for patrolling policemen. If she was discovered she would be escorted home and her plan would be foiled. Moreover, if she was found with a knife in her bag it would certainly take some explaining at the very least.

Suddenly a bright red glow lit up the sky and she stopped dead in her tracks. Steadying her breathing, she realised it was the furnaces opening their doors, something that was done every night, but being at home she never usually saw.

Fliss moved on stealthily from one shadow to the next, her heart beating rapidly. She wanted to run but knew that would be foolish and suspicious. If she walked and was challenged about being out in the middle of the night, she would say she was catching the milk train to Birmingham.

Eventually she arrived at her destination – Marshall's. As with everywhere else, the place was in darkness. All would be in their beds sleeping peacefully. Skirting the building, she hid herself in the privy. Taking the knife from her bag, she settled in for a long wait.

What she didn't know was that in the silver

moonbeams, Polly Fitch, sleepless with grief, had been watching her every step.

* * *

Dilys was up early, dressed and eager to use the privy first before the rush. When she entered the kitchen, she was surprised to see Polly sitting at the table with the first rays of sunshine through the window lighting her face.

'God, Polly! You gave me a start!'

Polly slipped a finger to her lips to shush the girl then beckoned with her finger. In hushed tones she explained what she'd witnessed during the night.

'Bloody hell!' Dilys gasped.

'Go and rouse our Adam and tell him and Joe to come quick,' Polly whispered urgently.

Dilys shot from the room and moments later, still dressed in their pyjamas, the young men appeared.

Polly related again what she'd seen.

'Is it Fliss, do you think?' Adam asked.

'I couldn't see that clearly but it was definitely a woman. She went round the back of the house and didn't emerge again,' Polly said keeping her voice low.

'It's her, I know it is. She's come to properly do me in!' Dilys said in a panic.

'Quiet, Dilys!' Adam urged. 'Let's think this through. If it is Fliss and she's here with intent to harm, then we need to be careful. Whoever is out there it's likely they're in the privy because there's nowhere else to hide themselves. Dilys, fetch Rodney and Digit because we don't know which side of the privy block that person is in.'

Again, Dilys did as she was bid. Once the other two had joined them, Adam laid out his plan.

'Dilys, you will need to go out first, but don't worry because I'll be right behind you. Digit and Rodney, you check the other side quickly and if you find nothing then come to our aid. Polly, you fetch Mum and Billy and tell them what's afoot.'

The maid began to shake as she recalled Fliss holding a knife to her face once before and she was petrified it might happen again. Adam laid a hand on her arm. 'It'll be all right, you'll see. Once we catch whoever it is, we'll call in the police.'

Nodding, Dilys unlocked the back door and walked

to the lavatory building, the others in her wake. Digit and Rodney moved to the right as Dilys and Adam went to the left. At Adam's nod, they all rushed in.

Fliss was on her feet in an instant. She had been taken by surprise but had still raised her arm, brandishing the knife.

'The game's up, Fliss,' Adam said as Rodney and Digit pushed their way inside to stand behind him.

Polly, Minnie and Billy were now in the yard, also still in their nightclothes. They could hear Adam talking quietly as he shoved Dilys back behind him. Escaping to the safety of her employer outside she gasped, 'It's Fliss and she's got a knife!'

Minnie's hand covered her mouth, the other holding her shawl ends together.

'Somebody get James, we'll dress then he can fetch her father,' Billy said.

'Oh God, Adam!' Minnie breathed.

'Don't worry, my love, I'll get him out and I won't take any chances with a knife.' With that he strode to the privy.

'Adam, back away, lad, let me deal with this,' Billy said calmly.

Adam did as he was bid, all the time keeping his eyes on the knife in Fliss's hand. Digit and Rodney moved out into the yard to give Adam room to retreat.

In no time at all, Adam had joined James and they were running hell for leather for St James' Square.

'Fliss, put down the knife,' Billy coaxed.

Shaking her head, Fliss hissed her contempt. She felt like a like a rat caught in a corner, so she tried to force her way out with a stabbing motion.

Billy took a step back. He saw her eyes roll back in her head for an instant and then they took on a gleam which made Billy shudder. He had to be even more careful as he realised the girl's mind had turned quite mad.

'You cannot win, Fliss, you're trapped,' Billy continued calmly in an effort to persuade the girl to relinquish her weapon.

Fliss, however, was having none of it. 'How did you know I was here?' Her voice sounded like a rasp on metal.

'You were seen,' Billy answered.

'That's impossible! It was dark and I was careful,' Fliss said, jabbing the knife forward again.

'You weren't careful enough though, Fliss.'

'I don't really care, anyway,' she said as she waved her weapon from side to side. 'Whatever happens one of you will pay for what you've done to me!'

'This is not the way. You need to drop the knife and come out where we can discuss this in more comfortable surroundings,' Billy cajoled.

'No! You send that maid in here. It was she who dropped me in this mess in the first place!'

Billy could see her agitation and he kept a wary eye on the blade glinting every now and then in the poor light coming in through the doorway.

Billy tried again. 'If you persist with this you will be in big trouble. We may have to bring in the constabulary.'

'You can do whatever you like, I don't give a damn!' Fliss yelled, then in a sing-song voice added, 'All I want is the maid.'

'Well, you can't have her, so make up your mind – are you coming out or not?'

'Not!'

'Have it your own way.' Billy stepped back,

slammed the door shut and turned the key in the lock, which Rodney had filched from the inside.

Almost immediately there came a bang to the door and Fliss's loud screams roused the rest of the household.

43

Completely unaware of the goings on at Marshall's, Una was reading the newspaper as she awaited her breakfast.

She tutted loudly as she read the article. Oscar Wilde had received a two-year sentence of hard labour for 'unlawfully committing acts of gross indecency with certain male persons'.

'It's unnatural,' she muttered, 'he got what he deserved.'

'Who did?' Cherry asked.

Una read the article out loud for the maid's benefit.

'Who's Oscar Wilde?'

'He's an Irish poet and playwright,' Una said with a sigh at the girl's ignorance.

'Well, he'll have no time to write anything else for the next two years if he got hard labour,' Cherry said flippantly.

Sausage and scrambled egg with onion was placed before her and Una nodded her thanks. She put the paper aside as Cherry sat down to her own morning meal.

'We'll have a wander around the boating park after...'

'No!' Una snapped. Seeing the girl's face crumple, she explained, 'That was where I had my heart attack.'

'It was your heart that attacked you, not the boating lake,' Cherry said calmly.

'All right,' Una acquiesced, despite still feeling a little unsure.

Cherry cleared the table, saying, 'Get your hat on. It's hot out there already.'

Una wandered away to the hall closet to pull out her straw boater. Fixing it in place in front of the mirror it occurred to her that the roles had been reversed since Cherry had arrived just a few days ago. Unsure how she felt about that, she stared at her own image. She saw she was looking old, and it frightened her. Age had crept up without her even noticing it. What else had she missed whilst working herself half to death in this place? Marriage was the first thing to spring to mind. After she and Billy Marshall had drifted apart and a wedding wasn't at all likely, Una had dedicated herself to the orphanage. With no husband, she had denied herself the possibility of having children of her own. Mind you, that point did not unduly distress her after years of taking care of other people's brats.

Happiness. Had she ever been truly happy? She thought not, and now she couldn't envisage it in her future. Making the best of a bad lot is all she could hope for.

'Yes, you look lovely,' Cherry said with a grin. 'So, stop admiring yourself and let's get gone.'

Grabbing a parasol each from the umbrella stand, they left and Una locked the door behind them.

Stopping frequently as Cherry gossiped with women she knew, Una saw the girl in a new light.

She was courteous and polite and appeared to know everyone.

During one of these conversations, Una was shocked to learn it had been Dickie Stanton who had been laid to rest. How ironic that he was stabbed to death whilst trying to protect the very allotment he had once wrecked.

Una kept the thought to herself as they strolled on. Eventually they came to the bandstand in East Park and sat to rest.

'Shame about that kid being stabbed like that,' Cherry said.

'He was a rogue,' Una answered.

'Did you know him, then?'

'Yes, he was in the orphanage with his two brothers for a while.' Una hadn't planned on telling the tale of the boys absconding, but she found herself doing so nevertheless. Somehow she was finding it easy to talk to this girl; something she'd never experienced before and it left her with a feeling of something akin to happiness. Maybe this was what she had needed all along – a friend.

Moving on, they meandered around the boating lake and it came to Una that she was enjoying herself. Was this the closest thing to being happy she would get? Whatever the case, she decided to grab it with both hands and hold on for dear life.

* * *

Over at Marshall's, Norvin Hargreaves, along with James and Adam, had arrived by cab and went instantly to the kitchen. With everyone now dressed, he was ushered outside to where Fliss's screams still echoed around the yard.

Unlocking the privy door, Billy stood back and the girl's noise ceased.

Opening the door, Norvin stepped inside.

'You stay away from me!' Fliss was heard to say. There were muffled voices then the sound of a sharp slap. Norvin dragged his daughter outside by her arm, the knife in his other hand. Fliss was struggling and crying but he paid her no heed. Passing the weapon to Billy, handle first, he asked, 'May we come inside?'

Billy nodded and they entered the kitchen once more. Still holding Fliss by the arm he forced her onto a chair. 'You stay there! Don't you dare move so much as a muscle!'

Turning, he addressed Billy again as the head of the household. 'Sir, you have my profound apologies...'

'It's Dilys you should apologise to, Mr Hargreaves, it was she who Fliss came to hurt,' Billy said.

Norvin inclined his head and looked at the maid. 'Dilys, my sincerest apologies for what you have suffered at the hand of my daughter. Could I beg your indulgence not to call in the police regarding this matter please?'

'What about if she comes at me again?' Dilys asked, clearly afraid of the prospect.

'I promise that will not happen. Yesterday I arranged, by telephone, passage on a ship bound for Ireland where I will see Felicity into the hands of the Sisters of Mercy convent penitentiary.'

'Oh, right,' Dilys muttered, almost feeling sorry for the girl, 'fair enough then.'

'My thanks.' Grabbing Felicity by the arm once more he said, 'Come, our ship awaits.'

As he swept her from the house, the mumblings began.

* * *

Due to the Fliss debacle, breakfast was later than usual and those with jobs to go to ate bacon sandwiches on route. As all the others settled down again, whistling could be heard outside. The Rewcastles had arrived and had begun their work.

Dilys was sent with a tray of tea and came back all of a lather. 'The boys are stripped to the waist and their muscles... Ooh, I feel quite faint.' As her hand went to her brow, everyone burst out laughing at her theatrics, but one by one the women nipped outdoors to have a quick look – all except Polly.

Throughout the day, the young men working under Josiah's supervision laughed and joked with those bringing a constant supply of tea and homemade lemonade. They whistled and sang and worked non-stop. They didn't leave until the sun began to sink behind the horizon.

Ray and his five sons were working like Trojans to get the foundations laid before the first of the bricks were to be delivered.

Adam enlisted Echo's help working out figures to purchase new furniture, as the old, which had been stacked outside, had been ruined by the weather. It could be ordered when they knew when the extension was going to be completed and ready for use.

One evening, as Polly and Adam sat together having their usual chat, she said, 'I wonder how Fliss is getting on in the convent.'

'Do you really wonder? Personally, I don't care. I know it sounds callous but after what she did to our James it would take an awful lot for me to even consider forgiveness,' Adam said.

Polly was surprised at her brother's words; Adam was the most forgiving of all the family. Thinking about what he'd said, she found herself agreeing with him to an extent. 'I know what you mean – but a convent?'

'Pol, even her father didn't trust her any more. Clearly he thought it was in her best interests. Anyway, forget Fliss, and tell me how you are.'

'I'm all right, why?' Polly asked, puzzled at his question.

'I was worried stiff for you after Dickie passed, but you seem a little easier with it now,' Adam responded.

'I am. That day Echo and I laid the wreath on

Dickie's grave I felt – lighter somehow. I said my goodbyes then, and knew Dickie would want me to get on with my life. I'll never forget him, Ad, but the pain lessens with each day.'

'I'm glad to hear that. None of us will forget him, that's for sure. Pol, did you know Harlan Rewcastle has been asking about you?'

'No, I didn't,' Polly said with a blush.

'Well, he has, and I don't know if you're aware but May and Trevor Rewcastle appear to have become something of an item.'

'No!' Polly gasped in amused disbelief.

Adam nodded with a grin.

'What does Arthur say about that? Is he employing his big brother tactics?' Polly asked.

'Apparently he's fine with it as long as Trevor behaves himself.'

'How did I not notice that?' Polly asked almost to herself.

'It's no wonder, with everything else that's been going on around here lately,' Adam replied. 'Do you think you've been neglecting May a little? Maybe you should talk to her more like you used to.'

'You're right, Adam. I will, starting tomorrow.'

After Adam went to his bed, Polly sat thinking about what he'd said. In the nicest possible way, he'd pointed out that she had been wrapped up in her own misery for so long she had been oblivious to the goings on around her. She felt a twinge of guilt at being so thoughtless, but Dickie's death had hit her hard and she had needed time to mourn.

Then she recalled what Adam had told her regarding Harlan Rewcastle asking after her. A tiny smile lifted the corners of her mouth and she felt a flutter in her stomach.

For goodness' sake, Polly Fitch, stop mooning about and get yourself to bed!

Jumping to her feet, she checked all was safe and well in the room before heading for the stairs, but she couldn't help the smile forming as she went.

44

It was a few days later and Norvin Hargreaves kept a careful eye on his daughter as they waited in the sitting room whilst the maid packed her mistress's clothes and saw the bags stowed onto the waiting cab. Then he grabbed Felicity's arms and led her outside, shoving her roughly into the carriage.

'Monmore Green Station please, cabbie,' he called out before climbing aboard himself.

Father and daughter had not spoken a word to each other since their return from Marshall's. Norvin was afraid he might strike her if he dared open his mouth. Instead, he had locked her in her room day and night to ensure she stayed where he could find her.

Felicity's mother, Verity, had suffered an attack of the vapours and taken to her bed, unwilling to face the terrible family upset. She refused to move until everything had settled down once more, never truly believing Norvin would carry out his threat to send her girl away.

Felicity, on the other hand, was mentally planning an escape. Norvin had said they were travelling to Ireland by ship so they would most likely be heading now for Liverpool. By dint of the fact they would be reaching the port by train, she felt sure there would be stops along the way and she tried to work out how she could slip from her father's grasp to disappear into the crowds and make her getaway.

Arriving at the station, Norvin again grasped her arm and walked towards the ticket office, whilst the cabbie unloaded the bags and a porter collected them.

'If you move one step, I will thrash you in front of all these people!' Norvin growled.

Felicity shivered, despite the heat of the summer. She had never seen her father so angry – or so determined. Standing meekly at his side whilst he paid for the tickets, she then watched her bags being loaded onto the train, which was puffing out great clouds of steam.

Cupping her elbow tightly, Norvin walked towards the first-class section at the front of the train.

The doors of the carriages were painted green rather than the dirty brown of the rest of the train. The driver leaned his elbow out of the open window and tipped his cap respectfully; Norvin nodded in return. Steam and smoke swirled like a fog along the platform, carrying with them the smell of soot.

Pushing Felicity aboard, Norvin climbed up the step after her.

Finding seats in an empty carriage, they sat quietly waiting for the train to chug out of the station.

Huge windows allowed daylight to pour in, highlighting the painted panelled ceiling. A polished centre leg oak table sat in the centre, flanked by long high-backed seating which was upholstered in a rich plum-coloured velvet, studded with deep buttons.

As she sat down, Felicity wondered whether to risk trying to talk her father out of the decision he had made, but thought better of it as he glared at her.

She still had the money she had stolen safely hidden in her bodice, which was a blessed relief. If she could escape, at least she wouldn't starve.

A whistle blew and carriage doors were slammed shut. Felicity suppressed a shudder, wondering if this is how it felt being locked up in jail. The train lurched, then slowly began to move forward. Felicity watched the smoke flying past the window as it picked up speed. She likened it to the only life she'd known disappearing forever. She wanted to cry at its loss but when she thought of Dilys her heart hardened. Somehow, she would claw her way back to Marshall's and finish that girl off for good.

Norvin opened the newspaper he had brought with him, completely ignoring Felicity, who sat opposite him. She stared out of the window but saw only the image of Dilys. A scowl crept over her face as she thought about how she had been thwarted. Who had seen her that night as she hid in the lavatory block? It could have been any one of a dozen or more people. It mattered not, for all she could think of still was her revenge.

Getting to her feet, Felicity returned her father's glare. Pulling down the window to allow some air into the stuffy carriage, she sat again, and Norvin returned his attention to the newspaper. It was going to be a very long journey if they continued to ignore each other.

Felicity began to tap her foot irritably. Without taking his eyes from the newsprint, Norvin laid a hand on her knee to still it. Felicity sighed loudly then returned to staring out of the window.

Every now and then the train called at minor stations for passengers to alight or board before the massive iron beast resumed its journey. Each time, Norvin watched his daughter closely, for fear of her dashing from the train before he could react quickly enough to stop her.

The clickety clack of the iron wheels on the track, combined with the heat from the sun through the window, made Felicity feel drowsy. Looking at her father, she saw his eyes were heavy too and before long they were both fast asleep.

The train's horn snapped them awake and the conductor slid open the door to clip their tickets.

'Crewe Station coming up, sir,' the young man said as he doffed his cap.

Norvin nodded and the conductor left the carriage, sliding the door closed behind him.

'Daddy, I really must get some air, I'm suffocating in here,' Felicity said.

'We will stroll on the platform together when the train stops, then we can board again and continue on towards Liverpool.'

So her guess was right, they were heading for Liverpool. Felicity gave him a little smile of thanks. This could be the one and only chance she would have to make her escape. She would have to time it to perfection. Crewe was a major station and it would be thronged with people pushing and shoving. She had to find a way to hide herself amidst the bodies filling the platform.

The train slowed and Felicity's pulse quickened. It wouldn't be long now. Brakes squealed as they ground to a halt and Felicity stood. With her father behind her she stepped down with a helping hand from a porter. She gasped at the amount of people who surged towards her, and in an instant she was swept along in their midst. She heard her father calling her name urgently and she caught a glimpse of him endeavouring to fight his way through the crowds.

On the other side of the tracks stood another train belching out filthy smoke, and everywhere people were rushing about. Pushing her way through, Felicity made for the exit; she had to get out now before she was found. Walking as swiftly as she could she finally emerged at the station's entrance. Breathing a sigh of relief, she headed in the direction most people were coming from. That, she surmised, must be where the town was situated.

Hot and tired, she continued on. She had to find somewhere to lie low, for she knew her father would already be seeking out a constable. Cutting down a side street she spied a tea shop. Here she could rest a while and plan her next move. Tea, and scone with jam and cream ordered, Felicity sat well away from the window for fear of being seen. It was unlikely her father would find her here, but if the constabulary became involved she could be spotted.

Whilst she ate, she formulated a plan. She did not dare return to the station to catch a train home; it was far too dangerous. So, what were the options left open to her? A cab would take forever and would probably cost more than she had.

Just then the doorbell tinkled, and in walked a woman in worn clothing, her shawl draped over her arm and a cotton bonnet covering her hair. She was carrying a basket of fruit, which she placed on a table.

Felicity listened to the conversation between the woman and the shop owner. It transpired the woman was a 'cut-rat' who was making a regular delivery. Taking her money and leaving the fruit, the woman departed. Knowing she had found the answer to her predicament, Felicity paid her bill and slowly and carefully followed the woman. With luck they would arrive at a wharf where Felicity might be able to pay for a ride on a narrowboat back to Wolverhampton.

* * *

Back at the station, Norvin had done precisely what Felicity suspected he would do and found a constable. With a quick explanation, the two then searched the train. Felicity was nowhere to be seen.

'We have to find her!' Norvin shouted above the noise as they stood on the platform once more.

The policeman looked around him. 'In this lot?'

Norvin sighed in despair.

'I'm sorry, sir, but your daughter could be anywhere by now. She could have legged it from the station; she might even have taken a train to another town!'

Norvin nodded resignedly and thanked the constable. Then he instructed the porter to remove the luggage from the baggage compartment.

As he watched the train they should have been on pull away, his anger mounted. Marching to the ticket office, he bought his fare home. Crossing over to the other platform, the porter and bags in tow, he fumed his disgust at Felicity's behaviour.

Once the bags were on board, he tipped the porter and found a seat. He would go home and await the return of his daughter, for he was sure that's where she would be headed. Not to his house, of course, but he feared she would find a way to avenge herself with that young maid, Dilys.

As the train trundled back the way he had come, Norvin decided to send the bags home by cab. He, however would not accompany them. Instead, he would face the decidedly unenviable task of informing the Marshalls that Felicity had out-witted him at Crewe station and absconded. He had to warn them to be extra vigilant, for it was his considered opinion that Felicity would return in an endeavour to finish what she had started. He was not looking forward to this one bit.

45

It was early evening when Dilys answered the knock to the door and showed the visitor into the kitchen.

Minnie's eyes widened in surprise when she saw who it was. 'Mr Hargreaves!'

'I apologise for arriving on your doorstep unannounced, Mrs Marshall...'

'Minnie.'

Norvin inclined his head. 'I'm afraid I have some grave news to impart to you all.'

Minnie frowned as she nodded to Mabel. The cook nodded to her underling Josie, who fetched a large cake from the larder. Dilys made tea without being asked.

'Take a seat, Mr Hargreaves...' Minnie began.

'Norvin.'

Minnie nodded. 'Have a sup of tea and a bit of cake then you can impart this grave news.' The smile she gave him assured him she was not being sarcastic – merely friendly.

Thanking the staff for the refreshments, Norvin took a deep breath. 'I'm afraid Felicity escaped me at the railway station and is at this moment somewhere in Crewe – possibly.'

'I think you should start at the beginning, Norvin, and lay it on the line,' Minnie said, 'if you'll pardon the pun.'

Norvin winced.

Once the explanation had been given, he went on, 'I am terribly afraid Felicity might come looking for you once again, Dilys.'

The maid turned white. 'I bloody knew it! I said so d'aint I?'

'Calm yourself, you silly girl!' Mabel snapped.

'It's all right for you, it ain't you she's after!' Dilys shot back.

'I can only warn you all to be extra vigilant in

your comings and goings,' Norvin said apologetically.

'Mum, we can't let Dilys go *anywhere* alone until Fliss has been caught!' Adam said full of concern.

'I agree, lad.'

'Christ, that girl will be the death of me!' Dilys muttered.

'Norvin, we were just about to sit down and eat, won't you join us?' Minnie asked.

'That would be most pleasant, thank you. I confess I have not eaten since this morning.'

With everyone standing in line to be served their food, Norvin smiled at the happiness radiating around the room. The youngsters were unable to remain in the queue as they chatted and formed a huddle. They laughed loudly as one whispered something, but no one looked around in fear of reprisals. Clearly it was a well-run and relaxed establishment, and when his turn came he held out his plate to Mabel. She piled it with food and he took a seat next to Minnie.

'I have to say, I'm famished,' he said, 'thank you for your kind invitation. This looks delicious.'

'Get it down you then we can go into the living

room and discuss what to do about keeping Dilys safe,' Minnie said with a warm smile.

Later, as they sat in comfort, Minnie began. 'So we need ideas about looking out for our Dilys.'

'...Dilys,' came the familiar echo.

'It looks like you'll be trapped indoors for a while,' Adam said to the maid.

'Oh, that's bloody marvellous that is! All this sunshine and I can't enjoy it.'

'You don't get out much, anyway, so quit your moaning,' Mabel remonstrated.

'That ain't the point and you know it!' Dilys fired back.

'Bodyguard,' Echo said.

'Good idea, Echo,' Polly said enthusiastically.

'The problem is all you lot have jobs to go to,' Minnie said.

'I'll do it,' Digit volunteered. 'I can be spared from the allotment.'

'Fair enough,' Minnie said. Then turning to Dilys, she added, 'You don't go anywhere without Digit, not even to the privy.'

'I ain't taking him in there with me!' Dilys retorted.

'You don't have to, soft girl!' Mabel interrupted. 'He will check the privy before you go in!'

'Oh, right,' Dilys said, feeling rather silly now.

Norvin watched and listened in silence. He was amazed at how this family came together in a time of crisis. He was also ashamed of his daughter for causing all this distress.

'Everybody, we have to make sure the windows and doors are locked tight at night, and with Digit being Dilys' bodyguard I don't see there's much more we can do.' Minnie looked around the room.

'We can call in the coppers,' Dilys muttered, not at all happy she was having to be babysat by Digit.

'I doubt they could do anything more than we are, Dilys,' Billy said kindly. 'They won't put a constable on guard overnight when he could be patrolling the streets.'

'I agree,' Minnie said, and satisfied there was nothing further to be discussed, she nodded.

'Oh, good grief! In all this bother I had completely forgotten about the cabbie waiting outside,' Norvin said, jumping to his feet.

'It's all right, Josie took him a dinner out whilst

we had ours. He's enjoying a puff on his pipe now, I shouldn't wonder,' Minnie assured him.

'Minnie, you are probably the kindest person I have ever met,' Norvin said by way of thanks. 'So now I shall leave you in peace, but please be careful, all of you.'

Saying his goodbyes, Adam saw him out to the waiting cab.

* * *

Felicity had no idea her father was enjoying a meal with the Marshalls as she trudged along the towpath looking for someone who was travelling to her home town.

For hours she had wandered up and down as narrowboats came and went, but no one was heading that way. Her stomach grumbled its discontent at being empty, and she knew she would have to go back into the town soon and find food before the shops closed up.

What if she had to stay here overnight? Where would she sleep? Would she be safe? What if she was attacked by some drunkard trying to find his way home? The more she thought on it, the more frightened she became. Was that maid worth all this worry and trouble?

Felicity knew she could never go home to her parents now, for they would surely have her thrown in jail, or worse still – the insane asylum. What would she do once Dilys was out of the equation? Where could she go and how would she live? She would have to find work of some sort but with no qualifications or experience it would be nigh on impossible to secure a job.

Spotting a bench, Felicity sank down onto it, grateful at being able to rest. The sun was going down and the air felt a little cooler. She heard the laughter coming from the boats moored up in a long line and she smelled food cooking. Her stomach rumbled again and she sighed. It was no use staying here any longer, she had to find a meal and shelter for the night. It would deplete her funds but she had no other choice. As she wandered away, she saw women lighting candles in jars which hung at intervals along their boats. It all looked so pretty in the coming darkness,

Striding out, Felicity kept her eyes peeled for a

café that might still be open. Her luck was in as she saw the little place's gas lights come on. Rushing inside, she found a seat and ordered a meal and a hot drink.

When her food came she asked the waitress if there was anywhere close by to spend the night.

'No, love, yer'll need to go back into town for that and I warn you it won't be cheap.'

Felicity thanked the girl and began to eat. It was looking likely that she would be sleeping on the bench beside the towpath.

She lingered as long as she possibly could in the café, until at last the waitress said, 'I'm sorry, miss, but we're locking up now.' Paying her bill, she left the safety of the café. Retracing her steps, she shivered. She had no coat and with the darkness had come a chill in the air.

The towpath was lit by the many lanterns lining the boats and she easily found the bench which was to be her bed.

Plonking herself down, she gave way to the misery surrounding her. For the first time in many years, Felicity cried tears she didn't have to force.

46

Dawn broke in a blaze of glory. The sky was scarlet with streaks of gold, giving the land a rosy glow.

Digit was up, dressed and feeding the range to boil the kettle when Dilys appeared. He preceded her through the back door and checked the privy block was empty before returning to the kitchen.

'I wish you didn't have to do this for me; it makes me feel guilty getting you up so early,' Dilys said a few minutes later.

'No problem,' Digit said with a shrug.

'You don't say much, do you?'

Digit shook his head.

'Have you always been the same?'

He nodded.

'Bloody hell, it's like trying to get blood from a stone!' Dilys said not unkindly.

Digit laughed and the maid joined in.

'It's nice to see somebody happy in their work,' Mabel said as she bustled in. 'Have you seen that sky? It's a beautiful morning.' Going to the larder she began to pull out the things needed for breakfast.

One by one the residents of Marshall's rose as the aroma of cooking bacon permeated the whole house.

Loud singing heralded the arrival of the Rewcastles, who were taking full advantage of the good weather.

Polly took a tray of tea and egg and bacon sandwiches out to them and was rewarded with a great cheer.

Once everyone was fed, those with jobs went on their way, snap tins in hand. The little ones were allowed out to play, under Echo's supervision, before their day of learning began in the classroom and soon the air was filled with their joyful shouting. James and Peter took off to the allotment, and Billy enjoyed a leisurely cup of tea before going to the chapel room to resume his boxing lessons.

Mabel sighed.

'What's eating you?' Minnie asked.

'It's just – well, to be honest, Minnie, I'm worried stiff about Dilys and that Fliss!' Mabel confessed.

'She'll be all right, she's got Digit by her side every minute,' assured her friend.

Mabel nodded but she was still not convinced. 'I'll be glad when she's caught.'

'Me an' all. I wonder what Norvin will do with her when she is finally apprehended?'

'He'll need some help, whatever he decides,' Mabel said with a snort.

'True. That girl is as slippery as an eel,' Minnie agreed.

'I don't think she's right in the head, Minnie.'

'If she is, I know where there's a house full,' Minnie replied. The women smiled at the age-old saying.

'I've planned shepherds' pie for dinner, enough to feed the workers as well, and with a cold tea we'll be right,' Mabel said as they returned to the kitchen.

* * *

Over in Crewe the crimson light and noise from the cut-rats rising early had woken Felicity. She had fallen asleep on the bench from pure exhaustion and now her body ached. Standing up, she stretched the knots out of her muscles and squinted around. A shout drew her attention and a narrowboat woman beckoned to her. Felicity ambled across and the woman called out, 'Come aboard and have a sup of tea.'

'Thank you,' Felicity replied as she hitched up her dress and clambered clumsily onto the boat.

'The lav is in there.' The woman pointed to an impossibly small cupboard and Felicity nodded. After a great deal of struggling she emerged and was given a small bowl of water and an old towel to wash her hands.

Sitting at the tiny table she was presented with a pannikin – a tin cup – of hot tea and an egg sandwich the size of a doorstep. 'This is very kind of you,' she said gratefully.

'You're welcome. You got nowhere to live?'

'I'm trying to get a ride back to Wolverhampton. My father wanted to put me in a convent in Ireland so I ran away during the journey.'

'Why ever was he going to do that?' the woman asked with a horrified expression.

Felicity took a moment to chew and think up a halfway decent lie. Then she said, 'I wouldn't marry the man he'd chosen for me; he was old and had one foot in the grave.'

'Blimey! I'm not surprised you ran off, I would have done as well.'

'Where are you headed?' Felicity asked hopefully.

'Manchester, we have family there,' the woman answered.

Felicity stood, having finished her food, and asked, 'How much do I owe you?'

'Nothing. Us cut-rats help out where we can. Here, take this, you might need it.' The woman wrapped a small pie in a scrap of linen and passed it over.

'Thank you very much, I'm grateful.'

'If ever you are in trouble, you will always be able to rely on a cut-rat for help,' the woman assured her.

Felicity jumped from the boat to the towpath, only just managing to stay on her feet, and waved at the woman as the boat engine started up.

Sitting on the bench once more, Felicity resigned herself to another long wait. As she watched the prettily painted boats sail past, she muttered quietly and wondered again about taking a train. Surely her father would be gone by now, and she could be waiting here for who knew how long before securing a ride on a boat going in the right direction. If she returned to the station, she could scout the area thoroughly for any sign of her father or the constabulary.

Making her decision, Felicity got to her feet and wound her way back through the network of streets. She would have to be careful and not act suspiciously if she was to carry this off. She had to appear like any other traveller waiting for a train.

As she walked, she tidied her hair and smoothed her dress. She couldn't arrive looking like she'd slept outdoors, even though she had done just that.

Nearing the station, she felt her nerves twang. Taking a deep breath, she straightened her back, held up her head and walked with purpose. Going straight to the ticket kiosk she paid her fare to Wolverhampton. Stepping onto the platform, her eyes scanned the area surreptitiously. Seeing a group of young women chatting and laughing, she sauntered their way. They nodded a greeting which she returned before finding a place behind them. Their noisy excitement grew as the massive iron train squealed to a halt in front of them, the clouds of smoke making them cough.

The porter opened the carriage door and helped each one to board, including Felicity.

Finding a seat, she heaved a sigh of relief, but her eyes continued to scan the platform for signs of danger. It was only moments before doors slammed, a whistle sounded and the train lurched into motion. As it gathered speed, Felicity finally relaxed – for a little while at least.

47

During the journey Felicity tried to decide her best course of action once she arrived in her hometown. She had to steer clear of her parents, for certain; she could not allow them to discover her whereabouts.

On the other hand, she couldn't hide in Marshall's lavatory again either. She was sure they would have been informed of her escape by her father, and would be on the lookout for her.

The money she had remaining would pay for one night in a cheap hotel and a meal; after that she would be penniless. If she could work out a plan, then one night would be all she would need to destroy Dilys.

Felicity determined she would have to hide herself somewhere close to Marshall's before deciding when and how to strike. Giving a little cackle drew attention from other passengers, but she ignored them. She thought about the building, knowing it would be busy in daylight and it was probable she would be seen, and locked securely at night so she would be unable to get inside. Would Dilys have a minder now? If so, how could Felicity get to her? Surely there would be a time when the girl would be alone, if only for a minute. With a sigh, Felicity knew she would have only one chance which meant it would have to be the privy block again.

The train finally pulled into the station and Felicity readied herself to leave. Once more she had to look like any other passenger. As she stepped down onto the platform, her eyes looked left and right, scanning the crowds. She strode out confidently towards the exit, all the time aware she could be apprehended at any moment.

Out in the street she hurried away, eager to be gone from the area. Following the towpath of the Birmingham Canal, Felicity climbed the embankment and crossed the bridge into Cable Street. Slipping between the buildings on her left, she was now behind a massive structure which hid her from view. She was so close to Marshall's she could hear the voices of the workers there.

Sitting on the ground, leaning her back against a wall, she pulled out the pie given to her earlier. It was not the tastiest thing she had ever eaten, but she was glad of it nevertheless.

Occasionally she peeped around the corner of the building which kept her safe from prying eyes. She could see clearly now the extent of the work being undertaken around the main house.

As she watched, she spied Dilys carrying a tray and a well-built young man at her side. He waited whilst she distributed the cups then escorted her back indoors. So, the maid *did* have a minder – Digit.

Leaning back against the wall again, Felicity thought long and hard about what she'd seen. This was going to make things a lot more difficult. However, she had all the time in the world to work out a plan.

The sun was hot on her face and she felt dry and thirsty after eating the pie. Moving further into the shade, she wondered what the time was and how much longer it would be before nightfall.

Unaware she had been asleep, she was woken abruptly. What had disturbed her? It was a moment before she realised it was silence.

With another peep around the corner she saw the workmen had finished for the day and had gone home. The sun had lowered to the horizon and she felt a little shiver at the change in temperature.

The time was almost right. Firstly, once it was fully dark, she would have to search for a weapon. Maybe there would be something on the building site. Then she could secrete herself somewhere where she could attack that maid, possibly *behind* the lavatory block.

Slowly darkness descended, and Felicity's body began to shake from cold. Slipping from her hiding place she ran as fast as she could towards where the men had been working. In the light of a pale moon she looked around for something with which to arm herself. Stumbling across a forgotten hammer, she picked it up and gave it a swing. This would do nicely.

Treading carefully, she made her way to wait behind the foul-smelling small building. Light still shone through the open back door and she hunkered down in the shadows. How long she would have to wait for an opportunity to strike was anyone's guess, but having come this far she was not about to give up now.

She grimaced as someone came out to use the latrine, and judging by the whistling it was a man. Trying to close her ears to the sounds, she covered her mouth to shut off the gag reflex. Then she was alone again. She hoped there would be no more *visits* unless it was Dilys. Her hopes were dashed when she heard a heavy footfall.

'It's all right, they're empty,' the gruff voice said. It was Digit.

'Ta, I won't be long.'

Dilys!

The heavy tread disappeared back indoors and Felicity took her chance. Rushing into the privy she saw the maid in the light of a candle balanced on the little shelf.

Dilys drew in a breath to shout for help, her hands full of her underclothes.

'Don't!' Felicity growled low in her throat.

Dilys whimpered as she pulled up her drawers.

'I told you what would happen, didn't I?'

Dilys nodded, her heart in her mouth. 'Please...' she begged in a whisper.

'Too late!' Felicity swung the hammer and the scream that followed could be heard for miles.

'What the bloody hell!' Minnie said as she jumped to her feet, but by that time Digit was out of the back door.

The shouting and crying had everyone crowding outside to see what on earth was happening.

Digit emerged, dragging a woman fighting like a wild cat. He man-handled her into the kitchen, where he forced her onto a chair.

Felicity kicked and screamed abuse as Digit held her in place. 'Washing line,' he said as he looked at Mabel who had followed them indoors.

Minnie had rushed into the privy to see a terrified Dilys cradling her arm, tears streaming down her face.

'She hit me with that,' Dilys sobbed, tilting her head towards the ground.

Minnie picked up the hammer from the floor and

led Dilys back into the house, talking soothingly as they went.

Felicity was now tied to the chair, muttering curses under her breath, with everyone looking on in astonishment.

'Dilys, tell us what happened,' Minnie coaxed.

'She swung that,' nodding her head to the weapon now lying on the table. 'I tried to cover my head and – I think my arm's broke!'

'Broken, you imbecile!' Felicity corrected the maid venomously.

'You! Shut it!' Digit said pointing his finger in her face.

Felicity made to bite it and Digit slapped her face.

Gasps sounded and Felicity fell quiet, her eyes burning with hate.

Polly was now looking at Dilys' arm. 'I think it is broken, Mum, we'll need the doctor to set it, otherwise it will heal badly.'

'Right, Rodney and Joe fetch the doctor. Tell him what's happened so he'll know what he needs to bring with him,' Minnie said in her usual supervisory manner.

'Maybe we should fetch Mr Hargreaves as well, Mum,' Adam suggested.

'Good idea, son,' she concurred.

'I'll go,' Adam volunteered.

'I'll come with you,' James said.

'James, it would be better if you went for a constable,' Billy said.

The four young men left together, running through the dark streets on their urgent errands.

Mabel pulled out the brandy she kept specifically for her Christmas cake and poured a measure for Dilys.

'I think we could all do with one of those,' Minnie said eyeing the bottle.

Mabel nodded and grabbed more glasses.

Felicity watched with eyes wild with anger, every now and then struggling to free herself.

Twenty minutes later the doctor arrived by pony and trap, Rodney and Joe hanging off the sides.

Taken into the kitchen, the doctor surveyed the scene. One girl tied to a chair, muttering obscenities as she rocked back and forth. Another cradling an arm and sobbing loudly. Clearly something catastrophic had happened between these two young women. People were milling around talking and fretting.

Moving to Dilys he asked, 'You are the patient, I take it?' The maid confirmed with a nod. 'Right let's have a look at that arm.'

Dilys winced as he prodded and poked, and after a quick and efficient examination he said, 'I will need some help here.'

'Our Polly is a nurse,' Minnie piped up.

'Trainee,' Polly said sheepishly.

'Excellent. I need you to hold the upper arm tightly. Don't let go until I tell you.'

Polly nodded and did as she was bid.

Dilys' eyes widened in horror, sure he was going to chop off the offending limb.

'Now, I'm going to pull hard to allow the broken bone ends to align themselves, so grit your teeth young lady,' he said to Dilys. Then to Polly, 'On three, ready?'

Polly nodded again, also gritting her teeth.

'One...' The doctor yanked hard on Dilys' wrist and smiled with satisfaction. Everyone else winced as Dilys let out a scream.

'You said on three,' Dilys said through her tears.

'I lied,' the doctor said with a grin. 'I needed you to be as relaxed as you could be under the circumstances.'

Felicity let out a laugh like a mad woman that chilled the hearts of all in the room. 'What happened here?' the doctor asked as he moved to Felicity and looked at her closely.

'This young woman attacked Dilys with a hammer,' Billy said, preferring not to go into any more detail than was necessary. 'We have sent for the police and they should be on their way by now.'

'Mad as a March hare, if I'm not mistaken,' the doctor muttered, with another look deep into Felicity's eyes.

Returning to Dilys, he took a large square of linen from his bag and deftly folded it into a sling, tying the corners into a tight knot. He bandaged the forearm tightly before sliding it into the sling which he then looped over Dilys' head. Passing a small round box of pills to Polly he said, 'Two now and then two a day starting tomorrow.'

Dilys watched tearfully as Polly took out two of the little tablets. She opened her mouth and Polly dropped them onto her tongue. The foul taste made her grimace so she picked up her glass of brandy. The doctor snatched it away, much to Dilys' chagrin.

'With water,' he commanded. Taking a sniff at the contents of the glass, he smiled, then drained it dry.

Minnie stifled a grin as she pulled out her purse from the drawer in the table. Paying the doctor, she went to see him out.

The cab that passed the doctor's trap in the driveway contained Norvin Hargreaves and Adam. The cabbie was requested to wait, and Minnie led the way to the kitchen.

'Minnie, I'm so dreadfully sorry,' Norvin began. In the kitchen his eyes bored into his daughter, but when she screeched out a laugh his demeanour changed. Now he looked on her sadly, finally convinced the girl was quite mad.

Turning to the maid, he saw the sling and gasped. 'Oh, my God!'

'She broke my arm with a hammer! It could have been my head!' Dilys spat angrily.

'I'm sorry, Dilys – so very, very sorry,' Norvin said as tears filled his eyes. Overcome with emotion, Norvin covered his face with his hands and wept.

Embarrassed glances passed around the room,

then, as Mabel set the kettle on the range, Minnie lowered the sobbing man to a chair.

Felicity began to laugh hysterically, and spittle flew from the corners of her mouth. 'I'll kill you all!' she yelled.

Recovering his wits, Norvin said, 'I need to contact the insane asylum and have her removed from your property.'

'What about the convent?' Minnie asked. 'Would they still take her?'

'Possibly, but I fear it's gone past that now,' Norvin said sadly.

'But the asylum? Dear God, what an awful place to spend the rest of your life!' Minnie said in horror.

'I agree, but I think she will have to go there for now. I will contact the convent and see what the sisters say,' Norvin conceded.

'Fair enough,' Minnie said resignedly.

Felicity had listened and watched intently, before beginning her struggles and wailing once more.

James came in with a constable, both puffing with the exertion of running back to the house.

It was Billy who explained the whole debacle,

and the policeman scribbled in his little notebook, nodding every now and then.

'I think my sergeant will want her in the cells until the Magistrate can deal with her.'

'Excuse me, constable, but I think it would be safer all round if my daughter was taken to the insane asylum as soon as possible,' Norvin replied.

'I'm not sure about that sir, it's my duty to...'

'What happens if she attacks someone else on the way to the police station? She escaped from me once before and you can see what she did to poor Dilys there. Please, constable, it will break my heart but Felicity needs to be in that facility rather than your station.'

The bobby blew out his cheeks and with a nod he said, 'I will remain here until it's arranged, then.'

'Cup of tea?' Mabel asked, and the policeman nodded his appreciation of the offer as he stood over Felicity, hearing her utter curses under her breath. As he watched her eyes roll back in her head he wondered if the girl was possessed.

48

May, Echo and Polly went to settle the little ones who had been woken by the noise. Some were crying and others were wandering about on the landing, wanting to know what was going on. Norvin addressed Minnie.

'I wonder if I may crave your indulgence yet again by asking you to keep Felicity exactly where she is until I return.'

'Of course. It saddens me it's come to this, but I can see the necessity,' she answered.

'Thank you. I hope all this won't take too long.'

Norvin Hargreaves left and climbed into the cab. The driver had heard all the screaming and yelling and when his customer called out the address of an-other destination, he knew why.

Arriving at the asylum, Norvin alighted the cab and yanked on the bell pull at the side of the mas-sive wrought iron gates. A moment later, a porter arrived.

'I need to speak with the person in charge,' Norvin said.

The porter made to unlock the gate but Norvin shivered and stopped him with, 'Would it be possible to conduct my business here? I realise it is an un-usual request but I cannot find it within myself to enter.'

The porter shrugged and climbing onto the bi-cycle leaning against his lodge he rode away to the huge building further up the long driveway.

The cabbie packed and lit his pipe as he watched his fare pace back and forth and his heart went out to the man. Whatever was occurring, and he was sure he would find out eventually, it was a sad busi-ness that had brought them here.

A little while later, a tall well-built man strode purposefully to the gate, the porter cycling behind.

'This is most irregular, sir...' the man began.

'My apologies, but I simply couldn't face coming inside!'

Seeing that his visitor was a gentleman of means by his attire, the man nodded. He could understand how the poor man felt.

'My daughter has assaulted a maid with a hammer, and I need to have her committed as I am now convinced she has gone mad. I ask she remain here until I receive a reply from the penitentiary convent as to whether they will accept her. Felicity is at this moment tied to a chair with a policeman watching over her, screaming she will kill us all!'

'I'm sorry to hear it. You will have to pay her upkeep whilst she is with us, I'm sure you understand.' The supervisor of the institution rubbed his hands together as he spoke.

'Of course. Please can you send someone to...' Norvin took out a handkerchief and blew his nose in an attempt to conceal his distress.

'Where is she being held?'

'Marshall's Children's Home in Major Street.'

'I will arrange to have her collected straight away, Mr...?'

'Hargreaves.'

'And payment, Mr Hargreaves?'

'I will arrange first thing in the morning for the bank to pay each week.'

'Very good.' The man turned on his heel and spoke quietly to the porter who had heard every word. Nodding, he cycled away once more.

With a wave, the asylum supervisor strode back up the drive and Norvin climbed back into the cab.

The driver shook his head in sorrow as he clicked his teeth to his horse. Poor man, having to commit his daughter to a dreadful place like this.

Within an hour, Norvin was back at Marshall's, followed by a carriage from the asylum. It had been specially modified to have bars on the windows and one lockable door on the back rather than two on the sides. Two burly men in grey uniforms climbed down from the driving seat and followed Norvin inside. Without a word they untied Felicity who was still shouting death threats, and holding her arms they trundled her outside to the wagon.

Norvin had followed and now watched as the door was opened and his daughter was bundled inside. One of the men closed and locked the door before joining his colleague on the driving seat.

Norvin's eyes locked with those filled with hate staring back at him through the bars as the wagon rolled away. Turning to head back indoors, he saw Minnie waiting for him.

Together they returned to the kitchen, where Norvin gave his thanks to all. Then he quietly left.

Unable to sleep now, everyone took fresh tea into the living room, where they discussed the events of the evening.

Digit sat near Dilys and suddenly said, 'I'm sorry.'

'It ain't your fault,' Dilys said with a drug-induced smile.

'I should have...'

'No one here is to blame for what has happened, it was Felicity who caused it all. And judging by what we've seen, I don't think she was responsible for her own actions,' Adam said quickly.

Nods affirmed his words and he went on, 'Now it's all over we need to get back to some sort of normality.'

'Like May walking out with Trevor,' Rodney called across the room. He was repaid for his remark by a cushion bouncing off his head. Laughter filled the air and the worry that had surrounded them all was finally lifted.

* * *

The following morning, Dilys stood outside in the sunshine, relating the tale of her broken arm to Josiah and the Rewcastles.

Josiah, who did not need to be on site very often as he was confident the Rewcastles were doing a splendid job, had called round to see how the work was progressing and was astonished at what he was hearing.

Returning to the kitchen, Mabel assigned her tasks she could manage with one hand, such as helping Echo to lay the dinner tables.

Still, the conversations centred on the Felicity affair, and probably would for some considerable time.

'Mum, I think we should have a telephone put in,' Adam said.

'Well, it's an idea,' Minnie said.

'It would have been very useful last night and would have saved all that dashing around,' Adam added.

'That's true enough, but it will be expensive.'

'I'll see to the paying of it, Mum, don't worry.'

'All right lad, why don't you get off and visit the Telephone Company and find out how much it will cost and when they can fit us in? After all this nonsense with Fliss I think we need it.'

Adam nodded and grabbed his jacket.

Polly slipped into her role of nurse again, ensuring Dilys took her medication on time – with water. Then she and Echo went to visit Dickie's grave, as they had lots to tell him.

It was when they arrived home again that Harlan called to Polly.

'You go on in, Echo, I won't be a minute,' she said before she strolled over to see what the lad wanted.

'Polly, I was wondering if you'd like to walk out with me like?' the Geordie asked.

'I don't think so, but thank you for asking,' she replied with a blush.

'Don't you like me?'

'Yes, of course I do,' Polly said in a rush. 'It's just that...'

'I don't think Dickie would mind,' Harlan said gently.

Polly was surprised. 'How did you know about that?'

'People talk, Polly. Ah know how much you cared for him and ah'm not trying to take his place. Ah'm heading for a place of my own in your heart.' His cheeky grin was infectious, and she smiled.

'It hasn't been that long since...' Polly began again.

'Agreed, but ya have to take that first step some-time so why not take it with me?'

'I'll think about it,' Polly said.

'No, you should do it. I tell ya hinney, I'll not give up asking, so ya might as well agree first as last.'

Looking at the handsome face she noted how blue his eyes were. His skin was tanned by the sun and his smile lit up his whole face. On impulse she said, 'All right!' Then she grinned as Harlan gave a whoop of joy.

'This evening, Ah'll come when Ah've had a wash and change.' Even white teeth sparkled in the sun-shine and Polly felt a flutter in her stomach.

With a little laugh, she went indoors. Polly saw that Adam had arrived back by cab; clearly he had some exciting news. 'Mum, the Telephone Company can come out next week.'

'Phew! Everything is happening at once, but that's good to know. Thanks, Adam,' Minnie said.

Then Polly related her own news. 'Mum, I've agreed to go for a walk with Harlan this evening.'

'I trust you to know how to behave, so you go and enjoy yourself.' Minnie gave her daughter a hug and thanked the good Lord for giving Polly a healthy mind.

Polly did enjoy herself as she told Adam later that night. He watched as his sister enthused about the new man in her life and his heart sang. He hoped with all his heart that everything would be all right for her now. She had been through so much in her young years and he prayed that she would finally be happy with Harlan.

Retiring to bed he felt all was well with his little world now Felicity Hargreaves was no longer part of it.

* * *

During the next few days, the gossip around the altercations at Marshall's reached Una's ears. She had sat in silence as Cherry disgorged a mountain of information but her thoughts had centred on Minnie Marshall. How was it that, no matter what was thrown at that woman, she came out of it smelling of roses?

A lunatic had attacked her maid with a hammer, and those living at Marshall's had prevented the girl ending up dead.

'Well, they've carted her off to the asylum now,' Cherry said.

Una snapped her attention back. 'Probably for the best.'

'Crikey, what a place though! I hate to think what it must be like inside,' Cherry went on, just as Una thought she might have run out of things to say.

'All those people crying and screaming; it would be enough to drive you mad – if you weren't already!'

'Indeed.' Una picked up the newspaper in an effort to deter the girl from any further speech. She was disappointed.

'Just think how awful it would be, knowing you would never come out again.'

If you don't shut up you could find yourself joining

them, Una thought, then immediately chastised herself. Cherry Banks had come to her in her hour of need. She had saved Una from a life of solitude which could so easily have set her on the path to insanity herself. In truth, Cherry was a blessing, her cheerfulness never wavering, no matter what. Her constant chatter drove Una to distraction at times but it was far and away better than the suffocating silence of an empty house. She had dreaded becoming thought of as *old Reedy the crazy woman* by the people of the town.

With the newspaper now lying on her lap, forgotten, Una stared into space as Cherry prattled on.

Una's thoughts sailed back to when she and Billy Marshall became good friends at school, then slowly drifted apart when Billy took up boxing, which she hated.

Her next memory was of opening the orphanage in Jenner Street with Ruth Ashby, who then deserted to Marshall's taking Celia Brock, the teacher, with her after they had all moved to the present location.

Polly and Adam Fitch came to mind: the latter absconding to find his sister after she was sold on.

Then came the break-out of their friends from Reed House.

Una could hear Cherry's voice but it seemed very far away now and a smile formed on her lips. Having led a full and interesting life she wondered how different it would have been had she become Mrs Marshall.

A strange feeling came over her as though she was floating away. She was warm and comfortable and she took a deep breath before letting it out again slowly.

It was as Cherry turned to look at her employer that she had a shock. Una Reed was very clearly dead, her unblinking eyes wide open, with a macabre smile on her face.

Cherry sat at the table, unable to tear her eyes from the ghoulish spectacle. Then with a deep breath she muttered, 'Rest in peace – old Reedy.' Grabbing her shawl, she went to fetch the doctor and undertaker.

49

Fresh fruit and vegetables had come regularly to Marshall's kitchen from the allotments. Some were used immediately whilst the rest were bottled to see them through the next winter.

The pantry shelves were stacked with jars of onions, cabbage and eggs all sat in pickling vinegar, as well as home-made jams. Large onions were tied together and hung from hooks set into the wall. Muslin bags held apples, also dangling from hooks. Milk, cream, cheese and butter each had a place on the cold slab. The larder was stocked to the brim with flour, tea, sugar and all the staple foods needed to feed a hungry household.

Early one morning, an unexpected visitor arrived. Norvin Hargreaves was welcomed and given tea.

'I thought it best to inform you that I have received a response to my letter to the Sisters of Mercy Convent in Ireland.'

Adam and Minnie exchanged a concerned look.

'Unfortunately, they have refused to take Felicity in her present state of mind. They can't have her upsetting their peaceful regime and she might be a danger to the nuns there.'

Minnie sighed loudly. 'I'm sorry to hear that, Norvin.'

'As am I,' he said sadly. 'This now means she will have to spend the rest of her life in the – where she is at present.' Norvin could not bring himself to say the word asylum.

Minnie noted that the man had aged considerably since that last time they had met. His hair was turning silver and his eyes seemed dead in their sockets. He appeared to have lost any lust for life.

'Is there nowhere else she could go? Somewhere less – austere?' Adam asked softly.

'I fear not. She is in the only place where she

cannot hurt anyone.' Norvin shook his head sorrow-
fully. 'I am assured she is being well taken care of.'

'I take it you haven't visited then?' Minnie asked
not unkindly.

'No, Minnie, I couldn't bear it. My wife takes the
vapours often now because of the whole debacle and
I have been forced to employ a nurse to see to her
needs. I'm afraid for what little health she has left.'

Minnie blew out her cheeks; she had no idea
how to reply to that.

Getting to his feet, he thanked them for the refreshments. 'I must be on my way now and be with
my wife. I merely came to inform you of the outcome
of the dreadful circumstances that surrounded you
not so long ago.'

Adam saw Norvin to his cab and watched as it
rolled away, his heart going out to the man who sat
inside. As he suspected, conversations were taking
place about their visitor when he returned to the
kitchen.

'At least she's safely locked away,' Dilys said, her
hand unconsciously going to the arm devoid of its
sling now that it was healing well.

'Dilys!' Mabel snapped.

'What? I don't care, Mabel. That girl tried to murder me! How would you feel if it had been you she swung that hammer at?'

'All right, calm down you two,' Minnie said sternly.

Mabel huffed and Dilys nodded curtly.

'We are safe from Felicity and that's all that matters. Life can return to normal now,' Minnie went on.

A bee buzzed around the range and Dilys flapped a tea towel, chasing it outdoors once more. There was not a breath of air and the heat was cloying in the stuffy kitchen.

'Oh, bugger this – everybody grab a chair, we'll go and sit in the shade outside and have a rest. Polly, go and tell Celia and Diana the kids can play outside for a while. It's too hot to be cooped up in here,' Minnie said as she mopped her brow.

Moments later, the adults sat in whatever shade they could find whilst the children ran around laughing and squealing, seemingly impervious to the heat.

It was as she fanned herself that Minnie spied a pretty young woman walking towards them.

'Mrs Marshall?' the girl asked, looking around.

'Yes,' Minnie answered.

'I'm Cherry Banks, Una Reed's maid.'

Minnie sighed. Another one looking for work, perchance?

'I thought I should tell you – Una passed away this morning.'

Shocked expressions looked at the girl who had brought the news.

'I'm sorry to hear it, despite never having been able to get on with Una,' Minnie said.

'Una talked often of you, Mrs Marshall...'

'Minnie.'

'Minnie, I think she held you in the highest regard,' Cherry said.

'That woman hated every bone in my body but it's nice of you to say that. Find somewhere to sit; we were about to have some cold drinks,' Minnie said as she glanced at Mabel.

Getting wearily to her feet, Mabel smiled as Josie said, 'You rest, I'll do it.' Mabel nodded her thanks with a smile and retook her seat eager, to hear what would be said next.

'What happened?' Minnie asked.

'Another heart attack, so the doctor said. One

minute she was here, the next she'd gone. She was sat at the table and it took me a minute to realise she was dead. She just looked like she was listening to me rattling on.'

Minnie shivered, despite the heat.

Cherry nodded. 'It was a bit spooky turning round to see dead eyes staring at me.'

'I can imagine,' Minnie said.

Polly and Adam exchanged a look. So, the woman who had caused them so much heartache was dead. Neither, if truth be told, could feel sorry at the news.

Accepting the glass of cool lemonade, Cherry said her thanks before continuing. 'I paid for the doctor and undertaker out of the household expenses.'

'That was good thinking,' Mabel put in.

'The funeral is the day after tomorrow at nine in the morning – St George's,' Cherry went on.

'So soon?' Minnie queried.

'The undertaker said it needed to be quick 'cos of the heat. I suppose he didn't want her stinking up his morgue,' Cherry said matter-of-factly.

Minnie stifled a grin at the girl's forthright manner, but Dilys couldn't manage to do the same and laughed loudly.

Mabel shot her a disapproving glance and the maid looked suitably cowed.

'Well, I thank you for coming to tell us,' Minnie said.

'I didn't mind. It was a nice walk in the sunshine,' Cherry said with a smile. Clearly death held no terrors for this young woman. 'The thing is, I don't know what to do about Reed House now Una is gone.'

'Has she left a will?' Minnie asked.

'I've no idea. I suppose I will have to look but if not...' Cherry left the sentence hanging.

'Would you like me to come over and help?' Minnie asked. She could see the girl was in a quandary as to what to do about going or staying at the property.

'That would be grand. I can cook and clean but I'm no good with papers – I can't read, you see.' Cherry was not at all embarrassed by her admission of being illiterate.

'Well, let's finish our drinks and then we can

head back and get it over with, then,' Minnie said as she reached for her lemonade.

Minutes later they set off and Cherry talked all the way back to Reed House whilst Minnie smiled inwardly. The incessant chatter must have been a nightmare for Una.

Back at the children's home, Polly and Adam were discussing Una's demise and Polly said, 'There's always something going on around here. First Fliss, then Dickie and now Una.'

'This family does seem to attract trouble or sadness,' Adam agreed.

There was a painful yell from somewhere in the house, followed by raucous laughter.

Polly and Adam exchanged a grin. 'It sounds like someone will have a sore thumb, I would guess,' Adam said.

'I wonder if a nurse is needed,' Polly said, and they burst into laughter themselves.

'Ad, when Mum comes home, I want to talk to you both.'

'All right,' he answered and instantly began to worry what secret his beloved sister was keeping now.

50

Minnie led Cherry to the office, remembering the way from her previous visits.

'I tell you what, I'll look in here and you go and make a cuppa,' Minnie said.

Cherry nodded, glad of something to do that didn't involve paperwork.

Minnie sighed then began her search. There was nothing to be found in the cupboards other than ledgers dating back years. Moving to the desk, she pulled open drawers and rifled through them. Nothing.

Sitting in Una's chair, her mind whirled. Una Reed was not the sort of person *not* to have made a will, so where was it? Could it be held at the bank like Dickie's? No, Una would have wanted it close to hand.

Cherry arrived with a cup of tea then vanished back to the kitchen.

Sipping the hot liquid, Minnie stared into space. Una was a devious madam so where would she have hidden her most important papers?

Minnie's eyes rested on the bookcase and she frowned. She'd never noticed that before but then she wouldn't have. The times she had been in here she would have had her back to the shelves. Would Una's will be secreted in one of the books?

Going over to look, she pulled out the first tome and flicked through it. Replacing it she tried the next. As she came towards the one on the end she had the shock of her life. Tipping the top of the book in order to pull it out she heard a faint whoosh and a section of books joined together on the shelf below slipped out of place. A secret drawer!

You crafty old bugger! Minnie thought, as she dipped her hand inside and withdrew an envelope. Checking there was nothing more in the drawer, she took the envelope and sat at the desk once more. She was glad she had, for as she read the contents she was stunned.

Minnie read the will through again in order to digest the words. Then she took it downstairs.

'Cherry, I need you to stay on here for the time being,' Minnie said.

'You found the will, then?'

'Yes. I have to have it verified before we decide what will happen, so how do you feel about being here on your own?' Minnie asked.

'Oh, I don't mind,' the girl answered. 'There's plenty of food and I can give the place a real good clean.'

'Good. I'll get this to the solicitor then I'll let you know the outcome,' Minnie assured her.

'Fair enough. Will you be going to the funeral?'

'Yes, we'll have representatives there so don't worry about a thing.'

With that, Minnie left the house and headed for the solicitor named on the envelope. As she walked, she passed grand ladies in their pretty summer dresses, lace parasols shielding their heads from the fierce sun. Down another street women dressed in rags were washing windows and yelling at their unruly children. Then she thought, *it's strange how you can see both sides of a coin at the same time!*

Eventually reaching the office she sought, she entered, glad to be out of the sunshine. Shown into an office, she handed the envelope to a man who sat behind his desk, sweating profusely. Taking the seat offered, Minnie waited whilst the solicitor read quietly.

'This all seems to be in order, Mrs...?'

'Marshall,' Minnie said, and she saw his eyebrows rise in surprise.

Looking at the paper once more, his gaze then returned to her. 'The will is legal and binding. I will add my signature to prove its authenticity.'

Thanking the man, Minnie left the office and hailed a cab. 'Marshall's, please, and I'll pay when we get there.'

The cabbie doffed his cap as Minnie climbed aboard. She couldn't wait to get home and tell the others what she had discovered.

Everyone was still outside when she arrived, and calling to Adam, she said, 'Fetch some money from my purse and pay the cabbie, will you, lovey?'

Adam nodded and went indoors. Once paid, the

cabbie turned his horse and the carriage rolled away slowly.

Echo and Flash were despatched to the chapel to fetch Billy. 'Tell him not to worry but I need to talk to him about something important.' The boys sped off, Flash keeping his speed down so Echo could match his step.

'What's going on?' Mabel asked.

'I'll tell you when Billy gets back,' Minnie said with a smile.

Frowns and puzzled looks passed from one face to another.

A little while later another cab rolled to a halt and Billy, Flash and Echo spilled out through the doors. Billy paid the fare before rushing to Minnie.

'Is everything all right?' he asked as he took Minnie in his arms and held her close.

'I said not to worry,' Echo said, clearly worried.

'He did, Minnie, but I couldn't help it,' Billy confirmed.

Echo beamed at being proved right.

'Billy, we found out after you'd gone this morning that Una Reed has died,' Minnie said gently.

'Oh!' Billy paled and Minnie led him to a chair.

Over the years of being wed to Minnie he had told her of his growing up with Una. How he took care of her and she helped him with his schoolwork. He'd explained that Una had thought they would marry some day until he refused to give up his boxing career. Then they had drifted apart, seeing less and less of each other as time went by.

Knowing all this, Minnie knew Billy would be saddened by the news of his childhood friend's passing.

'The funeral is the day after tomorrow and I thought we should attend,' Minnie said softly.

'Yes, of course,' Billy said in a whisper. The news had hit him like a poleaxe; he had thought Una would outlive them all.

'Billy, there's something else,' Minnie said as she handed him the will.

Reading quietly his head then shot up and his eyes met his wife's. 'Good grief!'

'What? Will somebody *please* tell us what's going on?' Mabel said in exasperation.

'This is Una's will,' Minnie said nodding to the paper in Billy's hand, 'and she has left Reed House – to Billy!'

'Bloody hell!' Mabel gasped.

'My thoughts exactly,' Billy said.

'She never did stop loving you, Billy,' Minnie said sadly, reaching out for her husband's hand.

* * *

It was the morning of Una's funeral and those wishing to attend gathered in the hall. Minnie, Billy, Adam, Diana, Ruth and Josie stood there; everyone else opted to stay home.

'I don't know why you're going,' Polly said to Adam.

'I'm showing respect for the departed, Polly,' was all he said.

'Well, I'm attending to assure myself she's really gone!' Josie muttered under her breath as she affixed her black hat. Seeing Minnie's disapproving look, she added, 'I say it as I see it.'

There were few mourners at the graveside in St George's churchyard. Minnie, Billy, Adam, Cherry, Josie, Ruth and Diana all crowded around, listening as the vicar spoke quietly.

Billy hung his head sadly as the coffin was lowered into the ground and Minnie grasped his hand in support.

Each said a silent goodbye to Una Reed before shaking hands with the vicar and leaving the cemetery. Cherry said a farewell and headed back to Reed House; the others turning for Marshall's. No one spoke as they walked home.

A couple of hours later they were back from the funeral, and once changed out of their sombre black, the domestic chores began again.

A couple of days went by, then one evening, as they all sat in the living room, Billy said, 'Minnie and I have been talking about Reed House and what should be done with it. We could sell it, of course, or we could open it as Marshall's second children's home. What do you all think?' Calling for order at the noise of everyone speaking at once, Billy said, 'Round the room and one at a time as always, please.'

'It would be wonderful to have another children's home,' Polly said.

Echo clapped his agreement.

'I'm not sure how much Reed House is worth, but I'm sure you could put the money to good use, Billy,' Ruth said.

'You have a point, Ruth, but I agree with Polly,' Mabel put in.

'So do I,' Dilys concurred.

'I'd want shot of the place if it were me,' Josie muttered.

'Knowing everyone and this place was here for me when I came out of jail was what kept me sane. There will be other kiddies who will need a loving home in the future,' Digit said.

'You can only re-home so many here. I was grateful you took us all in,' Joe said, his eyes on Billy.

'Without question,' Arthur added.

'Or standing in judgement,' May slipped in.

'Minnie, we won't have to go back there, will we?' Pip Stanton asked with a worried look.

'No, sweetheart, your home is here with us now.' Minnie gave him a warm smile and watched as he relaxed again.

'It was Reed's or the workhouse for us, but I'm glad we're here now,' Kit said.

Therefore, after much discussion it was agreed to change the name and open it as another children's home.

'What about staff?' Ruth asked.

Minnie said she had told Cherry the contents of Una's will. She had explained to Billy that she'd asked the girl to stay on rather than cast her out onto the streets. Billy was in full agreement that his wife had done the right thing.

'We thought about asking if you would take it over as manager, Ruth, after all the money and hard work you put into it in the first place, we think you should be given the choice,' Minnie said.

'I'd love to!' Ruth said. 'Thank you both.'

'Cherry has agreed to stay on as maid because she has nowhere to go otherwise,' Billy added.

'You'll need a cook, so can I apply for the job?' Josie asked.

'You're hired,' Minnie said with a grin.

'I would recommend you consider Diana as your new teacher, as she's more than capable of running her own classroom,' Celia said.

Minnie looked at the woman in question who nodded. 'I'd be honoured. Thank you for having faith in me, Celia.'

'Done!' Minnie said as she clapped her hands once.

'What's it to be called, Mum?' Polly asked.

'Same as this, Marshall's Children's Home,' her mother answered.

'Billy, another thought. Maybe you should have a telephone put in there, too, then Mum can have a natter to Ruth any time she likes,' Adam suggested.

Titters sounded as Minnie grinned her delight at the notion.

'Good idea, son,' Billy said. His endearment gave everyone a warm feeling.

'If you need any work done on the place, we could take it on once we're finished here,' Harlan said. He and Trevor came every evening to visit their lady friends.

'I'll have a word with your dad, son, a bathroom will be needed at least,' Billy said. As each of the lads made a suggestion, Billy answered them all with the same endearment – he called them all his sons.

'What about electricity?' Polly asked.

'That will be needed too – daughter,' Billy said with a little laugh.

'Running water?' May asked.

Billy answered as he had to Polly.

Minnie sniffed away the tears of happiness as she listened to them come together as a complete family.

51

The weather held as day after day the Rewcastles arrived early and left late. Then the building work itself began. Everyone was surprised how quickly the shell went up, with holes left for windows to be fitted later. Before they knew it, the roof was going on.

The first of the bathroom fixtures arrived and were fitted. Pipework was laid and Minnie was ecstatic. Dragging Polly along, she visited the market for fabric for curtains for the new bedrooms.

In the extension the plastering was underway, and the glazier's cart arrived with the glass for the windows.

Minnie was outside watching, and marvelled at Josiah as he orchestrated the work.

Saul and Merton Rewcastle unloaded the panes of glass, each packed in thick cardboard wrapping, and placed them where they would need to be fitted. After a word with Josiah, the glazier waved and left them to it.

Harlan was working on the staircase and Jordan Rewcastle was slapping plaster on the walls and smoothing it out before scoring it. Minnie gasped as she saw him stride outside on a pair of short home-made stilts. Dropping an empty bucket on the ground, he deftly leaned over and picked up a full one. With a grin, he returned to continue plastering a ceiling.

Seeing Saul and Merton fit the first window in place, Minnie rushed indoors to excitedly tell the others how the work was progressing.

It was Harlan who returned the tray of empty cups and plates with, 'By, that was grand.' Seeing Polly struggling to drag the mangle from the scullery, he went to help.

Minnie watched from the corner of her eye as the two chatted quietly. She was relieved her girl was finally coming to terms with Dickie's death, and wondered if Polly was developing a relationship with the young Geordie. Minnie would welcome that, as they were all fine lads in her estimation.

Harlan went back to his work and Polly began to fill the large tub with cold water from the standpipe whilst May filled another with hot. Ruth and Josie carried sheets and pillowcases into the yard to be washed.

Minnie started as Josiah knocked the open back door and walked in.

'Good morning, ladies. Just to let you know, this afternoon the boys will be starting work on your kitchen.'

'What?' Mabel blurted out. 'I have meals to prepare and...'

'The pipework needs to be laid and sink and taps fitted so you can have running water. We will try to inconvenience you as little as possible,' Josiah assured Mabel.

'Minnie, I have incorporated an outside tap into my plans so there will be no more pumping that dreadful standpipe. I do hope you don't mind.'

'It's fine with me, Josiah, and the girls will be glad

of it, I'm sure,' Minnie replied. Then to Mabel she added, 'We can have a cold meal this evening, nobody will mind. We can take everything into the dining room and prepare it there.'

Minnie, Dilys and Mabel began that job so the kitchen would be clear and so ready for the lads to move in to replace the sink and lay the pipework.

'This is the start of the upheaval for us, I suppose,' Minnie said, 'but it will be lovely when it's all done.'

'The sooner the better for me,' Mabel grumbled.

'Those lads have worked bloody hard, Mabel, and continue to do so, all so that we can have more room and running water.'

'Don't get me wrong, I praise their efforts,' Mabel agreed.

'I should think so, too,' Minnie muttered.

'It's just the thought of all that dust whilst we're trying to prepare food,' Mabel explained.

'Well, if we have cold lunches we can do that in the dining room and cook after the boys have gone home. I'm not sure how long it will take, but look on it as an adventure!' Minnie said with enthusiasm.

Mabel couldn't bring herself to do that and wandered away mumbling as she went.

Minnie burst out laughing as she watched her friend shuffle out through the back door.

* * *

By October, the extension was finished, having been fitted with electricity like the rest of the house. A new telephone had been installed in the hall and Minnie willed it to ring just so she could answer it. The kitchen had a new sink and taps and running water, much to Mabel's delight.

Adam and Joe had moved into their new bedroom, still preferring to share as they had always done, and furniture for the other rooms began to arrive. Now the Rewcastles were busy installing the second bathroom in Adam's old room.

It was much later, after all the work was done and Harlan and Trevor had gone home, that Polly again asked for a word with Adam and her mum. Going to the office, Minnie asked, 'What is it, sweetheart?'

'Mum, Harlan has asked me to marry him!' Polly said in a rush.

Minnie smiled, as did Adam. 'Is there a problem with that?'

'What about Dickie?' Polly's question was filled with anguish.

'Pol, Dickie is gone. In my heart I know he would be pleased for you,' Adam said.

'How do you feel about Harlan, sweetheart?' Minnie asked.

'Well, I...'

'Do you think of him first thing when you wake?' Polly nodded.

'And last thing before you sleep?'

Another nod.

'Then you love him. Now, clearly he loves you because he's proposed,' Minnie said wisely. 'So, the question now is – will you accept?'

'I'd like to,' Polly said with a fierce blush.

'Then do it!' mother and son said in unison. With hugs all round, they returned to the living room so Polly could tell everyone her good news whilst swearing them to secrecy.

'Please don't say anything until I've spoken to Harlan, though,' Polly begged. Nods confirmed they would keep their mouths shut until she said otherwise.

Hugs and congratulations were given by all until Polly's eyes strayed to Echo. He sat quietly watching the excitement.

Polly drew Adam aside. 'Ad, what can I say to Echo?'

'Ask him to give you away,' Adam said with a loving smile.

'I was going to ask you!' Polly gushed.

'I wouldn't mind,' he assured her, but Polly was having none of it.

'It has to be you, Ad.'

'Then ask him to be an usher. Tell him how important a job it is and that you won't take no for an answer.'

'Thanks, Ad, you always manage to have the right answer,' Polly said with a grin.

Going to Echo, she sat down beside him on the floor and said, 'I have a *very* important job for you Echo. I'd love you to be an usher at my wedding. Will you do it?'

Echo's face lit up and he clapped his hands like a

little child. 'Yes!' With that he stood up and danced around the room to everyone's amusement.

The following morning, whistles and clapping sounded from upstairs.

'Polly has accepted Harlan's proposal formally, by the sounds of it,' Minnie said with a grin.

'Mmm,' May muttered quietly.

'All right, out with it,' Minnie said.

Drawing a deep breath, May whispered, 'Trevor has proposed to me.'

'That's great news, May. Have you accepted?' Minnie asked.

'Not yet.'

'Why not?' Minnie asked, perplexed.

'I didn't want to steal Polly's limelight,' she answered timidly.

'Oh, May!' Minnie threw her arms around the girl.

'I love him, Minnie,' May said.

'That's it, then. Come on, everybody.' Minnie grabbed May's hand and yelled for the others to follow her.

Upstairs, Minnie called the Rewcastles out onto the landing where everyone was crowded.

'As you all now know, our Polly and Harlan are going to be married.' Clapping and hurrahs sounded, and Minnie waved her hands for quiet. 'Now it seems there could be another wedding.' Minnie tilted her head to Trevor.

Taking the hint, he stepped forward and bent his knee to May. 'Will you marry me, May?'

Flushing scarlet, she nodded, 'Yes.'

Polly's mouth dropped open in surprise then formed into a wide grin as she caught May's eye in the midst of yet more applause. Trevor was jostled by his brothers and Minnie called out to Ray Rewcastle. 'Seems we're to be family.'

'I couldn't wish for better,' Ray said with a laugh.

Polly went to May, and they hugged as only true friends could.

Having first met at Reed's orphanage, the girls had shared each other's happiness and sadness. May had cried buckets of tears when Polly had been sold, and had never thought to see her again. But fortune favoured the bold and their little group had struck out on an adventure which had resulted in them all coming together again in the end.

Polly and May both knew they would be close

friends for the rest of their lives.

It was later when Polly went to spend some time at Dickie's grave, and as she tidied around the plot she spoke quietly. 'I've accepted Harlan's proposal, Dickie. I will still come and visit but probably not as often, I'm sure you understand. Fliss has to stay in the asylum, which is awful, but I suppose it's for the best. Trevor and May are betrothed, which took me by surprise but I'm really happy for them both. Una Reed has passed on and left her house to Billy – would you believe it? The Rewcastles are putting the finishing touches to the extension now and it looks amazing; however, Mabel was at her wits' end with all the dust. Kit and Pip are doing well but they miss you, as is to be expected. I promise to keep an eye on them, although you were the one who always seemed to get into trouble. Well, I need to get back now as there's lots to be done at home. Sleep well, Dickie, and I'll come again before too long.'

Polly stood and gazed down at the grassy mound as a shadow fell across her vision. A pigeon landed close to where she stood, tilting its head to look at her. Satisfied she was no threat, it walked away, its head bobbing as it went.

Was it a sign from Dickie that he approved of her decision and was glad Polly was happy at last? She wanted to think so, but of course it may be the bird was merely searching for food. Polly returned home feeling better than she had in a very long time.

When Minnie came back from visiting Cherry, Polly said gingerly, 'Mum, I'd like to get married soon.'

Minnie eyed her daughter and asked, 'What's the rush, gel?'

Polly smiled. 'No, I'm not pregnant before you ask. It's just that Dickie had talked of marriage and he died before it could be arranged.'

'Are you afraid Harlan might die?' Minnie asked, horrified that her daughter might be harbouring such thoughts.

'No, but if we are to be wed then the sooner the better, so we can spend as much time together as we can.'

'I can understand that. Maybe you should ensure your intended makes a visit to the vicar, then, to arrange a date,' Minnie said with relief.

'Tell him to take Trevor with him,' May said as she came into the kitchen with a tray of empty cups.

'May, it's only a thought but – how do you fancy a double wedding?' Polly asked suddenly. 'I'll understand if you don't...'

'What a smashing idea!' her friend said, placing the tray on the table.

Minnie and Mabel watched with grins as the girls enthusiastically began to make plans.

'You'd best inform the lads of your decision, then get off into the town and start looking at wedding gowns,' Minnie said, beginning to feel their excitement build within her.

The girls ran from the room as they laughed and called out to their future husbands.

Much later, Polly and May settled in the kitchen discussing wedding plans with Mabel and Dilys.

'Can I come? Only Fliss wasn't going to invite me to her wedding to James,' Dilys said.

'Of course you can, Dilys! You're part of the family. So, you'd better get that new hat you talked of buying,' Polly said, trying to dispel the girl's uneasiness.

Dilys beamed her pleasure and looked to Mabel.

'There'll be time tomorrow and then you can

take your time in choosing,' Mabel said with a warm smile.

A disappointed look crossed Dilys' face. She wanted to grab her bag and shawl and skip out of the back door in order to be making her choice in the hat shop in town today.

'The boys are seeing the vicar today,' May told Mabel.

'How did they take the idea of a double wedding, then?'

'They were delighted,' Polly answered. 'Two brothers being married on the same day appealed to the whole family.'

'What did their mother say about it?' Mabel probed.

'She died some years ago, apparently. They don't talk about it much, I think they still miss her dreadfully,' Polly explained.

'So, when you are both *Mrs Rewcastles* will your husbands will move in here with us?' Mabel asked.

'I expect so, although it's not been discussed with Mum as yet,' Polly said making a mental note to address the subject soon.

An hour later, Harlan and Trevor bowled in

through the back door.

'The vicar said the first of December at one o'clock!' Harlan said as he tried to catch his breath, still panting after having run all the way back.

Polly and May hugged each other, and their men clapped each other on the back.

'Get upstairs and tell your folks then, because there's a lot to organise,' Minnie said as she walked in on the happy scene. 'Then you girls will have to sort out who will be moving rooms once you're married.'

'We were just discussing that, Mum,' Polly said with a blush.

'Well, it will need to be sorted out, so it's up to you who moves where because your husbands-to-be will have clothes and such to move in.'

Polly ran to Minnie and gave her a hug and when she let go, May took her place.

Minnie watched as they followed their men upstairs to share the good news, and a tear filled her eye. Her girl was getting married and Minnie was becoming a mother-in-law. Maybe in time she would be a grandmother after all. The thought made her smile.

52

Ruth, Josie and Diana had moved back to Reed House and Billy instructed the Electric Light Company to begin their work straight away.

The Rewcastles were once more employed to undertake the laying of the pipework for running water to the kitchen before converting a bedroom into an indoor bathroom. The privy block was to be demolished and the land turned into a flower garden.

One by one, the women took time to buy their new outfits for the weddings as the big day drew ever nearer.

Harlan joined Polly one evening to visit Dickie's grave, and as they laid some wild flowers on the plot he said, 'Dickie, I promise to love Polly for the rest of my days. I thank you for your blessing on our union, and swear I will make her happy.'

Polly wiped away the tears his words had brought forth and she nodded as a pigeon landed close by. Was it the same bird she had seen once before? She liked to think so. Turning, the couple walked away hand in hand.

The morning of the weddings saw a flurry of activity, and Dilys was so excited she wore her new hat at the breakfast table. The food for the party afterwards was all prepared and stored on the cold slab in the pantry.

After their fast was broken everyone dashed away to don their outfits. Minnie wore a blue organza dress with a feathered hat to match. Dilys was in a green two-piece which once on looked like a dress; her hat was fixed proudly into place with a pearl hat pin. Mabel had opted for a pink flowing dress with a mulberry hat and shoes. The men all looked very smart in their suits.

Minnie went to Polly's room where the two brides-to-be were laughing, their excitement knowing no bounds. She helped each into their wedding dress and stood back to check everything was in place.

Polly looked serene in white silk, a coronet of white roses in her hair, which held a small veil in place. She held a bouquet of matching flowers in her hands.

May had chosen champagne silk overlaid with a darker shade in lace. A long veil trailed down her back and was held fast by a little gold tiara. She carried a bouquet of yellow roses.

'Perfect,' Minnie said as her eyes filled with tears.

'Mum, don't, you'll have us bawling as well,' Polly said.

'I'm so very proud of you both,' Minnie said, and with that she went to join the others gathered in the hall. Spontaneous applause erupted as the girls emerged onto the landing, looking like two angels.

The sun beamed down as they left the house and in true tradition of living close by they walked to the church.

Women and children came to their gates to wish the girls well as they passed by. Men took off their caps and waved them in the air as they whistled loudly at the procession wending their way along the busy streets.

Polly and May waved their thanks, their smiles rivalling the rays of the sun.

Joe and Echo had gone to the church early to be ready for when people started to arrive.

Echo showed Cherry, Ruth, Diana and Josie to a pew and returned to the doorway.

Next came the Rewcastles. Ray, Jordan, Merton and Saul were taken to the pew the other side of the aisle before Echo returned to escort Harlan and Trevor to the front of the church to await their brides.

Both young men were dressed in mulberry frock coats with a white double-breasted waistcoat beneath. They each sported a flower in their lapel. Grey striped trousers and black top hats completed the ensemble.

As he saw the family arriving, Echo, dressed similarly to the grooms, clapped his hands with glee. Polly and May waited patiently whilst he settled everyone in place, including Joe, then he came back to tell them all was ready. He took his own seat, having congratulated himself on a job well done.

May linked her arm through her brother's. Arthur smiled down at his younger sister and whispered, 'Good luck and be happy.'

Polly linked hers with Adam. 'I'm proud of you, sis,' he said, 'I know you will have a wonderful life with Harlan.'

'Everything is going to change now, isn't it?' Polly asked a little sadly.

'Yes, I suppose so. We've all grown up now – it had to happen eventually,' Adam said with a smile, 'but I'll always be your big brother and will continue to look out for you.'

Polly's smile radiated as she kissed his cheek. 'Thanks, Ad.'

Arthur and May watched the little exchange with a tear in their eyes.

The sound of the pump organ said it was time.

Polly and May giggled excitedly.

'Here we go,' Arthur said.

'Ready, Pol?' Adam asked, and smiled as she nodded.

As the four sedately made their way down the aisle, oohs and ahs sounded.

Billy passed Minnie a handkerchief when he

heard her sniff. 'Polly looks beautiful – just like her mother,' he whispered.

Minnie's tear-streaked face smiled at the man she loved with all her heart.

Mabel slapped Dilys' hand away as the maid continually adjusted the new hat she was so proud of.

As quiet descended, the vicar's voice was loud and clear.

'Dearly beloved...'

A short while later, the sound of applause echoed around the church. No one was aware of the pigeon which had flown to perch on the church roof.

MORE FROM LINDSEY HUTCHINSON

We hope you enjoyed reading *Minnie's Orphans*. If you did, please leave a review.

If you'd like to gift a copy, this book is also available as an ebook, digital audio download and audiobook CD.

Sign up to Lindsey Hutchinson's mailing list for news, competitions and updates on future books.

http://bit.ly/LindseyHutchinsonMailingList

The Children From Gin Barrel Lane, another gritty Black Country saga from Lindsey Hutchinson, is available to buy now.

ABOUT THE AUTHOR

Lindsey Hutchinson is a bestselling saga author whose novels include *The Workhouse Children*. She was born and raised in Wednesbury, and was always destined to follow in the footsteps of her mother, the multi-million selling Meg Hutchinson.

Follow Lindsey on social media:

f facebook.com/Lindsey-Hutchinson-1781901985422852

🐦 twitter.com/LHutchAuthor

BB bookbub.com/authors/lindsey-hutchinson

ABOUT BOLDWOOD BOOKS

Boldwood Books is a fiction publishing company seeking out the best stories from around the world.

Find out more at www.boldwoodbooks.com

Sign up to the Book and Tonic newsletter for news, offers and competitions from Boldwood Books!

http://www.bit.ly/bookandtonic

We'd love to hear from you, follow us on social media:

facebook.com/BookandTonic

twitter.com/BoldwoodBooks

instagram.com/BookandTonic